The author hails from a modest working-class background with minimal early education. Joining the Royal Air Force as an airman in 1980, Paul Hart took steps to make good on his chequered early life. Commissioned in his early twenties against all odds, he went on to a varied nineteen-year career in the RAF, leaving in the rank of squadron leader. Working in an intelligence role and with the British Army, the author has a perspective which brings life to his fiction writing. Subsequent career manifestations include being a hotelier and owning a successful commercial estate agency. Taking early retirement, he now resides in Inverness, Scotland, with his wife, Mandy, and between bouts of golf and various forms of exercise, he has turned his hand to putting pen to paper (figuratively).

Operation Fulcrum Storm

Paul Hart

Operation Fulcrum Storm

Vanguard Press

VANGUARD PAPERBACK

© Copyright 2023
Paul Hart

The right of Paul Hart to be identified as author of
this work has been asserted by him in accordance with the
Copyright, Designs and Patents Act 1988.

A CIP catalogue record for this title is
available from the British Library.

ISBN 978 1 80016 625 7

Vanguard Press is an imprint of
Pegasus Elliot Mackenzie Publishers Ltd.
www.pegasuspublishers.com

First Published in 2023

Vanguard Press
Sheraton House Castle Park
Cambridge England

Printed & Bound in Great Britain

I dedicate this book to the many people who supported and guided me during my formative years. To those who encouraged me and gave me the tough love that helped me get on the right track. These people motivated and reassured me during the many challenging periods of my adult life. This book is theirs, as much as it is mine.

This novel has only been possible with the generous and highly-competent editorial support of Annie Diver-Stamnes, our friend from across the 'Pond,' who resides on the West Coast of America. Annie's help inspired me to keep on track throughout the process. A genuine angel.

Prologue

Oxford University, England – May 2016

Professor Janet Williams was presenting her final lecture to first-year students on the effects of viruses throughout history and their impact on mankind. Her two-hour presentation was concluding.

'In summary, throughout human history, widespread outbreaks of infections and illnesses have laid waste to vast populations. We think each time we observe a fresh virus emerging it is new, but that is certainly not the case. In all probability, it is an old virus or bacteria in disguise.' she paused for effect. ' "In disguise", I hear you ask.'

She held her hand to her ear.

Some bright spark on the right shouted, 'In disguise, Professor?'

The students laughed.

'Funny you should ask that,' she proceeded.

'Viruses don't spring from nothing. They mutate from a former version of themselves, their predecessor, much like we all have mutated from our ancestors. One example of our human mutation is that, as a general rule, people today are taller and stronger than our forebears.

'Pandemics have been around since records began, and we can only assume long before then. In H.G. Wells's iconic novel, "War of the Worlds", the Martian invaders were killed by the microscopic organisms that inhabit the earth, resulting in their total destruction. Taking that work of fiction and placing it alongside history and science, it is not beyond logic to assume the final days of humankind could be brought about by a pandemic, one so virulent and totally devastating that it causes the extinction or near-extinction of all humankind, resulting in the dawning of a new age of life on earth.

'In early recorded history, we have observed typhoid fever decimate entire cities, such as the plague of Athens in 430 BC, which killed up to one hundred thousand people. The Antonine Plague and Plague of

Cyprian from 165 to 266 AD killed more than six million people from possibly measles or smallpox infection. The first recorded bubonic plague was the Plague of Justinian from 541 to 750 AD, believed to have killed up to half the population of the world. The second great plague was the Black Death from 1331 to 1353, which reduced Europe's population by around half. This was the first epidemic in a series of about one hundred or so in Europe. The last major one in the UK was the Plague of London in 1665, where one hundred thousand people died in the city alone. Science has shown these devastating diseases all originated from sources in Asia, as did the Third Great Pandemic in 1855 which spread to the United States of America and killed around ten million people worldwide. Since cholera became widespread in the nineteenth century, this bacterium, which is spread through infected food and water, has killed millions of people.

'Flu pandemics have also been a common feature of modern history. The first one was described in the sixteenth century, and, since then, pandemics of influenza occur between every ten to thirty years. The 1889 Russian flu outbreak was responsible for one million deaths. In 1918, the incorrectly named Spanish flu was responsible for the deaths of up to one hundred million people. The Asian flu of 1957 caused the loss of two million lives globally. In 1968, the Hong Kong flu epidemic killed about one million people worldwide, lasting four years. Recently, the Swine flu of 2009 killed up to five hundred thousand people. These viral epidemics are only a few of the headline acts. Nearly every nation will have a localised flu epidemic killing tens, if not hundreds, of thousands of people at each occurrence every ten years or so. The numbers are debatable purely because historic records are limited.

'However, what is not a matter of conjecture is the social, economic and structural impacts they had on countries. These plagues were claimed to affect the ability of the Roman Empire to endure and had a great impact on the armies of Christendom to fight the later crusades.

'Throughout our history, humans have spread diseases such as smallpox, measles and whooping cough to the Americas, Australasia, Pacific Islands and other unsuspecting population groupings. For centuries, European conquerors developed herd immunity to these diseases, while the previously unencountered indigenous peoples had no such protection. Sadly, newly introduced and aggressive viral strains are so devastating that they infect nearly everyone in the new socio-economic community with varying impacts and wipe out millions of people. They burn out eventually as herd immunity kicks in. As viruses mutate, our immune systems do as well, but the latter are always behind in the process with sometimes catastrophic outcomes. As such, a new pandemic may well be upon us in another ten to fifty years. Many viruses and epidemics become pandemics because of people's movement and the fact that since Roman times, people increasingly live in closer proximity to each other.

'It is impossible to predict when and from where the next pandemic will come and what its source might be. However, every new illness, bacterium, virus or fungus, if deadly enough and if transmittable, could lead to the annihilation of humankind. Thank you.'

The students enthusiastically and loudly applauded.

'Thank you again. Any questions?' asked the Professor.

A spotty, serious-looking young man in the front row put his hand up.

'Yes, Geoffrey, what's your question?' she asked.

'Professor, how likely is your scenario regarding the elimination of humankind to happen, and if it is likely, why hasn't it happened so far?' Geoffrey asked.

'Those are good questions, Geoffrey. Let me answer your second question first.

'The only reason why you, Geoffrey, are here today is because of several random events in your life and the lives of your forebears. These events, and the inter-relationships they have with other unconnected happenings, made it impossible for your predecessors to predict where you would end up on this day. The further you go back in generations, the more impossible it is for people to predict what the future will hold for their descendants. What was the chance that your parents would meet? What were the chances they would get married? What were the chances they would have a son who would choose this course at this university? These are the key factors, but within every key factor exist millions of other influences. Did you decide to take this course because someone you knew was taking it, or did your favourite teacher point you in this direction, or did your family encourage you to attend? If I were to ask you what your grandchildren would study, at which university and what tutorial they would be doing, say in fifty years on a given day at a given time, you would rightly say that you have no idea. Who is to say that the university you chose would even still be around?

'Some people call it fate. Some might see God's hand in what happens. As a scientist, I see inter-connecting coincidences. Take a meteor hitting planet earth. Would that be anything other than an unfortunate collision? So, in answer to your question "why has it not happened thus far?", it is simple: the events or coincidences that would bring about such an outcome have not yet come together to make it happen.

'Let's say, to create an anthropomorphic analogy, at some point in the future two viruses meet, fall in love and reproduce. Their offspring is vicious, and its only aim is to replicate. By doing so, it kills people very effectively, without mercy or indeed conscious knowledge. Rather than some flu which kills millions of people, the new virus kills billions, and it keeps mutating, so we cannot find a way to fight it. It's not beyond reason to suggest that this could happen.

' "How likely is this to happen?", I think was your first question.

'Well, we know that all creatures, including viruses, mutate. Darwin's theory in its crudest form tells us that for a species to survive, it has to evolve and become stronger. If we keep killing viruses through the use of chemicals and medicines, it is reasonable to suggest that of the ninety-nine point nine percent killed, the point one percent remaining are the strongest or most robust. If these are allowed to mutate and, through evolution, become even stronger, logic would tell us that at some point, they will kill off humankind. This could take thousands of years, possibly longer, but I would suggest that it will happen. We are talking about an extinction-level event. We just need that love affair to develop between something that is slightly more deadly than Ebola and a virus with the ability to transmit itself like the common flu; albeit the flu isn't that common. At each future mutation of the killer-virus, those who had missed the initial outbreak could be susceptible to the new variant and die. I would say an extinction-level pandemic is just as likely to occur as an extinction-level meteor. When will these happen? No one knows.

However, my money is on the virus hitting us first. As a culture, human nature is such that we strive for knowledge and power. In the same way that humans introduced animal-breeding strategies to increase our food sources, I suspect that someone someday will develop a virus in a bid to control the world. It might sound like science fiction, but germ and biological warfare are real. They exist today. Viruses could be the next weapons of mass destruction. What is science fiction today is science fact tomorrow.'

Professor Janet Williams held her audience in the palm of her hand.

'Thank you, everyone. Have a great holiday.'

Students called out that they would see her in September, and she simply smiled and waved.

She knew she would not be there in September because she had been offered a post at the Ministry of Defence establishment at Porton Down where she would join the bioweapons research team.

Chapter 1

Bombshell

24th May 2024

One of the smallest creatures on the planet was wreaking havoc with the dominant species, and researchers around the world were tossing about countless theories as to why the present mutating pandemic had taken hold. Hundreds of millions of people had already died. One in twenty-five people who had been alive at the pandemic's start only four years ago had perished. An equal number of patients were suffering from illnesses that would shorten their lives and place a growing burden on those left to care for them. The carnage was still raging with no end in sight. Death had become a feature of everyday life.

The extreme impact of this worldwide plague called The Great Pandemic was caused not by one virus, but by a continuing vast range of mutating organisms. The changing threat attacked all in society. It offered no hiding place except to those who could isolate totally: the mega-rich.

During the early months and years, people offered the theory that the virus had been manipulated scientifically, and that it was, in fact, man-made. Scientific communities across the world explored this possibility, but the randomness of the virus's impact made it difficult to see how any one entity could benefit from it. Those few countries that had a fairly easy time early on were affected more aggressively during the later stages of the pandemic. The multiple waves of infection devasted economies and impacted populations across the planet.

In the first two years of Covid-19 and its associated mutations, more than ten million people died worldwide. The follow-on waves from 2022 to the present day were more impactful because resources had been depleted, and hospitals were losing staff through attrition at an alarming rate. Major economies were devastated and finances were not available for the same level of support structures and bailouts. Poorer areas like India and Africa were hardest hit, and it was estimated two hundred million died in four years across the planet. The deaths attributable to Covid-19 and its ancestors probably were much higher because many countries played politics with their numbers to hide the catalogue of errors made in the handling of the virus. Most Western European countries stopped testing those who had pre-existing medical conditions of which, in the view of the certifying doctor, the patient would have died within a relatively short period. For the general public, their lives had become mundane, and during the various phases of the lock-downs most people felt they had lost many of their freedoms. The periodic lifting of sanctions made the reintroduction of new limitations on movement and activities feel more devastating, a further regression of their quality of life. The ramping up of rhetoric by leaders across the world, the imposition at times of a semi-martial law and the heavy-handed police in most countries made populations rebel, leading to greater restrictions and people being jailed without trial. Society was eroding everywhere.

Between December 2023, and January 2024 it seemed that the world was making progress against the latest manifestations of the virus, and a semblance of normality and order was being restored. People began living their lives again, albeit cautiously. In the small village of Sankt Veit im Pongau, Austria, the sense of relief that the worst was over brought the tiny hamlet together over Christmas and New Year. The village was a strong and close community that had suffered from many deaths over the preceding years. It was delighted to welcome a few holiday-makers who had returned to enjoy the plentiful snow on the many ski slopes in the area. It wasn't like the good old days, but it was a small mercy for those whose livelihoods depended on the visitors and who had scraped by during the barren years just passed.

Then, in February 2024 after this short period of liberation and rejuvenation, crushing news sounded from Austria. A new strain of coronavirus had surfaced at Hotel Metzgerwirt. The morning's peace and quiet were brutally assaulted by the sirens of an ambulance coming to a screaming halt outside the hotel, one of the larger establishments in the village. It was there for only a few minutes. A light-weight hospital trolley was taken through the main exit of the hotel to the idling ambulance. The patient on the trolley was fully-covered head-to-toe, obviously dead. The paramedics looked furtive and were talking in stressed tones to their command centre many kilometres away. They made sure no one could overhear them.

They issued an order to the hotel Duty Manager that no one was to leave or enter the hotel. Guests were to stay in their rooms and not allowed to mingle. The paramedics stressed their message again as they adjusted their full PPE.

The reassuring words that everything would be OK did not provide the desired comfort.

The Duty Manager went to his office mumbling, 'Shit, shit, shit.'

Six additional fatalities were recorded in the hotel over the next four days. Ultimately, the population of St. Viet was decimated by this new virus: Covid-24. Over half the village succumbed to its clutches, as they were the new frontline with no prewarning or adequate defences to this revised and more deadly strain of the existing covid variant.

Covid-19 and its many off-shoots were pussy cats compared to Covid-24. The previous vaccines for Covid-19 and its successors were ineffective with this new variant or strain; Covid-24 had developed a resistance to all known vaccines. Certain strains of Ebola kill ninety percent of those who come into contact with it. Covid-19 of 2019/2020 was innocuous compared to Ebola, with a low lethality rate of less than one percent. Covid-19 went through approximately one hundred and twenty notable mutations, which for such viruses was not excessive but most were relatively harmless. Flu viruses constantly change and adapt, and that is why some years flu vaccines are pretty ineffective. Over the virus's developmental stages, it transformed into a much more deadly adversary: Covid-24 had a death rate of twenty percent plus and when contracted, it stayed dormant within its host for seven to fourteen days, then striking with a lethality seldom seen on such a scale. Once a person felt the symptoms, death could occur within twenty-four to forty-eight hours. Those coming into contact with the virus had a fifty-fifty chance of it becoming serious, causing them to be admitted to hospital. Once in the care of the medical staff, half of the patients would recover but many would suffer from major on-going respiratory illness for the rest of their days. The other half died. This new virulent form of coronavirus had the very traits that most virologists feared: the ability to be passed on easily, a lengthy dormant period during which it could be transmitted unwittingly and an aggressive active phase resulting in a high-death rate for those infected. It also seemed that those who contracted the disease but never became ill could continue to transmit the virus for weeks, possibly months.

Covid-19 did not impact equally across society. It hunted down the old and infirm, the feeble, the young and of course, the unlucky few who were fit and healthy but who succumbed, nonetheless. The poor and certain ethnic groups suffered disproportionately. Covid-24 was a truly indiscriminate killer, affecting all ages and ethnic groups. Those from the poorest families remained its easiest targets but everyone was fair game for this newest assassin.

The scientific community was quick to postulate that this new virulent strain of the Covid-24 virus was just a routine evolution of nature. The virus was instinctually learning to adapt and survive. These traits are "hard-wire" in the viruses, set in their DNA. The majority of creatures evolve, and the less complex an organism, the simpler it is to make the next change; to mutate.

The world had changed and, unless something could be done to deal with the virus or its source, in the short span of ten years, the planet's dominant species would no longer be the human race.

Professor Johnathon King, a virologist at Bristol University, supported the mutation theory, but he also observed the presence of markers within the virus indicating the mutation might have been manufactured. He noted that the changes from the first recorded samples of Covid-19 were critically different from the Covid-24 strain. This adaptation needed further investigation, and Professor King had been deep into this research with his students at Bristol when he came to the disturbing conclusion that he had found strong evidence the virus may have been engineered. He needed someone at a higher level to review his alarming findings proving someone might have deliberately created and released the virus which was wiping out so much of the world's population. He tried to alert the authorities to his work, but the current chaos in Government due to the pandemic resulted in little being heard above the deafening background noise of death, destruction, disharmony and political in-fighting. His colleagues were overwhelmed with their workloads. Most professionals across the country were running on empty after years of the crisis. He had contacted every person in the Government that he thought could or should help – by email, letter, and telephone, expressing his concerns in tones of increasing alarm and urgency. He had either been ignored or rebuffed. Everyone seemed to be asleep at the wheel.

Jon, as he was known to his friends, was an unassuming man, an academic who was a capable and solid researcher. He believed in his work. It was inherently sound, and he knew it needed to be placed in front of someone in a position of authority who could act upon it. A man of principle, he had decided given his lack of success in garnering attention for his research, he had to take matters into his own hands and, thought, 'bugger the consequences.' He knew his intended action would be life-changing but he could not sit idly by.

A little before seven a.m., he arrived at the BBC Campus, Broadcasting House, Bristol, located on Whiteladies Road, and now he was standing by and ready to be interviewed. A television appearance was new and somewhat uncomfortable territory for him. Professor King had rehearsed his lines over and over, very much as he did when presenting a paper to a large audience of colleagues at a professional conference.

He sat three metres from the interviewer, and she nodded at him indicating they were on the air.

Smiling into the camera, she began,

'Our guest this morning is Professor Johnathon King, a virologist at Bristol University who is with us today to talk about his research findings. Professor King, welcome. Would you explain your theory on the origin of Covid-24 and its relationship with the original Covid-19 virus?'

'Certainly. Such a huge change in the structures of Covid-19 to Covid-24 indicates either an evolutionary rate never before seen in nature for a creature of such a cell structure – or indeed in any creature – or it indicates that the virus has been intentionally tampered with and scientifically developed in a laboratory.'

A quiet man with no axe to grind and zero desire to be in the public eye, Professor King was confident in his work, and this was reflected in his delivery style. He knew his topic and exhibited the sort of presence that made people feel what he said was rock-solid.

He added, 'Of the two options being discussed, the former might point to an exponential rate of evolutionary development that could indicate this virus in twenty or thirty further mutations could lead to a near world-wide extinction of humankind.'

The broadcaster was visibly startled and exclaimed,

'World-wide extinction of the human race?'

Jon kept his gaze steady and said,

'Yes, that is correct, a near world-wide extinction.'

This comment was entirely unexpected and put the whole BBC crew in Bristol on the backfoot. The news reporter heard various voices talking at once in her earbud. She struggled under the pressure of trying to listen to the panicking voices whilst appearing calm and collected.

Hesitantly, she asked, 'If it is true that the virus is mutating at an exponential rate, how does this work exactly, and how long would such an outcome, as you describe, take to be upon us? What level of casualties could we envisage?'

Professor King paused, breathing in deeply. He had prepared to answer this exact question. He raised his head to again look straight into the camera.

'First, how does mutation work? Well, it can occur in many different ways, but suffice it to say that all creatures mutate. Less complex organisms mutate faster than complex ones. Viruses are very simple organisms. Covid-19 mutated into Covid-24 over about four years. Of course, no one can be exact on that particular assessment, but this is a mid-range calculation.'

The reporter's eyes widened, but before she could get the next obvious question out, Professor King continued,

'It will, of course, depend on how far any mutation can change and the limitations of those mutations. However, if we see the same incremental changes over new mutations, the impact on the human race could be devastating. The next significant mutation could be with us in two to three years, thereafter, a further one in five to six years and so on.

We do not know if the mutation process will speed up or slow down. It could be that Covid-24 is the last mutation phase, and the virus will die out. Historically, viruses have simply burned out and thus ceased to be a threat.'

The reporter asked, 'Is there any evidence that this virus will die out?'

Johnathon King again looked at the camera and predicted,

'There is nothing on a biological level which would indicate that this virus will cease the dramatic change it has seemingly undergone from Covid-19 to Covid-24. We have all heard of the many variations over the past four years. It is unlikely to burn itself out if it keeps mutating. The simple answer is an emphatic "no".'

'Professor, surely this is all science fiction, but if your prediction were to come to pass, what sort of impact would it have?'

Not wanting to seem confrontational, Johnathon said gently,

'This is certainly not science fiction, and today's death rate is an indication of science fact. Please, do not try to belittle the science here.'

Without hesitation, he continued,

'The casualties we are experiencing today from Covid-24 would be a drop in the ocean compared to what we can call, "Significant Mutant Strain Five," or the next major iteration of the virus. What we are dealing with here is not one pandemic but multiple yet connected individual pandemics, each more devastating than the previous one. We can all appreciate that, in terms of fatalities, Covid-24 is exponentially worse than Covid-19 by a magnitude of twenty. Imagine if each subsequent pandemic had an incrementally increased effect. The impact would be incomprehensible to most people.'

The staff in the newsroom gasped, and what followed knocked the wind out of the whole audience watching.

Johnathon said, 'I'd expect ninety to ninety-five percent of the world would be detrimentally affected by the compounding effect of a mutating virus.'

'What does that actually mean?' was the news reporter's sharp response.

She was just hanging on by a thread. The production team back in London was speechless. The small crew in Bristol was completely out of their depth, not knowing where to take this. Should they stop the interview, or let him run with his views? They were completely unprepared.

'Keep it simple,' Johnathon thought to himself, and then said, 'Ninety to ninety-five percent of all people will die or will be so adversely affected by these waves of viruses that they will cease to be viable functioning members of society.'

Professor King had a detailed model in his head about how the figures could be justified. His calculations were complex and took account of an intricate change in societal attitudes resulting in a steady decline to a new Dark Age. He kept his own counsel. He could see the abject fear on the newscaster's face. The basic human emotions of fight or flight were evident, but, in this case, she froze, and there was a long pause.

Filling the void generated by her silence, Professor King stated,

'Of course, there could be other rationales as to why the virus mutated. One such theory could be that a power, be it a national government or someone within industry, carried out scientific trials to develop this new strain of virus. The reasons for such scientific development are numerous. Should that be the case, we would need to identify who it was and why anyone would take this course of action.'

The reporter recovered from her shock and challenged him.

'Surely this is fanciful! It sounds like a plot from a James Bond movie! Who could possibly benefit from taking such an action? How could they do it without us finding out? Who would do such a thing?'

'Societies around the world possess secretive aspects, and we simply do not know who would do such a thing. However, it is not beyond reasonable doubt that a foreign power or industry mogul could produce this virus for monetary, political or military power motives. It's either one or the other: naturally mutated or scientifically developed. This is what we must investigate, or else we will never know.'

He unclipped the wireless microphone from his lapel, saying,

'Thank for you your time,' before getting to his feet and walking off the set.

The reporter was caught off-guard, and with more voices in her ear, she said,

'We will be back after this short break.'

The same old public notifications about washing hands, social distancing and wearing protective coveralls and masks when outside or working, came on TV screens around the country. Those who had listened to the Professor's broadcast were stunned. A rush of frenetic voices poured over the various comms channels within the TV studio and back at the London control desk.

One producer, sounding outraged, asked,

'Were we expecting this bombshell?'

Another fumed,

'For Christ's sake, I thought this guy was going to tell us all the science around the differences between Covid-19 and 24, not predict Armageddon!'

The Bristol-based producer caught his breath and asked,

'Tell me, people, did anyone know this guest was going to raise the likely destruction of the human race?'

It was all quiet in his headphones. He waited until it was clear no one was going to respond then said,

'Let's move on to the next segment for now, but someone get this guy back and see if we can get a more in-depth story. Also, can we find another expert to verify, or at least comment on, what he said?'

By the time the television production team was moving to follow his orders, Professor Johnathon King was heading towards the exit of the BBC offices in Bristol. He wanted out immediately. Having multiple cameras pointing at him was an unsettling experience, and not one he wanted to repeat.

Johnathon had calls to make. He knew his life would never be the same. He would either become known as the mad professor of Covid-24 or the man who unleashed the truth about its derivation and potential impact. As soon as he was on his way in his old silver Mitsubishi Eclipse, Jon called the University of Bristol and was put through to the Dean. Dumbfounded at what he heard, Dean Evans told Johnathon to take a leave of absence and to keep his head down. When he hung up after the seventeen-minute call, Johnathon found he had missed seven calls on his phone. He reviewed the voicemail messages, all from friends or work colleagues, many of which included some choice language. While listening to the messages, he received five more voicemails and nine new text messages. News stations asked him to do radio and TV appearances. The Sun and Daily Mail would be happy to pay him for exclusivity on his story. Some of the calls were from clearly unbalanced people who threatened him.

'Today is going to be a long day,' he sighed as he deleted all the messages.

Chapter 2

Intelligence Intervention

Millions of people were watching this latest news update and could barely believe their eyes and ears. Depending on individual dispositions, people thought they were all going to die as a result of wave after wave of viral attacks or that some evil country was developing a kind of germ warfare which they had unleashed on the world. People's levels of tension elevated dramatically, and they demanded an immediate official response from the Government regarding Professor King's revelations.

One particular individual watching the news report was Squadron Leader Claire Walters, sitting in her office in London in the Headquarters Secret Intelligence Service (SIS). Claire had a BSc in Microbiology which included the study of microorganisms, and she knew about the biology of bacteria, viruses and fungi. Much of what Professor King was saying made sense to her and in a way crossed over into her work as an Intelligence Analyst on secondment to the SIS, better known as MI6. Her job was to analyse the worldwide threats of weapons of mass destruction, and biological warfare was within her remit.

She had been instructed to review the current crisis some weeks previously as a consequence of the outbreak of Covid-24. Her task was to assess the likelihood of this new virus being an attack by a Hostile Intelligence Service (HIS) or some other external or indeed internal faction or terrorist group. Sources of pure intelligence on this matter were scarce. Claire had put out a Category One request to all agencies seeking any human intelligence, electronic intelligence or otherwise physical intelligence, that might indicate a pathway to further investigation and had met with little success. Government Communications Headquarters (GCHQ) came back with more information than any reasonable person could trawl through, so she needed additional filters to make the task of sifting through the data provided possible. This is what she was working on just now. Getting a follow-up response from GCHQ would take time, as other priorities were taking precedence.

The various desks internal to MI6 came back with snippets of information, the most interesting and somewhat puzzling coming out of the USA, but nothing concrete came of that lead. The Far East Desk was also forthcoming with some contradictory information on the virus, both from official and unofficial sources in China. Other extracts were often items in the mainstream news media. The pure volume of information and data was just too vast for a team of four analysts to process.

Claire was giving the Professor's news report some serious thought and was inclined to want to speak to him. Just then another obvious illustration of how modern media was taking over: a surge of activity within her inbox with messages landing at a frenetic pace.

"This Professor King has poked the hornet's nest,' she thought quietly.

Like the millions listening to him, she was impressed with his character and sincerity. He seemed to be in his early fifties, some twenty years older than she, but he didn't come across like the dry professors she had encountered during her studies in Liverpool. She found him intriguing but didn't know if it was because of the information he had imparted, or his personality and obvious earnestness.

She picked up the phone and called her administrative Staff Sergeant, Yorkie Charlton, asking,

'Staff, did you just watch the BBC coronavirus update?'

She heard him pause.

'No, ma'am.'

'OK, get me the telephone number of Professor Johnathon King of Bristol University as a matter of urgency. Immediately after that, I would like to meet with Section Chief Rankin. Can you get that sorted for me, Staff?'

She heard a pause again from Staff's end of the phone as he scribbled a note, and then he said,

'Professor Johnathon King, Bristol University, and Section Chief. Got it. I'll report back in ten minutes, ma'am.'

She rolled her eyes and thought,

'Silence, no goodbyes or have a nice day. Fucking Army grunts – no manners, but they get the job done.'

Both Claire and Yorkie had come to work for MI6 after stellar military careers. Aged forty-eight, Yorkie was still serving as a Senior Non-Commissioned Officer in the British Army when he landed at MI6 Headquarters. A battle-hardened special forces operative who had spent nearly twenty years working with the premier military outfit all across the world. He had worked in Special Air Service, spending two years with Delta Force in the US and working with NATO special forces. He had responded to a signal indicating SIS Section Chief Special Weapons Section Bill Rankin was looking for a specialist in Weapons of Mass Destruction. Yorkie felt it was time to find a different career path because, although he was in top physical condition, he was aware that he was getting older and didn't want to jeopardise a mission due to the possibility he couldn't keep up. He also emphatically did not want to take a training role or a behind-the-scenes job with the Regiment, and his knowledge of weapons of mass destruction was as good as anyone's in the military. Bill explained to Yorkie that they were setting up a new cell within the Special Weapons Sections formed with a mix of serving military personnel and civilian operatives which would be headed by a Royal Air Force squadron leader. That squadron leader turned out to be Claire to whom Yorkie was introduced in the meeting with Bill Rankin.

Claire's path had led her to undertake a BSc in Microbiology at Liverpool University. Thereafter, craving to make a larger difference than she could by spending her life in a laboratory, applied to Officer Training at RAF College Cranwell in Lincolnshire. She went through intelligence training and commenced work as a Photographic Analyst. In her spare time, she worked out at the gym, took up Judo and Karate, and learned survival techniques from an unarmed combat instructor. After eighteen months and aged twenty-five years old, she was posted to the Joint Principal War Headquarters for UK Forces in Northwood, Middlesex, and promoted to the rank of flight lieutenant. She developed mountaineering skills and undertook a military parachute course at RAF Brize Norton. With short operational tours of duty in Afghanistan and out of Cyprus in support of live missions, her attributes grew. Her next role was an exchange-post with the United States Air Force in Germany as a specialist Nuclear Chemical Biological Warfare Analyst at Ramstein

Air Base. In all her posts, she excelled. When her time at the USAF base was coming to an end, she, like Yorkie, knew she did not want a sedate desk job and saw the writing on the wall that this was where she was headed: even as a squadron leader, she would be making the tea for some two-star officer, or worse still, a civilian equivalent. She was delighted when her Wing Commander gave her Bill Rankin's name and telephone number, saying, 'This guy is looking to form a specialist team within the SIS, and you might be a reasonable fit. Give him a call, if he likes the cut of your jib, this might be a great opportunity. If he doesn't, it looks like you will be doing a staff job next.' She interviewed with Bill and then with SIS Deputy Director Operations Tom MacDonald, and was offered a place on the field training course. MI6 took her on secondment for three years, after which point, she could decide if she wanted to stay in the RAF or perhaps continue in MI6.

Looking through her emails, Claire saw it was the usual wave of crap that many of her current and ex-colleagues generated, some because they were bored, and others because they were, in her opinion, dimwits. Often, they were just looking for a quick win without doing the necessary hard work. Claire thought back to her old instructor in intelligence training who said numerous times, 'The only place you find success before work is in the dictionary.'

Peter Tomkins, thought of as the posh kid on the block and who was very ambitious had sent an email to all staff on the mailing list Zulu, entitled, 'A Warning.'

'This Professor King should be questioned, and if he has any information, we should review it.'

Peter lacked the effective intelligence and motivation to have a thought and do something about it. Action and following through on his thoughts were not his forte. Sitting back in his chair, Peter would be thinking that was a great coup. He was probably waiting for a commendation from Bill Rankin or some other Head of Section with instructions. Tonks, as he was known, lacked any substance, but he knew how to play the game. With him, bluster counted for everything, and it was easier than thinking through to a positive outcome. He was connected, smug and never had to work for anything. He thought he was superior, coming as he did from Kensington and old money.

'Tosser,' thought Claire, but she kept those thoughts private.

Other emails came in. One was from the Prime Minister's briefing team looking for a response to the recently aired news report.

'Fuck me,' Claire muttered, 'it's rattled someone at a fairly high level already. It could be the PM, but that's unlikely. We are living in unsettling and difficult times, and we have the least capable PM of a generation leading us.'

Claire had often wondered why the Conservative Party had selected consecutive buffoons to lead them. Everyone knew the current PM's character and professional limitations. She often wondered whether there was a "Mr Big" somewhere yanking the chains of the political elite.

Looking at the inner workings of the SIS, one just could not help thinking that way. The higher echelons of the military and the intelligence services all seemed to make decisions whilst on Rohypnol; the benefits of sedation and amnesia sometimes seemed to be key qualities for senior staffs. The distraction of the emails was welcome. Claire's mind was racing. At ten-twenty a.m., the phone rang, an internal call, and it was the Staff Sergeant.

In his gruff West Yorkshire accent, he said,

'Ma'am, Section Chief happy to see you at 1200 hours. I told him it was partly about the TV report this morning. Mr King is out of the office and won't be back today. His admin people would not give me his mobile or any other details over the phone so I got the tech boys in the basement here to dig it out for me, plus a little bit of background for you. Do you want me to raise a file on Mr King and his team?'

'That would be perfect, Staff. Could you also ring Professor King,' emphasising his station and qualification, 'and ask him if he would be free to meet me tomorrow, say eleven-thirty in the morning here in London? If he seems happy to come along, send a car, no escort required at this stage and play it down. Explain who I am and our interest in his work. Suggest he brings his research along with him. Sort out a standard visitor pass, and if you could meet him on arrival, that would be great. We will play this tight to start with. I will confirm authority for everything after I meet with Mr Rankin. I am sure he will approve this course of action.'

'That's fine, ma'am. Just to confirm: raise file on Professor King and his team, book meeting for tomorrow at eleven-thirty a.m. I will use Meeting Room Three. Organise wheels and reception. Do you want me to organise accommodation for the night? If not, I will have the car on standby for a mid-afternoon return. Anything else, ma'am?'

'Thanks, Staff, that's all great. Not sure about the accommodation, but book something provisionally. This is a potentially important visitor. Hold the transport on standby.'

Claire gave an uncharacteristic pause, wavering in her next response.

'If for any reason he cannot come to us, we'll go to him. Whatever happens, I need to see him immediately, but we don't want to be too heavy-handed. If we go, get a wire, no guns. We need his expertise.'

Staff snapped, 'Clear, ma'am.'

Squadron Leader Claire Walters, ever the professional, read through the summary of the MI6 report into the Covid-19 outbreak. It read:

Summary - MI6 - Covid-19 outbreak.

There is ample evidence demonstrating that China misled the world about the coronavirus by trying to cover up the outbreak of Covid-19. The assessment produced by the Special Weapons Division categorically demonstrated that the Chinese have mishandled the disease and were culpable in the virus being opened up to society. It was evident that President Xi Jinping's government was complicit in the cover-up, having both knowledge of the virus and its potency. However, there was no evidence to prove that this virus has been produced for any ulterior purpose. The fact that Chen Wei, a Major General of the People's Liberation Army, was flown into Wuhan in February 2020, after the coronavirus broke out in the city, according to Chinese state-run media and supported by other sources, indicated a closer link to the military than first thought. Chen Wei was the senior military bio-warfare specialist. She took over control at Wuhan Institute of Virology, and her appointment provoked claims that the classified facility was an Army-run operation. This indicated that Beijing may be developing bioweapons in Wuhan. These were always strenuously denied, and the Chinese government stated that they had drafted in military personnel and resources to assist and support the beleaguered staff in Wuhan. There were suggestions that the virus could have been created there, but the leak was an accident. A director at the lab has denied the allegations and called for an investigation; that director was subsequently removed from his post. Chen Wei is a leading specialist in genetic engineering vaccines in China, which raised a few eyebrows. It was openly reported that she developed a medical spray during the SARS outbreak in 2003, preventing around fourteen thousand medical workers from contracting the virus. She is famously known in China as the 'terminator of Ebola' for leading a team which helped create the vaccine against Ebola. Her boss was Major General (Retired) Lei Wei; they are not related. Wei is one of the most common family names in China.

Widely credited as the source of the coronavirus, the wet market in Wuhan was the location of the first detected case in October 2019. The Chinese revealed that the laboratory in Wuhan, close to the wet market, had studied the deadly bat-derived Covid-19. The lack of transparency by the authorities in China was not considered anything beyond the normal cultural default position. Evidence of human-to-human transmission was known possibly as early as October 2019, but the Government of the People's Republic of China maintained their denials until January 2020. Part of the blame for the shrouding of the evidence was due to the complacency in the international communities and the World Health Organisation. The few countries or colonies nearby who expressed concern before the end of the year in 2019 were ignored.

The SIS Executive report concluded that the Chinese Government acted recklessly in not alerting the broader national communities to the human-to-human spread during the early and critical stages of the outbreak. The delay in passing this information was assessed to be between six to eight weeks. Earlier notification and full disclosure of the virus's effects and its communicability could have facilitated better preparations and controls by governments around the world. The delays in notification and the failure to distribute samples of the virus at the earliest opportunity put back the world's response to this pandemic by up to two months which in simplistic terms could cause another five hundred thousand deaths worldwide.

As part of their program, those doctors and scientists who were working on the virus and who spoke out or were suspected of whistleblowing were silenced, and presumed killed, by order of the

Government. Evidence indicated that the laboratory in Wuhan had been studying deadly bat-derived coronaviruses but had not developed it, as either a scientific test or a bioweapon. There were clear indications that nonsecure evidence of the virus was destroyed in a bid to hide the full nature of the impact of the virus. These actions, though alien to Western democracies, are not uncommon in China.

Though there is only scant information regarding the actual motivation behind the secrecy and disinformation, it was concluded that part of the inaction could be blamed on the habitual nature of the Chinese to be secretive. The other rationale was that there were concerns that, if the information was fully disclosed, China would become a leper colony in terms of trade, travel and general economy. Though there are some indicators that the President was informed that this could be controlled, it was apparent to those on the ground, that containment was not possible. The only way to prevent the global pandemic was to close down China for the betterment of humankind. This was never going to happen as long as there was a remote possibility that the virus would just burn out.

Finally, no clear proof exists that this virus was engineered, and most scientists around the world concur with this assessment. There are a few notable exceptions claiming that the virus displayed markers showing some element of human development.

Covid 19 and March 2020 seemed a long time ago now. After reading the summary, Claire thought, 'These voices suggesting that the virus could be manmade were lost in the background noise being generated by the virus's presence. Critically, it was the damming comments made by Donald Trump, who voiced his support for the theory of the virus being engineered, despite going against all his advisors. Trump had made so many gaffs in his dealing with the virus, including advocating injecting disinfectant and taking malaria tablets, that anything he said was immediately discredited.'

It was good that Trump was now off the political map. The final and most significant point of note is that, if Covid-19 was a biological weapon as had been suggested by limited sources, it was a pretty pathetic one. The report covered eight other conspiracy theories, suggesting they were all implausible.

Claire was now thinking that maybe Covid-19 could be a pathway development of a bioweapon which had not yet been finalised. The release of Covid-19 may have been a genuine mistake but one which would allow the current strategy of a mutating virus to be propagated. The hiding of an intention in military terms was not new. The surprise attack philosophy often catches the enemy off-guard, but the only weakness in this argument was that Covid-19 had impacted China similarly to most other nations. However, when comparing the death ratio against the population, the Covid-24 death toll in China was one of the lowest in the world. The virtual lockdown in China was thought to be the main reason for this. The only way that China as a nation could come out of this in a beneficial position was if it was essentially unaffected when a new vaccine became available. Certainly, no effective vaccines for Covid 24 were on the horizon in the Western world. Another significant harmful mutation of Covid-24 would be a real game-changer and would lead to a real breakdown of the world's social structures. Signs on the news showed that this was already happening. Daily media reports heightened the fear and apprehension being felt across the UK, Europe and many parts of the world. In around four years, the world had changed beyond the wildest thoughts of even the writers of doomsday novels.

Jon arrived home, letting all his calls go directly to voicemail which he checked every fifteen minutes or so. Then finally he received the message for which he had been waiting since the broadcast. He breathed a sigh of relief when he heard a man's voice saying,

'Professor King? Mr Charlton here, sir, from His Majesty's Secret Intelligence Service in London. Please return my call on the number on your phone. I would appreciate it if you would act quickly. Thank you.'

The return call was made at eleven a.m., and a meeting was arranged for the following day. He was to be collected by car at nine a.m. from his house. He was told what kind of car to expect.

'Any change of plans, call me back on this number at any time,' said the voice at the other end of the phone.

The no-nonsense discussion offered Jon some consolation that the Secret Intelligence Service was taking his broadcast seriously. It was time for reflection but not for regrets.

Johnathon now had to show the courage and resolve that he expected others to display. He showered and got his files and papers together. He realised this was a one-shot opportunity. He hoped with all his heart that they would understand or at least take it seriously enough to put his work in front of someone who could grasp the science and make an intelligent judgement.

Chapter 3

Section Chief

24th May 2024

Squadron Leader Claire Walter's meeting with Professor King was in the bag, and she was buoyed with enthusiasm. It was now 1150 hours. She had spent the last thirty minutes putting together an outline proposal for a provisional investigation. She had to hand a summary of the TV news article and a brief on the primary person of interest – Professor Johnathon King. She collated some fundamental aims of the investigation which centred around the suggestion that Covid-24 was possibly a manufactured virus and could be being used by a hostile agency or possibly a terrorist cell.

Claire knew this level of work was above her current pay grade, but she wanted to take the lead. Keen to show off her qualities, she was familiar with the science, albeit not having studied the subject for eight years. She had been reviewing the whole Covid-19, Covid-24 outbreaks and everything in-between to assess if anything obviously untoward was going on. She had suspicions – many people suspected foul play, but despite the large volume of disparate material out there, no substantive leads existed. The boffins at Porton Down, the Ministry of Defence's Defence Science and Technology Laboratory, had provided nothing of value or promise regarding Covid-24. She had studied reports surrounding Covid-19 and its origins. In summary, it was generally reported as most likely not being manufactured.

Anyone engineering a lethal virus for nefarious purposes would obviously try to hide their involvement. In truth, the team at Porton was actually only drawing on the work of several other scientific centres of excellence, so it was difficult to judge what research they had carried out internally, if any.

Thinking of her strategy going forward, she knew the people at

Porton would have to be involved but was confident she could hold her own on an academic level. If she could recruit Johnathon King, she might be able to set up an MI6 cell within Porton Down but realised that might be a difficult sell, both internally within the SIS and to those in control at the Wiltshire laboratories. Once other Government agencies knew what she was planning, they would all want to get in on the act. However, this virus, if it was developed by another country or external terrorist group, would be classified as an external threat and not a domestic one, thereby falling neatly into the remit of MI6.

Walking along the corridor, she knew that the first two minutes of her presentation were critical. It was the first time that such an elevator pitch would have a massive impact on her career. Claire assessed that if she was still in the Section Chief's office after five minutes, she had a real chance to do something monumental. Her ambition was only equal to her desire to prove herself. She knew she had good qualities but also possessed doubts. Working in MI6, with its plethora of highly capable and driven characters, made even the most professional and able people question their place and position.

Section Chief Rankin was a good boss. He permitted her and Staff Sergeant Charlton to do their own thing within reason. She didn't really know him well from a personal perspective, but he seemed even-handed and reasonably intelligent. Claire had sensed Rankin was a bit cautious, a rule follower who was averse to making difficult decisions quickly. A career intelligence officer, Rankin was in for the long haul and was more politically than operationally motivated. This project had to be pitched as a career-enhancing investigation. This would have to come over as a team effort, and Bill Rankin was, after all, the Team Leader.

Entering the Section Chief's outer-office, Claire saw his secretary, Emma, look up and say,

'Go straight through, Squadron Leader.'

Without even time to draw breath, she found herself in front of her superior, staring at the top of his full head of hair.

'Give me a few seconds, Claire, and grab yourself a coffee,' he said, pointing to his right.

She looked to her left and saw the small table to the rear of the office with a pot of coffee, milk, sugar and oatmeal biscuits. She loved oatmeal biscuits but could never take one in a meeting. She was always self-conscious about eating in front of colleagues.

As she stepped over to the table, he said,

'Could you pour me one too? Thanks. White, no sugar.'

'No problem,' she replied cheerily, knowing that this was not a sexist request.

Claire took solace in the fact she would at least be given the time it took to drink a coffee which should be ample to get her key points over. Bill Rankin took out his earphones which were connected to his iPad. He had been reviewing the TV interview with Professor King. Shaking his head, he lifted his face and locked eyes with the small and attractive squadron leader.

His first comment was borderline aggressive,

'What a fucking mess this is going to be. If people take this twat seriously, we'll have even more riots on the streets regardless of which of his scenarios might come to pass.'

He shuffled from behind his desk with notepad and pen in hand, grabbing a chair. He took his time to get settled and said,

'Give it to me. What's your prognosis on this bloody situation?'

Rankin was clearly rattled. Claire had not seen her superior wound up like this before. He was always fairly bland in his responses to situations.

'Sir,' she said, 'I will not go over the Professor's comments made on TV. They are pretty self-evident, and I saw that you have had the opportunity to appraise yourself. However, for completeness, I have a full transcript here for you.

'I agree entirely, sir, this Professor has really set the cat amongst the pigeons. He could be a crank, but I think not. He has strong personal and professional credentials. Therefore, I recommend we treat him as a serious person of interest, at least for now.'

Rankin said, 'That's fine, but expand further. I need more information.'

She had her green light to proceed.

'Firstly, what we need to do is formally assess what sort of character the Professor is. If he is a nut, then we need to let the boys at MI5 discredit him.'

Looking down at her notes, she added,

'However, I suspect that he is a sound character. He's a highly-regarded academic, an expert in his field, and this is the first time he has put his head above the parapet. Before today, he has never been on TV or other national or local media outlets. From a superficial review, seeking publicity is not how he works. He is a considered and steady character. A bit of an introvert. Definitely not an alarmist or activist. No recorded political affiliations. We would need to do a deeper background check if we are to take his ideas seriously. From a character perspective, the only fly in the ointment is the fact that his wife died of breast cancer about two years ago and she had also contracted Covid at the same time. That could be an indicator suggesting a behavioural change, but what we have seen thus far is not outwardly unbalanced. In his private life, he has no kids, and no significant other that we know of. He works long hours, has had no disciplinary issues, and finances are in order but I have to note that we have just scratched the surface. Suffice it to say that a cursory initial search on all available national registers is clean.'

Rankin's response was, 'That's a good initial look at the principal subject. What's your suggested game plan going forward? What is the key first step?'

Without hesitation, Claire continued, 'We aim to put his claims into perspective. It is not just about the external threat but also the naturally evolving virus theory. If what he says is true, either way, we may be all screwed anyway, but it would be nice to know.'

She hadn't meant to say that last bit and inwardly winced.

Refocussing she continued, 'Our fundamental objective is to determine if his comments regarding the possible involvement of a foreign hostile intelligence service are viable. We have to find out if his assumptions are based on solid research. It's a bit too early to say with confidence, but I don't think he's the guessing type or a bullshitter. My gut tells me he is genuine, that he has a real belief in his work, but we cannot dismiss the possibility that he may be just a plausible crank. What I would like to do, sir, is have a face-to-face meeting with the Professor and see what he knows. Also, I want to get a sense if he's on the level or not. I suspect I will be able to determine pretty quickly if there is something of significance we must act on. If it is crap, or he's a fruit cake, we'll cut him loose and burn him. On the other hand, if it stacks up, we need to take it further. I have a brief written proposal which outlines a positive course of action.

'Firstly, we need to meet with Professor King and determine the veracity of his external threat theory. Next, if his premise has credibility, and a potential hostile threat exists, we must take immediate steps to contain the Professor's work and the flow of information via open-source forums. At the same time, we must control all future communications by King and his team of researchers. Needless to say, we should confiscate all materials, faculty or personnel about the subject matter. This next point may be slightly contentious, but I believe we could enlist King, and possibly his team, to assist in a fuller review on a scientific level. Finally, we would need a coordinated plan to engage with field assets to see if any other sources would support King's findings. His science alone will not be enough to consider further action.'

Rankin knew that Claire was a relative newbie in the MI6 intelligence world, but her qualifications and effective reasoning made her a most capable resource. Her lack of experience, on the other hand, made her a bit of an unknown in pressured situations. Claire's lack of operational exposure made her a bit of a risk. He was assessing what she was saying whilst judging her as an individual.

'Boss,' Claire said, 'I know that I am on secondment to the SIS, and my experience levels here are not strong as others, but this job was made for me.'

She paused.

'For us,' she added. 'I am ideally qualified to deal with the scientific elements of this situation. I will have to brush up on some aspects, but I know my stuff and could be up to speed within days.'

She looked for a response in her Section Chief's demeanour, and, seeing nothing, she waited.

'He must be some poker player,' she thought.

The silence was difficult, a bit uncomfortable, but she could wait.

'Look,' Rankin said, 'we are going to have to take this one step at a time. Let's not get any hares running just yet. What I will sanction is a formal meeting with this Professor. Let's see what he has to say for himself. I want everything recorded and I mean everything. Get a team ready to lift his stuff from the University and home. Also place surveillance on standby to monitor his research staff. We will have to involve MI5 - shit, but do it by the book. I will fill the gaps in your plan but remember this is your plan. I am not stealing your thunder. This was your find, and you have shown the balls to take pre-emptive action.'

Claire, knowing she had pitched things fairly well without having to get pushy, stated,

'Sir, Porton Down will need to get involved to review Professor King's findings.'

Rankin nodded.

Claire continued, 'We will need to take the Professor under our wing and possibly some of his research fellows as well. There will be a cost, and we need to get a case number.'

The Section Chief stifled the moment by snapping,

'Firstly, we do not want to bring every man and his dog on board; restrict your activities to the Professor for the time-being. More importantly, what you are talking about, is inter-agency collaboration which requires Director-level involvement. Do nothing official until we have just cause. I do not want to look like an over-exuberant schoolboy with nothing to show the teacher. Tread carefully. Do not discuss this case with your immediate team and this office until we know we have something to run with. Once the shackles come off, that's when we move like the wind.'

He tilted his head, observing a slight mood change in the Squadron Leader's face and maintaining an authoritative tone.

'Anything we do with this matter stays within this office for now. If we have justifiable cause to take action, we will need to involve the Deputy Director Operations. We had better be pretty damn sure our evidence is sound; we don't want to end up with egg on our faces. I am sure you know that when we elevate this to the next level, at that point only God knows what will happen. The DD Ops loves task forces on given operations; we could be out of the picture at that point. We have to make sure we control what we can for the good of the country and our careers. If it goes forward, this will be a UK Eyes Only and Codeword Operation. Until we are clear about what we have and what we are working with, I am sure the boss will not be involving the Americans –

the NSA or CIA. If we did without a clear picture, it would lead to the President being briefed and, fuck me, if that would not result in World War III. Am I clear on this?'

'Yes, sir,' came the swift and firm response from Claire.

Rankin changed his speech pattern, taking a more temperate tone

'So, the course of action is: ask Professor King to pay us a visit. Any unwillingness to attend of his own volition, I am happy to get an arrest warrant. Speak with him and develop a sense of who he is, but most importantly, find out if he is playing with a full deck. Assess if his theories have merit. Do you need to bring in anyone to help in the latter point?'

'No, boss,' snapped the junior.

Rankin continued barking out instructions.

'I want a transcription of the meeting on my desk within two hours. I will watch the meeting covertly, and if I need you to come out, my secretary will pop in asking if you would like another coffee. Record everything, even casual contact. Get a fuller profile on this guy, his deceased wife, and the research team. I will leave you to determine how best to conduct the meeting, but immediately when you sense there are reasonable grounds to investigate further, inform him that we will be seconding him. You know how to put it.'

Claire thought now, 'I will let him know what I have done thus far.'

'That's all clear, sir. I have a car picking him up at nine a.m. tomorrow. Professor King has agreed to come in to meet with me at about eleven-thirty a.m. The interview will be conducted in Meeting Room Three. Full recording and technical support are booked. The car and Staff Sergeant Charlton will be wired. I have also arranged overnight accommodation, but he is not expecting to stay. I did not want to set alarm bells ringing, so I did not ask him to bring an overnight bag. What I think would be good, if you agree, sir, is for me to chat with him, take him for a spot of lunch and then conduct a further meeting with you at say two-thirty p.m. This will give us time to make a judgement on the next steps.'

Rankin offered an approving grin.

'Claire, it appears you have got your ducks lining up nicely. Crack on, and we can have a quick catch-up, say, ten tomorrow morning just to cover anything new that comes up. Tell Emma on your way out to pop our meeting in my diary. That's all for now, and well done. Let's see where this takes us.'

Both Rankin and Claire stood up in unison, and to her surprise, he put out his hand. The convention of shaking hands had died out during the pandemic, but she understood the significance of the gesture and offered hers in return. He shook it and said,

'Until tomorrow.'

Claire bounced out of the office past Emma and down the corridor, suddenly stopped and went back.

'Whoops,' she said, 'I am back in at 1000 hours tomorrow, Emma. Cheers.'

She turned and marched off, pulling hand sanitiser out of her pocket, squirting a dollop onto her hands, and rubbing them together vigorously.

She was thinking that the meeting had gone well. She was happy to be dealing with step one, and if she played her cards right, it could be her project lead. Her first one.

Chapter 4

Preparation

25th May 2024

Whilst Professor King was enduring his mostly silent journey to the meeting the following day, a team of engineers was preparing audio-visual equipment in the Annex to Meeting Room Three. Every word, expression and movement would be captured as a permanent record. Each system had a back-up plus a third redundant system ready for use. With three cameras in use, Johnathon King would be captured from multiple angles. An infrared camera would also be employed and the guest chair would read critical biometrics. In addition, an automated transcription system would produce a written report of the meeting. A specialist secretary would edit it live, as the IT system endeavoured to put every audible sound into recognisable words and phrases. Notepaper and pens were readied for use by the observers. Their job was to identify areas of further questioning and to add commentary to the report, mainly surrounding the credibility of the principal subject. Unknown to Claire, she would also be assessed. Her ability to control the interrogation and draw out salient points through in-depth and thorough questioning would be key. Those watching this encounter unfold would be Peter Tomkins, one of Claire's colleagues and not someone she could warm to, and a specialist in human behavioural science who would assess Johnathon King's mental state and general demeanour. If the Professor were to have a role going forward, he would undergo several psychological assessments. Squadron Leader Walters's potential future role would also be under scrutiny. These psychologists take every opportunity to analyse key staff when in a natural work situation. The role of the Section Chief would be to draw all these elements together and prepare for a supplementary meeting but only if he assessed the merit of such. All the usual administrative requirements for receiving a guest were being put in place.

Squadron Leader Claire Walters sat in her office, mobile on silent, her office number diverted to Staff Sergeant Charlton to have absolutely no interruptions. Within the Section, the news was circulating that Claire was taking the lead on this matter. A few less energetic and indecisive staff had tried to approach Bill Rankin in the late afternoon the previous day, only to be rebuffed. They were told that the matter was already in hand. This got tongues wagging to see who had gotten ahead of the game. Peter Tomkins was a bit miffed because he thought that Claire had stolen his thunder. The truth was, whilst he sat on his arse waiting for coffee and others to come to him, he had lost any initiative. In his assessment, she was only on secondment, not even a real MI6 member of staff, and so she got the role because she was being treated with kid-gloves, and of course, the trend was to put women in lead roles to offset years of gender bias. From Tomkins's point of view, the level of negative bias, while not as aggressive as that of the BBC, was still present. However, in this case, the truth was that the better person got the job and deservedly so. Claire knew that he would be a secondary assessor, and she had every cause not to allow him to stick the knife in. Even minor gaps in her questioning or any faux pas would surely be highlighted to the Section Chief, or worse still, put in the report being passed up to the Deputy Director Operations.

From leaving Rankins's office yesterday lunchtime, Claire had worked tirelessly on all aspects of her up-and-coming meeting with Professor King. She watched his twelve-minute TV broadcast six more times and annotated the transcription with her notes in the margins. The technical aspects of his comments were fairly bland for someone of her academic background. It was obvious he had prepared his statements so that a layman could grasp the enormity of his message. The TV content provided precious little to work on, but the insight into the man was a good starting point. Using her limited neuro-linguistic programming training, she scanned every discernible character trait to see if she could identify anything that might offer some additional insight into this obviously capable and intellectual high-achiever. King came across as confident and in control. He exhibited calmness and a degree of respect towards the floundering news reporter, treating the clumsy questioning from the news presenter with due deference. It was obvious that King

45

intended to keep the focus on the message, not himself. After dissecting the TV footage, she realised that it was time to understand the man more fully.

She scrutinised everything in the Professor's personal life: family, friends, finances, hobbies and interests. The Tech Team had raised a file showing some published professional papers on a broad spectrum of microbiology subjects. Keenly studying the report authored by Professor King on the source of Covid-19, Claire found that it made good reading. Re-acquainting herself with some of the current terminologies within this specialist area, Claire had a warm sense of confidence, as this was her field of expertise. Professor King's assessment was precise, clear and well-supported. Claire liked the way he thought and expressed himself. With no embellishment, the narrative was written in a simple and flowing text, the work of an honest man, comfortable in his skin who had nothing to prove but the facts themselves. If anything, the report showed a lack of professional ambition.

She trawled the usual social media platforms to determine the extent of the man's private life: Facebook, Twitter, Linked-In. She reviewed various communication sites, but she found little substance. She also reviewed anyone who had a relationship with Professor King to gain insights into his character with little effect. It was not unusual for a man in his early fifties not to be engaged fully with social media. Professor King had no affiliations with political organisations. Claire noted that he had no role within the faculty except the Head of the Department taking no part in inter-departmental politics or extra-curricular activities. Socially, the Professor seemed to be well-liked but led a fairly solitary life, not unusual in the current pandemic. His employment assessments from the University were all glowing with never a derogatory comment. King was popular amongst his students, peers and seniors, considered hard-working and professional. He appeared to be a highly respected man. He kept fit by running and swimming but had no club memberships on record.

His family life provided only sparse information as well. He was from a middle-class family originally living in Bath. As a young student, he did well at school, really well, Claire corrected herself. Sauntering through his 'A' Levels, Johnathon then entered Oxford University, progressing to achieve a master's degree. He married his first wife at twenty-five but divorced four years later. They had no children. He worked in industry for a few years, mainly in research laboratories. At thirty-four, Johnathon applied for a teaching post at Bristol University and had been there ever since. At forty, he remarried but sadly, his second wife died of breast cancer after a very short illness a few years back. It must have been a shock to him, but other than a few days of leave, to everyone's surprise, he went back to work. He and his wife had no children. Claire wondered whether that had been a conscious choice. Did he put his work before family, and maybe that's what he wanted? He had a dog to whom he referred as his 'fluffy puppy' – cute but hardly useful information. He owned a lovely house with no mortgage, had plenty of cash in the bank, and had an excellent pension fund; essentially well set.

Professor King came across as a generally sound and honest man, professionally strong and highly regarded, happy with his job and not particularly ambitious. He appeared balanced about the loss of his wife, in so far as Claire could glean.

The next question was how to approach the technical aspects of the science. His assertions on TV seemed quite pronounced. It was as if he had every confidence in what he was saying. Balancing the man's character against his assertions, it was difficult to see how he was anything less than nearly one hundred percent certain of his facts. He was coming to see her without any duress being applied. A willing participant, and even better, it was his action that initiated the meeting.

A question to be resolved was whether his objective was to be put in front of the SIS all along.

The uplift had been confirmed by the codeword indicating everything was on track. Did Claire have to assume that he would be an open book, or would there be the need to apply pressure? The latter seemed extremely unlikely. She wanted to focus on having him explain what evidence he had to support the theory that Covid-24 was manufactured. Depending on how much technical detail he was willing to go into, this could be a short meeting or could last for days.

She thought that if the Professor was talking in purely scientific terms and drew deeply on his academic knowledge, poor old Peter Tomkins would be out of his depth. Peter was surely given access to the file she had just reviewed, but doubted he would have read much of the information, giving only a cursory glance at each of the summaries in each aspect.

This took a bit of the pressure off Claire, but her inalienable desire to be professional surpassed every other emotion. Scanning pictures of the Professor, she observed that he had a full head of sandy hair with direct blue eyes, and he looked to be in good shape. She realised that he was twenty years her senior although age differences did not intimidate her. She was used to dealing with older men, given her military background. Claire felt the need to be that bit sharper than her male colleagues to prove her worth. With this man, that could be a challenge. She was going to be quizzing him on a subject matter that was his principal professional reserve. Essentially, they would be playing the game on his turf. Given his television interview, she figured that he wanted to play the game and by whatever rules to get him to his objective. What did he want out of all of this?

Chapter 5

The First Steps

25th May 2024

Professor King's house was in Calne in rural Wiltshire. His home was a pleasant late-Victorian property, an old manse with a massive garden sporting a lush green lawn and a substantial orchard at the bottom. The front aspects were impressive featuring an in-out driveway circumnavigating a large central rotund raised flowerbed displaying an array of colourful bushes and spring plants. The gravel drive gave adequate warning of anyone approaching either on foot or by car. At the sound of a heavy car, Professor King rose out of his favourite armchair and peered around the bay window in his sitting room. He was being collected by an MI6 service car. Johnathon thought the Jaguar XF was very smart, and was expecting it.

'This must be it,' he said to himself, feeling both excited and nervous in equal measure.

He looked around to say goodbye to his usually attentive and bouncy seven-year-old Sprocker Spaniel, but she was staying with Auntie Jackie next door. Jackie was a close friend and had been very pally with his wife, whom he still missed with all his heart. More importantly, just now, Willow, a mix of Cocker and Springer Spaniel, missed her too but also loved her holidays with Jackie. Johnathon was always a bit sad to leave his house and Willow. He picked up his day-bag and bulging worn tan leather briefcase. As he approached the car, the driver opened the rear left-hand door and greeted him, saying,

'Sir. Professor King?'

Johnathon smiled and nodded.

'Good morning, sir. I'll take your bags,' and the driver took both placing them in the boot of the car.

He swiftly reappeared in the car doorway just as Professor King was getting comfortable and closed the door. The driver, a middle-aged man of about fifty-five years, was an MI6 employee and a fairly normal-looking chap. 'Nothing like James Bond,' Johnathon thought and smiled. The driver and passenger exchanged few words as they progressed along the M4 corridor into central London. Johnathon King wondered to himself what you say for small talk to an MI6 employee. It's not, after all, like engaging with a taxi driver.

After the driver negotiated the busy London city centre traffic, they arrived at Vauxhall Cross which houses the Headquarters of the Secret Intelligence Service, the United Kingdom's foreign intelligence agency MI6. Jon had looked at the MI6 website the previous night and was pleasantly surprised at how welcoming it was. It stated:

We are SIS – the UK's Secret Intelligence Service – also known as MI6.

Our people work secretly around the world to make the UK safer and more prosperous. For over one hundred years SIS has ensured the UK and our allies keep one step ahead of our adversaries. We are creative and determined – using cutting-edge technology and espionage.

We have three core aims: stopping terrorism, disrupting the activity of hostile states, and giving the UK a cyber advantage.

We work closely with MI5, GCHQ, HM Armed Forces, law enforcement and a range of other international partners. Everything we do is tasked and authorised by senior government ministers and overseen by Parliament and independent judges. People who work for MI6 come from all walks of life, with different skills, interests and backgrounds.

MI6 is an organisation where integrity, courage and respect are central to what we do. We encourage and admire difference. Many MI6 staff are based overseas while others work from our Headquarters in Vauxhall, London. Although our work is secret, everything we do is legal and is underpinned by the values that define the UK.

Johnathon had wondered about all the acronyms and had to look them up, disappointed that the MI in MI6 stood for Military Intelligence rather than Mission Impossible. Johnathon Googled it to be sure.

They drove into an underground parking area and an escort was waiting for him, a burly sort of gent, one that you thought could be a proper spy, unlike the driver.

With no introduction, the man said,

'You don't need your overnight bag, sir. Please follow me.'

Johnathon thought that this chap sounded like the man on the phone yesterday and did as instructed. After reaching the reception area, a mumbled chat between the burly escort and a receptionist ensued. Then Professor King was presented with a visitor pass which was annotated with the words, 'Must be Accompanied at all Times.' They proceeded through standard airport-type scanners and baggage check.

'Professor, please take out your laptop and mobile phone. We will hang on to these until you leave. This is standard practice for all visitors,' said his escort.

Yorkie had just lied, but the Professor was none the wiser. Johnathon waited for his leather briefcase.

Again, he was given the order, 'Follow me, sir.'

They went to a lift and proceeded to the fifth floor. The lack of serious conversation between being picked up at nine a.m. and now, eleven-twenty a.m., was a bit disconcerting. He was shown to a fairly substantial meeting room and told to have a seat, and that someone would be along immediately.

A charming woman came in, and Johnathon stood up. The courtesy was not missed by the observers.

'Would you like tea or coffee, Professor?' she asked.

'Yes, coffee, please. That would be lovely.'

He smiled in appreciation.

The room had a central table with ten chairs, all well-spaced out as required under Covid-24 regulations, with all the usual material to conduct a meeting laid out in a tidy and professional manner. He saw a mirror at one end of the room which was set slightly too high in the wall. Johnathon wondered if it was a secret window and he was being observed. The coffee came, and he tucked into the pre-wrapped oatmeal biscuits. In fact, he had two packets and was now on his own, hoping that this was not going to be a hostile meeting.

Chapter 6

Meeting of Minds

25th May 2024

Squadron Leader Claire Walters strode into Meeting Room Three, shoulders back with a ramrod straight posture. She had made the extra effort to power dress that morning; attired in a formal dark blue suit with a smart plain white blouse, and her skirt was knee length, her patent leather heeled shoes made her five feet eight inches just over five feet ten inches, the same height as the Professor. She wore no make-up or jewellery. Upon entering, the Squadron Leader placed a bulky folder on the desk just in front of where she would be seated.

Making eye contact with the Professor, she introduced herself, and as was the extant convention, they both nodded. They did not shake hands and sat about three metres apart. Claire explained her role within the Special Weapons Section of MI6. He seemed passive through her explanation until she mentioned that she was a Nuclear Chemical Biological Warfare Specialist. As she explained her brief history, he was impressed with her academic credentials.

Johnathon thought, 'Here is someone who should understand the gravity of what I have to say.'

However, the most stunning aspect of the person before him was her obvious energy and drive which seemed to be coupled with a responsive personality. This was not some career automaton looking to just make her mark. He sensed she had a passion for what she was doing on a human level, not just to enhance her career. He desparately hoped his initial assessment would prove correct.

The Professor found himself relaxing and taking a liking to this military person. As a rule, he did not usually warm to military types. Before long, the Professor and Claire were chatting about their respective careers and stands on various current issues. They seemed to agree on most things. They shared some humour as well. An outside observer might not realise the fact that this was possibly the most important meeting that they both had ever attended. The friendly conversation ended, leaving them both feeling that they had established a rapport, and Claire decided time to get down to serious business.

She got the real purpose of the meeting underway. Taking a slightly more formal tone, she got straight to the point.

'Professor, let me formally thank you for meeting me at such short notice. I saw your appearance on the BBC and was taken aback by your comments. I would like to pick your brain as to why you have intimated that Covid-24 might be man-made. I have also read your report that stated fairly categorically that Covid-19 was the result of the natural process of evolution rather than a product of laboratory engineering. Have you any indicators that the new coronavirus, Covid-24, was produced, modified or developed through known scientific techniques?'

After drawing a slight breath, Johnathon replied,

'You may not know that as part of our research programme, we were asked by the World Health Organisation back in early March 2020 to study the Covid-19 virus. Our task was to draw comparisons to both the MERS and SARS coronaviruses. We were just one of many academic institutions which became involved. Our research faculty is held in reasonably high regard, but there are other centres, as you know, that would be considered better-placed. We relished the opportunity to get involved with one of the greatest microbiological issues of modern history.'

Claire nodded her understanding and smiled at his modesty.

He continued, 'The research carried out was on the molecular components of Covid-19 in comparison to those of the SARS virus. As you will have read, the viruses had differences, but the commonalities would indicate that Covid-19, in all probability, was a natural development from this existing virus, the key differences being Covid-19 was more robust in terms of its transmission ability but less potent in terms of lethality when compared to SARS. The problem with the Covid-19 outbreak was, we thought, it had not been dealt with as effectively as it could have been. Had China acted more aggressively and immediately, I suspect that the worldwide pandemic could have been averted. With hindsight, the Chinese sort of admitted their gross error, but by that point, it was too late, the virus had impacted the world. Any opportunity to trace and control the outbreak was lost. Our job at the University was done. We summarised that the virus appeared in all senses a close relative to the SARS virus. Furthermore, we could deduce with some confidence that the viruses were from the same genus and had sufficient similarities to confirm that Covid-19 was, in all probability, a mutation of the SARS virus.

'Just for the record, in my report, we did say that it was not impossible that the virus could have been engineered, but rather that it was improbable. Part of our reasoning was that the virus lacked the potency to be an effective military bioweapon. As an economic weapon, its application was too indiscriminate, and it appeared that with small margins most nations were suffering equally. That latter statement has been supported by the impacts of the subsequent waves that occurred post our reporting date.

'Time went by, and then the Covid-24 hit Austria in February this year, and before we knew what was happening, we had a major second pandemic before the first had managed to completely burn itself out. In modern times, this was unheard of, but the increased fatality levels and reproduction number from about two to three in Covid-19 to five to six in Covid-24 were catastrophic for all populations. These two factors were significant shifts in impact, akin to comparing the flu to Covid-19, if not greater. It was a whole different level of threat. Our university had managed to get samples of Covid-24, and, before being asked, we undertook a research programme into comparing Covid-19 to Covid-24. Again, we found obvious similarities, but the differences between these two strains of the supposedly same virus were so significant that we thought that there had been some mix-up in the handling of samples. Obviously, we checked and found no mistakes. We were flabbergasted with what we saw.'

Taking a sip of now cold coffee and seeing that he had Claire's full attention, Jon continued,

'During our research on Covid-19, we checked its markers against the SARS virus of which I assume you have a knowledge?'

Claire nodded, her face looking deeply engrossed in the subject matter.

The Professor carried on, 'The differences in our research between

SARS and Covid-19 were obvious, but they also had an eighty-four percent similarity of genomic sequencing. Though SARS had a higher lethality rate, one of the key differences was that the Covid-19 spike proteins were ten times more effective at latching on to the host cells. This meant that Covid-19 was more efficient at attacking cells. Moreover, it also could attack more than one organ at a time which resulted in severe illness with a rapid onset, but especially in those with underlying health conditions who struggled more. As you know, many ended up dying.'

Claire thought it was time to clarify a few points for those observing and to make sure her virology knowledge was as it should be.

'Just for the avoidance of doubt,' she started playing to her audience, 'the spike proteins in Covid-19 are more effective at binding to the membrane of the human cells that they infect. This improved binding process, is it because the cell structure is more accommodating for human cells, or are the activated cell enzymes more potent?'

Johnathon was impressed with her quick understanding. He explained using his hands as a visual aid,

'Imagine the gaps between my fingers represent the spike protein. As it comes into contact with the host receptor cell, the latter excrete an enzyme called furin which causes a minor but significant response in the attacking virus to modify the binding contact, and bingo, the virus has landed. Because all human organs have furin, it means that all organs are fair game and thus can result in multiple and concurrent organ attacks by Covid-19.'

Johnathon waited a moment to see if she had any follow-up questions. An important point he was keen to make was that he and his team had done this research off their backs. No one had requested their faculty support.

'Getting a sample of Covid-24 was fairly simple,' Johnathon stressed. 'Using the same techniques of genetic sequencing and comparing spike proteins, my team concluded that Covid-24 demonstrated only fifty-five percent similarities to Covid-19. In essence, it appeared that the lethality rate of SARS had been combined with Covid-19's ability to bind to the membrane of its human host. In our findings, we postulated that the mutation values were too great to suggest a single point of transition and probably indicated an element of genetic engineering. It would appear that the new coronavirus was purposely developed as a pathogen.

'I have my full report on my team's findings for you.'

He pulled out a huge four-ring binder crammed to bursting. It made a resounding thud when it hit the table.

He said, 'These are all our research figures and values.'

He then took out a smaller document, professionally-bound in a smart cover with a plastic spine, adding,

'And this is the summary text.'

Claire reached over and pulled the summary to herself. Flicking through the pages for about ten minutes, it looked comprehensive. Written in an almost identical format to the Professors Covid-19 report, it helped her in assimilating the knowledge.

Looking up with a hint of stress on her brow, Claire said,

'Professor, can I be blunt with you? What did you hope to gain by bringing this to our attention?'

Johnathon looked puzzled at her question and replied,

'If someone is developing this virus which is murdering our population, surely the Government would wish to do something about it? Wouldn't they?'

He continued in a slightly more confrontational voice,

'I hope I have not made a huge mistake highlighting this to you, so that your organisation can sit on their arses, pondering over it endlessly.'

The Squadron Leader, slightly shocked by the change of tone, upped the ante and stated firmly,

'Of course, you are correct. We will not ignore your work and what you have said here today. If we find your work can be verified, we will act. It is worth adding that we will act on a level you could probably not anticipate. The work of the SIS is seldom in the public domain, and for a matter of this gravity, if borne out, could be crucial to the world. Professor, we are going to have to ask you to hand over all your research work, hard copies, all computers, drives, and notes. This may seem a slight over-reaction to you, but if your research is deemed competent, I think you have identified a risk to our national security. As a consequence, you may be asked to help the SIS and our partners who are specialists in this field at Porton Down in Wiltshire. They will be testing your theory and may need your input to justify evidence of your findings.'

She gave this issue a moment to settle, but the Professor seemed to appreciate her directness.

Claire continued, 'Everyone privy to this report will be required to sign an Official Secrets Act Declaration and on the disclosure of even the smallest detail to an unauthorised person, could be charged with treason. Your findings are sufficiently important that I must tell you that a breach of the Act could lead to imprisonment.'

Johnathon was not expecting anyone to mention being incarcerated.

Slightly taken aback, Johnathon stated,

'We are all aware that what we have discussed here has been circulating in open public forums. Anyone can Google it.'

Claire knew he was right and replied,

'Yes, you are correct, Professor, but most people believe that any suggestion of a hostile intelligence service being behind the introduction of Covid-19 and 24 is just a conspiracy theory. The crucially important point here is that you have brought that conspiracy theory into the realm of an evidence-based scientific finding. You have upped the ante to a matter of significant national security, and we request your help in taking this to the next level. The work that we will be asking you to assist in, I suspect, will be as important as the breaking of the Enigma Code at Bletchley Park in World War II.'

She then made a statement that vexed the Professor.

'Of course, going live on TV with your announcement was reckless, and for a man of your obvious intelligence, you must have known that it would have repercussions.'

Slightly pink in the face, the Professor parried what he perceived as an insult by saying,

'Well, by being on TV, I finally got your attention. I am here, and it would appear that if you in the intelligence community were so bloody smart, all you would be saying is, "Thank you".'

Claire was feeling slightly stung by his response and the indirect attack. She recognised that it would be a good time for a break.

'Professor, please remain seated for now. I will be back in ten minutes but will arrange for you to have another coffee. Thank you for your time so far.'

Claire Walters had been instructed to keep the Professor in the Headquarters, and her immediate supervisor would meet with him at two-thirty p.m. if needed. She was well aware of the impact of the Professor's TV appearance, which had spread panic and fear quicker than the virus itself could. People had become immune to Government advice; life with the full suite of restrictions was no life. However, hearing the news broadcast caused people across the UK to go into even tighter lockdown than before. People were already cautious, but this news report raised tensions further. As the news spread, these reactions were replicated across the world as rumour and counter-rumour spun out of control.

It was against this dysfunctional social backdrop that future decisions on Professor King's assertions would be made. If the Professor was right, then all eyes within the SIS would be on him, and immediate action would be required. If a foreign intelligence service was involved, who knew what their game plan was?

She met Bill Rankin in the hallway, and he said,

'Take him for lunch. He seems fairly willing to help, and in truth, he will have no choice. Leave all his reports in Meeting Room Three. Staff Sergeant Charlton can get them disseminated so that we can get immediate input from a scientific perspective and a threat-level assessment.'

Claire went back to the meeting room and invited the Professor to lunch, instructing him to leave his bag and documents as they would be safe.

He looked up, still a bit annoyed with her, and said with a hint of sarcasm,

'If not here, where else would they be safe?'

'Please follow me,' she said, not rising to his dig.

Within minutes of leaving the meeting room, the documents were copied and sent to key departments within the SIS and over to Porton Down. Other key actions had also been instructed. Waiting could cost lives. They were potentially dealing with the greatest threat that had faced humankind. If the Professor's assumptions were borne out, and the Covid-24 virus had been engineered, they were at war, but only a few people knew it.

Chapter 7

The First Lunch

25th May 2024

Johnathon King was escorted to lunch in silence and struggled to keep pace with Claire as she strode purposefully along the corridors. Johnathon was not sure if she was in a strop and walking quickly to show her displeasure, as his wife had done on occasion when he had riled her. He concluded she was just athletic. Upon arrival at the staff canteen, he queued at the two-metre distance on the now-standard markings on the floor in all public places. Upon reaching the servery counter, he asked for a bowl of chicken soup and picked up a packet of ham sandwiches doubly covered in cling film. He had said nothing to anyone until he thanked the serving staff.

The dining facility was not busy as most MI6 staff had taken to bringing a packed lunch into work. This was another cultural shift which was brought on by the on-going pandemic. Staff could not sit and chat with friends in the same way as they could in what was now thought of as the good old days.

Claire was behind him in the queue and had said very little since leaving the meeting room. It was evident that she had ruffled the Professor's feathers. Sensing her reading of the situation was a little off-key, her concern was that she may have damaged her opportunity to move things forward. Johnathon sat down at a four-seater table and put his tray down. Claire pulled in diagonally to him, throwing him a half-cocked smile. He reciprocated. The ice wasn't broken, but at least it was a gentle thaw. Johnathon asked for a salt sachet which was set to the left of Claire's elbow.

She dutifully complied with, 'There you go, Professor.'

'Thanks,' he replied and continued. 'Look, we both want the same thing here. I am not the enemy, and, therefore, why don't we just agree to treat each other with professional respect and be allies?'

Claire was a bit disappointed that she had not taken the lead in the reconciliation but responded,

'I am happy with that, Professor, but as you will find out, I am not in charge here. Indeed, I am one of the smallest cogs in a monster machine.'

'But,' he said, 'you have the academic knowledge to get me to the right people to put my theories across, and, unless I am mistaken, not many people within the SIS have your expertise and qualifications.'

'Thank you,' she said, 'but there is an organisation that deals with all nuclear, chemical and biological warfare matters, and I suspect they may claim primacy on taking this matter forward in the national interest.'

'Are you referring to Porton Down?'

She smiled and said, 'Yes, Professor, that's right. The conversation regarding who will be working on this project going forward will be had at a higher level than mine.'

'Claire, call me Jon,' he said. 'Can we be straight with each other? What I have told you requires action on many different levels. We can prove the science, but we need people with different skills to mine to get to the bottom of this. To be honest, I don't know where to start, but start we must. Pretty damn quickly too. If we delay unnecessarily, we leave ourselves open to a whole range of risks, some I cannot even comprehend. I think this is where MI6 comes in. I need your support to convince the senior decision makers that I have not lost my marbles, and we are facing a clear and present danger.'

He smiled and said, 'Well, that's how Tom Clancy referred to it.'

His attempt at humour was to ease tension. It worked. Luckily, Claire understood the reference.

'We better eat,' Claire said.

After having some of his soup, Jon turned to Claire and said,

'Do you really understand what I have said, and if so, do you feel you can trust my judgement? I know this is all fanciful stuff, but I cannot, in my heart of hearts, come to any other conclusion than what we discussed.'

Claire glanced around, recognising that open conversation in this location was not a wise choice. She said softly,

'I am convinced of what you have said, but I would like to read your report for completeness. It will need to be scrutinised further by others, and only after that, will they wish to develop their own data and maybe, just maybe, those other actions you have spoken about could be set in motion. This isn't the place to discuss details. We are seeing my Section Head after lunch. He's a good guy with an open mind. Let's finish lunch, and we can talk later.'

'That's a deal.'

Jon tucked into his soup and gnawed at the fairly tasteless sandwiches. Coffee followed, and they chatted about where they both lived. Claire had a dull flat in North London, and he had a five-bedroomed house in the country. The Professor was a stay-at-home sort of guy who liked M&S ready-meals, good books, movies, and long walks with Willow. Claire had a different lifestyle before the pandemic. She was out most weekends seeing friends and family, taking in theatre shows, going to the cinema, and eating out which was her favourite pastime. The current situation meant that her life was put on hold. It was hard to absorb such a great deal of change but her job was a real lifeline. They looked at each other, both slightly envious of the other's life. He made off-the-cuff wisecracks about some of the people in the canteen being the antithesis to James Bond, and she laughed. He enjoyed seeing someone laugh at his silly humour; it had been a while. She found herself opening up to him, partly to make him feel relaxed. The other reason was to keep him amenable to what they were expecting from him, but also because she genuinely enjoyed the interaction.

He briefly mentioned the fact that his wife had died a few years earlier. It hit him hard, he admitted, but coped after a period of adjustment. Johnathon was very forthcoming. He said that his wife was not able to have children due to a medical issue. It was a major disappointment for both of them. With the onset of the Covid-19 crisis, Johnathon conceded it was easier to put any romantic involvement on hold. Using the virus as an excuse, Johnathon just accepted that finding the right person in the future would be difficult, but he had his dog. It was obvious to Claire that the dog was the significant other in the Professor's life. Apart from research, which by its very nature required full over-pressure suits and PPE, all his lecturing and university work done mainly online. He hated the impersonal nature of video conferencing, preferring the closer interaction of a lecture room. It was clear to Claire that he was quite a personable and probably sensitive man who was in tune with his feelings. The world of the SIS was one in which controlling feelings was quite important to maintain sanity, along with developing a slightly warped sense of humour and thick skin.

Claire also mentioned that she married at twenty-seven and suggested that her ambition was the cause of the marital breakdown. Her ex-husband was a doctor and wanted her home when he finished his shift and was most unimpressed with her commitment to the RAF.

Claire said, 'I should have realised it was doomed to failure before I got married because he had mood swings every time I went away on detachment, and when I returned, we argued.'

The lunch hour flew by, and Claire refocussed.

'We do need to be making tracks. Section Chief Rankin will be expecting us in thirty minutes.'

Hesitating just a moment, she added,

'I hope we will be able to work together on this,' she said, smiling slightly.

'I hope so too. It could be good for both of us,' he said agreeably and warmly.

'Tell me,' he said. 'That mirror in the meeting room, were there people observing me on the other side?'

Claire said, 'Observing us! If I cocked up, my job would be on the line. Every meeting in this place is recorded both in picture format and sound. Some meeting rooms have IR readers, along with a few other sneaky tricks to read your demeanour and physical condition.'

Under his breath, Johnathon said, 'Oh fuck!'

They arrived outside Meeting Room Three having built a few bridges and having a better understanding of each other. Whilst waiting to see Section Chief Rankin, Staff Sergeant Yorkie Charlton came in with a fairly stern look.

Yorkie introduced himself to Johnathon and then put on a TV monitor, saying,

'There's something you both need to see.'

The breaking news was of food riots in Liverpool and Yorkie's home city of Leeds. Both incidents led to a considerable number of deaths. The riots were growing in number and violence with rioters appearing with petrol bombs, crude explosive devices and weapons. Homes were on fire and people were beaten indiscriminately and taken into custody. It had turned into carnage on the streets.

Claire said, 'These scenes are unlikely to improve as the death rates climb, and fear becomes the backdrop in society. Soon, I suspect, each city will become its own fiefdom with local rule of law. Even within large towns and cities, smaller sub-communities could barricade themselves in, starting sub-cultures. In such cases, this could lead to a localised civil war and bloody conflict. All this makes our job here much more critical.'

Claire paused to reflect and then, changing her tone, said.

'Right, Professor, we need to get to work. It's time to introduce you to Section Chief Bill Rankin.'

As Johnathon was walking out, he turned to Yorkie and asked,

'Is she always this bloody cheery?'

Yorkie pulled a quizzical face and replied,

'She's a laugh a minute, don't you think? And you've caught her on one of her better days.'

Chapter 8

Judgement Hour

25th May 2024

After their brief visit to Meeting Room Three and meeting with Yorkie, Professor King collected his bag, and Claire picked up her files, before heading down the corridor to the Section Chief's office. Johnathon had not noticed that whilst they were at lunch, the contents of his briefcase had been emptied and recorded, the papers copied and returned, then left as if untouched. Copies of his report were sent to all relevant sections, including the Deputy Director Operations staff.

As usual, Emma was in Mr Rankin's outer-office and greeted them.

'Good afternoon. I hope you had a nice lunch.'

'Very nice, thank you,' they both replied in unison, casting a sideways look at each other.

Emma added, 'Please take a seat, and Mr Rankin will be with you presently.'

She buzzed through announcing the visitors. Bill Rankin was going to keep them a few minutes just to give himself a bit more time to collect his thoughts. He knew what was on his mind and what he was looking to achieve. As Section Chief, he wanted to show that he was in control and would get that across by keeping them waiting for a little.

Ten minutes later, Emma said,

'That's fine, Squadron Leader, if you would like to take Professor King through, Mr Rankin would be pleased to see you now.'

Emma motioned to the office door.

They stood, thanked Emma, and headed into the office.

Bill Rankin was already sitting at the small conference table with a coffee in front of him. He looked at the Professor, ignoring Claire, and said,

'Welcome, Professor. I hope we have been taking good care of you.'

Knowing his place, the Professor answered clearly and confidently,

'Your staff and the good Squadron Leader here have been perfectly accommodating, sir.'

He was relieved when Bill Rankin said,

'Call me Bill, and let's get down to business.

'Let me start, Professor, by saying that we were greatly alarmed by your TV appearance of yesterday.'

This came out slightly stronger than he had intended, but the Section Chief held his ground and followed up saying,

'I suspect that it has set in motion a sequence of events, of which our meetings today will be very much the tip of the iceberg. I want to be straight with you. We have had a great deal of interest in your appearance on the BBC. The PM is aware that you are visiting today, our allies are asking for access to you and, as I understand, every news station across Europe is looking for your further input.'

He paused, and both Claire and the Section Chief looked at the Professor for a response. Johnathon sat quietly waiting to hear something he had not yet considered, and the Professor's passiveness irritated Bill Rankin. However, Johnathon wanted to avoid a similar confrontation that he and Claire had to endure and thought that his new interrogator was not as sharp or personable as his initial one.

'May I call you Johnathon?' asked Rankin.

'Jon is good for me,' said the Professor.

'Thank you, Jon. We are also slightly concerned about your safety. Our communications teams have seen a noticeable level of chatter about you personally and the subject matter you raised more generally. As you may be aware, I can say no more on these sources but that they are reliable.'

What Bill had not mentioned was that there were indicators that several foreign countries had decided to monitor Professor King's movements and communications. Both the Chinese and Americans had been alerted to Professor King, plus a few European allies were curious. MI5 counter-intelligence teams had been alerted and were watching the watchers within this cat-and-mouse game.

'As a consequence,' Bill Rankin continued, 'we would recommend that you do not have any contact with media outlets, and when any further release is required, we will arrange this for you in a controlled environment.'

Jon looked at the Section Chief, commenting,

'You want me to speak with no one else without your explicit authority. Am I correct?'

'That's correct, Professor.'

The Section Chief continued observing Johnathon King's response but assumed he was in general agreement thus far.

'If what you have said to the Squadron Leader this morning is true and reliable, and I have no reason to doubt your integrity, it would be sensible to assume that those responsible for the manufacturing of the virus will be looking to, at best, discredit you or erase you and your findings.'

The Professor's eyebrows rose just a little, and he thought, 'Erase me? Fuck!'

'Consequently,' Rankin carried on, 'we have put agents on your university to physically secure your computers and files. With your approval, we would like to uplift these, along with your personal notes, and have them placed in a secure location. Do you agree with this?'

Professor King openly smiled just to allow the MI6 personnel to understand that he knew the rules of their game, saying,

'I suspect that should I say I am not happy with your proposed action, it would not have any significant impact on the outcome. True?'

A clever man, thought Rankin, it's a pity he doesn't know that all his IT equipment and notes, had already been taken into custody.

The Section Chief carried on,

'I think we also need to consider your personal security, and if you agree, we will provide you with a covert personal protection team; you won't notice they are there. Until we can get to the bottom of your research and put in place appropriate protocols, your safety is a key priority. I would like to suggest that you stay at one of our safe houses in London for the next few days and that you keep off all electronic communications until further notice.'

Johnathon said pointedly, 'You already have my phone and laptop. They were confiscated from me at reception, so it looks like that's taken care of.'

Rankin nodded and continued, 'Do you agree with these suggestions, and is there anyone you need to let know you will be off-grid for the next few days?'

Johnathon gave a brief list with the only one not anticipated being his neighbour, Jackie, who was looking after his dog, Willow. Bristol University had already been informed of Professor King's absence for the foreseeable future. Johnathon's phone had been downloaded; all texts and all calls were being transferred to an agency call centre. The phone itself was being sent out of London to give the impression that the Professor was travelling. This would keep hostile intelligence services reasonably well-engaged and at arm's length. A cover story was being put out indicating that he was secretly housed by an unnamed news agency who was preparing a scoop. Every media outlet was denying it was they who had the Professor under their wing, but they would, wouldn't they? For now, the Professor was oblivious to these actions.

Rankin kept up the momentum of the meeting, saying,

'Within your report, we have identified those students who assisted in your research and findings. Most of these people, we believe, are at home in lockdown. We are putting in place covert personnel protection teams for their safety and security until we determine a way forward. We are content they are not being targeted presently, but if any potential hostile intelligence service cannot get you, they may just want to speak to your students. Is there anyone on your list of research fellows that you feel is critical to any future research?'

Johnathon thought. The team was fairly young and inexperienced, all brilliant in their own ways, but in truth, mainly they were observing and recording more than providing the academic direction that the research required; he supplied the majority of leadership and management.

'Not really,' he said. 'It might be better to distance me from my students, but I would, however, recommend that you allow Squadron Leader Walters to be my research assistant if I need one. I believe she has the right academic background and who better to watch over my every move and report back to you.'

This was an unexpected curveball, as the Americans would say. Rankin put his head to one side as if considering, then responded,

'It is too early to say who we will have monitoring the next few stages.'

'The thing is, I am not asking. This is a precondition of my involvement. I do not intend to be difficult, but I need someone who can represent what is going on professionally and with complete honesty. I feel Claire fits the bill. She is academically qualified, and I suspect will represent matters appropriately.'

Rankin felt himself becoming annoyed at the Professors insistence.

'This is not entirely my call.'

'Then make it your call,' was Johnathon's reply.

Rankin's face for the first time since Claire knew him betrayed his emotions: he looked seriously pissed off. It took him a few seconds to compose himself, but it was evident that he had not been happy with the Professor prescribing the terms of his involvement.

'For now, let's assume your request can be acceded to, and I will confirm this within twenty-four hours,' Rankin responded forcefully, indicating that they were moving on.

Rankin pushed on in a slightly less friendly tone.

'The next phase is to have your research verified and, where necessary, put in place the necessary resources and support to see if we can learn anything further from the virus on a molecular level. We aim to get to the point where we can reasonably accept your assessment and then determine the next actions by HM Government's Secret Intelligence Services. Your input throughout this whole process will be required. What I suggest is that we reconvene tomorrow at nine a.m. in Meeting Room Three, and what I require you both to do is determine a strategy for achieving our first objective. In the morning, I will have some paperwork for you to sign, Professor, putting you on the SIS payroll with benefits.'

Section Chief Rankins's tone had moved from conciliatory to demanding. The warmth that was evident earlier was now long-forgotten. Claire knew that this change in tempo would not engender the best response from the Professor, nor indeed her immediate supervisor, and she was stuck in the middle. Her anxiety levels were rising, and she had not even taken part in the pissing contest between these two men.

'Do either of you have any questions for me just now?' Rankin asked, sounding stern and alternating his gaze between his two visitors.

'Sir,' Claire spoke for the first time in the meeting, 'can we assume that we will have the full resources of Porton Down, and will we be able to work with a team there who can verify Professor King's findings?'

Rankin slightly snarled the response,

'I feel that is a safe assumption.'

'Also, sir,' she added quickly, 'can I keep Staff Sergeant Charlton as my admin support, if I am to work with Professor King?'

She admired Yorkie, as he was known by his SAS colleagues. He was a man of many qualities, but one which shone the brightest was his ability to not take shit from anyone. He was a rock, a true tough guy, despite trying to adjust to the civilian SIS world.

Rankin was again caught on the hop.

'If, and only if, it is accepted for you to work with Professor King, then I am happy to authorise this. Do not say anything to the Staff Sergeant until all is agreed.'

Abruptly, Rankin ended the meeting.

'Thank you both for your time this afternoon. Professor, can you wait outside in my outer office? I have a few admin points to discuss with the Squadron Leader.'

'Of course,' the Professor said and made his way out of the office, shutting the door.

Once in the outer office, Jon began making pleasantries with Emma.

Claire could sense the tension in the room, and Rankin took in a huge intake of breath. 'Oh, fuck,' she thought, 'what is coming now?'

'What the bloody hell was all that about, Squadron Leader?' Rankin snarled again.

'Sir?'

'All that shit about King wanting you to be his research assistant. At what point in these proceedings did we allow this dick to take control,' he said with ferocious eyes depicting his anger.

'Boss, this came out of the blue to me as well. I had no idea he was going to suggest that,' Claire said defensively.

Rankin could not help himself.

'If this comes back to bite us in the arse, no one will come out of this smelling of roses.'

Then came a bombshell.

'I had already asked the Deputy Director Operations if you could co-lead this project, and the answer was definitely 'no!' You are too inexperienced, not formally on the SIS staff list, and you don't have the clearances.'

What Claire did not know was that Rankin was lying. Her boss wanted to put his subordinate in her place.

Claire blushed and retorted,

'But sir, I do have plenty of experience, otherwise, I would not be here. I suspect that within this building my qualifications for this job are as good as anyone else's. Secondly, I am happy to resign from the Royal Air Force and come onto the strength of SIS if that were to be required. Finally, sir, both you and I know that clearances are just a case of someone signing a piece of fucking paper.'

She hadn't meant to swear, but she could not take it back and had to demonstrate she possessed the necessary backbone to succeed in this.

She could see that Rankin was not used to insubordination, so she added,

'If you want me to tell Professor King that I do not want to work with him, I can do that. I am happy to tell him any untruth that would placate him. If it will be because someone else wants the job, that's fine. But I will not accept that my credentials for this operation are not up to scratch. Anything else, sir?'

'Yes,' he snapped, 'you are responsible for looking after Professor King. Get that assessment done and back here fed and watered at nine a.m. tomorrow. You are authorised to stay in the same safe house as the Professor tonight if that will aid you in getting a plan together. Until tomorrow, Squadron Leader.'

There was no pleasant hand-shake this time. Rankin had the last word but was still pissed off. He motioned his hand towards the door in a get-the-fuck-out-of-my-office motion.

It was now three-twenty p.m. Claire and Jon went back to Meeting Room Three. The whole mood had changed, and they both sat down.

Yorkie presented himself, filling the doorway. 'Sir, do you want any coffee?'

He knew Claire wanted one. He could always tell.

'Yes, please. Can I call you Yorkie? And please call me Jon. I fucking hate being called Professor, and I think we might be working together.'

Johnathon grinned like a naughty school boy.

Claire looked up with an incredulous expression on her face. She thought, 'Oh Christ, we were told not to say anything to the Staff Sergeant, and he's gone and blown it within two sodding minutes.'

Claire looked Jon in the eye and noticed a sort of boyish mischievousness she had not observed before, and said,

'What makes you think I want to work with you?'

'I don't,' he said matter-of-factly. 'However, I do want to work with you.'

'You know that Rankin was not happy with your dictate, and, although I don't know the man that well, I suspect he might have a different idea of what to do than what you think.'

'We'll see,' said Johnathon. 'I heard you both in his office sounding angry. Remind me from time to time not to piss you off.'

They both laughed in a slightly hollow way, drank coffee and started working together. It was going to be a long few days, but she and Yorkie had been working on the available options already. As far as the Professor was concerned, this was not going to be an easy ride, and it would require him to dig deep into his character.

Chapter 9

The Science Argument

25th May 2024

After the welcome coffee, they knew they had to get to work. Both Johnathon and Claire were feeling fatigued as the last two days had been manic and mentally draining. Yorkie just plodded on. Each drew strength from knowing that the prize was to convince senior staff that they could justify the science argument. The action after that, the three agreed, required input from people with different skill sets to theirs.

Claire started, 'Johnathon, we need to look at how we can verify your work. I think the best way forward is for you to explain your thinking and research yet again. Regardless of whatever we say here and now, it will rest on the judgement of the team at Porton Down. I know a few of the microbiologists there, and they are good people. In truth, they are absolutely working flat out, and they know their shit.'

Johnathon knew that he would have to jump through this particular hoop of justifying his work time and time again. Once it was accepted as good science, then MI6 could do their job, whatever that might be. He already sensed that he was reaching his limit of usefulness.

Johnathon quizzically looked at Yorkie and asked,

'Are we being videoed, mate?'

'We certainly are,' came the matter-of-fact reply. 'So, you had better speak up, nice and clear, sir.'

Johnathon grinned and began quite nonchalantly as if discussing the weather.

'As you know, viruses contain genes which allow them to mutate and evolve. The accepted understanding is that DNA within viruses carries genetic instructions for their development, functioning, growth and reproduction. Consequently, all living organisms inherit features or traits from their ancestors. Using recognised genetic testing techniques and methodologies, we can use DNA comparison to identify which traits are inherited and sometimes explain their provenance. More on this later.

'We can use records of known viruses to denote where certain inherited characteristics originated, hence the commonality in naming them. Where a virus has mutated from one generation to the next, clear DNA markers will show a family link. The differences between Covid-19 and Covid-24 are so significant that none of the major tell-tale generational signposts in its DNA were present. We observe similarities of course, but you would expect most viruses to have some of the same characteristics as others. It is like all humans have similar characteristics in DNA, and although we are not all directly related, it is fair to say that we all originated from the same gene pool. However, the differences are such that Covid-19 has more in common with other non-lineage viruses than it does with Covid-24. It was also impossible to identify any direct and significant commonalities between Covid-24 and other known viruses, which raised some red flags. It was assessed that every virus we considered was at least five generations younger than Covid-24. Most living creatures within an anthropological grouping have commonalities, and viruses are no different, but it does not mean they are all from the same family tree and are therefore not recently related. That can only mean one of two things: a freak mutation, which is as likely as a meteor hitting the earth within the next two hours, or someone tampering with nature. That's the baseline of my findings in a nutshell.'

Claire listened intently. She had read the report on Covid-19 and knew the science. This coupled with the gravity of the situation and acuteness of the impact of the subject matter held her captivated but she was still judging the Professor, as well as his argument.

Professor King proceeded.

'However, I appreciate that we need to explain my findings in more detail. I have stated in my research paper that virus source identification with the constant emergence of new, diverse viral populations will be a challenge. Trying to identify the absolute origin of a virus or its creator is nigh on impossible. This is due to the number of generations and mutations that have been undertaken. It's like trying to determine who your forefathers were thirty generations back; without clear records, the task is impossible. With viruses, we are talking about thousands and even tens of thousands of years. The major processes that give rise to viral diversity are mainly mutation, reassortment, and recombination. The problem is that modern science has been able to replicate all these naturally occurring strategies, and where, over time, a particular virus has developed through the manipulation of a number of these pathways, it is almost impossible to identify the originating source.'

Johnathon stopped to sip his coffee and did a mental check to ensure that he was keeping everything in sequence and his audience were still engaged and alert. Yorkie was trying to take notes but was lost in the complexity of the subject matter. Claire had been teaching him about basic microbiology, but the Professor was going too fast. As far as Yorkie was concerned, the Professor might as well be speaking Arabic.

Jon put his cup down.

'As more and more variants or generations are produced, the hazier the evidence to indicate the creator. Where this becomes even more challenging is when the work is carried out in secret, and no published records exist. Across the world, everyone is saying there are no records of Covid-24. Even the Chinese deny any knowledge of it. They claim that the virus originated five-thousand miles from China in Germany.'

Claire spoke up, saying, 'I know this is basic virology one-oh-one, but we have to explain this in a way that the non-scientific community can understand and make appropriate decisions. We have to work to our audience's capabilities and, dare I say, limitations. Rehearsing our arguments is important; we have to be credible and clearly understood.'

Johnathon King pressed on.

'Viruses themselves do not replicate. They enter the hosts and cause the host cells to copy the invading virus. Reassortment occurs when two such viruses with compatible genomes simultaneously infect a single cell and combine to make the host cell produce a completely new strain. This new virus will have many of the characteristics of the parent viruses. In a laboratory, where they have taken on the required characteristics, the virus could be mass-reproduced. This process could occur on multiple levels, and at each mutation, a more robust and virulent strain is generated. This form of mutation occurs naturally, but often the results are not aggressive. Examples, where the impact was devastating, were the Russian flu of 1889, the Spanish flu of 1918, the Asian flu of 1957, and the Hong Kong flu of 1968. Such mutations are not uncommon, but they tend to have elements within them that allow most people to fight them off through natural defences and antibodies. You will, of course, note that those outbreaks listed were all cases of flu, and this is crucial in understanding how these came about. There are millions of varieties of the flu virus, and as such, the probability will always exist that every twenty-five years or so, two flu strains will meet up and generate a more lethal variant. The good news is that in modern times cases of flu are generally, but not always, easy to vaccinate against. Even without a vaccine, flu viruses will burn themselves out because the human immune system is well-developed to cope with them. Simply put, flu viruses are very common, and we have developed generally efficient immune defences. The Covid virus is not so common, and we, as a species, have not developed the same level of immunity. On the plus side, Covid is not as robust or widespread as flu viruses, making it an almost impossibility that it could mutate as described and survive.

'I suspect given the DNA make-up of Covid-24, several techniques on multiple occasions have been used to engineer the virus to increase its potency. Achieving this level of development and outcome would have taken a fairly large team working tirelessly for years, possibly across multiple sites. It is my theory that the Covid-19 virus was one of the developmental stages leading to the end-virus, possibly Covid-24, but there may have been an even more terrible outcome sought – or if we want to be completely pessimistic, still being developed. You just don't know if the person, persons or country that is mad enough to want to inflict a pandemic on the world might not want to wipe it out.'

A little in desperation, Jon added, 'I have checked my research dozens of times. You might reasonably ask how I was able to undertake the assessment so swiftly. The answer is simple. I retained all my data on Covid-19 from the report produced during my clinical work on the comparison of SARS and Covid-19. When we conducted our research on both these early viruses, I can assure you that we had bullet-proof protocols in place. This allowed each research student to undertake his or her work independently of the others. I scrutinised all their findings. Just as a belt and braces precaution, I had an external auditor from Oxford come in to verify our deliberations. In our work, we found and verified eighty-four percent of common markers within DNA, proving it was highly likely that Covid-19 had mutated from SARS. Both came from China, and that made logical sense. What we don't know is whether there was any manipulation of the mutation because we found so few differences. The change between SARS and Covid-19 was at a reasonably low level of mutation from one virulent source to another. As you know, Covid-19 was, relatively speaking, quite impotent compared to SARS, the latter being more lethal. That said, Covid-19 was a much more aggressive virus in that it was more communicable, and though its lethality rate was lower because it affected a huge number of people, the death rate has been much higher.'

Johnathon sat quietly for a minute, then continued,

'But you know that in my report we did say that we could not one hundred percent discount any human input into the manipulation of the virus. I wonder if we had started this process earlier, we might have saved more lives.'

Claire said, 'Let's not go there, Professor. We can only influence the future, not the past. Let's focus on the here and now.'

Johnathon nodded and, concentrating on the science, proceeded to explain.

'Because the testing protocols were embedded within our laboratories at Bristol University, we used the same IT platforms for recording and assessing Covid-24. Consequently, we were able to come to our conclusions much faster. This was not an academic exercise this time. Our research team was genuinely concerned about our future lives and wanted a solution to this situation. Within weeks of the sample of Covid-24 hitting our laboratory, we knew something was wrong. We tested our samples again and again, but we got the same results. We even started quoting Einstein because we were refusing to accept our outcomes. You know the one that says, "Insanity is doing the same thing over and over again and expecting different results?"

'We were in such a quandary that we even re-checked our results on Covid-19, and we were not surprised to find our initial work was accurate. We agreed amongst ourselves that we should start again without reference to our previous findings on Covid-24. It came as no shock to find our results were wholly accurate. The reason for our astonishment was that the differences between Covid-19 and Covid-24 were so vast that, under any reasonable assessment, they could not be directly related. We believed we had either found a completely new virus or Covid-24 had been manufactured. We discounted the new virus theory because Covid-24 had too many similarities with Covid-19 which proved that elements had been taken from this virus. The geographical starting points of both viruses were so disparate, making it unlikely that one virus would naturally have a number of similar qualities. There were also markers showing similarities with SARS and MERS, and due to the limited outbreaks of these viruses, we knew it was almost impossible for this to be a naturally-occurring event. Because of this, we worked out that the likelihood that all three viruses could combine naturally was almost an impossibility. Our only conclusion was that it had been manufactured. Someone had developed this virus and infected the world. The reason for doing so eludes me but I am positive, well, ninety-nine point nine nine percent positive.'

To cement his argument, Johnathon thumbed through his stats, graphs, DNA and diagrams. They went through the range of tests and discussed methodologies and protocols, and all seemed in order. Claire's knowledge was rusty regarding her understanding of all aspects of the study, but the paper seemed, beyond a reasonable doubt, to justify its conclusion.

Johnathon King looked up from his papers, smiled at the small camera on the ceiling pointing at the table, and said,

'That, then, is the case. Convinced?'

Claire exhaled a huge sigh, then said,

'I hate to say it, but I am on board.'

Looking at her watch, she saw it was five-thirty p.m. Because she had not told Jon, when organising the meeting, that it might result in an overnight stop, she had presumed that he needed some supplies.

Just then, Yorkie stood up and checked his phone.

'More coffee, ma'am, Professor? Oh, Jon, your overnight bag is at reception. You can pick it up when you leave.'

Claire was quietly impressed with Yorkie's level of perception.

'We will, however, be hanging on to your mobile and laptop,' Yorkie added comically, pulling a face.

'Coffee would be great, Staff,' Claire said.

Looking directly at the Professor, she said,

'What about dinner? May I suggest that we eat on the premises, have a working supper, and get a car to our accommodation at about nine p.m.? Is there anything that you do not eat, or do you have any food allergies?'

Johnathon replied, 'Just get me any form of comfort food. I'm not fussy.'

Claire ordered, 'Make that two, Staff, or three if you are hanging on.'

'Ma'am,' Yorkie replied and continued, 'I will hang around until you leave, just in case you need something.'

She smiled her approval, 'Definitely better make it three suppers then.'

He nodded in appreciation, about-turned and left. Coffee landed ten minutes later, and supper arrived at six-thirty p.m.

After a period of chatting about the other remote possibilities, they took a ten-minute break from the science. They agreed that for HM Government to take action on the report, an independent review of the science paper, line by line, would undoubtedly be undertaken, perhaps even fresh research from scratch by a completely new team. Professor King believed that he could contribute little more of value to the research. Any verification work, due to its nature, should be concluded without his input or influence. This would prevent any natural bias or cognitive dissonance.

Johnathon turned to the Squadron Leader saying,

'Claire, the evidence to prove where this virus came from is beyond my skills. That will require physical evidence. Without that, it is only conjecture. We need to find the centre that produced the virus and obtain hard data. In truth, I feel pretty impotent at this stage. I suspect my skill sets will be of limited contribution once the science is complete.'

'Your knowledge of the subject matter still has a key role to play. Let's just discuss matters and see where the science and effective intelligence take us. How does that sound?'

Bouncing ideas around, they knew that Covid-19 was first identified in Wuhan, China. Every indication was that the labs there were either developing the virus or were part of a wider team of scientific review.

Even the Chinese accepted that it was a laboratory accident that caused the virus to escape and was the start point of the initial pandemic; it was either poor seals on the storage units or mishandling. They agreed they would never really know the truth as the lead scientist and many of his team had died of infection. At least that's what the official Chinese news agency broke. It would not be a surprise if they were casualties of the regime. Punishment killings for gross incompetence were not unheard of in China. They did know that a disproportionate number of Wuhan's doctors succumbed to the virus, notably when they were trying to alert the outside world of the pending disaster.

Johnathon mused, 'I would put money on there being evidence at that site regarding testing. I would think that this facility also holds keys to other sites used in production. There must be a communication trail leading to a key decision-maker. I suspect a military element as well, otherwise, why produce the virus?'

He was sure of it.

Claire was impressed and added,

'The problem might be that this could be a rogue element, operating outside the leadership's knowledge. We know the Chinese are culturally secretive, and within a secretive society, it's easier to hide things. It is true to say that keeping one thing secret is easier when all things are secret.'

She took a sip of coffee and went on with her thinking.

'The state may have a role in this but it would not be beyond belief that a single person in a position of power and influence is playing a dangerous game.'

Johnathon said, 'Ha! The mysterious Dr No.'

'That is not as odd as you might think. History is littered with despots, dictators and emperors who started in lowly positions but had a vision. A bonkers vision but a vision all the same. Think Hitler, Stalin, Napoleon plus the range of tyrants across the Middle East. Killing millions of people for personal gain and power is not new. Genocide is more common than you might think. The Balkan Wars were only a relatively short time ago. Throughout Africa in recent history, there have been inter-tribal genocides. Let's not kid ourselves that history might not repeat itself. Even our own illustrious history is pretty blood-soaked.

Many kings have slaughtered thousands of people, sometimes on a whim; Richard the Lion Heart massacred thousands of Muslim prisoners during the Third Crusade. The world can be a cruel place; our job here is to keep it safe and to protect our people first and foremost.'

Switching gears, Claire said, 'We need to have a plan of action for tomorrow morning. We cannot go into the meeting with nothing of significance.'

After a bit of discussion, they formulated a list of actions. They went through them again to get the delivery right. Claire was desperately hoping that she had not pissed-off Bill Rankin too much earlier in the day. If so, it could mean that she might be side-lined.

It was agreed that Claire would take the lead at the presentation. She needed to show herself as a worthy Project Officer.

The staff car came and took Claire and Jon to a safe house at nine p.m. They went to their respective rooms without delay. Their heads were racing with facts and figures; the 'what ifs?' were the most challenging thoughts. Claire desperately hoped that she had not burnt her bridges earlier in the day. She lay in her bed, worrying she had over-stepped the mark in Rankin's office and then let her insecurities run free. She reviewed every step of the day, questioning whether she had done enough, her approach was appropriate, she had treated the asset (the Professor) with detached professionalism, was she really cut out for this shit, and on it went. Her eyes closed at two a.m., and the alarm went off at six a.m.

The SIS car across the road was a Close Protection Team that stayed there all night. The MI6 service car arrived at seven-thirty a.m. and took the two passengers back to Vauxhall. The close protection vehicle followed behind at a discreet distance. The two watchful personnel had nothing to report from the last twelve-hour period of surveillance: a tough and pretty dull shift which was true of the majority of babysitting cases.

Chapter 10

Changing Gears

26th May 2024

At eight a.m. the arrivals went through reception security and collected a pass for Professor King. They were at their tables in Meeting Room Three within twelve minutes, hot coffee at the ready. Yorkie came in and ran through the slides they had asked to be made as part of their presentation. They rectified one minor spelling mistake and then deemed that they were perfect. Claire had emailed the briefing notes, stamped, "Top Secret UK Eyes Only". The Secret and Confidential Registry had copied these and recorded them. They presented the notes, professionally bound, to Claire who signed for them. She had six copies for distribution. She had passed a copy directly to the Section Chief so he could review it. It would give him the chance to be one step ahead of everyone else and add constructively to the meeting. Claire wanted him to be in a good mood today and see she was a team player.

At eight-thirty-five a.m., Emma rang the meeting room telephone in her usual chirpy voice.

'Squadron Leader, can you come along to Mr Rankin's office immediately, and would you please let the Professor know that the meeting has been put back to ten a.m.?'

'Certainly, Emma, I'll be with you presently,' she said, trying to disguise the concern in her voice.

She looked up and saw both Yorkie's and Jon's eyes fixed on her. Not waiting for them to ask her if everything was OK, she quickly reported,

'The presentation has been put back to ten, and the Section Chief wants to see me now.'

She added, unconvincingly,

'Nothing to worry about, I'm sure. I'll be back shortly.'

She hastily gathered together the briefing folders and left, avoiding questions so she didn't give away her feeling of trepidation. Claire hoped she was going to be asked to explain some detail of the paper or to add a point here or there. Her heart was racing.

'Get a grip of yourself, you arse,' Claire directed herself, and she put her shoulders back, plastered a smile on her face, and entered her boss's outer office.

'Morning, Emma, how are you today?' Claire said in a borderline cheerful voice.

Emma was as pleasant as always, saying,

'Perfectly well, thank you. Just grab a seat for a minute, Claire. Bill has got someone in with him just now.'

Claire's mind was racing to think who it could be. She forced herself to settle down. It could be anyone so what was the point of worrying? She wondered if she should apologise for her unorthodox and aggressive behaviour yesterday and then decided not to bring it up.

'Right, Squadron Leader, in you go,' Emma nodded with her usual smile.

Claire entered the office with a slight swagger to disguise her true feelings and saw Bill Rankin and two other people seated at the conference table.

'Come in, Squadron Leader, and take a seat,' Mr Rankin said formally, pointing to an empty chair. The Chief of Section showed no emotion; he was stone-faced.

Bill introduced Tom MacDonald, Deputy Director Operations, whom she had first met briefly at her initial interview and on infrequent occasions after that. DD Ops lived in the rarefied atmosphere of Field Work. The other chap was David Jones, Section Chief of the Far East Desk. Claire nodded to each man as his name was given.

Rankin kicked off with a confrontational tone.

'We are here to cut to the chase on this matter of Covid-24. We have all had access to the reports of yesterday's meeting, the study produced by Professor King has been reviewed by external sources, and we have scan-read your briefing document for this morning. No bullshit, Walters, do you think this guy is legitimate?'

His tone of voice was borderline contemptuous. They all waited for a response. Tom MacDonald casually tossed her briefing guide to one side, as if saying it was rubbish. He could not look any more disinterested, and Claire felt her palms perspire.

She gathered herself and, ignoring the rude attitudes of her superiors, said,

'I think he is most credible, sir. He seems switched on and knows his stuff. I know the report will need verification, as outlined in my comments, but his logic is credible. He is convinced that his assessment is correct, and I believe him.'

Tom MacDonald spoke, looking directly at Claire with a dour expression on his face.

'Is it not that you want him to be right so you can lead this project? We saw from the tapes of your meeting that he was playing you on an emotional level, and you responded positively. You are suggesting undertaking a major operation, against possibly one of the most powerful countries in the world. Are you putting your ambition before everything else?'

Claire felt her neck go red and was happy she was wearing a high-neck blouse. Her ears were getting warm which was an indication she was under pressure, but she was not going to put up with this crap.

'Sir,' she said, with gusto and finding herself getting wound up again, 'this man came to us without any need for duress. We didn't need to put a bag over his head to get him here. Professor King has shown us everything he has on the situation and was open about his research. Basically, he is co-operating as fully as we could ever hope. Regarding my position, I have already been told in no uncertain terms that I do not fit the bill to run this operation. Consequently, once the presentation is concluded today, I suspect I will be side-lined, and someone more suitable will be appointed. Mr Rankin was clear on that matter yesterday, whilst bluntly highlighting my weaknesses as the reason for doing so. I will say that I did not agree with him and still do not agree with his arguments but accept them with the greatest respect for his professionalism.'

She paused for a split second, and each man at the table showed no change in demeanour, they all seemed to be indifferent to her comments and pleas.

Claire thought, 'These bastards are going to hear my real thoughts.'

'Regarding my relationship with Professor King, I think you are insinuating some sort of flirtation which is both absurd and insulting. He's a nice man but old enough to be my father. I'm a professional, and I have not compromised myself or this investigation nor would I ever.'

She paused and took a further deep breath.

'If you want, as you called it, a no-bullshit assessment of where we are at, I suggest that you take his report seriously, get it checked out and pass our recommendations onto someone who can review them professionally. Once they come to the same conclusions as I have, you can take immediate effective action on them. The longer we wait, the greater the threat that a hostile intelligence service will be able to get the next generation pandemic launched, killing millions more people. If Professor King happens to be wrong, we will all still be floundering in the dark regarding this pandemic and what to do next.'

The atmosphere in the office had changed. It felt electrified.

'Wow, Bill, you said she was a firecracker yesterday. She stands her ground well. Tell me, Squadron Leader, do you ever take any prisoners?' said Tom MacDonald, his bearing changed.

Claire sighed inwardly at the sexism amid the veiled compliment.

'Squadron Leader, be assured we are taking this very seriously. Indeed, we have been since you briefed Bill here two days ago. You were quick off the mark, and I can see you have put a great deal of effort into this so far. My gut tells me this is going to be one difficult and complex matter to get our heads around. Consequently, we need our brightest and most capable minds on this. What do you say, Squadron Leader?'

Claire looked at the imposing figure of Tom MacDonald, not sure what he was asking her.

Just as she took a breath to speak, MacDonald raised his hand, saying,

'Good. You will be the Project Officer for this operation. You now have clearance to see everything on Operation Fulcrum Storm which is the operational name for the investigation into the potential manufacture and use of biological agents by as-yet-unknown hostile agencies or country. This is Top Secret (UK Eyes Only) for now, and if I have my way, it will remain a wholly National matter. This is a codeword-level operation, and only the people on the list David will share with you are authorised as of now to be involved. Until we know who and what we are dealing with, we will keep this list tight. If you want to expand the list of those requiring access, you need my explicit approval. You will co-ordinate all technical aspects and liaise with David Jones, who will directly control all operational matters.'

Having laid out his direction in a clear simple form, he eased his tone a tad.

'I think it is safe to say we see either the Chinese Government or a rogue unit within the Chinese Special Weapons set up as our primary targets. I have reviewed your action plan, and it's bloody good, but it needs some refinement. David will talk you through my thoughts, but we have a "Go". Let's do the meeting as planned. I want to meet this Professor King; I have a few questions for him. Get a taskforce together and get the ball rolling. Your first meeting is at two p.m. this afternoon. That's all for now. Let's get focussed.'

Claire stood up, looked directly at Bill Rankin, and said,

'Sir,' hoping the tone of her voice would convey her appreciation. She guessed that he had gone to battle for her and had persevered. Little did she know that Tom MacDonald was already earmarking her for this role, and her boss was less enthusiastic about her participation. Tom was impressed with her work thus far. He had told Rankin to tell her that he had misgivings because he wanted to test her resolve. Tom saw the tapes from the initial and secondary meeting with the Professor, plus the chat with Rankin yesterday. He knew she was the best person for the job.

Bill nodded, receiving her message of appreciation, and said,

'Good morning, Squadron Leader. On your way out, Emma has an Admin pack-up. Go through it with Professor King. He has to sign-up to everything, or we cut him loose.'

She left, feeling that all the anxiety from earlier had lifted. Claire went to the ladies' washroom just to be on her own for a few moments and gather her thoughts.

'Bloody hell, that was an intense twenty minutes,' she muttered shaking her head. 'Shit, I have to be more self-confident.'

She questioned if she had been too aggressive, but the outcome was what she wanted. Her conclusion: the means justified the ends. This was the once-in-a-lifetime opportunity so many people dream of, and she knew she had identified the opportunity and taken the right steps to be given it. Others were more passive, and such opportunities just passed them by. Over time they might think the system is unfair or biased, but it all came down to taking your chances when they presented themselves. Her watch words were energy, intelligence and action.

Hitting Meeting Room Three in full-stride, she flung open the door. Both Professor King and Yorkie were chatting. They turned to see Claire enter the room, smiling broadly.

Jon took a sip of his coffee and said,

'Good meeting, Squadron Leader?'

The response was a shrug of the shoulders and relaxed expression; she made it straight to the coffee pot, poured a drink and added a splash of milk and sugar.

Claire sat down and took a big gulp. Gathering herself, she turned to her team and said,

'This is where the hard work starts.'

She went on to apprise them of her meeting, enjoying ribbing the Professor that they had questioned his sanity. He didn't care. The crisis was being taken seriously and who had not wondered about their sanity in these troubled times? She went through the admin pack-up with Johnathon, and he signed everything without reading it.

He looked at Claire and said,

'You'll keep me right, won't you?'

Yorkie smiled at the cavalier attitude to these life-changing documents.

'Do you ever take anything seriously, Prof?' he asked.

Claire said jokingly, 'The Professor just signed his in-service Death Benefit over to me along with all his future pension payments. I could retire now if he pops his clogs.'

Both men laughed.

Chapter 11

The Team

26th May 2024

Claire Walters, Yorkie Charlton and Professor Johnathon King had spent the last two intense hours going over slides and briefing notes. This was a crucial moment in their lives. The presentation to the in-house team authorised to be briefed on the whole of Operation Fulcrum Storm was about to start. Claire was the one speaking, and Yorkie was looking after the visual aids. Coffee and the standard pre-packed biscuits were out. In attendance were:

Tom MacDonald – Deputy Director Operations

David Jones – Section Chief, Far East Desk

Phillip Wong – China Desk

Bill Rankin – Section Chief, Special Weapons

Lee Ford – GCHQ Signals Intelligence Liaison

Major Tim Churchill – Special Forces Liaison

As usual, Deputy Director MacDonald wanted to set the tone. As a former field operative he didn't pull any punches. An outwardly large and intimidating man, he enjoyed the challenge of making people raise their games. He would not let his team hide behind political correctness or allow people to be 'fluffy in their attitudes,' as he put it. He thought that kind of inept behaviour was slowly incapacitating British society and was quite vocal about it. He was a tough guy and just a few years off retiring on paper, but he never wanted to retire. The much younger and so-called free-thinking staff across MI6 thought he was a dinosaur in terms of his attitudes and behaviour, but in his younger days Tom was considered a rebel and a bit of a problem child. As a young working-class boy, he didn't fit the mould of an MI6 operative, and his style of action was somewhat unorthodox, which got him in trouble with his superiors many times over. Technology had left him a tad behind, but he respected modern intelligence-gathering methods. Tom had been at the forefront of many of the innovations over the past thirty years or so. The team within his Directorate referred to him affectionately as Uncle Tom, and he was held in high regard. Those personnel in the field who came under his control considered him next to God, and for some God was in second place. He never made promises that he did not keep. Tom's straight-talking and outstanding leadership gave confidence to those personnel putting their lives on the line. Few people challenged him because he was an expert at reading people and had more than his fair share of intellect. This coupled with a staggering amount of practical experience meant that there was little he did not know. Tom was open to new opinions and attitudes but held the fake-it-until-you-make-it brigade in contempt. These people, he knew from experience, were lazy and had expectations beyond their ability, intellect and drive.

He started the meeting in his no-nonsense briefing style.

'Good afternoon, everyone. I want to put into perspective today what we are dealing with, should our worst fears be realised. Were we to prove that a hostile intelligence service has actively and maliciously released Covid-24, and possibly Covid-19, on the world's population, whoever this person or persons are, they have committed an act of war. The use of a virulent biological agent can only be deemed as a war crime by international standards. Despite the nature of the virus, we are talking about the deployment and use of a weapon of mass destruction. I mention these phrases for two reasons. Firstly, to impress upon you that already the instigators of this act have killed more people than died in World War I and World War II combined. Secondly, if the architects of this virus are allowed to develop further strains, they could kill up to six and a half billion people. To put that into perspective, that is about six percent of all people that have lived on planet earth for over the past fifty-thousand years. People, these are big fucking numbers and dwarf anything your brains or mine can take on board. If we do not identify the perpetrator of this crime and put a stop to these actions, we not only risk placing our society, family and friends in total jeopardy but also humankind as we know it. I must ask, does everyone appreciate the enormity of what we have before us today?'

Everyone nodded or quietly accepted the Director's assessment. For

Johnathon, when put like that, it made everything he had set in motion seem overwhelming.

'During our peacetime operations, the Intelligence Service Act provides various levels of oversight which are completely inappropriate to what we are facing here today. Consequently, I have been assured that we are treating this situation as being at war. That means the gloves are off, and we must do whatever it takes to get to the bottom of this. We will need to anticipate field force casualties and, where necessary, bring to bear the full force of our intelligence service, special forces and military assets.'

He paused for effect looking in turn at each person seated; his message had landed.

'The Secretary of State for Foreign and Commonwealth Affairs has granted immunity from British prosecution to all SIS and attached support personnel when engaged in Operation Fulcrum Storm worldwide. For the avoidance of doubt, this includes immunity for all actions, up to and including murder but excludes genocide or treason. Our ability to use fully no-holds-barred interrogation methodologies as a means to extract information is authorised. However, people, let's not leave evidence, especially if we stretch accepted conventions. Be assured that if you are caught with your fingers in the till we will deal with you internally. For those uninitiated, this means if anyone pulls stunts for self-benefit or gratification, I will have their nuts. Get your people whatever they need to do their jobs. Anyone engaged in this operation will have full and enhanced pension support. Our venture has no budget limitations, but we will not be frivolous either. Make sure you get the best intelligence available, do not take "no" for an answer and leave no stone unturned. All assets will be given over to this operation as a priority. If we need to piggyback on the NSA, we have a few favours to call in, but I will only consider this as an option of last resort. Let me remind you this is a UK-Only Operation. Anyone who is not a fully paid-up member of the UK is not to be involved at any level. The only exception will be if we need in-theatre assets to assist in direct action but that will be on a need-to-know basis only. This is a UK operation for now, but should we need to call in NATO or US assistance, we will. Remember this is the most important operation we have run in years, possibly ever, and it is extremely sensitive, therefore we must maintain operational security at all costs.

'Let's get a result here and fast as every day we delay, more people die, and if we let the hostile intelligence service loose with another virus, that's a real game changer. Get everything right the first-time round.'

Taking a sip of water, Tom could see the shock on Professor King's face. He coughed to clear his throat before continuing.

'For those of you being exposed to SIS operations for the first time, you will have to understand that to keep the nation safe and to take on nations that do not allow our freedoms and support our values, we sometimes have to fight dirty. We take no pleasure in doing so, but if we do not take the fight to the enemy employing their tactics, we will be putting our people in harm's way with one arm tied behind their backs. More importantly, we risk leaving ourselves open to defeat and not achieving our objectives. The resultant impact would be millions, if not billions, of lives needlessly lost. Under no circumstances can we, through lack of courage or resolve, allow this to happen. I hope we are all clear on this?'

The whole audience nodded, including Professor King.

Tom MacDonald turned to Squadron Leader Walters, offering a confident nod.

'Claire, we have all seen the science on this matter. We have preliminary advice from our experts at Porton Down, and they concur with your assessment and the Professor's work, so thank you both for that. For future justification, they will undertake their own research, but they feel it is an exercise in going through the motions. For brevity, I would suggest we forgo going over the science again. Just now, my poor little brain couldn't take any more but be assured we very much appreciate both your hard work and that of the Professor over the past few days.

'Let's move on to the operational action plan you have proposed, and we will focus on getting the right next steps in place. However, before we do this, I have a question for the Professor. Professor King, please explain to me, why the hell did you go to the BBC to make your point rather than coming directly to us? What possessed you to announce this to the world and cause the panic that it has?'

This was a question that he had been waiting for the past two days.

'Tom, I think it is important for you to know that my attendance on National TV was not the first instance that I tried to gain the attention of His Majesty's Government. As will be borne out by my laptop and mobile phone which I am sure your teams have reviewed, I made countless attempts to engage with Senior Ministers, but all my efforts fell on deaf ears. I didn't leave it there. I tried to ring Porton Down. I contacted the Foreign and Commonwealth Office, MI5 and MI6. I sent a copy of my report to all those departments and organisations. I rang my MP and again received no response. All this occurred over three weeks. Not one person in a position of responsibility had the time or intelligence to see the importance of what I was trying to say. Frustrated and pissed off, I just did not know what to do next. I couldn't get anyone to listen.

'Thus, I felt I was left with no choice. I got myself on TV, and within one hour, she,' pointing to Claire, 'she took the right action to put us in the position we find ourselves today. So, to put things into perspective, it was the failure of the intelligence services to act intelligently that forced my hand.'

Professor King scanned the faces of those assembled and saw they looked thoughtful and concerned. Deputy Director MacDonald was pleased with the response. Had King crumbled at his question, that would have been the end of him in terms of being embraced by the intelligence community. Instead, he showed both courage and integrity.

'He's a keeper,' MacDonald thought.

Tom said, without a hint of cynicism,

'Thank you, Professor, for your eloquent reply. Moving on, Squadron Leader, let's hear your plan for resolving this situation.'

Apart from a small problem with the slides, the presentation was slick. It was a complex plan with several key activities all taking place simultaneously. Some were stand-alone activities, and others had aspects that needed careful planning and to-the-minute coordination. As she noted in her comments to the group, there were many areas where the whole thing could come crumbling down. For the plan to succeed, they needed an element of luck and good fortune, but everyone in the military knew such was the nature of conflict. However, she also knew that the harder you work and train, the luckier you get. Much of the proposed action was challenged, not because it was not well-considered but to check its robustness and the confidence of its authors. Elements were improved, and as the detailed planning progressed, further enhancements would be expected and introduced. The experience of the senior personnel came to the fore, offering insights of which Claire, Yorkie and the Professor had no knowledge or experience. Indeed, the Deputy Director's input across a swathe of matters impressed everyone. There seemed to be little in terms of live operations that he had not come across previously. This wily character had a sharp mind and was able to see all the connected activities, just like seeing a chess board and knowing your next ten moves. DD Ops Tom MacDonald was a true master at this game.

At the appropriate time, Tom got to his feet, surveyed the room, and said,

'People, we have the makings of a bloody good team here, the best. The plan is robust and taut, but we need to keep reassessing matters constantly. Success will depend on getting the details right and communicating with each other. This is not a rigid plan but a living one. We have no room for individual pride. If someone challenges you, raise your game and get to the right answer. Do not challenge needlessly but help and support each other fully. I would like to remind you all, often it is friendly fresh eyes that can see and highlight weaknesses in action, so within this team, get others to review your ideas and findings. The objective is to succeed, not to look good. Success will make us all look good. We have to keep our heads because those of our forces on hostile ground rely on us to do our jobs so they can have a reasonable chance to get back home to their families. We have no time to waste. You have all been allocated individual operations. Get your planning done and take affirmative action on time. Our follow-up meetings are scheduled; make sure you are prepared for them. Do not let the country or me down. Remember operational security is to be so tight that I don't want to hear of any cock-ups. If I do, the person making the slip-up will find themselves face down in the Thames.'

He smiled and left the room. Tom liked to leave such meetings with a parting statement that left a lasting impression.

Everyone immediately started to speak to those nearby. The complexities were daunting, but now they all had a starting point. Certain aspects of planning were based on assumptions that could be widely misleading. Thinking time was in short supply, but the combined intellect in the room was impressive. More importantly, the assembled group members were supremely motivated and had a great desire to get their specific jobs done.

Chapter 12

Operation Prune Pie – Part 1

26th May 2024

Professor King was now firmly ensconced in MI6, and it had only been three days since his TV broadcast. He had a permanent pass with his photo on it that read, 'Access all areas.' Johnathon had all the induction requirements completed and was on the payroll. After the meeting with the team, he was instructed to lock himself in his new office and get to work on a paper which proved that Covid-19 and Covid-24 were not related but in essence discrediting his own research. Staff Sergeant Charlton was on-hand to assist. He arranged for the kitchen to prepare meals for their new team member. He had a large pot of coffee constantly on the go in the office. It felt strange to Johnathon, but he aimed to craft manufactured proof that he and his students had delivered the wrong conclusion. Essentially, the study was a sham and would portray him as an academic idiot having gone on television and frightened the world, and now to retract his statements that Covid-24 had been engineered. Whilst he was getting down to changing the details of his work, every copy of the real study was being taken out of circulation and held in a secure location, indeed, at the same location as his computers and all other related materials confiscated from Bristol University were held. It was going to be a long night as the amended report needed to be finished and verified by ten p.m. tonight. He was relieved that he wasn't doing this all alone. Access was given through direct secure communications to Professor Janet Williams at Porton Down. She was providing helpful hints on how to undermine his findings and, by inference, his professional credibility. Whole new data sheets were being reproduced, and diagrams were altered very slightly yet significantly. Professor Williams would not be going home tonight either; she had her report to produce which would attack the Professor's work and impugn his professional credentials.

The BBC had been ramping down their interest in Professor King's revelations because they lacked evidence to substantiate them, and, despite their best efforts, they had not been able to communicate with or locate him. Senior Executives were actually wondering if the whole thing was a hoax. No one at the University of Bristol was available for comment, either formally or off the record. The Corporation had come in for some serious criticisms for allowing someone with, what now seemed to be an agenda about which they did now know, to take up valuable air-time and placing the audience in a panic. The public reaction after the broadcast set the mood racing, but, as always, the general population had a short attention span. Moreover, across the news and via the internet a few extremists had grossly overplayed the comments. These radical voices effectively took the attention away from Professor King. More balanced heads were trying to assess what was said on an intellectual level. That said, every outcome seemed like a doomsday event with the consequent breakdown of civility between panellists, leading to a free-for-all shouting match. To suggest that either outcome was plausible, made the person voicing it sound like a fanatic. The official line from HM Government on that first day was to ask Professor King to provide a copy of his study and findings. The nation's experts would be happy to review the research and make appropriate comments, but only once the report was seen. The sting in the tale was that the Government scientists and other esteemed academics looking at these viruses previously had not come to the same conclusion as Professor King. It was stressed that many experts were working with the viruses to develop vaccines and determining the best way to deal with all other aspects of the pandemic. It was suggested that these individuals who were working 'at the coalface' with the viruses were in a stronger position to comment than the probably well-intentioned academic whose full-time job was teaching students. Little digs at the Professor, both his character and his academic reputation, were becoming more prevalent and cutting.

That evening on the BBC Nine O'Clock News and every other mainstream news outlet, it was briefly reported that Bristol University had suspended Professor King indefinitely on full pay due to 'irregularities in his research methodologies and other improprieties.' The report concluded, 'It is the University's policy not to comment on on-going disciplinary situations.' Fortunately, Johnathon had not heard the news broadcast as it would have deeply wounded him, especially the thought that his father, sister and friends would hear this.

In the basement of the SIS Headquarters, the Tech Team, under Claire's watchful eye, was drafting some texts to be sent from Professor King's mobile number. His laptop was also going to be used to contact those few people with whom the Professor had communicated, albeit intermittently, via social media.

The first text was sent to his friend, Jackie, and simply said, 'Hi Jaq, I am not well. Things have just got too much for me. Will call soon. Look after Fluffy Puppy for me. Any problems, just text. Cheers, Jon.'

A message was sent to his father, 'Hi Pops, things are a bit messed up just now. Don't worry, I'll be in touch soon. Any problems, just text. Love, Johnathon.'

A similar message went to his parents-in-law, his sister Julie, his close pal Colin and a few professional contacts.

A further text went to those students who had been involved in the research. It simply read, 'Hi, sorry if my unconventional TV appearance has caused you any distress. I am taking a leave of absence to sort out a few personal things. If you have any queries, contact the Dean's office at the Uni. Keep safe. Prof King.'

In all, texts were sent to thirty-seven people to let them – as well as those monitoring his communications – know that he was not well and needed a bit of time. The texts were transmitted, spaced out over an hour or so, to emulate how a person would normally communicate. Those people watching and probably listening to the Professor's phone would be experienced in analysing misleading messages. Some would be the newspapers who had become so adept at intercepting such messages. Others might be hostile intelligence services or inquisitive allies. Every phrase used in these latest texts was an exact copy of previous ones used by the Professor, with the same salutation and the same sign-off the Professor used for each different person. The Tech Team spotted a spelling mistake that Johnathon consistently made and ensured that they did not change it. They noted he used no emojis or slang.

A post was put on his Facebook page which would hit his seventy-five contacts, some of whom would be the same folk who had received texts earlier. It said, 'Hi everyone, things have got a bit messed up, and I need some time off work to get well. I am seeing a doctor tomorrow and will be off-line for a while. Will be back soon. Keep well and safe. Jon.'

Not a great fan of social media, the Professor only had a Facebook page because his wife had created one for him. He did not want to appear as a technophobe, so he kept it going after his wife passed away. Weeks could go by, and he would not even think of reviewing his page, but then an email would land saying that he had a message on Facebook. He did not respond to much.

Back in his newly acquired office, Professor King found it a bit difficult to hand over his credit cards to an unknown youth, but it was part of the plan. They had to be used in various places to show that he was travelling. He felt more than a slight discomfort in thinking that this spotty-faced fellow might forget why he had them.

Johnathon said, 'Be careful with these. The last time I let them out of my sight, my wife went on a spending spree. I am just getting over it now, and that was over two years ago.'

The young man looked at Johnathon as if he were speaking another language. He didn't realise that Johnathon was joking.

Jon thought, 'This place must suck the humour out of every living thing.'

The youth then immediately took the cards and reported to his supervisor and Claire. To make it appear that Professor King was elsewhere, and in the same area as his phantom phone, a small number of transactions were undertaken. It appeared that he had just paid for some groceries in York. Coincidently, that was where his sister, Julie, was living in the village of Strensall, just outside the historic city. Julie and her husband were accommodated in Officers Married Quarters at Queen Elizabeth Barracks; her husband was a Major in the British Army. York was one of Johnathon's favourite places to visit. It was also his wife's preferred weekend getaway location. They both loved the Minster, the cobbled old streets called the Shambles, the museums, the castles and the Jorvik Viking Centre. York was one of the places that they had visited on numerous occasions during his wife's illness. Julie had been a great support during that difficult time. Jon and his wife loved walking along the old City walls on a warm spring day and at the end, sitting by the River Ouse. The Tech Team chose York as his hideaway place because they surmised that it was the place name that featured most in all his online history and bank statements, after local shops and amenities close to home. He had not been overseas for five years and clearly was not much of a traveller.

The shopping list had been carefully crafted: razors, toothbrush and toothpaste, shower gel, towels, deodorant, two packets of paracetamol, some snack food plus soft drinks and a bottle of single malt whisky, just to indicate a change in habit. He was not a great drinker, but they wanted to give a small indication that he was behaving abnormally. There were two newspapers because he liked the feel of printed matter. A notepad and some pens concluded the modest purchase. All brands were the same as he used at home. The Tech boys knew this because, during a covert search of his house twenty minutes after he left for the first meeting on twenty-fourth May, a team of six counter-surveillance specialists had combed his place. They videoed every nook and cranny, including his bathroom cupboard. They were looking for something that might indicate a motive for his actions, anything signposting political allegiances, substance abuse or anti-social behaviour. They took all electronic devices and put in a suite of monitoring equipment to keep an eye on the house and see who might also be looking for something. They found nothing untoward. They concluded that this man led an unremarkable life. They packed an overnight bag, and took a glass and a bottle of his opened whisky. Picking up a nice pen and a pack of beautiful quality writing paper, the team of six left the place exactly as they found it. The gloved and overall-clad team wore head coverings, leaving no DNA traces or fingerprints.

A further transaction later that same night was to take two hundred and fifty pounds out of his bank account in cash. The camera that normally worked on that machine had been smeared with a substance that made any pictures undecipherable. Tomorrow Professor King would take a taxi to Newcastle and pay for it by card. At that point, he would check into a special clinic, pay a deposit, also by card, and go off-grid. This would be supported by a couple more texts sent to a selected few people, mainly his family, to let them know he had arrived safely.

Back at the London Headquarters, at 2100 hours, Yorkie popped his head around the door, and said to Johnathon,

'Just give me a buzz when you're ready to write your suicide note,' pulling a funny shock horror face.

Johnathon suppressed a shudder at the turn of events in his life in such a short time.

'OK, mate, I'll be just another thirty minutes or so.'

When they had raised the idea of a suicide note that afternoon, Jon was more than a bit apprehensive. He could not help but feel that if they wanted him out of the way, he had just signed his death warrant. He realised that he was being paranoid, but looking at what was happening, never in his wildest dreams did he see himself in this situation.

The Staff Sergeant's facial expression seemed to make it a bit less real. He refocussed on his sham report. It was still a work of genius but of fiction this time.

At 2115 hours Claire met up with Yorkie.

'How's it going, Staff?'

'Fine, ma'am,' Yorkie said, 'but I think the Professor just shit himself when I asked him if he was ready to write his suicide note.'

They both chuckled with Claire adding, with a shake of her head,

'Military humour – it takes some getting used to.'

They agreed on the style of note and created a rough draft. The Professor would have to write it in his own hand, maybe two or three versions, just to give the impression that he was struggling with it. They would need to place DNA on the note in case someone was diligent about checking. The suicide note, email and text messages were all designed to show that Professor King was not well and had become unhinged.

Yorkie added, 'If he isn't now, he soon will be. It's this place.'

The decision to discredit Professor King had started before the afternoon's meeting had even kicked off. At the University, only the Dean was involved in the subterfuge regarding Johnathon's fall from grace. A letter of complaint about some minor inappropriate behaviour had been received. It seemed compelling. A note on file indicated the Dean had met and spoken with Professor King three days before his BBC appearance, and during the meeting, Johnathon did not deny the accusation but suggested that it was an exaggeration.

Another recent note on file was an informal discussion between the Dean and Johnathon indicating that Jon's professional standards were slipping and that maybe he was taking on too much. The Dean commented in the note that Jon was unkempt and appeared tired.

Previous entries on file from when his wife died indicated that the Dean suggested that Johnathon take time off to come to terms with his loss. In the recent note, the Dean Commented that it was possible that Jon had never really come to terms with this bereavement and that this might be a factor in the current situation. The question of inappropriate use of non-prescribed medicines was raised as well.

All the equipment from the Professor's office and laboratory had been returned but with modified hard drives and email records. Tomorrow, an engineer undertaking a routine Portable Appliance Test on electrical equipment would upload the data regarding the revised research document and supporting emails. At the same time, a few discreet motion-activated cameras would be installed. If they started recording, an immediate notification would be sent to multiple locations including the Tech Team in MI6, as well as the Counter-Surveillance Cell at MI5. The Professor's home PC and devices had the same treatment. As of nine-forty-five p.m., no one had entered either Johnathon's office or home.

Having met his deadline, a weary Johnathon called into Meeting Room Three which was the temporary Operations Office.

'Coffee, Jon?' Yorkie asked.

'Not for me, I'm all coffeed out, mate. Anything without caffeine, please.'

The Staff Sergeant looked at his boss and said,

'Ma'am, I have a bottle of single malt in my desk drawer.'

'Not for me, Staff,' Claire said, 'but you boys deserve a swift one. I'll have a herbal tea.'

'I'm with you, Staff,' said Johnathon, 'but only a wee one.'

That last part was in the worst Scottish accent Yorkie had ever heard, and he winced by way of friendly critique.

Five minutes later, Yorkie returned with the bottle of whisky: Glenmorangie twelve-year-old.

Johnathon said, 'This is my favourite.'

'What a coincidence! Prof, why don't you pour?'

Yorkie passed over the bottle, a glass and a plastic cup.

The Staff Sergeant was wearing surgical gloves, Jon noticed.

Yorkie added, 'I'll have the plastic cup, and you can use the Waterford cut-crystal glass.'

Jon poured a fairly large shot into the receptacles.

Claire said, 'I'm knackered, but we need to get this suicide note finished before we get off tonight.'

With a big sigh, Johnathon approached the drafted version on the table. He pulled out a chair and slumped over the paper that resembled the stationery he had at home.

He read the draft and it was a good version of what he would say if he was as depressed as they wanted him to appear. He picked up an ink pen, also just like one his, and started writing. It took two minutes to get the main note done. The two shunned efforts with errors and words crossed through were crumpled up.

'Job done,' said the exhausted Professor.

'Not quite,' said Yorkie. 'Get the pen out of your pocket and pop it in here, Prof.' Yorkie was holding open a plastic bag with a sealable zip.

Jon placed the pen in the bag without comment. Yorkie reached into his pocket and took out a finger prick used by nurses for testing for diabetes and the like. He removed the outer plastic sleeve.

He said to the Professor, 'Jon, put your arm out straight and give me a thumbs-up.'

Looking puzzled, he did as he was told in silence.

Yorkie smiled and said, 'Don't worry. This won't hurt me at all.'

He applied the finger prick to Jon's thumb, and a bright spot of blood appeared. Using a thin piece of sterile paper to pick up a sample of blood, Yorkie applied it to one of the crumpled letters, just on the edge and barely noticeable. Someone would only see it if they were looking really hard.

Yorkie instructed, 'Jon, if you'd pop the letters into this bag, that would be great.'

He held open another bag. Again, the papers were despatched without comment.

'And all the unused sheets in this one, cheers,' said the tiring Staff Sergeant.

The whisky bottle and glass would be put in sterile bags as soon as the Professor was out of the way.

Yorkie thought, 'No point putting the poor bastard through anymore.'

Both he and Claire had noticed a slight welling-up in the Professor's eyes when he got to the point in the letter which referred to his deceased wife and how much he loved and missed her. The letter said that he felt like he just couldn't carry-on.

'That's a wrap,' said Claire.

All tasks set for today had been completed. Every bit of work would be reviewed, and anything not convincing enough would need to be done again. If needed, they would be dragged out of their beds; the deadline was that tight. Yorkie delivered the plastic bags, including the whisky, to the Tech Boys and told them not to drink any. He left straight for home. The tube ride was less smelly and awful than it was when he first came to work here at MI6. The virus meant few people were working in central London. Less people were travelling on public transport which, in turn, made it safer for those that did. Regardless of who was on the train, facemasks were worn by everyone, and the carriages were so quiet, especially at night, that spacing was never an issue.

Claire read the revised research document and found it impressive. The data and arguments seemed really convincing. She was sure that if she hadn't seen the first study, it would have fooled her. The contact at Porton Down had OK'd the report which was good enough for everyone at MI6. The research just needed to be distributed and made accessible to those wanting it. They all knew tomorrow was going to be another tough day. Many more demanding days were on the horizon, and this was just the start.

Chapter 13

Operation Worcester Sauce – Part 1

25th May 2024

They had two ways to discover the evidence they needed to prove Professor King's theory. The first would be to pop over to Wuhan, break into the facility where the viruses were purportedly kept, go through the cabinets, steal the documents and take samples from the fridges. This type of physical intervention could be messy and possibly cost lives. The Chinese would probably not be too pleased with this if it became known. Certainly, President Xi's State Visit in June would be in some doubt. It would probably lead to an international incident with serious consequences. Therefore, they had to be sure they could prove they were right before setting foot on another nation's sovereign ground. Regardless, the Chinese would deny everything and claim evidence had been planted to frame them. China would suggest that the UK was a puppet-state of the USA and was acting on behalf of the President. No doubt, there would be executions in China, and extremists would want retribution. Consequently, the world would be put on DEFCON 2, on the verge of World War III.

The alternative was to see if they could find a virtual backdoor. The best electronic locksmiths in the business were the GCHQ: Government Communications Headquarters. The role of this highly secretive organisation in modern society was wide-reaching; providing intelligence and security services for the Government, the SIS and military. Based in Cheltenham, the doughnut-shaped home of GCHQ possessed some of the most up-to-date cypher systems and could listen into conversations worldwide. The digital era provided challenges but also great opportunities for those engaged in espionage. It was generally accepted that if people used any internet-based communication system or any standard telephone, GCHQ could listen in. It didn't matter if people had taken the trouble to have their accounts password protected, GCHQ could hack into any mainstream system.

Complex systems could provide a test for analysis, but in truth, not many areas of technology existed that they could not access. The key arm of the hackers on the Government's books under the GCHQ umbrella were, in fact, based in London. The National Cyber Security Centre (NCSC) employed some of the sharpest minds in computing who were an invaluable asset in the cyber battles raging constantly around the world. The threats and attacks from Russia, China and countless other countries, including those considered to be allies, were daily occurrences. This motley crew of geeks, being paid handsome wages by GCHQ, were also committed to breaking into highly-protected systems. Like a thief in the night, they left no trace of their pilfering of information. They were the best.

GCHQ were masters at intercepting all types of electronic emissions. The activities under this heading were known as Electronic Intelligence, including interceptions of electronic-emitting equipment, such as radar, targeting systems and telemetry. In fact, if anything produced a pulse of energy, a bleep or squeak, GCHQ was listening. Also, radio and other voice communication intercepts were supported by language specialists who helped translate the data being collated.

For MI6 to get the best out of GCHQ, Lee Ford, who was the GCHQ Signals Intelligence Liaison Officer, would take a road trip to Cheltenham. Explaining the complexities of their requirements in face-to-face meetings was not essential but much easier. Such encounters forged better personal connections, something that the younger generation had yet to learn to appreciate. Since nearly everyone and most businesses were still in lockdown mode, any justified excuse to get out of the office on a trip was worth taking.

The other reason for having personal meetings and keeping operations in hard copy, was to frustrate the enemy's ability to hack into what they were doing. It would be complacent to assume other leading world intelligence agencies were not trying to gain access to the UK's classified systems. Plenty of examples existed of the CIA and FBI having been hacked. Who was to say the SIS systems were completely safe and could not be accessed? Keeping other aspects of the operation a secret from GCHQ was important so any leak would only have limited information and not the full picture.

It was essential that the efforts being sought by MI6 were clearly targeted. Lee, who was a former GCHQ supervisor, was meeting with an old colleague and good pal. After the usual shenanigans of getting access to one of the most sensitive places in the UK, Lee was shown to a secure briefing facility with refreshments at the ready. His escort was a fresh-faced woman in her late-20s, who had the confidence of someone much older.

'Mr Ford, my name is Ellie, and I will take you to meet Director Jacobs. Derek told me to watch you. He said you would lift anything not bolted down.'

Lee laughed. He knew well Derek Jacob's sense of humour. He had probably heard his limited repertoire of jokes a dozen times over. That said, Director Jacobs was a good man, a bit longer in the tooth than he was. Derek was his last Supervising Director before he left, what they called, The Doughnut. Indeed, it was Derek who promoted Lee so he could get the London-based job.

As Lee and his escort walked through the door, a familiar voice said, 'Oh, I see you got the memo about the dress then.'

They were both wearing identical jackets and blue striped shirts. Lee hadn't heard that joke since the last time they met.

Both men held out their hands and shook vigorously in direct contradiction with the rules about minimising contact.

'That's it, you're contaminated now,' said the older man, who then took out a small spray bottle of hand sanitiser, sprayed his hands and then rubbed them together energetically before handing the bottle to Lee.

Lee looked at his old friend.

'Director, that must be the only exercise you are getting,' referring to the robust hand-rubbing, 'because you're putting on the beef, mate.'

It was a standard game with these two to see who could take the piss the most. Neither of them took offence because they knew it wasn't malicious. Also, working in a sterile PC environment like GCHQ could drive people a little scatty. Director Jacobs started with MI6 and had a record of achievement that read like a toned-down spy novel.

'Why the late call?' asked Derek.

Lee went straight to the point.

'Well, it's like this. We are running an operation to see if there is any truth in the matter that Covid-24 was a developed, manufactured virus, and whether any indicators point to the source being either the Chinese Government or a rogue element within China. I know that we did a similar operation concerning Covid-19, but the Chinese all but admitted that Covid-19's source was from Wuhan. They also provided data stating that it was a naturally-occurring virus which was released due to a handling cock-up. The information your team provided seemed to support their assertions. Additionally, there was also a bit of research undertaken independently by various biological warfare laboratories around the world, and they concurred with the Chinese. This was put into the public domain confirming the Chinese assessment. I also saw your reports, just recently, that the head of the facility in Wuhan was executed along with some lower staff members including a couple of scientists.'

Lee Ford waited a few seconds before continuing.

'If we fuck up in our jobs, we get our arses kicked or, at worse, a P45. It's a tough gig for those guys in China. If they make a mess of things, they are killed, and their families are put outside the protection of the state.'

Lee continued, 'Did you see that nut-job professor on the TV a few days ago? King, I think his name was. Needless to say, the whole SIS is getting an arse-kicking from the PM's office, asking why we didn't know about this. You will have seen the shit on the TV and that git, Ross Thompson, kicking off with all that anti-Chinese rhetoric again. When Covid-19 hit the ground, you will recall he said, "China isn't going to play by our rules", and he was right. This time, it's an "I told you so".'

Derek responded, 'Come on, Lee, tell us something we don't know. The Chinese, Russians and Americans all play their own little games by their own rules.'

'But then, don't we?' Lee asked.

'Point taken,' Derek said, adding, 'What are you looking for?'

'Simply put,' Lee answered, 'I have a list of key words and names here. We are looking to see if there is any traffic, the more sensitive the better, on these guys. Specific reference to Covid-19 and Covid-24 would be nice, but if Covid-24 was being manufactured, it may have a different name. So, anything that is a frequent reference with or to Covid 19 would be a start.'

'Go on, make it easy, won't you?'

'There's more,' Lee interjected, 'and you'll love this one. Can you task those clever fellas at The National Cyber Security Centre to see if they can get access to the Research Centre at Wuhan? I trust you have some data stored from last time, but I was not privy to how far you got in terms of infiltrating their systems. Also, whether or not you can get back in now.'

Taking a sip of coffee, he pressed on.

'We have a couple of boffins seconded to us at Vauxhall who are top-notch whizz-kids on the science end of the pandemic. As soon as you can provide data and transcripts, we can get them to work. If you could pass over anything from your last trawl, when looking at Covid-19, that will get them moving.

'The timescale on this is fairly tight. For operational security reasons, I cannot tell you why, but we would appreciate it if you could give me an indication as to the time frames needed to access the data required.'

Lee kept going before his friend could interject, 'I know this is an unknown, but the best guess would be appreciated by tomorrow lunchtime.'

As a master of his craft, Derek put his business face on and said,

'We will know within two days if we can get access to their systems. If they have not upgraded their software, I think it's a gimme.'

The inference coming from Director Jacobs was that they had hacked it before during the Covid-19 operation.

'We can have the data we secured on the Covid-19 Operation put on a coded memory stick for you tonight before you go. We will release the code over a secure line tomorrow when you get back in the office. We also have archived but unrefined communications data on intercepts over, say, the past six months; give me forty-eight hours to sift this lot and get a workable amount of information to you. If something sticks out as an obvious lead, we will send it over as a priority. For current communication intercepts, I will have a team focus on transmissions into and out of the Wuhan facility. We will target the mobiles of all key personnel you have identified here. Plus, if any new key figures pop up, we will add those. Likewise, for their landlines. I don't think there was much by way of radio comms at the Wuhan Centre, just internal security networks, but not surprisingly, these low-level guards often have poor RT security. We can also monitor local military and civil air traffic chatter; it might give us a clue regarding movements. As you know, nothing important happens without the Chinese People's Liberation Army or the local Communist Party getting involved so we will put an eye on them as well.'

Lee then reviewed his notes, written in such a way that would mean nothing to anyone else.

'Ah, one last thing. We need plans of the facility, any details of security systems; the usual stuff if you were thinking of a holiday there.'

The reference was understood.

Derek said, 'Look, it's seven-thirty. Let's get some dinner here, and you can fill me in on what Mandy and the kids are up to. In that time, we can get you your carryout pack ready, and if there is anything else required, you can let me know.'

Lee thought, 'As thorough and professional as ever.'

'That sounds great, and you can tell me how you manage to keep cheating at golf without being found out,' Lee said.

They both laughed and set off for some dinner.

'You could stay at mine tonight if you wanted?' Derek suggested.

'I'd love to, but this, as you can gather, needs my full attention, and I will need to be at my desk before Uncle Tom gets in tomorrow morning. He has this one under his wing.'

'Fuck, that makes it sound more serious than I thought,' Derek said.

Lee replied with caution, 'Yeah, it is. We don't want to drop any balls and give the Chinese advance notification that we are interested in them just now. If they shut up shop at Wuhan, based on any indicators that we are paying the place too much attention, we'll end up chasing shadows.'

They had a relaxing dinner of roast chicken and stuffing with mashed tatties, along with a shared pot of coffee afterwards. Ellie appeared with a package, for which Lee duly signed. Passing on regards to their respective wives, they parted, and Lee set off back to London at nine-thirty p.m. with important information in his charge. This would keep the Deputy Director Operations happy. It was a significant step in the right direction and with more information due within forty-eight hours. The icing on the cake would be full access to the computer systems at Wuhan; this could mean access to security systems. Satellite stuff was OK, but it had its limitations. Knowing what the Chinese knew and even data that they didn't know they had would be invaluable.

Lee had much to consider on his journey home. Shortly after arriving at the M40 junction, he noticed a black Range Rover on his tail. It was two cars back, but it looked like it had more aerials than usual. The M40 was normally a busy road, but the lockdown had reduced traffic levels everywhere, and at ten p.m., Lee would have expected to experience next to no traffic. He thought he would keep an eye on this vehicle; it never hurt to be too careful. He rang the Operations Room back in London on his secure mobile, reporting that he would be back about midnight with a sensitive package. The envelope was secured in a container under the passenger seat. He asked if any agency assets had been assigned to him as covert counter-surveillance.

The desk typed a few digits into a computer and said, 'Nothing reported here, sir.'

'No worries,' said Lee. He knew he was often a bit too paranoid which was natural and helped in this kind of job. 'I will report in twenty minutes. If you do not hear from me, get the local police to my location. Check you have my transponder on the system.'

'That's affirmative, sir,' the Duty Ops officer confirmed. 'Have a good trip.'

The phone went dead.

Travelling within the legal limits, the MI6 Jaguar F-Pace was coming to the village of Andoversford. The Range Rover had kept its distance, and when Lee slowed down to exactly forty miles per hour in a zone of road works, the following car kept to the same speed. Even after the road works, Lee was slow to get back up to sixty-five miles per hour, but the suspect vehicle kept to about sixty metres back. He was feeling a bit uncomfortable about his shadow. It was now nineteen minutes since the last check-in.

He rang the Duty Operations Officer for the second time that night,

'I need an intervention on a black Range Rover which is tailing me.'

Lee gave details of a partial number plate.

Eight minutes later the London Operations desk rang him back.

'Your intervention is set up at the junction of the A429, sir, that's about three minutes out. The local Police Armed Response Team will pull the vehicle over. We understand there may be a second police asset on-site.'

As the Jaguar quietly motored past the A429 junction, the Range Rover was still sitting at about the same size in his rear-view mirror. The roads were deathly quiet. Once both cars had passed the junction, the skies lit up with the blue flashing police lights. The sirens were clearly heard despite being around one hundred metres away. The police flashed their lights, and the shadowing car was pulling further back.

He called the Operations Room and reported intervention was completed and that he was putting his foot down.

The Duty Officer replied, 'I can see that, sir.'

Lee said, 'Let the local plods know I am going blue.'

He put on his own blue lights but not the siren.

He arrived back safely at MI6 Headquarters just before midnight, dropping off the package then headed home to Stoke Newington, North London. All was quiet at home when he arrived at one a.m. He slept in the spare room so as not to disturb his wife, Mandy. His alarm went off at six-fifteen a.m. He went to see his wife with a coffee and toast; that was the first time they had seen one another in three days. He left home at seven-fifteen a.m. and was at his desk at seven-fifty a.m.. Among the benefits of the lockdown were the empty roads, reduced pollution, clear blue morning skies and bird song.

'Maybe the world would be better without mankind polluting the crap out of the place,' he mumbled to himself.

Chapter 14

Operation Prune Pie – Part 2

27th May 2024

Whilst Professor King, Claire and the Staff Sergeant were in their respective beds, a two-man MI6 team had set out from London to Wiltshire, heading for the sleepy community of Calne. Their target was a smart house on the outskirts of this quaint market town. They had all the various items that had been generated by the Special Weapons Section the previous evening. Their mission was simple: gain access to the house, put the bottle of whisky and used glass on the writing desk and place the final suicide note on the top of the desk with the pen and the two drafts in the bin. They would also upload the final version of the Professor's new research report onto his PC and leave the property without being detected. The counter-surveillance team watching the house, based in a van around the corner, had been advised that there would be "blue team" visitors at about four a.m. After the visit to the Professor's house, the agents from Vauxhall would then drive to Bristol to give the Professor's IT equipment in the University similar treatment. Thus far, there had been no reports of unwanted visitors to either location. The incident regarding the Range Rover shadowing Lee Ford, the GCHQ Signals Intelligence Liaison Officer, had set adrenalin flowing. All field monitoring teams were given the heads-up of hostile intelligence interest in the operation. The rest of the disinformation task went smoothly, and the MI6 team returned to London at about ten-thirty a.m. with nothing to report other than DCO – Duty Carried Out.

Meanwhile, Johnathon's phone was being escorted to the New Priory hospital just outside Newcastle. The onset of the viruses brought a new wave of depression around the country. People were suffering from the effects of PTSD from worrying about catching the virus, and they needed treatment: yet another hidden impact of this horrendous pandemic.

The pre-booked taxi was in the name of Jon King with a collection time of seven-thirty a.m. It picked up his stand-in from a bed and breakfast on Fulford Road, York. The guest paid for his room for the night by card and, rather stupidly, left some items of clothing and a hair brush behind in his rush to get out, along with an empty bottle of whisky sitting in the wash hand-basin full of water. The faux Johnathon had the smell of whisky on him as he left his accommodation. This man looked like Johnathon with the same height, build and general features, and from a distance, people who really did not know him well would think it was him. Arriving at the clinic two hours later, he paid for the taxi by card.

The man impersonating Johnathon booked himself into the centre. The reception staff casually checked the new arrival's driving license against the details on the credit card presented. They took the first three days' payment by debit payment: the cost was four-thousand five hundred pounds, and there was no VAT. The newly-arrived patient looked tired, and he was escorted to his room and made comfortable. He had his first set of medical readings taken within thirty minutes. His heart rate and blood pressure were slightly higher than expected, but for a man of his age, he was in fine health. Unbeknown to the medical staff, the patient had taken a course of Prozac which usually treats depression but also raised the patient's heart rate. Bloods would be taken later as the staff saw no point in stressing the new patient any more just for now. When the blood samples were taken, they would show an unusually high level of alcohol and an element of substance abuse. His consultant psychiatrist had a brief session with him, just to make him welcome, relax and reassure him that they would make him better. The patient was not considered a high risk of suicide and would not require any additional supervision. After all, he came in under his own steam and seemed balanced. The false Johnathon would have another short session that afternoon but was given a menu card for lunch. It read like a trendy restaurant, but at one-and-a-half thousand pounds per day, you'd expect decent food. He was asked if he needed anything else; which he did not. The nurse left him in his five-star treatment room to rest. It was time to send those texts and let close family know he had admitted himself to the hospital with depression.

Whilst imposter Johnathon was sitting back and relaxing in the Priory, the real Professor King was heading back to the office in London. The car collection this morning was a bit tenser. A decoy car was sent first and left with two other people. Then Claire and he jumped in a second car and were taken to work. As he sat in the vehicle, Johnathon noticed for the first time that the windows to the rear were blacked out, and a fine mesh ran across the side and rear windows. He had never before seen what he thought must be heated side-windows. Claire noticed his puzzlement and explained that the element was to prevent eavesdropping on conversations and prevent anyone from getting a clear heat-signature reading.

'It's over the top, but most counter-surveillance cars have them nowadays,' she said. She never mentioned that it also blocked signals getting into and out of the car, unless you were plugged into the vehicle's system.

Upon arrival back at Headquarters, they were briefed on the shadowing incident involving Lee Ford coming back from GCHQ.

Looking shocked, Johnathon turned to Claire, and said, 'This is a bit much, isn't it?'

Claire studied his face before replying.

'The situation we find ourselves in today, by your estimation, is this virus, if developed further, could cost billions of lives. Your input is absolutely critical to forging a way ahead here. This is a strange world that you have chosen to be drawn into. You are going to have to learn to adapt whilst adding value.'

Unlike the university, which was his professional world, MI6 operated only in the real world, and the real world was a lot harsher than most people could imagine. He realised that he was feeling out of his depth.

Sitting quiet for a few minutes, lost in his own thoughts, Jon realised he could do a great deal of good here, more so than he could have ever imagined.

He made a pact with his conscience: 'As long as we do more good than harm, I can live with this.'

Johnathon accepted he would have to reset his moral compass to some extent, but he knew he could do this. He was sure that everyone had to recalibrate their thinking from time to time, to make sense of changing circumstances. The situation demanded that he adapted to an alien environment and quickly.

He looked over to Claire who had her head down and was reading a report, and said,

'You're right. I need to see the big picture here, but I hope you can appreciate that this is a new universe for me with things going on that I only ever thought happened in movies.'

Claire realised his sincerity from the obvious tension in his voice.

'Look, Jon, the situation we find ourselves in today is unique. I suspect that this could end up being the most important operation for British Intelligence ever, but in truth, it is too early to fully grasp the magnitude of what we are facing.'

At that point, she slid a four-page report over to him. Claire knew that this would be heart-wrenching for Johnathon. It could break his resolve, but he could not be sheltered from what was about to happen any further. The Professor could not believe his eyes. The report said in summary that at two p.m. tomorrow, the Prime Minister would be taking the daily briefing which was normally conducted either by him or a senior cabinet member. This was how it would transpire.

At 1400 hours on the 28th May, Allan Knowles would conduct the standard presentation on the pandemic and open up to questions. An ITV reporter would ask a question about the BBC news item that pronounced the end of the world as we knew it, demanding that the Government had to either renounce this reckless piece of journalism and chastise the BBC for causing undue upset and harm, or secondly, provide a clear indication that Professor King's work would be followed up on with further details being made public. The Prime Minister was to take the latter course of action.

At the conference, the Prime Minister would seem surprised at the question – it was not on his list – but would revert to type when dealing with such matters off-the-cuff, saying, 'We have been looking at the research that Professor King had undertaken, and frankly, though he has a sound reputation, or so I am told, the report is completely inaccurate. I have seen the study myself, and the experts in the field have said that it just doesn't stack up at all.'

The Prime Minister would sound convincing because he would come across as ill at ease. He would look around the room momentarily as if seeking acceptance for his fictitious statement. He knew he would get away with another whopper, so he would add, 'I am happy to release a copy of the report and the official findings of our specialists, so we have complete transparency on the subject.'

After stammering again, he would chastise the journalists stating, 'Those comments on the BBC – and this is a warning to all media outlets – if you allow this sort of thing to be aired without checking the veracity of the story first, we will be inclined to revoke broadcasting licenses. As you know, every unnecessary death is a tragedy, and my medical advisors' have informed me of a spike in suicides within hours of the Professor's revelations. This was the most reckless piece of news reporting in recent times. I cannot allow this to happen again.'

The Professor sat back in his chair mentally hearing every word that Allan Knowles, the new Prime Minister, would say as if he were in front of him now. Johnathon grasped that his whole reputation was about to be lost. His family would see him as a failure, and essentially his life as he had known it was over.

He asked, 'The comment about suicides, is that true?'

Claire shook her head impatiently and said,

'Of course not. All that crap about suicides is horseshit. Just like those comments on your report are completely fictitious. This is subterfuge, and we have to keep up the deception going forward. When we are out of this, everything will be put right, and your brave actions and support of the SIS will be applauded. I am sure of that.'

Claire knew that all files would be locked away in some deep vault for at least fifty years. Some semblance of rehabilitation would occur, but the whole truth would never come out.

'Are you sure?' he asked, trying to grasp hold of the situation. 'What about my family? Is there any way I can let them know the truth of it all now?'

'I am afraid not, Professor. It is for their safety and national security that these actions have been taken. Your contribution and sacrifice will not go unnoticed or unrewarded in the fullness of time,' she said, endeavouring to soften the blow.

She knew that there was more planned that might put the Professor and his family into a greater calamity. It was probably best to let Uncle Tom know what had transpired. It might need special handling. Not aware of Claire's thoughts, Johnathon was partially reassured. Claire noted that he looked vulnerable, took him a coffee and patted him on the shoulder.

At that point, Yorkie walked in with a buoyant, 'Good morning!'

He had been reading the full counter-surveillance report from Lee Ford's previous night's escapades. Claire put her hand to her throat moving her fingers in a cutting action. Yorkie immediately knew to shut up.

Yorkie paused and said, 'Any instructions for today, ma'am?'

She acknowledged his quick response with a nod,

'Staff, any chance you can go see the GCHQ Liaison and see if he can come here for a catch-up? Of course, if he wishes, we can pop down and see him.'

'Not a problem, ma'am.'

Yorkie smartly about-turned as if he were on parade and vanished.

'Look, Johnathon, we are all pretty well strung-out. Why don't you take thirty minutes to gather yourself in your office? There's nothing to do here that a few minutes down-time would harm, and it might even help,' she said with a reassuring tone.

He looked up.

She said, 'Everyone needs time to deal with difficult thoughts, and we have all been there.'

Jon nodded his agreement and thought about taking the PM's press release with him to read again but instead just pushed it away to the centre of the table. He stood up hunched like a beaten man and walked out of the meeting room. After a few moments and being happy that the Professor was not going to come back in, Claire picked up the internal phone and spoke to Bill Rankin.

He said, 'My office in ten minutes.'

She arrived, and Emma said, 'Go straight through, Squadron Leader.'

Tom MacDonald was standing in the office, his large form shielding Bill Rankin from view. She stepped to a side and came to attention.

She thought, 'Old habits die hard.'

Tom MacDonald spoke first.

'Well, things seem to be going well for now. Give us an update on your work and on how the Professor is coping.'

Claire gave a succinct briefing on the operation so far, covering everything in sufficient detail but with no superfluous elements. Neither of the senior staff had questions for her. They waited for her to move onto the issue that provoked the call from the Section Chief to the Deputy Director earlier.

With a slight touch of hesitancy in her voice, she added,

'I am a bit concerned about the Professor. He sees his life unravelling and is concerned about the impact of all this on his family and also on his professional reputation.'

She followed up with the detail of the conversations of the morning and described his physical disposition.

She added, 'I believe he is going to be OK, but we might need to handle the next phase slightly differently, more sympathetically.'

It was clear she had professional respect and a growing regard for the Professor.

Bill Rankin cut in, 'Well, Squadron Leader, what is it you propose?'

Claire articulated her views with simple clarity.

'Sir, we need to maintain operational momentum, and if it comes to pass that we need to ditch the Professor, so be it. However, he is undoubtedly an asset and worthy of keeping on-side. What I would propose is that we give dispensation to bring his family into the fold, in that they are told he is not dead but working for us – that's it. I have done a bit of research into his family. I think they can be trusted.'

Claire added in a concerned voice, 'We must remember that the Professor is not a field agent. He has no special training and is just a citizen, a regular member of the public who, by accident, landed in our laps.'

Tom swiftly weighed up the risks and the benefits of looking after this man. The expected input required of the Professor could be crucial.

Tom made a decision, and stated,

'Let his family know what is going on but the bare bones only, as highlighted. We will let the Professor make the call to his father and sister, but only to them. We must make sure they are not being watched. Any discussion is to be over secure comms only. Controlling the information release is key. Clear?'

Both responded, 'Yes, sir.'

Tom continued, 'Actually, I will inform the good Professor. I take it he's in his office?'

Claire nodded but then added, 'Sir, it might be better to leave any further chats with him until tomorrow morning. He has been through a lot today and might respond better if he has had some time to assimilate everything. Also, we have a briefing with the GCHQ Liaison at midday, and I want him to focus on what the next step will be for him.'

They agreed. Claire and Deputy Director MacDonald walked down the corridor together.

'You are doing a fine job here, Squadron Leader, a really fine job,' said the senior man.

Claire felt herself glow with pride.

'Thank you, sir.'

She got back to the Professor's office, opened his door and popped her head around.

'Hi,' she said. 'How are you feeling?'

He looked up and could sense her genuine concern yet again.

'I feel a bit of a git, to be honest,' he said. 'You must think me a self-centred, spoilt arse. There I am thinking about my reputation, whereas millions of people are dying all around the world. I am embarrassed.'

'Look, Jon, this is a fucking difficult time for you. Everyone here knows your qualities and the commitment you have made. The SIS world is a queer place. You have the unfortunate position of being the outsider which must make you feel a bit isolated. You are encountering a new kind of work, and sometimes the task is so perplexing that even the old guys are rocked back on their heels. This is one of those times. The Deputy Director will have a word with you in the morning, and I hope that will allay some of your concerns. However, for now, let's grab a cuppa and get ready to see Lee Ford in the Wire Room.'

She sensed Johnathon had regained some of his usual bounce and this made her feel more relaxed about what lay in store.

Chapter 15

Operation Worcester Sauce - Part 2

27th May 2024

The downside of being a Liaison Officer is that you don't have a large staff. Of his team of three, one was ill with Covid-24, one was pregnant, which under the Government's new guidelines meant she had to stay home, and the third always got in on time at eight-forty-five a.m. That meant Lee Ford had to get his own coffee this morning. Usually, that was fine, but today he was anxious, chomping at the bit to open his package, given to him last night by his friend and mentor, Director Derek Jacobs of GCHQ.

Lee, with his back to the door pouring a hot filter coffee, heard a voice he recognised, say,

'I'll have one of those too, white, no sugar, thank you.'

Without turning round Lee responded,

'That's fine, sir. Pop into my office and grab a seat. I'll be with you in a moment.'

Tom MacDonald went through as requested. Lee poured out two coffees, hurriedly thinking about all that transpired the previous day. Under normal circumstances, when Uncle Tom came to see you, it meant a screw-up, and you could prepare for an arse-kicking. The alternative was that a mountain-load of work was going to descend from a great height. What Lee did not appreciate that morning was that every off-shoot operation related to Operation Fulcrum Storm, including his Operation Worcester Sauce, was tagged so that any reports being raised were passed to DD Ops directly. This morning, before anyone else had the chance to get access to the report on the intervention during the previous night, Tom MacDonald had scoured the details. He had a voracious appetite for information and a great capacity to retain it. His greatest gift was to know when to act and when to wait.

The black Range Rover had been stopped by the police on the fabricated assertion that it was being driven erratically. The vehicle occupants were Chinese Consulate staff allotted to the Cultural Attaché's Division. Within the world of espionage, this meant they were almost certainly spying. The police were shown the requisite diplomatic immunity documents, but for completeness, the officers went through the full verification process. Had the offence been a serious one, they could have arrested the two men, but as it was, they were just required to wait in the back of the police car until it was confirmed that they were bona fide embassy staff. The two spies just sat there quietly saying absolutely nothing, answering only questions that were relevant to their employment. This procedural delay allowed the MI6 car to get clear of these unwanted observers. Copies of their paperwork were taken by the vigilant traffic cop, using his mobile phone, and these were with the report.

When Lee came in, Tom MacDonald praised him, saying,

'You were certainly on the ball last night young man. Your observation indicated that the Chinese have paid particular attention to us, but as of yet, there is no direct link to Operation Fulcrum Storm.'

Both men checked the footage provided by the Operations Room Support Team from various road traffic cameras and saw no indication that Lee had been followed from London. It appeared that Lee's car was picked up outside GCHQ but had not been followed previously.

Tom stated, 'It could be a routine surveillance job; they certainly will have our fleet number plates and know what types of pool cars we use. Let's not overreact just now, but we do need to brief the team to be on their guard when travelling around. If we get any more instances of our team falling under Chinese scrutiny, we will declare a lockdown operation.'

'That's a good idea, sir,' said Lee, whilst thinking, 'Not a fucking lockdown!'

His heart sank. Lockdown meant he would be living and working in the Headquarters until the Operation was over. This not only would be a grave inconvenience, but his wife would also go ballistic. She was struggling with the worry of Covid-24 and the effects it was having on their family. The kids couldn't go to school. Her parents had died within the past year, possibly of Covid, but because of their age and underlying health issues, they were not tested. Not knowing was hard but the fact that they died alone without family contact hindered the grieving process. The whole operation could go on for weeks or even months. Lockdown was not a pleasant thought, and he would have to move his wife to her sister's in Barnwood, near Gloucester, for the duration.

Tom saw the reaction to the lockdown and knew it was not a desirable outcome, but then demanded,

'Now tell me what you achieved yesterday on your jolly to Cheltenham, and how was that old sod, Derek Jacobs?'

Lee had sensed the affection in both men's voices for each other but similarly a professional respect that transcended the normal level of admiration. Lee pointed to the Secure Memory Stick and explained its contents.

Tom said, 'That's a good start. Get the data to the basement and set it up in one of the wire rooms on a system unconnected to the main server. I want the Chinese Desk and the Special Weapons Section to get working on it as soon as possible. Also, get the Professor cleared to handle this level of intelligence. Be sure to remind him if this information is leaked now or at any point in the future, I will have his balls; even if I have to come back from the grave to cut them off myself. Anything from GCHQ has a six-person access list only – you know the drill. Anything coming out of the Wire Room is to be seen on an as-needed basis. Reports are to remain in this building, Top Secret – UK Eyes Only. Just so you are aware, the Chief is briefing the Prime Minister and the Chair of the Joint Intelligence Committee today on the potential threat but I believe, will play it down, at this juncture.'

The Chief of the Secret Intelligence Service (MI6) was George Main, who was Tom MacDonald's immediate boss. The incumbent was a career Intelligence Officer and was well-regarded by most people in the world of espionage. Tom thought he was too career-minded and that this sometimes clouded his judgements, making him too political. He was what Tom would call a slippery character with tunnel vision, with his eyes on the next promotion. However, Tom knew you needed team players who could handle the politicians and the growing number of oversight committees. It certainly wasn't his cup of tea as he was an operator, not an administrator.

Discussion between the two intelligence officers surrounded what could be reasonably expected next via the GCHQ conduit. Lee reported that within the next few days, he hoped to be notified that they still had access to the Wuhan computer system. If not, GCHQ would worm their way in again, but until they knew what they would be facing, it would be difficult to put a timeframe on this outcome.

Lee said, 'If GCHQ get into the Wuhan system, this should give us all we need to know, one way or another. A pile of data should be with us in terms of intercepts over the next forty-eight hours, and thereafter we can expect daily reports.'

Lee added, slightly nervously, 'Sir, you do know that this will be a shit-load of work, and the four-man team sifting through it will not be enough to do the job if this becomes protracted.'

'Thanks, Lee, I fully agree with you, but I do not want this operation growing arms and legs regarding exposure to personnel. Because of the potential end-game, we need to keep the lid on what we are doing, and the more bodies involved the greater the risk of a leak. Again, I appreciate your sentiments, but let's run with whom we have for now.'

Sitting back on his chair, Tom said, 'I want all information physically transported by secure means as encrypted data on man-portable systems. Nothing over our servers. Minimise risks of intercepts. Each delivery must have a two-man team, armed with a support car. Use counter-surveillance vehicles, not the main fleet from here on in.'

Tom was old school. He saw how easy it was for SIS to get information from other countries computer systems and could not believe they were the only ones actively hacking other nations' systems. He likened it to the Second World War: at some point or other, everyone knew everyone else's codes, and the only way to keep something secret was not to transmit information using the airwaves. The internet and computer systems were the new airwaves.

Tom said, 'We will review matters in a few days, and if we need to recruit some additional bodies, we will do so.'

He threw back the last remnants of his coffee, and his internal beeper went off.

'Bill Rankin wants to see me as a matter of urgency. Lee, make sure we have the wire room and people working on this stuff by lunchtime. I will not tolerate any delays.'

He pointed to the secure memory stick and continued, saying,

'Well done, son. We have a good starting point but keep the pressure on that old fool, Jacobs, and tell him I told you so. Remember to tell the Professor about his imminent castration if anything is leaked.'

Tom left smiling.

Lee contacted the Tech Team and secured the use of Wire Room Two. These rooms were called Wire Rooms because no radio waves could get in or out. They were one hundred percent impregnable. The rooms themselves looked like normal offices, but every electrical circuit had dampeners, so residual radio waves could not be detected. They had no aerial points or any other wiring which could be usurped. The IT systems in these rooms were stand-alone with six workstations linked to a single server but with no internet or intranet access. Every page copied by the printer was recorded and accounted for. Waste was shredded daily in the room and then immediately incinerated. Everything was hardwired for security.

When the Wire Rooms were allocated to a specific operation, only those on the access list were allowed in, plus Deputy Directors and the Chief. Everyone going in was scanned for electronic devices, and bags were searched or left outside, with the latter being the preferred option. When information was to be taken out, it needed the signature of the leading Section Chief or Director-level authorisation.

Lee contacted Yorkie in the Special Weapons Team and set a meeting at midday in Wire Room Two, telling him to bring Professor King and Squadron Leader Walters. Phillip Wong of the China Desk was also asked to attend. Section Chief Special Weapons Bill Rankin would take the lead in this aspect of the operation, and, counting himself, this would make the six. Lee set off to allocate chairs and make sure the room was clear of prior operational clutter; he wasn't expecting to find anything. The first task was to download the data he had on his Secure Memory Stick. He would ring his pal, Derek Jacobs, to get the access code on the secure line. In passing, he would make mention that he was followed the previous night, and if his security boys wanted details, he would send them over. Maybe they were more interested in GCHQ than his visit. It could be possible that he was just a target of opportunity passing on a quiet night and worthy of shadowing.

Lee knew that the hard work of being an intelligence officer was about slogging away, day after day, going through reams of drivel to find the one golden nugget of information. Strategic intelligence is neither fast nor exciting. It was long hours often of endeavour with nothing to show for the work until that eureka moment, and these, to be fair, were few and far between. However, this felt different. Everyone seemed motivated and hard at it. It was obvious that the Deputy Director Operations saw this as the biggest operation for years, and it might lead the way to a further promotion for all involved and possibly a move back to GCHQ for him. That would make his wife happy, to be close to family.

Lee was in the Wire Room at eleven-thirty a.m., and his guests started arriving just after eleven-forty-five a.m. They left all items not required in a locker outside the room. Thereafter, each undertook their physical security checks, entered and took up a position at their allocated workstation in front of their computer. One file showed on the screen. That file contained twenty-six sub-files, and within each major heading were hundreds of documents. Each document had its original Chinese transcript with a translated version. Some of the technical documents ran to thousands of pages and data. This was a mountain of information.

The first to arrive was Phillip Wong of the China Desk. Next, were Johnathon and Claire, followed closely by Yorkie. Eight minutes past midday, Bill Rankin sauntered in late. He gave his apologies and a feeble excuse for being tardy in which no one seemed the slightest bit interested.

'Welcome to the game of looking for a needle in a haystack,' Lee offered as a light introduction. By way of briefing, Lee went through the rules of the Wire Room. Only the Professor was taken aback by the level of security. Johnathon could not get his mind around the fact that within one of the safest and supposedly most secure buildings in the UK, they needed extra secure areas.

Once the administrative details were dealt with, Lee said,

'Now we have to focus on the important operational task before us. Before you are the files containing all the information relating to Covid-19 and other matters that our chaps at GCHQ thought might be relevant. This is the old information obtained as part of a search into the question,

"Who was responsible for Covid-19?" If the work to develop Covid-24 was done by the same characters, a clear link may be hidden here somewhere. Our job is to find that link. It will be long and laborious work, and we are the people who do it.'

Lee informed those present, 'I have arranged with GCHQ to run a set of standard algorithms to undertake some sequencing of data, in particular of the known key players, to determine communications patterns which would indicate where decisions are being made and the scale of involvement within each topic area. It is imperative that if we find new keywords, for example, names of new viruses, a procedure or a codeword, you let me know, and I will pass on the information for a more in-depth search. The better the essential specifications for any data progressing, the more reliable the results of these searches will be and the quicker we will be able to target the key intelligence. These initial data searches are being conducted as we speak against our first set of values, but let's keep refining our requirements.'

Everyone nodded in agreement.

Pausing for breath and glugging water from a see-through plastic bottle, which had also been scanned, Lee continued.

'We have separated the files for ease of focus. You will note that the source of information is indicated next to the file name. There are general conversation transcripts which could be the key to identifying the main players. Please be aware that those people who are now deceased are annotated DEC in red. Obviously, we will be hearing no more from them. There are files allocated to research documents which look like gobbledygook to me. I am sure you, Professor, and the Squadron Leader here, might make some sense of them. Philip will be on hand from time-to-time to help with any translation anomalies or to assist with any cultural understandings. These happen all too frequently with technical and scientific documents. If something is not making sense to you, please note where it is, and Phil will help translate. My role here is to act as the interface with GCHQ, so if we wish to refine a search on a given word, person or topic, let me know without delay. Any instruction from us will be their next priority. Likewise, if you need any searches carried out on the system here, and you are not familiar with how it works, I will be on hand to assist. Remember, absolutely no one else is allowed in this room.

No cleaners are permitted in until the system is wiped completely, so keep it tidy.'

Looking towards Bill Rankin, Lee asked,

'Sir, is there anything you would like to add?'

Bill had thought that Lee would never shut up and began to speak without notes.

'The mission of our work here is to find evidence of Covid-24 being manufactured. Other key objectives are to find where further developments may be. We need to identify the decision-makers in this process. Of critical importance is to be able to identify if the People's Communist Party is behind this, or whether rogue elements are at play. We should also be looking for any indicators of research into vaccines. Common sense would dictate if some entity has intentionally unleashed Covid-24 on the world, they would have an in-house protection plan to minimise the impact on their own people. If they have one, let's find where it is and get our hands on it.'

Rankin continued, 'The features of the evidence we are looking for are clear voice discussions between recognisable individuals detailing irrefutable facts. These discussions need to be supported by documentary evidence – emails, letters, research documents, etcetera. The evidence model we are working towards is near one hundred percent justification. Anything left open to interpretation will not convince the powers that be to take action. We are not going to take invasive action based on best guesses and hunches. Therefore, we are looking for multiple levels of information showing a clear pathway to decision-makers and illicit actions. When valuing the data and evidence, we do not want any "I think", "we suspect" or "possible maybes". If you have these thoughts, keep looking and following up on hunches. The level of confidence we need to see is categorically, "This guy did this, and here is what proves it". Essentially, find the smoking gun in the hands of the perpetrator. Anything less than that will be unactionable. Before any assessment leaves this room, the evaluation criterion is that two people need to sign off on the intelligence, and I will then countersign. Before presenting anything to me, get everyone's eyes on the information to check for veracity and validity. Every source is to be fully referenced: format, date, time, originator, receptors and cross-referencing. The evidence has got to be bullet-proof.'

'We will have to brief this going forward, so aim to develop a stronger and more coherent understanding of what we are dealing with here. What is unfolding in our cities and towns right now might just be a forerunner of what is to come. Weigh the value of one particular piece of information against another, and let's present the best evidence we can find. Understand the interplay between the key characters in China, and make sure your own beliefs and worldview do not limit your abilities to identify what we need here. The Chinese think and act differently to us, and their culture is not the same as ours. Keep an open mind and endeavour not to manufacture evidence to prove a thought process. Let the evidence determine what it can prove. Keep your minds open to indications of disinformation. If, and just if, someone inside the Party is doing this of their own volition, they will be hiding their intentions from those above them. If it is someone who is hell-bent on killing off half the world's population, there will be personality markers. They will be exceptionally intelligent. Do not underestimate anything or anyone in this work.'

Looking around the room, Rankin checked to make sure everyone was being attentive. Knowing he could sound like a lecturer in these situations; all he saw were keen faces, so continued,

'I have asked our behavioural specialists to see if they can draft a personality profile on any key players. I have passed over the details of the head of the centre at Wuhan and the three lead scientists. We have identified the three tiers of control above the facility and each of the heads of these departments; these individuals will be subjected to a desk-top character review. If you find anything about these guys in your analysis, highlight it to me, and I will pass it on. Remember: anything could have a bearing here. Reflect on the words of the Deputy Director Operations: the clock is ticking and we need results as soon as possible. If you think you have something, no matter how small, raise it, and we will discuss it as a team. The start of the search, regrettably, will need to be broad-brush, but as soon as we find one lead, it will point to others. Obviously, it may take weeks to find something worthy of further investigation. This is a backbreaking and mind-numbing job, but getting this aspect done right and at the first attempt may save thousands of lives.

I would suggest that for those analysing the data, you get some lunch and get started immediately thereafter. Any questions?'

There were none.

After lunch, the Professor sat at his terminal with his head down. He was desperate to prove his theory, but strangely, he would also be happy to be wrong. Claire took up the screen to his right, and Yorkie was on his left. At least Johnathon was surrounded by people he knew and respected.

Yorkie quipped, 'Jon, you must feel like Jesus Christ because he died between two crooks.'

Everyone grinned.

Yorkie was not a natural analyst. He struggled to concentrate and would periodically stand up and walk around the small office. He wanted to chat about anything, his beloved Leeds United, but the others were masters of studying. At five p.m., everyone's eyes were becoming heavy with near-constant staring at the screens. Yorkie noticed Johnathon had a few notes and a diagram with arrows. Claire had more notes, and it looked as if she was counting something with the farm-gate method of recording in fives.

'Anyone for afternoon tea?' Yorkie asked, exaggerating his Yorkshire accent.

The two other analysts pushed back their chairs, stretched in unison and followed the large soldier out the door without saying anything.

Halfway to the canteen, Yorkie turned to Claire and said,

'Fuck me, ma'am, but I don't know if I am cut out for this reading and writing shit.'

She gave him a wide grin. It was the first time that she had ever seen him unsure.

'Don't be a prat, Staff. This is easy, boring, but easy. But you know, this is how most intelligence information is found, and that's why it's so invaluable.'

Looking her in the eye, he responded, 'Give me twenty minutes with one of those scientists in that facility. Me and my pliers would get to the bottom of this in short order, no worries.'

They both laughed.

Johnathon wasn't sure if he should laugh. He wondered if Yorkie was being serious. Surely not?

The rest of the day was a mirror of the afternoon's endeavours producing a few more notes but nothing yet to get excited about. The Professor and Claire discussed some matters surrounding genes and DNA. Yorkie thought he would have more chance of understanding the Chinese text. They left at nine-thirty p.m., tired, but at least they could see a routine starting to form. Throughout the SIS, people were working hard across a great many specialisations, but only a few understood the gravity of the big picture and fewer still appreciated what the end game might be.

Chapter 16

Operation Prune Pie – Part 3

28th May 2024

Tom MacDonald had suggested an early morning meeting with Johnathon and wanted Claire in attendance. Both were in Meeting Room Three at seven a.m. Johnathon was in a slightly better state of mind than he was yesterday morning, but Claire knew another bolt from the blue was about to land. The coffee was on the go, and they were having a heavy conversation about how they would most likely stumble over the information they needed. Claire had to reassure Jon, if they kept focussed with the support of GCHQ, the Tech Team and the other odds and sods in the building, they should be able to get to grips with things fairly quickly.

She explained, 'There may only be a few people who have any real clue as to the whole operation but be assured, there are hundreds of people working towards an outcome. It's a bit like a jigsaw. Someone is working on the sky pieces, another is putting the bottom left-hand corner together and so on. Each individual is oblivious to the full picture but trusts that those who do, know how to provide the pieces.'

At seven-thirty a.m. in strode the Deputy Director with a box full of Danish pastries.

'Good to see you have the kettle on. Mine is a white one,' he said bullishly.

Obviously in a buoyant mood, he sat down, opened the box and took out a pastry that filled nearly the whole tea plate. Claire popped a coffee in front of the now-munching senior intelligence officer, walked around to the other side of the table and plonked herself next to the Professor about two metres away.

'Whilst I devour my breakfast, Squadron Leader, give me an update on Operation Prune Pie,' said Uncle Tom.

Claire started to go over the progress thus far, essentially summarising the discrediting of the Professor, the fact that his impersonator was in hospital in Newcastle and that the next and final phase was to be undertaken today.

The Deputy Director added, 'Just so you are aware, Professor, we have a team watching your house, the University of Bristol has an element of surveillance, and we will later today, with your consent, put someone on your father's home and that of your sister. These are precautionary measures to protect the work we have undertaken up to today and going forward.'

Cramming in the last bit of his sweet pastry breakfast, Tom cleared his throat and said to Johnathon,

'We have a further difficult choice to make today, Jon. Your impersonator in Newcastle will not be able to maintain the ruse of being you for too long. Should anyone think to investigate that it is you in the hospital, our man will not pass any more than a cursory check. We need a better and final solution to get people off your trail.'

Tom MacDonald continued, 'Professor, you are aware, I think, that we are going to have to stage it so that it appears you have died. Don't worry, it's only a temporary removal.'

Johnathon had written the suicide note so he was well aware that this could happen, but hearing the words shook him. Before he could form any sensible sound, Uncle Tom continued,

'We think it is prudent to allow you to let your father and sister know you are well so that they do not become distraught. It is important that you disappear quickly. We now know that the Chinese have accessed your report, and they are looking into your whereabouts. It may be they are concerned about the negative coverage your report has generated. If we are to succeed going forward, we need to help them relax about their involvement in anything. The whole aim of this slightly over-egged subterfuge is to keep them off-guard concerning our next few actions. Though what I propose is quite unorthodox, I am going to arrange for a few of our chaps to contact your father and sister to arrange a conference call over our secure systems at about nine a.m. You will be limited in what you can say. Essentially you will confirm that you are fit and well, they can disregard anything they hear about you in the news and, finally, that you are assisting the Government in important work. They will ask you questions but limit yourself to those three answers. Your family will be advised of the same matters when our boys meet with them initially. Naturally, they will undoubtedly only believe it when they hear your voice. Finally, if you need to prove to them that it is you, think of some fact only you will know that you can impart to them.'

Tom let this sink in, and asked, 'Are you comfortable with what I have said, Professor?'

Johnathon was relieved he would get to speak to his family, which was a huge consolation.

'Yes, I am, Deputy Director,' he replied.

Tom added, 'Finally, Professor, I would like you, the Squadron Leader and the Staff Sergeant to go into internal lockdown. That means you will stay on the premises here in Vauxhall until we have a breakthrough. We would suspect that this will be no more than three to four weeks. If we are getting nowhere at that point, we might just have to accept we are not going to be able to prove your theories without taking a different avenue of approach.'

The room was silent for a minute. Johnathon was processing all this information and gathering his thoughts.

'Tom, thank you for that,' he started, 'but what happens when this is all over? What happens to me?'

The Deputy Director smiled.

'Well, that is entirely up to you. You could go back to work in academia if that is what you want. Alternatively, you could retire. I am sure your university final salary pension plus what we could sort out for you would leave you comfortable enough to lead a pleasant life. If you would like to keep working and feel happy here or, say, at Porton Down, maybe we could find a job for you. Good scientists with the sense of duty you have displayed are hard to come by. Whatever you choose to do, we will support it. When this is over, you will be rewarded and recognised for your efforts. Of course, no one outside the SIS will know that you were here or about the work we did together. That is the very nature of what we do. It can be frustrating at times.'

Johnathon looked at the senior man opposite him, and said jokingly, 'Shit, another career change at my age! I'll have to see how things work out, I guess.'

They spoke about the future and the unprecedented and unpredictable situation they were in, and the meeting was called to an abrupt end at seven-fifty-five a.m. with a parting comment from Tom.

'Squadron Leader, can you escort the Professor to the Tech Team for nine a.m., so that he can make that call to his family?'

The box of pastries had not been touched by anyone but the Deputy Director, who left them where they were. As soon as Tom was out of the meeting room door, Johnathon and Claire each grabbed one along with coffee. They both needed a sugar rush and some time to go over the meeting that had just taken place.

As Tom was heading back to his office, he called the Tech boys and said,

'Get the comms open to the Professor's family and the ball rolling in Newcastle.'

The next few minutes were frantic in the cellar where the Technical Department was located.

They contacted the two surveillance teams outside the homes of the Professor's family, who approached the front doors and knocked. After a brief discussion on the doorstep and a showing of IDs, the visitors went inside. This, of course, was against the lockdown protocols, but any news about Johnathon was worth the risk. The surveillance teams had not seen any suspicious activity at either location but still asked if either household had any visitors. Given the lockdown, it was no surprise that the answer was 'no'. They were offered a further question of whether the houses had been left unattended in the past week. Again, both sets of occupants provided negative responses.

A fuller explanation was offered as to what was going on, but it was sparse in terms of the details. The MI6 operatives had secure mobile phones which rang exactly at nine a.m. The Professor was almost in tears at being able to speak to his dad and sister. He gave the key messages: don't worry, I am safe and well, and don't believe anything you hear or see about me on the TV. He passed on his love and said that he would not be able to phone for a few weeks, but that the agents with them now would leave an emergency contact number. If they had any real problems, they should ring them, and the agents would get a message to him. At nine zero seven a.m., the call ended. It was over all too soon, and Johnathon felt as if he had not explained enough.

The MI6 operatives then went through several scenarios that the families may be confronted with and what their responses should be. They were told they may be informed that Johnathon had committed suicide. This was not true as he is in a secure location.

'Please keep up the pretence,' the MI6 Agents asked. 'Thousands of people's lives depend on this.'

Both Johnathon's father and sister were confused, but the agents could tell that they had absorbed the information. After the initial shock, they started to gather themselves.

Just outside Newcastle, a Police car and NHS ambulance had arrived and pulled up to the front entrance of the New Priory. A body was taken out of the Centre, covered from head to toe. Patches of blood were clearly visible to the staff looking on in dismay. The ambulance driver spoke at length with the consultant Doctor, and the vehicle pulled away with lights flashing but no sirens.

The Doctor briefed the staff saying, 'The patient killed himself in the night. It was Professor King who was on the news recently.'

The background chatter from the staff was loud.

The Doctor added, 'I do not want any outside talk about this case as the newspapers might be interested. Staff are not to breach any confidentiality rules. Anyone who does so will be sacked immediately.'

As he turned to leave, he said, 'Think of the poor family members.'

Unbeknown to the Priory, an anonymous call had been placed to the Sun Newspaper providing information about Johnathon's suicide. The caller was looking for payment but wanted to remain anonymous. The Sun was going to run the story. They rang the Priory in Newcastle for comment, but none was given by the staff. They rang the Priory later pretending to be a friend of the Professor asking to be put in touch and were told he was dead. When she put the phone down, the young receptionist knew she had made a mistake but said nothing. The newspaper also tried to contact the family for comment, to no avail.

The suicide story hit the internet, and the connection with Johnathon's outrageous revelations was made. The usual conspiracy theorists came out with all the wrong assumptions: the Chinese had silenced him, or the UK Government was behind the death. The more chatter that occurred, the better it was for MI6. All this free publicity was grist to the mill, especially since none of it was anywhere near the truth. Senior politicians and noted celebrities were interviewed for their comments, but the lack of any new facts meant that it lost traction on TV with serious broadcasters.

Within minutes of the news flash online, the Chinese consulate began discussing it because the Professor was a person of interest; he was very much on their radar. They had been monitoring all media channels, as was common practice. A small team were readying to see if they could verify if the Professor was dead or if instead, this was some sort of deception. They had his published work which was now in the public domain via the UK Government plus a handy summary from Porton Down. This, of course, had been passed back to China, but it would not be treated with any great interest by the Party. It was just another fabrication by an unbalanced Westerner of significance, yet one of the many falsehoods the Chinese Government had been forced to face up to and deny. Donald Trump, in his last years as the President, had been on their case since the early days of Covid-19, and his alienation of the Chinese people from the Americans did not help him maintain his position. He constantly told the American people they were under attack. He had no facts to support this, but that didn't stop him from tweeting his incoherent thoughts. The Chinese were developing a thick skin thanks to the "Donald Effect" due to his incessant tweeting of lies and disinformation, and, in truth, so had the rest of the world. As soon as Trump started talking, sensible people stopped listening, all apart from the satirists who found the ex-US President to be a non-stop source of comedic material. The Intelligence Chief of China reported there was nothing in this discredited scientific survey, and he passed his report up to his seniors who had no further interest in reading it. The report had been disputed by the UK Government. The whole thing was a non-event.

The Chinese Cultural Attaché's staff decided to do a bit of groundwork, to see if everything was as it should be. Their chunky file on the Professor gave his home address. They might just take a look. They would engage a private detective via a third party to go to

Newcastle just to get to the bottom of his death. If there was anything suspicious, they could relay this to their masters in Beijing. They also had a few Chinese nationals studying in Bristol who might be able to throw a bit of light on matters. A visit to the University, which was virtually a ghost town like most areas of suburban Britain, might be fruitful. This was not a priority, but there was precious little else to do. The Chinese equivalent of a road trip for the afternoon was on the cards.

The black Range Rover left the Chinese embassy at one p.m. heading out of London towards the west, picking up the M4. Following their Sat Nav, they approached Swindon and pulled off at junction 16. Passing through the village of Royal Wootton Basset, which was the focal point of deceased British servicemen returning from Afghanistan many years earlier, the Chinese agents knew they were not being followed. They were about nine miles away and would take no more than fifteen minutes to find themselves outside the Professor's house. They arrived and continued driving past, did a U-turn and drove past once more. They saw no signs of surveillance or activity within the garden or house. After a further drive past, one of the vehicle's occupants jumped out and walked up the driveway, holding a package in his hand as a reason for being there, if challenged. He tried the doorbell, then knocked loudly on the door. Pressing the door handle to see if it was open, he found that it was not. The Chinese agent looked over the inside of the house through the side windows, seeing no sign of movement or indications that the house was alarmed. The main lock on the front door was a basic Yale-type. Pulling out a few key-picks, the Chinese agent had it open in seconds. Whoever left the house last, exited by the front door and was anticipating coming back in the same way. There were no bolts or chains to negotiate. The Chinese agent cracked the door open and put his head through. Seconds later he was fully in the hallway.

He called out, 'Professor King, are you home?' without expecting a reply.

Making a swift search of the house and finding nothing unusual, the agent radioed his colleague. This second agent drove their large car up the driveway and parked it facing the main exit, just in case they needed a quick getaway. Within minutes, they were taking videos and photos of everything. They found the suicide note and took a photo. They picked the partially-finished copies out of the bin and copied them. They kept the copy with the blood stain, putting it in an evidence bag. They took hairs from the bathroom sink and fingerprint impressions from the glass on the table, which still held an aroma of whisky although it was dry. They checked the fridge for food. Most of it was going out of date, an indication that the Professor had not been shopping recently. The kettle and oven were cold, the heating was on very low, and the hot water was switched off. The stack of mail by the door provided another indication of his absence. They photographed each letter, opened a personal letter and a bank statement, copying both of them. They resealed the envelopes and carefully put them back on the floor by the front door. One of the agents went upstairs. He went into the spare room being used as an office, turned on the Professor's computer and copied his hard drive. He did a superficial check of the bedroom drawers and found a money box with twenty-pound notes in it and a jewellery box with women's jewellery. Photographing them both, he left them as he had found them. Three wardrobes still had women's clothes in them. The other fitted wardrobe had a few suits and shirts. The laundry basket was half-full.

As the agent upstairs finished his search and was heading back down, he heard a woman calling out sharply, 'What are you doing here?'

The agent quietly moved further down the stairs until he could see a middle-aged woman with her back to him. He took out a truncheon and hit her on the head. She immediately fell unconscious. Her dog was now barking, still tethered to her hand. The agent bent over and whacked the dog on the head, which yelped and then was flat-out too. The agents exchanged words in rapid-fire Mandarin and were gone within a few seconds. They assessed that they had what they needed, leaving no indication of who they were, wearing gloves and facemasks; the latter now being a part of the normal dress. Baseball hats covered their hair. They both wore black polo-neck jumpers with leather jackets, black cargo-style trousers and black trainer shoes. Everything about them was nondescript.

'If she comes round, she won't be able to identify us,' one of the men said.

Before they left, they checked the woman still had a pulse. She did. They did not check the black and white dog which was still and unmoving. It would be better for them if the woman lived. Burglary was a fairly common crime in the UK, or it used to be. The police were too busy to follow up on these types of crimes, especially without evidence to indicate who the perpetrators were. Murder would be handled differently, but they had immunity. The Chinese duo discussed their situation and believed that the police would conclude that the lady walked in on a burglary in progress, and the criminals left in a panic. The saving grace was that she entered from the rear garden and had not seen their vehicle.

Before the Chinese had left the Professor's driveway, the MI5 counter-surveillance team watching the house was ready to follow the black Range Rover. Alarms had sounded at MI5 and MI6 operations desks. The imagery was being pulled from the hidden cameras before the intruders had reached Chippenham. The surveillance team was in a Ford Transit van disguised as a central heating firm, ideal for low visibility. They had no other support so they would have to call off the pursuit shortly. The Chinese team stayed on the A420, and the MI5 agents peeled off to go back to the house. When they arrived at the Professor's home, a police car was already in situ with an officer on the door. The lead agent in the van showed his credentials and walked into the house. The woman was out cold with a low pulse; an ambulance was on its way. The police were told to report this as a burglary gone wrong. Back in MI6 Headquarters, Tom MacDonald was pleased about the effectiveness of the surveillance and the planted information. This would go part of the way to cement the deception plan surrounding the Professor's demise. Sadly, he would have to break the news to Johnathon that his friend was in the hospital with a serious head injury, and his dog was in a coma. Tom told the local police to pay the vet's bills and do whatever it took to save the dog. The loss of his 'fluffy puppy' would be hard on the Professor. It was his last link with his deceased wife.

The Chinese duo, feeling entirely secure in the thought that they had executed a perfect job, drove to Bristol University. After parking, they easily gained access to the Professor's office and downloaded his files from his computer. They saw a few people, but no one challenged them. MI6 agents had instructed the Dean at the University that these people were not to be hindered in gaining access. The Dean saw the intruders, and they saw him. The University had plenty of Asian students so they did not look out of place. The Dean just gave them a hearty, 'Good afternoon!' from behind his mask. Again, all the work of the Chinese agents was caught on camera, including their jocular comments about how easy this was. The foreign intelligence agents were heading back to London by six p.m. having reported briefly with the codeword to say that they had completed their mission successfully.

The next day in the northeast of England, the special investigator, surreptitiously employed by the Chinese, would provide all the evidence needed to show that Professor Johnathon King was dead and that he had registered into the Priory Newcastle. Also, he had stayed in a bed and breakfast on Fulford Road in York. The guest house owner was happy to pass over the Professor's forgotten belongings to the investigator. These were packaged up and sent onwards, through a third party, to the Chinese embassy which paid handsomely for the report and physical evidence. They were happy that Johnathon King was dead. His report was a sham, and it was all a waste of time. The Chinese report back to Beijing was an administrative function and recommended no further action.

The Chief of the Ministry of State Security who controlled all Intelligence and Secret Police matters quickly read the summary and put it in the 'no further action' pile. He had too much else on his plate to worry about some wayward professor in the UK who had been discredited and was now dead.

'The lack of response from the hierarchy in China in itself was a noteworthy response,' thought Tom MacDonald, sitting in his London office overlooking the near-empty Vauxhall Bridge.

The whole episode surrounding the Professor's revelations and the Prime Minister's comments on TV did not stir the Chinese intelligence apparatus at all, which seemed to be making no effort to discredit the report.

Tom MacDonald sat and thought to himself, 'If I was developing an illegal weapon of mass destruction, and I thought that someone had indicated my actions, I would be a bit anxious. However, China has shown no mood change. There's been no increase in communications between Government departments. Absolutely nothing. Strange.'

Though it was a fleeting thought, the lack of action by the Chinese forced its way to the front of his mind again.

'Either they are playing a counter-bluff, or we have got this wrong. The only other option is someone inside China is pulling the strings of their biological warfare research facilities and keeping it secret. The last option is surely unlikely, but not altogether impossible to do, especially within a big and unwieldy secretive society.'

Chapter 17

Death by a Thousand Documents

28th May 2024

Johnathon had regained a spring in his step having spoken to his father and sister. Feeling much relieved, he genuinely believed he was now part of the team and that the Deputy Director and Claire had his back. This was only day five of his adventure into the world of the SIS, but it felt like he had been here for a lifetime already. Claire could see the weight lifted from Johnathon, and she would be sure to thank Deputy Director MacDonald for his forbearance in allowing the Professor to speak to his family. It was evident that they meant a lot to Jon.

They marched to Wire Room Two, both realising that the day ahead would be a grind. Yorkie was there already and had been trying to work out the communications links on the diagram that Lee Ford had brought earlier.

'This stuff is just a mess of lines. What the hell should we do with it?' he asked. 'Using it for toilet paper would be my preferred option.'

Philip Wong was also present, and he had marvelled at the lack of dexterity Yorkie had shown handling the diagram, constantly twisting it this way and that way. Both Claire and Jon smiled at him. Clearly this wasn't his forte. He was a man of action, not administration.

Yorkie passed on the briefing from the GCHQ Liaison Officer,

'Lee said that this diagram shows the numbers with names in brackets making calls with key words in them. Each keyword has a colour-coded arrow. The arrows show the direction of flow of the call and the number in brackets shows how many calls within the dates shown. I must have some sort of ADHD because my poor little brain can't take it all in.'

All four staff were standing around the diagram now and agreed with Yorkie. It was just too complicated for them to be able to draw any meaningful conclusions; it was information overload. The Professor suggested that it might declutter the information if there was a separate plan for each keyword. Claire agreed and suggested they work on the most promising keywords first, looking at those communications and associated documents.

Philip contributed, 'In Chinese culture, knowledge is power, and anything that is most important is hoarded by senior staff. I would therefore suggest that we deal with communications to and from the Head of Centre. Those secure communications off-site to a higher authority are most likely to have clues. Also, the volume of external communications is not going to be full of admin nonsensical claptrap.'

Philip was only in his late twenties, a bright lad who probably got the job because he was fluent in the two best-known and most-spoken variants of Chinese: Mandarin and Cantonese. He was a language major at Oxford University (Queens College), First Class honours in modern languages. He also had Spanish and Russian in his repertoire.

Claire put a call into Lee Ford and made the request for new maps and asked for two sets for each keyword: one for off-site communications and the other for internal ones. These were presented to the team within the hour.

Yorkie asked Claire, 'Ma'am, what were you counting yesterday?' This question had been buzzing around in his head all night.

Casually, she said, 'Well, I came across the words "Yellow Petal" being used in a context of a codeword. I started counting its use out of boredom more than anything, but I have a hunch that it could be something.'

'That's strange. When I was looking at some transcripts from telephone conversations yesterday, I came across that term a couple of times as well, but I dismissed it. I thought it was just a misspelling or something innocuous.'

Philip was listening to their conversation and, apologising for interrupting, added,

'Yellow flowers symbolise the bonds of friendship. Also, they represent success and pride. Joy is also one of the meanings of this colour of the flower. Flowers in the Chinese culture have strong symbolism.'

'Thanks, Phil,' Yorkie said. 'That's really interesting. Maybe it is a codeword, and the author is looking for success to bring back pride or something like that. Just a thought.'

'You're right, Staff. Let's check it out, and if we see anything else that stands out like this, we'll raise it with Lee Ford and get his boys at GCHQ to do a full analytical search using those criteria. We must follow this through to a natural conclusion. I will ask Lee to get us another expanded communications roadmap with the keywords "Yellow Petal".'

When she spoke to Lee Ford, he remarked, 'Bugger me, that was quick off the mark!'

Back in the Wire Room, they determined to work in pairs, Yorkie and the Professor and Claire and Phil. The rest of the morning sped by, and the only piece of information that had practical use was that Yorkie found out that the Professor was a West Ham fan. No one else found anything constant although there were reoccurring strings 'IV35NR' and 'IV13HD' relating to virus strains. They found nothing significant relating to Covid-19 or Covid-24 and just a few more mentions of "Yellow Petal".

The team went for lunch, and as it happened, the Professor and Yorkie sat at the same table. The large Staff Sergeant had his usual: anything with chips. Today it was haddock in breadcrumbs. The Professor had broccoli and stilton soup, plus a small avocado salad.

Yorkie said, 'So, why West Ham? You're not from London.'

'I don't know,' said Jon. 'I suppose that when I was taking an interest in football West Ham stood out.'

Yorkie gave the Professor a hard time, saying,

'Pathetic. It's eating all that veggie shit. It puddles your brain, Prof.'

Grinning, he continued, 'You just cannot have a conversation with someone who doesn't take footie seriously and won't eat meat regularly.'

Yorkie knew Johnathon was not a vegetarian but was having fun ribbing him.

They ate in companionable silence, and then Johnathon asked a question that had been troubling him for days.

'Why would someone want to kill millions of people so indiscriminately? Surely, if there was a plan to take control of China or even the world, a better solution could be found?'

Yorkie looked at the Professor and suspending his fork aloft, said,

'Professor, I know that the Squadron Leader has mentioned some of the maniacs that have been on this planet, but the truth of the matter is that there are always those types of people around. I would guess that many of the leaders of countries throughout the world today are unbalanced psychopaths or sociopaths. As to why use a virus to secure political ends, these people are only interested in domination and possession of power. Killing people is not an issue to them. One, twenty, ten thousand or a million, for them it makes no difference. It's just a number. If it's a bullet, bomb or virus, what's the difference?'

He paused and continued, 'For these maniacs to take power, they often have to displace an existing power broker which is normally a stable government. To gain power you have to undermine what is established, and more often than not, it involves conflict, war and killing. People do not go "quietly into that good night" when they have power. Look at that moron in Syria, Bashar al-Assad. He has completely ruined his country; after nearly thirteen years of fighting, everyone loses. It was the same with Gadhafi, Saddam Hussein and Hitler. All power-grabbing bastards who find it hard to let go. They are not interested in their people, just themselves, and most don't give a toss about their families. This is the way it has always been, and it's the working men and women who get slaughtered and their families bombed senselessly. It's futile stuff, but it keeps happening.'

Yorkie gulped water and continued,

'Professor, what we suspect those chaps overseas are trying to do is no different from our own system, except that we work by different rules.

'You have to remember that one hundred percent of all people die. Worldwide travel helps the transmission of viruses, leading to pandemics. The relative cleanliness of modern society restricts the virus's ability to transport itself, but like in the two great plagues, it is the poorest who are hit the hardest. I am only a simple soldier, but I grasp the nature of man and how strategies can change societies and bring about new dictators, who, incidentally, often start off being seen as saviours.'

Johnathon looked at Yorkie and nodded his agreement and thought, 'There is nothing bloody simple about you, mate.'

They finished their lunch in thoughtful silence and returned to work.

Claire and Philip were not finding a lot of references to "Yellow Petal", but what they were uncovering was making interesting reading, including one call to the site at Wuhan from Two Star General Lei Wei to the Head of Facility. He and the Facility Head discussed the progress and the timing of when "Yellow Petal" would be useable. The Facility Head was anxious and asked if it were sensible to release this second strain without there being a finished vaccine. Calls within the laboratory in Wuhan showed a strong dissention about "Yellow Petal". It was obvious that they were not referring to Covid-19, as these discussions were in May 2022, after the outbreak and slightly later. They documented a further call to Major General Lei Wei, again asking for restraint which was met with an angry response. Days later, the Head of Facility was removed, ostensibly due to ill health, and a few days later two senior scientists were also replaced. Why would a two-star general get involved in this level of work and be so aggressive if he were not trying to hide something? There were no other contacts from the centre to external bodies on "Yellow Petal". This was obviously a sensitive project, but there was no direct evidence as to what it was. Further references were being made regarding "Yellow Petal" and a vaccine for IV35NR. Could it be possible that "Yellow Petal" and IV35NR were the same substance or virus?

Major General Lei Wei made a call to the New Head of Facility on the thirteenth February this year, regretting the loss of the previous Head and his two supporters, stating he only wanted staff who wished to see China as a world leader. He would not allow anything to stand in the way of "Yellow Petal". A further call informed the Head of Facility that the vaccine was now proving effective, and testing was taking place, saying that "Yellow Petal" will be a more potent weapon than the destructive nuclear weapons on which they had wasted money.

Taking all this in, Claire briefed Bill Rankin, who realised that it was time to brief upwards. A meeting was booked for the next day with the Deputy Director.

Chapter 18

Stand-by Dark Force

28th May 2024

It was eleven a.m. The last few days had passed in the blink of an eye. Because of the priority of Operation Fulcrum Storm, everyone involved had been working pretty near flat-out. The meeting with Tom MacDonald was put back from yesterday. He had things of greater precedence to deal with, and the day just overran. Tom was genuinely apologetic to Major Tim Churchill for putting back their meeting, but in truth, Tim was happy for the extra time. Planning time was always in short supply for operations involving the SAS, so Tim was pleased to have the space to go over his thoughts yet again with Yorkie Charlton. He had spent considerable time preparing an operational options paper which he had presented to Tom. Today they would discuss which of the options they thought were most prudent.

Yorkie had just arrived in the Deputy Director's meeting room, pleased to have a rest from reviewing documents. Tim had been there a few minutes earlier to get a few slides of maps ready for showing. The truth was that he had insufficient information in hand to formulate a full plan but could offer a range of options. He knew that Tom would have his own views. Philip Wong of the China Operations Desk arrived for the meeting and chatted quite happily about the busy schedule and the challenging days ahead. He was a relaxed man with a very sharp intellect and an unpretentious warmth. David Jones, Section Chief of the Far East Desk, was the last of the members of the meeting – apart from the Deputy Director – to arrive. David went straight to the coffee that had been prepared which led to everyone else queueing up behind him. This was a good place for coffee as it was well-known that Tom did not like crappy small cups, preferring mugs. That meant everyone had a decent drink in front of them. Uncle Tom walked in holding a coffee in one hand and a bacon roll in the other. Behind him, June, his PA, held a tray of bacon rolls.

Yorkie said, 'Now this is what I call a meeting.'

Everyone scurried to their places, Tom taking the end seat. Two metres to his left was Tim Churchill with David Jones similarly spaced to his right. Yorkie was two metres further away on the same side as Tim, and Philip Wong was opposite him, technically next to his boss. Everyone has a place, and it was set in order of seniority.

Tom took another bite of his bacon roll, chewed, and then said,

'Tim, give us a brief overview of your potential operation.'

Everyone around the table knew that there was a ninety percent chance that an operation on mainland of China was highly unlikely. It was assumed no one would even propose such a thing to their political masters unless indicators pointed to a near one hundred percent possibility of wrongdoing by the Chinese. Tim started with a risk assessment of any such operation. This had already been considered by everyone around the table, but a reminder kept things in context. The SAS Major went through a few similar operations that he had reviewed to see what lessons could be learnt.

Tom MacDonald interjected with a joke, 'Just don't involve the colonials.'

Tom had worked with the Americans many times, and in truth, he admired many of the individuals with whom he came into contact. The only thing that made him wary of the CIA in particular, was their culture of being heavy-handed when it wasn't always necessary or even the best option. The cultural differences were also a factor, but the professionalism of agents tended to supersede the difference in approaches. The same applied, in the main, with special forces operatives.

Not wanting to dick about too much and in sound military tradition, Tim stated the mission,

'To infiltrate a small team of SIS personnel into the facility at Wuhan, and or any other target identified, to extract evidence of the intent to produce a biological weapon.'

The objectives were briefly outlined as:

1. A covert incursion into the area surrounding Wuhan.

2. Infiltrate the target facility, secure the necessary evidence and withdraw leaving no sign of the team's presence.

3. Withdraw from the target area and exfiltrate the country.

4. Destroy all virus-producing facilities and samples.

5. No contact with either the military forces or other security forces of China.

6. Any taking of life must only be under exceptional circumstances to maintain the clandestine nature of the operation.

7. Operational personnel were not to be taken prisoner; serious medical injuries could not lead to the apprehension of live participants.

8. If the operation at any point would compromise the UK government, it would be aborted.

Up to point six, everything was pretty normal.

Tim noted, 'This would be a suicide mission if things went wrong on the ground. The team would have nothing on them that would indicate they were from the UK. Their equipment would be non-standard special forces issue and some planted information, indicating the corpses were from a private organisation.'

'Someone like Greenpeace,' Philip Wong suggested naively.

Tom felt the need to say, 'We have to accept the risks and be straight with the team going in. We all accede to the fact that there may be casualties, and we have to be realistic about what we do.'

He did not comment on the disinformation alluded to. One of the key objectives not mentioned was the non-attributability and plausible deniability of the UK Government. MI6 were the masters at this game and would do anything to prevent the possibility of a World War starting prematurely.

Tim listed the options for the Action Force. First, was a clandestine Special Forces group of four but with in-theatre operatives providing support as required. This had proven successful previously. Given the location and nature of the task, the second option was to engage a team from entirely in-theatre assets. The final proposition was to utilise a mixed infiltration force; the SIS / SAS could provide specialist skills accessing and exiting the target with indigenous elements providing direct operational and on-the-ground support. The option of putting a team on the ground posing as a group of visitors was out of the question with the worldwide travel lockdown.

Infiltration was the next issue to highlight. Drawing the meeting's attention to his first map, Tim highlighted the difficulties of the location of Wuhan. He had indicated the key distances to the coast that were from eight hundred to nine hundred and forty kilometres from the target area. Shanghai was about nine hundred and forty kilometres, making it a steady twelve-hour drive by car. The roads were major thoroughfares with tolls at numerous points which would also have armed security. The route to the southeast towards Wenzhou would be shorter, but the roads were less modern and still had tolls and checkpoints. Backroads would take forever, and every extra hour in-theatre increased the chances of compromise.

'That makes this more than a basic road trip,' he said wryly.

Everyone appreciated the difficulties that long-range penetration in a potentially hostile territory could present. Tim showed Map 2 depicting an area of ground thirty kilometres southwest of Wuhan which would make a great DZ for a small team infiltrating by parachute. A new map, fifty thousand to one scale, provided greater detail: a rural area with no discernible buildings within a five-kilometre radius. The landing area was flat ground, not cultivated, and surrounded by a small forest belt. The roads into this locality were essentially dirt tracks. Initial imagery indicated that it was a floodplain with hills running southeast to northwest. The hills were in fact mountains, sitting at about three thousand feet which would provide a degree of shielding from radar coverage located at Wuhan. The nearest military units were also in Wuhan, and it appeared that there were no military training areas nearby. The site would offer an excellent location to set up a lay-up point after a late-night drop. This would give the team time to rest and prepare for the mission on target at dusk.

Tim discussed the options of a coastal incursion, but the risks just seemed to increase the chances of things going south. Getting a four-man or two-man team ashore with kit and having the need to ditch either boats or breathing apparatus, would leave a serious record of their presence and increase the possibility of an ambush upon return. Of course, they could use different landing and disembarkation points, but the knowledge that something surreptitious was happening would have the coast crawling with security and army personnel.

The exfiltration of the team was going to be more complex and possibly occur under the threat of being pursued by a hostile force. The longer an operation was in train, the greater the chances for things to go wrong. The team on the ground had to be taken from Wuhan to the extraction point as quickly as possible. All the technical possibilities of getting uplifted by a friendly aircraft were just too precarious and offered the greatest danger to the UK Government becoming embroiled in a diplomatic nightmare. The team's extraction would have to be overland with a coastal pick-up. Trying to get to the Embassy or taking standard passenger routes out would lead to disaster.

'Of course,' Tim added, 'if we use in-theatre forces only, they may not need to be extracted, but the acquired samples and kit would require an uplift. Having only indigenous people driving around would not be unusual and would negate the need to furtively hide the special forces operatives.'

Tom MacDonald went straight in.

'Right, guys, I see it this way. Drop in using the piggyback off either a commercial flight or some form of military logistics pick-up. The RAF are constantly going over to China to get more PPE. This will need a great deal of thought and planning. The drop zone looks good, but let's check out for other hot spots. We will need every type of satellite imagery going: visible spectrum, infrared, synthetic-aperture radar and everything in between. If there is something at that DZ, we want to know about it. I think hitting the ground is not an issue. Philip, getting to the target and out is an in-theatre issue so take the lead and coordinate with Tim. Tim, keep the Staff Sergeant as your Number Two for planning.

'Tim, I will give you a list of technical equipment you will need to acquire for your team to get the samples and data needed. Basic arming and night vision operations kit will be needed, but heavy weapons will not be taken. If we need to fight our way out big style, we are fucked. So, let's avoid the need to get dirty. You will need one Chinese speaker within the compound; two would be better. In terms of the infiltration team, we need an IT specialist and someone who can work their way around a lab. All on-site personnel must be explosives-trained. Remember, what is in the labs may be more deadly than Covid-24. Let's not start pandemic number three. All members have to be up to scratch in fieldcraft; no passengers on this one. I am not worried about ditching stuff, but we'll need to deny the enemy the use of it and make sure it is not found in a hurry. I want a full equipment list based on a four-person incursion team down to make, weight and notes on how to disguise its origins. No numbers on weapons. I want things from off-the-shelf civilian sources and readily available, nothing too specialist and no UK manufacturers. The team will need Chinese rations for, say, two days; in-theatre support will provide the rest. I want no UK rubbish but plenty of Chinese. I will sort out the deception plan and pass to Dave and Philip for scrutiny.'

David Jones and Philip Wong both nodded in acknowledgement.

Director MacDonald was in his element. He kept speaking.

'Tim, would you and Staff Sergeant Charlton look at the options for infiltration into the site and laboratories? I am hoping to have full details of the security systems within the next day or so. If I have not got them to you by cease of play tomorrow, I want to see you kicking my door down the next morning. Once we have plans for the site, I would like you to test the feasibility of accessing the site and exiting without detection. If we feel we can do it, we might pass it to the boys in Hereford, but for now, keep this internal; external calls or communications could alert the Chinese. The fewer people involved at this stage the better operational security will be. Staff, you have done this thing before, I seem to recall from your file. We need an operator's eye on this. Don't be afraid to ruffle feathers, and if you feel key points are being overlooked, kick up a fuss. Tim, if you are not getting the data and analysis work you require, make a noise. As I said in our initial briefing, this takes priority over absolutely everything.'

Turning to David Jones, Tom said, 'David, I want you to report back to me with an option to use only in-theatre assets on this. I want a full man-by-man brief on whom you could use. We need a committed team just in case we lose the plot. This means people who know to not get captured alive. Philip, look at the infiltration option in conjunction with Tim and Yorkie. We will consider an airborne drop. I need options for delivery systems, preferred techniques and an alternate DZ in case your initial option Tim has unforeseen issues. Also, getting the team out, determine what support you need to get from Wuhan to a coastal pick-up. Routes are critical here. We will be monitoring radio chats, so if something goes wrong, we need secondary and tertiary routes. Consider changing vehicles and possibly decoys. You know the drill. Chat with the RN Liaison about a pick-up and a possible location for a covert job. I am assuming it would be a submarine with a mini-sub collection from shore but look at other options. Without giving away anything too much, find out what assets we have in the seas of China. David, once the Chinese know of the operation, every suspected foreign agent in the country will be lifted. If we have anyone whose cover is suspected of being blown, get them out quietly now. Anyone involved in the operation can exit with the team but no family. This will mean that if it is discovered who has helped us, their families will be executed. Give this some thought, we do not want civilian casualties, but there is always that potential.'

Tom MacDonald started his summing up.

'So, we are looking into how we will be getting on the ground, how we get the merchandise and how to get the fuck out of Dodge. I cannot stress too greatly that the success of any operation rests on the details in the planning. We have to think of everything now because if we leave it to the team on the ground, every time they have to improvise, they are one step closer to being compromised. Every unforeseen problem they have to negotiate is a potential further nail in their coffins. Therefore, test your plans, check them and run them again until you are perfectly happy with the outcomes. If you would not go on the mission because of doubts, don't expect others to do so.

'I am hoping to know in the next five days if the operation might be possible. Get all your plans ready in three days. However, bear in mind that we might be sitting on our hands for weeks. Therefore, I don't need to remind you to keep up to date on what's happening on the ground in-theatre. David and Philip, I will leave it to you two to keep us all abreast of anything pertinent. We have guys listening to the chatter but keep an eye on what's coming out of the region, even general news. Any questions? No? Then let's leave it there and get to work. Major, you and Yorkie stay behind briefly.'

When the room was cleared, The Deputy Director Operations said to both men,

'I know you have pals back in Hereford, but do not chat to anyone yet. The lads there, if they get wind of what we are planning, will get excited and blab. What I want you to do is put together a dream team of around ten guys that you feel would suit this type of operation. We can whittle numbers down later. Keep it to single or divorced lads, if possible. Where you have a key player who is married, that's fine, but remember this could be a one-way trip.'

Major Churchill asked, 'Director, would it be possible for me to go along as I have done a couple of operations?'

Tom replied quickly, 'Tim, your skills and intellect are needed here controlling what's going on. From your briefing, I am thinking possibly one or two UK personnel. One will need to be explosives and the other competent in the handling of viruses. Both will need to know each other's job inside-out. Maybe one SIS employee and an SAS minder, but until we know what we have on the ground at the target, we will have to keep an open mind.'

Tom finished, 'Thank you both for your endeavours on this. I appreciate it is hard to pull together a plan without having all the information and intelligence to hand. As I said, I hope that will change in the next few days. Before you go, Yorkie, in my office I have a folder for the Squadron Leader.'

'Yes, sir,' said Yorkie.

Yorkie went into the Deputy Director's Office and was told to close the door and sit down.

The Staff Sergeant knew there was no folder for the Squadron Leader and was excited about the next conversation.

Chapter 19

Coming Together

29th May 2024

A formal wash-up was called regarding the outcomes of the deception plan surrounding the Professor's untimely demise. Also, a brief was prepared to bring Tom MacDonald up to date on the intelligence review going on in the Wire Room. Claire and her Section Chief, Bill Rankin, were present in Tom's main office.

Tom, looking down at his huge file on Operation Prune Pie, started the meeting with an unexpected, 'Fuck me.'

Claire thought, 'Shit, that doesn't sound promising, I wonder what has gone wrong?' Her brain was scrambling around to think about what her senior boss was referring to.

Tom paused and then forcibly said, 'We went to all this sodding effort and expense to throw the Chinese off the heels of the Professor, and the net level of interest from them was borderline mind-numbingly lacklustre. I have asked our China Team to ascertain if they suspected any subterfuge going on here but not even a whisper or murmur. We have been leading ourselves on a merry dance.'

'From our perspective, sir,' said Bill Rankin nervously, 'everything went like clockwork. Most of the evidence that we planted was intercepted and, as far as we can tell, was verified as being valid by the Chinese. There has been no reason to think that we have failed in achieving our objectives.'

'Bill,' Tom responded, sounding a bit irritated, 'my concern is not about what we did. It's the bloody lack of response or even interest the Chinese had in the whole thing. Let's put the boot on the other foot. If we wanted to know the whereabouts of someone to see if we could find out what he knows, what would we do?'

He answered the question himself.

'We would do all the things the Chinese did, but we would have taken it so much further. They have thousands of nationals in the UK and more agents than we can cover. Surely, they would have attempted to contact the University, the students who wrote the report with the Professor, the Professor's family, his friends and colleagues. There were so many more avenues of investigation that have been either completely ignored through incompetence or by way of rational decision-making and seen as totally unnecessary. The Chinese are not incompetent, so we must assume it to be the latter.'

Tom went on, 'My frustration is simply this. If we, the UK, were trying to hide the fact that we had in our midst something of national critical importance, we would have a deception plan. Our plan would cover many layers of information, and once it was over, even we would believe our own lies.'

Both Claire and Bill nodded in agreement together.

'We have heard nothing out of the Communist Party apparatus in China regarding this matter and nothing from their State Security sources. It is like this means bugger all to them. This fact has been niggling at the back of my mind for the past two days. It is stopping me from getting my beauty sleep,' he said.

Claire thought, 'No wonder the old git sounds so grumpy.'

Tom went on, 'In sum, the deception operation was well-executed, the titbits prepared for the other side were picked up on, but the Chinese barely could be bothered to report it. Finally, when all the facts were on Chinese soil, it merited no further action. The level of apathy from the Chinese on Professor King's revelations was stunning.'

Tom looked at his audience, smiled and said,

'Look, I know I have just repeated myself, but do you see the dilemma?'

'Deputy Director,' Claire replied, 'we are pretty sure now that there is development work going on at Wuhan, but that was no surprise. Our boys are rechecking our data of communications channels on certain codewords that we have encountered. We have not found the smoking gun that Section Chief Rankin has asked for, but I am sure with a bit more time on task, we will find the person or persons holding that gun. One unusual thing, within the Chinese culture of secrecy, is higher levels demanding to know everything of strategic importance going on below them. As you know, most commanders and the political hierarchy are control freaks. One of the codeword viruses, "Yellow Petal", does not go beyond a Major General Lei Wei, who is the senior person directly responsible for their biological warfare infrastructure which includes Wuhan plus at least two other such laboratories. From our cross-referencing of "Yellow Petal" in all communications in and out of Major General Lei Wei's office, he corresponds directly with only four people. Every communication on this virus is marked as Top Secret and has limited eyes distribution. By our estimation, only five people know of its existence. There is a crossover reference of IV35NR on two occasions to "Yellow Petal" which is an indication that the two names refer to the same product. We also have seen chatter that the production of a vaccine for "Yellow Petal" is well advanced with trials going well. Indications are that this codeword virus is either Covid-24 or a derivative of Covid-24; if it is the latter, sir, that could mean another wave of a new, more lethal virus.'

'Get to the point, Squadron Leader,' said the impatient senior intelligence officer.

"Sir, to put it in a nutshell, we think that a senior intelligence officer controlling the biowarfare cohorts in China is developing a virus or viruses without Government or Party knowledge or authority.'

'OK, how sure are you of this?' he asked.

Bill Rankin thought he'd better have some input.

'Boss, the team is doing a great job, but our confidence rating is only about fifty percent on this intelligence.'

Both Claire and Rankin had discussed the confidence level before the meeting, and they had agreed that it stood at about sixty to seventy percent. Claire knew that the Section Head was a political beast, but this was no time to be anything other than straight.

'Possibly sixty or seventy percent,' added Claire defiantly, 'but we have to tie up a number of loose ends. As you know, sir, a few of the key people in Wuhan were executed, we believe on the direct orders of Major General Lei Wei. These could be simple punishment killings for the Covid-19 cock-up, or it may be something more sinister. We found weak indicators of some dissent at the work being undertaken in Wuhan by senior scientists. The murders could have been ordered to silence detractors from the project and maintain security.'

Grasping the situation, Tom MacDonald said, 'If this is true, and let's assume it is, you are telling me that Major General Lei Wei has manipulated the whole bioweapons department of China into following his orders to which no one else above him is privy. Over years, I am guessing, he has developed some strains of killer viruses and has managed to keep them secret. Is that not farfetched, Squadron Leader? A leap of imagination further, and does this Major General Lei Wei have a fluffy white cat that sits quietly on his lap?'

The last questions were asked in a condescending, disbelieving way. Tom knew how to press people's buttons, and he had just done so with Claire Walters' hitting the roof switch.

Before Claire could leap to her own defence, Tom looked at Rankin and said,

'Bill, do you accept this bunkum?'

Bill showed his true colours by answering with a shoulder shrug. This infuriated Claire, even more, to find her immediate boss had no backbone. She pointed her attention squarely towards her Deputy Director.

'Bunkum, sir? Do you not realise that the best place to keep secrets is within a secret society or organisation? This is entirely feasible. Our Operation Fulcrum Storm, how many people know its full extent? Six or seven maybe and even some of those do not know all aspects. If you wanted to erase all records of this operation, how difficult would that be? You would only have to buy off, bribe, blackmail or kill a few people. If you wanted to run an illegal operation, could you do it, sir? I suspect so. How many times have people in positions of authority in our agency made off-piste decisions and then hidden them?'

Claire could feel her body temperature rising. She was shooting from the hip again, but she couldn't help it. Continuing, a milder tone, she asked,

'And tell me, sir, don't you have a white West Highland Terrier who undoubtedly sits on your lap?'

Claire sat back, taking a slow, deep breath.

'Bloody hell, Claire, relax,' Tom said. 'I was only pressing to test your resolve on this one.'

He turned to Bill Rankin, 'How often does she go off like this?'

Bill replied cheekily, 'Only when you're around, sir.'

'By the way, Squadron Leader, I have never left the reservation, as the Americans would say. MI6 plays by the rules we have been given, albeit sometimes they are flexibly interpreted.'

He smiled at her.

After a moment's silence, Tom MacDonald said,

'We need to refocus, people. Let's summarise. From what you are both saying, there are strong indications of a rogue element operating within the Chinese intelligence apparatus without the knowledge, either direct or indirect, of President Xi Jinping or the Central People's Government or the Communist Party and the People's Liberation Army. Is that fair so far?'

'That's right, sir,' Bill Rankin responded.

Tom continued, 'We have strong suspicions that this "Yellow Petal" either refers to Covid-24 or a new virus and that the facility at Wuhan is the centre of production. Also, it could be possible that a vaccine may exist at other facilities. Correct?'

'We are not one hundred percent sure that the virus is produced at Wuhan, but we are pretty damn sure it was developed there. We suspect from telephone conversations that at least two other sites exist either for the production of the virus and or the vaccine. Other than that, you are right,' said Bill Rankin wanting to get back in on the act.

'OK, what's the plan going forward?' the Deputy Director demanded.

Bill Rankin quickly replied, 'We need to bring our confidence levels on the summary up to above ninety percent, confirm "Yellow Petal" is Covid-24 or a new virus, determine who is the controlling power and decision maker regarding the production of "Yellow Petal", develop threat scenarios regarding "Yellow Petal" and finally see if this reported vaccine exits. Also, sir, we must stay attuned to other options.'

Tom said, 'Bill, perfect. I will take the lead on threat scenarios. Also, I will rush through the personality profile of Major General Lei Wei. I agree it would be possible for someone at his level to have a separate and personal agenda. I will see if we can have these to hand by tomorrow.

'Squadron Leader, keep your team hunting down these facts. Do you need more bodies, or can you cope? How about I give you a couple of days to see where we are at and review matters then?'

'That's perfect, sir, but I think we will go with who and what we have here,' said Claire.

'Now, Claire, tell me how are you and the boys coping with being on internal lockdown?' Tom asked.

'It's not too bad, sir. Not having to travel to and from the safe house is good. Not having to cook is great, but the beds are crap. The facilities are a bit basic, but we'll be fine. The boys are good company, but most of the time we are only focused on work.'

'That's great to hear and thank you both. Now piss off,' said the Deputy Director in a jovial voice.

'Squadron Leader, just one last thing if I may? The only person I usually let talk to me like that is my wife, and how the hell do you know I have a Westie?'

She looked at him and smiled, 'Sorry, sir, a good intelligence officer never gives up her sources, but you might want to think about the personal photos you have on the wall behind you.'

Tom turned and saw a picture of his wife with their dog. He had forgotten all about it and laughed heartily.

She kept a straight face, turned and left with Bill Rankin.

In the corridor, Claire said, 'I think that went well.'

Bill said, 'We've done well. We just have to deliver some better intel.'

'What happens from here?' Claire asked.

'To be honest, I really am not sure what the next moves will be. If we can prove our findings beyond any reasonable doubt, there are some incredibly difficult decisions to be made. I could provide you with a list of my thoughts, but I will hold my own counsel just for now.'

Claire knew he would have various options to ponder, but sometimes it just didn't help to get ahead of yourself. His lack of decisiveness in the meeting was playing on her mind. She wondered if he would really have her back if the whole thing unravelled. Her guess was he would hang her out to dry.

Rankin added, 'Claire, we have made some great progress in a relatively short space of time, and the team seems to be holding up quite well. I know you are all pushing the envelope regarding working hours, but we need to keep up the impetus and squeeze every ounce of effort out of every man jack.'

'Copy that, sir.'

Bill went back to his office, and Claire moved on to join the team for an early lunch. It was clear that the team members were flagging. Long days and sleepless nights were taking a toll on all of them. The lockdown meant that there was no way to really switch off. Their days were all the same: Breakfast – work – lunch – work – afternoon tea – work – dinner – work – bed – repeat.

Yorkie was keeping the mood fairly light with his somewhat inappropriate humour. She didn't mind, figuring they were all adults here. The truth was that everyone laughed at his jokes, and even the Professor got in on the act which just encouraged Yorkie to raise the ante into another, as yet, untouched taboo subject.

The Wire Room was bland, and as Claire walked back in after lunch, her heart sank. However, she knew there was a job to be done. In reality, the four intelligence officers in the room needed no kicks up the arse because they were all supremely well-motivated individuals. Each had a track record of endurance either in study, sport, battle or work. The trick here was to stimulate more than bully. A bit of motivational sweet-talking would have the desired results. She decided that a brief update on her meeting with Uncle Tom was in order. It was a welcome distraction to her colleagues. She gave a potted version of what was said but made the most of the positive aspects, saying how pleased the DD Ops was. The main discussion point was around the lack of interest of the Chinese Intelligence teams and how the senior Party machinery was totally apathetic to any accusatory remarks about the supposed wrongdoing by their country.

Philip said, 'It was not the Chinese way to ignore something that might threaten an operation. They pride themselves in having the intelligence to foresee the game unfold. They will have contingencies for every eventuality. Being passive is just not their way. A lack of communication above the position of Major General Lei Wei might indicate either that the Party wants plausible deniability, or they don't know what's going on. In truth I would think the latter is most likely.'

Yorkie said, 'Any country that produces a game like Mah-jong can't be completely balanced!'

Philip retorted, 'Mah-jong is what intellectuals give to the peasants to engage their brains, so they don't notice they are being over-taxed. You should try it, Yorkie.'

Yorkie got the point slowly, having had to replay it through his head a few times. He really was tired. He gave Philip a weak grin.

With renewed vigour, they agreed that the thrust of their attention was to prove what "Yellow Petal" was, identify if a vaccine existed for "Yellow Petal" or Covid-24 and finally, prove if Major General Lei Wei was acting unilaterally without any controls from the higher echelons within the State Security apparatus or the People's Republic of China Government.

Chapter 20

The General Evil

30th May 2024

Deputy Director Tom MacDonald introduced Mrs Mary Westwood from the Behavioural Sciences Team who had prepared a personality profile on Major General Lei Wei. The audience included Johnathon, Claire and Yorkie. Philip Wong was also sitting in, but he knew the General well, given that he was responsible for the China Desk. As usual, Bill Rankin was running late, getting seated at nine zero nine a.m. just before Mrs Westwood got underway.

Mary was not a natural orator, but she was enthusiastic. She flicked through some slides of photographs depicting a slightly plump, short person wearing a general officer's uniform. This was a man who was neither athletic nor took pride in his appearance. Each shot showed an expressionless round face with no warmth in his features. Lei Wei's eyes looked as if they could be black holes, pulling in all life that encountered them. After a few minutes, Mary started her formal presentation.

'Major General Lei Wei had a glittering career in the Army making it to two-star general status in charge of the Strategic Rocket Forces. This role also placed under his control the military's Chemical and Biological Warfare Specialisations. He was born to a mid-range influential family from Shanghai and was appointed to his current role in the Directorate of State Security as the Under-Secretary for Strategic Weapons. This role included oversight of all things surrounding Nuclear, Chemical and Biological Warfare. Within his Army career, he was ruthless and used his power and position to rise through the ranks, whilst hiding his psychopathic qualities.'

Yorkie suggested, 'Sounds a bit harsh. We've only just met the guy!'

Tom MacDonald chuckled, and the others followed suit. Bill Rankin laughed only when it was clear the DD Ops genuinely found the comment humorous.

Mary smiled and continued.

'From an early age, Lei Wei attended a special school as he struggled to fit into mainstream education. As an only child, he was a great disappointment to his aged father who was a high-ranking Party activist. His mother was thirty-eight years younger than her husband and came from a peasant background, marrying at the age of seventeen, a fact that other students at Lei Wei's school teased him about. Lei Wei loved his mother deeply and could feel her pain at being in a loveless and, at times, brutal marriage. His father was abusive to both his mother and Lei Wei. Sexual abuse was a regular occurrence for his mother and his father encouraged his friends to join in the abusive behaviour. For Lei Wei, it was a great shame he carried with him all his life. He knew how depraved his father was and how his mother would accept the affliction to protect her son. The family home was a plush but awful place to be. It is believed at the age of twelve, the son vowed to kill his father, and it is rumoured he fulfilled that promise at twenty. It occurred when Lei Wei was home during leave from Army training one weekend. His father was suffering from pneumonia, and Lei Wei suffocated him. There was no investigation as his father was seventy-six years old and had a history of respiratory disease. Both Lei Wei and his mother outwardly grieved for their loss but were both relieved to be free from their abuser and tormentor.

'During his education up to university standard, Lei Wei struggled to form real emotional attachments with other students. He constantly lied and deceived others. A clever and habitual cheat, he saw being devious not as a flaw but an admirable quality; these traits being evident throughout his life. Forming artificially shallow relationships, these were designed to manipulate people and improve his standing in the eyes of his tutors. Lei Wei treated these acquaintances as pawns to be employed for his benefit. When his unfortunate friends were adversely treated for carrying out his instructions, Lei Wei felt no guilt regarding any punishment to which they were subjected. Indeed, in one school report, his science master astutely noted, "Lei Wei enjoyed seeing others being disciplined too much". Latterly, Lei Wei developed into an intelligent student and had learnt to mimic good behaviour, being able to hide in a social crowd.

'During Army officer training, he was often seen by his training officers as being charming and trustworthy. However, there were disciplinary issues in which Cadet Lei Wei was noted for issuing harsh punishments to subordinate cadets. He was always able to distance himself by inflicting punishment beatings through third parties, enjoying the actions of others vicariously. Pushing the limits of disciplinary beatings beyond that which was considered reasonable, he was adept at passing the blame on to the person carrying out the beating. He had no issues incriminating others. It appeared to his superiors that he either was innocent or had covered himself so well that it was impossible to prove his evil intentions. There were doubts as to his character, and these were alluded to in his assessments, but nothing of the magnitude inhibiting his rise to power.

'In his early military career, Lei Wei was prone to outbursts of verbal and physical misbehaviour. An abusive and extreme officer, he was universally disliked by his troops. It was suspected that, as he was a small man, he feared direct physical conflict, displaying an aversion to being physically dominated. Those who threatened him were often dealt with indirectly. He was an expert at framing his peers by planting discrediting information in their offices or steal files, showing up their incompetency. Patient and scheming, Lei Wei would select the right time to inflict the gravest damage to his target.

'He showed no remorse or regret for humiliating his peers who competed for advancement and ruining their careers. A risk taker, he had no compunction to throw his subordinates in the fire to increase his profile. He rose through the ranks quickly. As a Major, Lei Wei would not tolerate his staff talking back to him in private but within group forums would try to appear to be open to the views of others. In essence, he was an autocratic leader in private but a more amenable person in front of his seniors. To them, he came across as being an ideal senior officer whose units were well-run.

'When Lie Wei engaged in unorthodox behaviour, he did so in a such way that minimised the risk to himself. He would remove himself from any transgressions and have contingencies to ensure he was not held culpable for any wrongdoing. Again, he would not hesitate to issue the harshest of punishments to those seemingly failing him. Lei Wei never showed any pangs of remorse or guilt for the pain others endured, especially when he was the architect of such hurt. When he ruined a fellow officer's career, he took great delight in watching him and his family being escorted from the military camp in tears and shame. He apparently took unbridled delight to hear the very same officer had committed suicide.

'As a general, he worked mainly within strategic arms but had a penchant for biological warfare. He left the service prematurely to take up the role in the State Security Directorate responsible for Strategic Weapons, what the West would call weapons of mass destruction. He has kept a low profile over the past eight years. However, it is believed that he was involved with the removal of his immediate superior who was found embezzling Party funds to procure young boys for sexual purposes. Major General Lei Wei turned down the opportunity for promotion two years ago due to his wife's ill health but hasn't taken a day's holiday in that time.

'In his current role, he has a strong leadership style bordering on dictatorial. He issues instructions and expects his team to perform without questioning his judgements or authority. A secretive man, he believes without any doubt that knowledge is the principal key to power. For that reason, Lei Wei often maintains much of his organisation's critical knowledge to himself, only providing snippets of information on a need-to-know basis to key staff. A man of few mistakes himself, any errors are always the fault of others. He has a repugnance towards those who embarrass him, whether in jest or through insensitivity. The architect of his humiliation is invariably sacked or disappears. The expectation regarding the performance of his staff is of the highest standards at all times. Lei Wei does not tolerate mistakes; minor ones lead to punishment and more grievous ones often result in dismissal or possibly worse.

'In summary, Major General Lei Wei shows all the qualities of a psychopath. In his current position, he can express his inner demons and control everything going on around him. It is believed he refused his promotion for reasons other than his family, possibly to maintain a tight grip on his projects in Wuhan and other biological sites.'

Mary took a long gulp of water. For her, public speaking was a true torment. She loved her work but would have been happier to issue a written brief only.

'Ladies and gentlemen, any questions?'

There was the usual pregnant pause during which everyone was waiting for someone to break the silence.

The drawling tone of a Yorkshire accent was heard.

'Ma'am, Staff Sergeant Charlton here. Just one question: is this the sort of man who you might consider to be a mass killer, someone who would not lose sleep over the deaths of millions of people?'

Without hesitation, Mary answered, 'That would be a reasonable assessment.'

Yorkie nodded a thank you.

Claire, leaning over to Johnathon, whispered, 'Well that's it. We don't need to know any more than that.'

Tom stood up and thanked Mary for her comprehensive report. He added,

'In all we do here, we have to be more than sure we come to the right judgements. For an intelligence officer to fully grasp what we are doing, our understanding of the characters at play is crucial. We must appreciate what makes our adversaries tick, their motivation and their deprivations. The man that has been described to us would have no compunction in sending everyone to their deaths in the Western world if it meant he had absolute power over all else.'

Keeping on message and being positive, Tom turned to Mary and asked if she could prepare a full written work-up on the General for presentation to an oversight committee. This would be the most detailed level of character assassination they needed to prepare, but Tom was thinking that this might be needed for the Prime Minister if invasive espionage was required.

He thanked Mary again for her professional and much-appreciated work, then dismissed the meeting.

At that moment, six individual pagers went off in the room; it was the whole Operation Fulcrum Force team. Marked urgent, the message said, 'Wire Room Two immediately.' The group all moved down to the bowels of the MI6 Headquarters.

'This has to be serious for Lee Ford to tell the Deputy Director Operations to get here now!' Claire said.

Bill Rankin responded, 'Well, it had better be important!'

Claire and her team were excited but trying to keep it under wraps. There was no planned meeting with the GCHQ Liaison Officer, and each was hoping for some new and more recent intercepts which might just have a few nuggets of information that would blow the whole thing wide open.

Chapter 21

The Open Door

30th May 2024

On arrival at Wire Room Two, everyone left their personal items in lockers outside and were scanned through to the inner sanctum. In this compact room, two men were standing with their backs to those entering. One was obviously Lee Ford. The other was unknown to the group members.

Claire thought, 'This seems like a breach of protocol.'

Who was this man, older than Lee, somewhat portlier and a tad scruffier? Both men turned to greet the assembled team.

Tom MacDonald stared at the red-faced fellow and said,

'Derek, you old bugger, I thought you were dead or at least retired.'

The visitor had a bold grin across his face.

'You are still a cheeky old bastard, Tom. Did they make you leave your Zimmer frame outside?'

The two men shook hands like long-lost friends with absolutely no consideration for the standard Covid protocols. Both pulled a small bottle of hand sanitiser out of their pockets and squirted a dollop in their hands before rubbing them together, still grinning at one another.

Tom MacDonald turned to his team and said with great warmth.

'People, the slightly decrepit fellow before you is my old mate, Derek Jacobs, who is the Director GCHQ.'

Tom went on, 'This fine fellow would not have travelled from his Ivory Tower in Cheltenham to be here unless it was something important. Does Shirley need you to shop at Harrods again, my old mucker?'

Everyone was smiling, not so much at the humour but just to see the obvious affection between these two old friends who clearly had a long history. It was a light-hearted moment.

'A bearer of bad news would not perform like this,' Yorkie

whispered to Claire. 'He would give his pal the respect of briefing him in private, especially if it were a terrible update.'

Derek questioned Tom, 'Mate, I take it we are all cleared to the required level in here? What I am about to tell you is at the highest level of sensitivity, but given my understanding of your requirements, I am assuming, the assembled team is all 'need to know'? The information is of such a delicate nature and importance, that outside of this room, there are only three people who know what it is and how we obtained it.'

Tom nodded and gestured for Derek to proceed.

'We have broken into the entire server system at Wuhan, accessing all areas including the Head of Facilities coded files and those of the previous incumbents of that role.'

Everyone gasped except for Deputy Director MacDonald and Lee Ford for they knew GCHQ's capabilities.

Derek continued, 'However, there is more.'

He paused for effect.

'Come on, you old drama queen! Get on with it. This isn't a game show,' said Tom MacDonald. 'I am nearly pissing myself in anticipation.'

Some of the SIS team had not seen Tom quite so animated before.

Derek grinned at his old friend restraining comments on old age and incontinence, then continued.

'We have not only gained access to all systems at Wuhan, but purely by accident, we located a back door into Wuhan's sister research and production facilities at Zhengzhou and Shanghai.'

Even Tom MacDonald was now wholly engaged, and his mind was running wild.

Seeing everyone's eyes widening in anticipation, Director Jacobs went on.

'Each facility is connected to each other's servers using the same encryption and passwords. We believe they have set themselves up in this way so that one person has access to everything. Fundamentally, what I am saying is we have access to everything, every single document, research data, email record and personnel files that they have.'

This wasn't the first time GCHQ had done this, but the reason for Derek's elation soon became apparent.

'In translating and sifting the information for you good people, we have found research that simply points to a new Virus labelled IV35NP codenamed "Yellow Petal" which is a derivative of Covid-24. The documents we have seen categorically prove that this new virus and Covid-24 were developed in Wuhan and produced in Zhengzhou. This new strain, "Yellow Petal", is more virulent, contagious and lethal than Covid-24 and makes Covid-19 look like a case of the sniffles, if what we read is to be believed.'

Professor King interjected, 'Have you seen the research and the test results?'

'Professor, we have not yet had the time to analyse all the data, and to be frank, that's not what we do. I suspect you and Porton Down are our specialists in this field, and you will be very busy over the next few days or possibly weeks. The headline though is "Yellow Petal" is being produced at an off-shoot facility at Zhengzhou University of Microbiology and Immunity Department. Indications are that this is going to be used as a bioweapon against the USA, the West generally, and the Indian subcontinent. However, let's not fool ourselves, people. Any nation not on the side of China will not be supported by the vaccine. It's a high-risk strategy for Major General Lei Wei, whom we believe is the architect.

'I mentioned a vaccine. We have also seen documents showing that at the Institute of Microbiology & Immunology, Shanghai Normal University in Xuhui District, a vaccine for Covid-24 is available but was not rolled out. The vaccine for "Yellow Petal" is a tertiary vaccine which will protect against all these strains of the virus, and it would appear is ready for trials. However, we must add, there seems to be an impetus to get this ready for use and to have "Yellow Petal" on the streets within the next few months. We suspect Major General Lei Wei is looking for a widely dispersed initial infection area commencing with key targets in late autumn, the end of November.'

Claire Walters said, 'Director Jacobs, are you saying that unless we can intervene, later this year we may encounter a virus even worse than Covid-24 which will be delivered across the whole of the Western World by a deliberate act?'

'Yes, you have that completely right.'

Everyone had questions.

'Professor, you first,' Derek said.

'Director, what do we know about this virus?'

Director Jacobs's face took on a pained look.

'Professor, I am no expert, but from our readings of their assessment summary it indicates, firstly, a transmittable R Number of between six and ten in open society. Secondly, the lethality ratio of infected unvaccinated persons is between sixty to eighty percent. The aspect that worries us most is that it has a gestation or incubation period in the host of between eight and twenty-one days. The next sting in the tail is when it becomes active in the host, the infected person will succumb to the virus between twenty-four to forty-eight hours. Those who survive, so the research papers tell us, will be ill for months with the possibility of lifelong diminished physical capacity.'

Claire spoke with a startled tone, 'Sir, if what you say is correct, that would mean whole cultures would come to a grinding halt. Our ability to defend ourselves would vanish in months. At that point, the West's only practical response to an attack would be a nuclear one. This is a doomsday weapon they have produced.'

Jacobs responded, 'But, if they thought they could infect the West before we realise its source, by that point they would have us over a barrel, and our only way out is to trade for the vaccine. Thereafter, world domination.'

The silence was prolonged as everyone tried to come to terms with what they had heard.

'What we have here, people, just to be fucking clear,' butted in Tom MacDonald, 'is a genocide weapon. This lunatic in China, I suspect, wants to weaken every other race and nation on the planet and move his people in to fill the gaps, what the Germans called *"Lebensraum"*, meaning living space. Basically, it is much the same as the Europeans did to the North American continent, and what the Spaniards and Portuguese undertook in South America. It's a policy of settler colonialism with territorial expansionism to control the world's resources. It might sound fanciful, but I think our man, Major General Lie Wei, believes he is the new Genghis Khan or Adolf Hitler.'

Derek chimed in, saying, 'Tom, whatever evidence your team needs, we have it. As of eleven p.m. last night we copied their whole fucking server and put in a worm so they cannot detect we have been snooping around. If we need to get back in, we can, but staying connected permanently would leave us open to detection.'

The competing emotions of shock and elation in the room were palpable. For Tom, this was like all his Christmases coming at once. The Professor was thinking he was exonerated for his actions. Also, his scientific work was completely validated. He felt a great sense of relief, but the fear of what lay ahead filled him with dread. Both Bill and Claire felt an element of satisfaction mixed with apprehension as to what would come next.

Yorkie said, 'Those fucking bastards.'

The next two hours were spent looking at key documents. This was irrefutable proof of the actions of a hostile nation which would justify a pre-emptive attack. If they involved the Americans, it would be World War Three. Before the senior team could recommend anything up the chain of command, they had to know categorically how far this extended within China. If, as was being discussed, it was a rogue operator and could be proved as such, a more sensitive plan might be required. Tom barked out orders of what he needed. He was clear and precise. Everyone in the team had their tasks and was told to get on with them.

Tom asked Derek if he could help, using Lee as he needed.

'Dig out all the security plans of the three sites. Anything to do with passes, access codes, combinations on safes and locks. We need to know procedures for entry, the number of guards at each post, their names, everything about everything, including the names of the guards' pets.'

He looked over to Claire waiting for a smart-arse comment about his Westie, but she just smiled. Tom guessed she was reading his mind.

Derek thought, 'Tom's pondering going in with a team or three.'

The only other person in the room who had similar thoughts was Yorkie. He knew the drill, what you needed on the ground to get in and out with minimal fuss. He was feeling the rush of adrenalin remembering past ventures, some fondly and others with an element of regret.

Lunch was late that day. People had renewed energy and could not drag themselves away from their work until they were ordered to take a break. They no longer felt tired and were pumped up on adrenalin.

Before they departed for lunch, Tom engaged with the team once more.

'This has reached new levels of sensitivity. Everyone is on lockdown tonight until we have a game plan going forward. Let me make this clear. No one outside this room is to know what we have here and what we have discussed. At four p.m. this afternoon, I want Bill, Claire and Yorkie in my meeting room. Derek, would you be kind enough to come along too?'

Director Jacobs said, 'Only as long as you have blueberry muffins and decent coffee.'

'That's a 'yes' then,' replied Tom.

At lunch, the Professor asked Claire, 'Have I done anything wrong? Why was I excluded from the meeting in the afternoon?'

Claire smiled at his lack of understanding.

'No, not at all. This is moving to the next phase, a non-scientific stage, more of a period requiring direct action. We have people who can do that sort of stuff, and we have friends who can help us.'

She signed SAS on the table, and said, 'Yorkie's pals.'

He looked at her, took a deep intake of breath and sighed in relief.

Claire added, 'What we will need to do, Jon, is validate the Chinese test findings for the viruses and vaccines, at least as far as we are able. Do you want me to draft in some support from Porton Down?'

Johnathon replied, 'I think we had better. It might be too much just for you and me. Professor Janet Williams seemed to really know her stuff. Maybe she would help?'

'I think she would be perfect, making a great addition to the team. I will speak to Uncle Tom to get her on board. As it is a theoretical exercise, she should come here, but there may be good reasons to work at Porton Down, and you might have to move there.'

Yorkie sat at another table across from Claire's with Philip Wong. They were deep in conversation, and it wasn't about the pie and chips Yorkie had in front of him. Yorkie was getting the measure of the young man whom he had grown to admire. It was a relief that Philip was in the Oxford University Officer Training Corps (OUOTC), an Army Reserve unit that recruits exclusively from university students. The cadets undertake a broad range of military training skills.

173

Yorkie thought, 'They are not the SAS, but it's a start and shows intention.'

Phil also won college colours for playing as a fly-half for the rugby union team. More importantly, he had undertaken the full fieldcraft training cadre at the MI6 training centre. Yorkie had also attended the MI6 field training at Fort Monckton in Portsmouth and was impressed with most of what they did. Many of his old pals were instructors, so he knew they were training for the realities on the ground. The SIS field operations training centre was where both basic and advanced fieldcraft training was given to MI6 personnel.

'Maybe the lad could do with a fresher?' Yorkie pondered.

However, the young man was fit, running ten miles in gym kit in about sixty-three minutes which was very good. He worked out as well.

Yorkie wondered, 'Does Philip have the necessary balls for combat?'

Philip Wong told Yorkie about getting interrogated at Monckton but was just grateful it did not involve a towel over the face, being held down and water being poured over him. He hated the Resistance to Interrogation Training. It was humiliating and painful, but he passed as well as the best.

Yorkie observed, 'No one ever passes interrogation training. You only survive it.'

After lunch and an hour into getting all the data that the Deputy Director Operations wanted, Philip managed to speak with Claire.

'Yorkie is acting funny,' he said.

She replied 'Yeah, I know. It is his instinct to get ready for battle. He's trying to get the operation clear in his mind.'

'But he got all personal and asked me about my background. The military training, I had done this and that. How I would feel about one thing or another? What's all that about?'

'He tried the same with me. I politely told him to piss off,' she replied.

'What do you think Uncle Tom will be suggesting this afternoon? I would love to be a fly on the wall at that meeting,' Philip said excitedly.

'Be careful what you wish for. What we are hurtling towards is the dangerous part of our work. Mistakes now could cost people their lives.

Focus on what you need to do now, OK?'

She turned abruptly towards her workstation and completed her tasks.

At three thirty p.m., both Claire and Yorkie left to go to the Deputy Director Operations' office. They headed off for a nervous pee before marching in time to the meeting.

'This is going to be bloody epic,' said Yorkie.

Claire looked at Yorkie and said, 'What's with you? You seem full of beans.'

Before Yorkie could respond, Claire added,

'And what the fuck are you doing winding that poor boy up? You know, Philip Wong! Asking him all those damn-fool stupid questions. He thinks you are about to ask him out!'

Fortunately, they had just arrived at the DD Ops Conference Room to find Derek Jacobs and Tom MacDonald waxing lyrical about the old days.

'You know, when we were young, we were tough. Not like these namby-pamby kids of today.'

Claire walked in and said, 'One young namby-pamby and,' giving Yorkie a sideways glance, 'one not quite so young namby-pamby reporting, sir.'

She mock saluted, and Yorkie followed suit. It got the desired laugh.

Derek tossed Yorkie a blueberry muffin, 'Here's yours, and you'd better get tucked in before this old git eats them all. I have never met anyone with an appetite like his.'

Derek was properly introduced to Claire and Yorkie. He then blew Tom's cover, saying,

'So, this is the person who keeps you and Bill on your toes.'

Tom glared at his pal, and said, 'She's twice the man you ever were and even now when you are twice the size you used to be.'

Director Jacobs looked Yorkie in the eye and thought what a true soldier he was: a warrior of old.

He said, 'And you, Staff Sergeant, a Leeds United fan by all accounts. I am a Liverpool boy myself. How the hell did a character like you get in here?'

Yorkie's answer was lightning fast, 'Well, sir, I just lied. I said I knew sod all about football and intelligence, and that seemed to do the trick.'

Derek punched Yorkie on the shoulder in a matey way and thought, 'Shit, he's made of iron.'

Since Yorkie arrived on the Special Weapons Team, everyone was laughing more. Voices were heard in the corridor, and the rest of the team came in.

Yorkie added, 'I bet Bill's late again. I am going to buy that man a watch!'

'You had better curtail that insubordination, Staff Sergeant, or we will have you peeling potatoes again,' said Claire.

Tom grinned at them both.

Chapter 22

Plan for Action

30th May 2024

A seven-man team gradually arrived at the Deputy Director's Operations Meeting Room. The two senior players, Derek Jacobs of GCHQ and Tom MacDonald had been present for thirty minutes or so. Claire and Yorkie arrived early with Major Tim Churchill, SAS Liaison Officer, close behind. David Jones, Section Chief for the Far East Desk, was in at three fifty-seven p.m. As usual, Bill Ranking was three minutes late.

'You do know, Bill, that you'll never get a knighthood if you are always late,' Tom said, winking at Yorkie.

Bill offered another feeble excuse which Tom waved away.

Everyone was seated with a coffee and a huge blueberry muffin in front of them.

'You each have a folder in front of you. This is the culmination of many days of hard work,' Tom MacDonald said.

The words stamped on the folder in bold red ink stated:

Operation Fulcrum Storm

TOP SECRET (UK EYES ONLY)

'No need to explain the sensitivity here. This will be the greatest operation of our careers,' Tom continued.

'After today, Operation Fulcrum Storm will be taken out of our hands in terms of decision-making. That is why it is so important that we get this right. No apologies for repeating myself. I want nothing left to chance. We need to calculate every step of what we are proposing with a full range of contingencies built-in. We aim to be fireproof, no room for anything other than one hundred percent success.'

Turning a page, Tom MacDonald stated,

'Our mission is to destroy the existing biological warfare capability of the People's Republic of China. In achieving this, it has been estimated that the Chinese ability to produce future viruses would be put back ten years. Whilst we are undertaking this direct action, other steps will be taken on a political level with which we will not concern ourselves just now. Are we clear on the mission?'

All assembled said, 'Yes, sir.'

Tom spoke again.

'This meeting is to look at phase one of the action plan going forward. We will concern ourselves today with the infiltration of our targets and cover off-generic points only. From this, follow-on plans will need to be drafted, but the detail of these can be discussed separately. The targets are as per sheet one and are in Wuhan, Zhengzhou and Shanghai. We will instigate teams to run the three separate operations, being implemented concurrently, with the primary objectives of:

1. the total elimination of all viral samples in all three sites,

2. the retrieval of all vaccine samples for Covid-24 and "Yellow Petal",

3. the destruction of all hard copy documents relating to virus research and production and

4. the incapacitation of all IT systems and virus production facilities.

Each mission will also have a secondary objective to recover samples of viruses for repatriation to the UK. Whatever happens though, we leave no samples of the live virus "Yellow Petal" for the Chinese to run with.'

Pointing to his folder, Tom persevered,

'Within your folder, there are three separate files about each location: the Wuhan Institute of Virology, The Zhengzhou Production Facility and the Shanghai Institute of Microbiology and Immunisation. Each target has a range of plans showing standard entry points, security systems and the location of critical items. Most areas are fairly compact, and therefore once we gain access, time on target should be fairly limited to a maximum of one hour, ideally thirty minutes.'

'Any imagery you need will be provided,' said Director Jacobs, 'and we have literally every plan and procedure they use at the target locations. What we will do is keep a close eye on the target areas until the operation is successfully concluded. Anything you need to know and is mission essential, we will get to you.'

Tom continued, saying, 'The date of the operation has been planned for the night of Friday the 21st June 2024. That's an on-target penetration date. Transit to and extraction from target dates will vary according to location. We have a window of opportunity from eight p.m. to three a.m. to breach the sites, lay explosives, extract the viruses required and get the hell out of there.'

Everyone assumed that these times reflected the hours of darkness, perfect for covert operations.

'The later the incursion, the less likely the guards will be alert or even awake. The facilities, from our understanding, are secured at six p.m. on a Friday and reopen at six a.m. on the following Monday. I was thinking, depending on guard patrols, around midnight would be a good entry time, but we can flex this so all three teams are on target concurrently. If we need to stagger entry times, that will not be an issue, but I suspect we can all move as one. There are security patrols and checks at each location, but seem low-key to not draw attention to their illicit activities, I suspect. We will have the full details of guard numbers, change-over times and patrol sequences by tomorrow, with a review three days before deployment. Any last-minute changes will be sent whilst teams are in transit or awaiting the "Go". Questions on timings?'

Claire asked, 'How closely do the teams need to coordinate regarding infiltration?'

Tom answered, 'Not really close, Squadron Leader. It is more important to get in and get the desired ordnance in place, extract the goods and make a covert exit. Onsite, we must be able to deliver the payload and position it so that it can be remotely detonated once teams are well away and back into secure hands. A backup is an airborne strike if we have no alternative. Our aim is to destroy our targets, minimise civilian casualties and give the Chinese Government an out, without resorting to World War Three. An air strike will leave us compromised and may leave the President of China up shit creek without a paddle. A blatant military attack without warning will lead to war, but if we have the vaccine, the risk is worth it.'

Tom looked at the alert faces of the people around the table, scanning for questions before moving forward.

'In terms of insertion into China, each team will have their own methodologies to consider. The Shanghai Team will have the simplest task in this respect in that we can take them in and out under diplomatic cover via the British Consulate. Diplomatic Immunity will apply to Team One only. The teams heading into Wuhan and Zhengzhou, Team Two and Team Three respectively, will both be completely clandestine, operating as rogue units with no connection to the British Government. If discovered and captured prior to placing the necessary ordnance, we will have no option but to terminate team members, so bear this in mind when planning. If a team is captured during exfiltration, depending on the political situation and timings, there may be a negotiated settlement.'

He sighed.

'Teams will need to be aware that this may not be possible. Those people going in-theatre will need to know that there is no chance of extraction if they are taken by the Chinese, and we will have to take precautions so they do not talk.'

'We are looking for detonation to take place at two p.m. on the 23rd June, London time; that's eight p.m. local in China. The detonation is to coincide with the state visit to the UK of President Xi Jinping. At two p.m., China's President will be at Chequers discussing with the PM a joint plan to tackle the current pandemic.'

Tom took a quick swig of coffee, and everyone around the table copied his action.

Then he pressed on.

'Let's get to the teams. Any thought on team composition?'

Everyone knew he, more than anyone, would know what the best ground force for each target would be.

Yorkie came up with the first few comments,

'Sir, what human assets do we have in country? Do we have reliable local people who can move us to a point where entry can be facilitated? Also, if we are handling sensitive viruses, it would be sensible to have training on such before setting off. From the look of the maps, all the targets are within built-up areas, and as such anything more than a four-person team would stand out like the dog's proverbials, thus increasing the possibility of compromise. With four people, you would need a driver who offers rear cover. An infiltration team of three could comprise cover support, explosives and an unfortunate bastard to handle the viruses. If one person was lost, it would be important that the others have had cross-training so they can cover each other's role. It would make sense to use people who looked like the indigenous population and could speak the language, ideally two.'

Tom said, 'Why two?'

'Simply, the one by the car or van, the getaway driver, just in case someone gets nosy. If the driver can blag a reason for being there, that would be better than starting an early body count. The other would be inside. There will be a lot of signs and instructions in Chinese. Plus, if we come up against someone, before killing them, we could get information out of them. I take it that if we are discovered onsite, to enable a clean getaway, we can take appropriate steps?'

Tom responded, 'Thanks, Staff Sergeant, that makes great sense to me. Team One, taking on the Shanghai job will be made up of two local agents and one of my boys in the Consulate. In addition, Major Churchill, we would like a specialist cover with explosives experience. My man in the country will deal with the viruses but can cover explosives too if called upon. We would like your man to be identified within the next few days. He will be the first man in China, so once in-theatre, he can recon the target with my chap, and they can learn the factors unique to their job. Immediately after the ordnance is set, we would look to get him to Japan by UK military medical evacuation, as he will be suffering from Covid-24.'

'Poor bastard,' Yorkie interjected.

No one laughed. They were all too focused.

'This will be the same exit route for all our UK-based team members but more on that later. However, a contingency will be planned for the in-country teams, just in case of delays, cock-ups, etcetera. For the avoidance of doubt, the SAS and SIS people on this operation with or without diplomatic immunity need to have their real identities expunged and will be given new ones. As usual, when they get back to Blighty, all will be restored. The distance from the Consulate to the target, The Shanghai Institute of Microbiology and Immunisation, is about a thirty-minute drive. If the team can get in and out without being seen, they are pretty much home and dry.'

Tom MacDonald then dropped a bombshell.

'The second team with the target of Wuhan, Staff Sergeant, I would like you to take the tactical lead.'

Yorkie nodded with a grin from ear to ear. Claire had sensed this was coming, but Bill Rankin had a shocked look on his face.

Tom continued, 'This type of operation is right up your street, Yorkie, and your experience would be invaluable. Your Number Two will be an SAS operative and our own Mr Wong. This will be the infiltration team for Wuhan. Liaise with Major Churchill in terms of who you want from Hereford. You are fully qualified on the explosives, and the man from Sterling Lines needs to be explosives qualified also. Philip will be the principal virus handler, with you and your oppo from Hereford being trained up too. I have a three-vehicle fleet to get you to the site and back again. We have four local agents, but only two will take you to the target area and back. They all have good English, Staff, so if you could learn to speak English too, that would be an advantage.'

Most people around the table laughed. Yorkie grinned and nodded in agreement.

Tom let the mirth quieten down.

'Just so we are aware, people, the complexity of getting into the site at Wuhan will be a bit tighter due to the press coverage and its strategic importance, but it's definitely doable. What I am about to say is gravely sensitive.'

He paused.

'We have a man on the inside at Wuhan, working as a laboratory technician. He is a low-value asset just now but maybe on hand to assist and guide you to the exact areas requiring our attention. If he supports the mission, we can rely on him to identify the viruses for retention, but once involved, he must form part of the extraction plan.'

They were all shocked: no one had known that they had an asset in Wuhan. Questions swirled through people's minds: Why didn't we know about the virus before now? How was it that we didn't have a wealth of information before now?

The Deputy Director continued, 'Wuhan is a ten-hour drive from Shanghai, so the quicker you get in and out, the more time you have to negotiate the journey back to Shanghai. The roads from Wuhan to Shanghai are pretty good, but there are plenty of tolls throughout the journey. Expect there to be several stops and starts. Make sure samples are stowed safely and that people stay down for the whole time.'

'That's OK, Tom,' said Derek. 'The team will be able to catch up on their beauty sleep.'

He looked over at the Staff Sergeant and said,

'Yorkie, no matter how much beauty sleep you get, you will always be one ugly...'

'That's enough, Mr Jacobs,' intervened Tom.

The room erupted into laughter, including Yorkie.

With some force, Tom added,

'Just to be clear here, the asset mentioned has been under fairly close scrutiny by his Chinese masters at work, especially since the Army moved into the Wuhan facility in February 2020. This young man lost all his immediate family to a Party reprisal about fourteen years ago. He is a solid asset but one which, as I said, is at a fairly low level and not directly involved in virus research. We have known since 2005 that the work in Wuhan was looking into the development of bioweapons, but which major country isn't doing that? This contact was the first person to secure information on Covid-19 and gave us the key, so to speak, to get our boys at GCHQ into their IT systems. Any questions?'

The room was deathly silent. The last question was a loaded one, basically saying, 'I have imparted too much information already. If this operation goes down badly, I have thrown this asset on the fire and added another casualty to my account.'

In a slightly softer tone, Tom MacDonald called everyone back to focus on the operation. Yorkie was pleased they had a friendly on-site and had a few questions, but these could wait for another time.

Taking point again, Tom continued,

'As for the Third Team to tackle the facility in Zhengzhou, Squadron Leader Walters will take the lead. Thank you for volunteering, Claire. Your primary role will be sample extraction, but you will have to become familiar with explosives. I see your weapon skills are as good as any person going through Fort Monckton, so no worries there. We have a field agent of Chinese extraction who can speak Mandarin like a native and will be your number two. His name is Scott MacGregor, a quiet chap but mentally and physically as tough as any man I have met.

'Again, Tim,' Tom was looking directly at the SAS Liaison Officer, 'we will need one of your boys with an explosives background to make number three on the infiltration team. As with Team Two, Team Three will be supported by a three-vehicle force with four drivers, all field-trained and fluent English speakers. Claire, Scott MacGregor knows the facility at Zhengzhou so he will be invaluable in putting together your infiltration plan but draw in Yorkie and your SAS appointee in coming up with the best options for entry and exit.'

In the slight pause, Yorkie pipped up in a jovial tone,

'Ma'am, it's normally the front door.'

She smiled over to him, 'Too simple, Staff Sergeant. I am going to emulate my hero, Ethan Hunt of Mission Impossible fame, and make it as complicated as possible.'

Again, some light relief worked its way around the table.

Drawing a mouthful of coffee followed by a deep breath, Tom kept going.

'Incursion for Teams Two and Three will be by fishing boat north of Shanghai. We have Royal Navy assets in the area taking part in a tri-nation maritime exercise who will be in support. We will work out detailed timings later.'

'Team members will travel light, silenced small arms only and minimal technical kit. The Quartermaster will have your fighting kit for inspection within four days. I have a suggested kit list in the folder here. Let me know if you need anything else. And yes, the Chinese-based teams will have local clothes for you and your day-to-day comforts taken care of. I don't want any complaints about fashion or food when you get back. The clothes will be smelly and worn so you blend in.

'In-theatre teams will provide local style bags for kit. 'Q' will provide a one-piece, tailored undergarment which will have the necessary pouches for weapons, phones and coms, etcetera.

'Regarding transport, the in-theatre teams will devise primary and secondary routes. You will be taught your routes. Know these in case you have to help with driving or in case of compromise. Face masks and clothing will help with hiding IDs and other sensitive items. One vehicle will take you to a mid-point to your targets where you will lay up for a while. On the 21st June, you will leave the lay-up point at about midday, take a drive with rest stops, and then proceed to the target. Returning, we may change vehicles from the ones used in the assault just in case there is an alarm; we will play this by ear. The more complex we make it, the more likely a cock-up. Then on to the return RV to join up with a cargo vehicle heading to Shanghai Airport. Should the cargo vehicle go tits-up for any reason, exfil will be by the same route as ingress. The plan is to keep it uncomplicated, travel fast but sensibly, and get to the point of exit within ten hours of leaving the target. There is some built-in flexibility but try not to use it. All transportation will be uncomfortable until we are in friendly airspace. For your information, the drivers will have cash to get by checkpoints; bribes are also a good way to move, even with the right paperwork. Getting the teams out is by way of PPE crates and RAF Transport aircraft. The final leg of the drive will be in a lorry with a huge amount of PPE. The UK Government has placed an urgent order for PPE, and the RAF will be uplifting it on the 22nd June at two p.m. by military emergency flight; our casualty from Shanghai will be on this flight too.'

Turning to David Jones, Section Chief for the Far East Desk, Tom said,

'David, you and your boys on the China Desk are our eyes and ears for the next few weeks. Knowing what's happening on the ground is crucial. Any changes to the infiltration and exfiltration plans need to be communicated to the agents in-country, but we don't want a significant increase in comms traffic, alerting our Chinese friends that something is happening. If your boys in China need anything, let's get it to them early. The infiltration teams will have limited capacity to carry additional equipment. Make sure our agents on the ground get a bit of extra cash support after the operation, and with the proviso that they don't go on a mad spending spree. Also, David, make sure there is an extra hidden space within the PPE consignment just in case my boy in Wuhan needs to get the hell out of there. Finally, can your team put together a brief for the teams going in regarding Escape and Evasion and protocols to enable them to blend in if needed?'

'No problem, sir. This will all be done,' David replied but not asking about conduct after capture which could still be a difficult situation to tie down.

'Major Churchill, put a training plan together for the teams in conjunction with the Chief Instructor at Fort Monckton? Yorkie, can I ask you to get everyone up to speed with the explosives training? For some, it might be a refresher, and for others, a new skill. Also, we need to ensure all teams are current in weapons and self-defence, especially knife work. The CI at Monckton will handle that side of things. For those who have not met him yet, you are in for a pleasant surprise. Claire, you take the lead on the science, especially sample identification and handling techniques. Also, Claire, use Philip and Scott to teach you the Chinese names. All teams are to learn a bit of Chinese. It might come in handy.'

Yorkie quipped, 'Especially "Don't shoot, don't shoot".'

Deputy Director MacDonald and Derek Jacobs, who had both spent years in the field and had been involved in more than a few combat situations, knew that humour was the best way to make sense of their bizarre world. Tim Churchill laughed and was envious of the Staff Sergeant's sharp humour and vast experience, then accepted the senior intelligence officer's instruction.

Bill Rankin, desperate to contribute, said,

'Our communications teams will get you the best discreet and secure comms going. Secondary secure communications will be provided, and at worst we will have mobile phones, even if they are insecure. The phones can only be used in a last-ditch situation and for codeword use. A list of codewords will be issued common to each team. Each codeword will be prefixed with team call signs as standard, to be allocated nearer the operation.'

It was Derek Jacobs's turn next.

'GCHQ will maintain an open link to all non-friendly radios and key telephone numbers throughout the operation. If we get any indication of problems, we will immediately contact the SIS Operations Controller. Additionally, we will have a voice-deception team on standby, just in case we have to add to the confusion for the Chinese on the ground. Also, we can cut power to various communications and security systems which operate via their IT Server, but we will put plans in place and discuss these with teams. If we fail to sever the security systems, we have the override codes. We will have access to all target camera systems via GCHQ, and the usual disinformation will be displayed. A communications plan for each incursion will be agreed upon, and Lee Ford will ensure you have tests and run-throughs. Any unresolved issues, come to me. I am informed that we have no funding limitations on this one.

'That's the overview. Tim, get your boys here as soon as possible plus a couple of reserves, but brief them on the stakes before telling them the plans. Anyone looking wobbly, send them home. We need the best The Regiment can muster; this is a momentous operation in the SAS's history. Put the request through back channels, nothing in writing. I will speak directly to Director Special Forces face-to-face tomorrow, so hold off until lunchtime. Remember it is important that team members gel, so no wild cards on this one.'

Everyone around the table knew what the Deputy Director meant. From time to time even the best organisation allows in a dud who doesn't last long. Also, sometimes experienced operators start to lose their way.

Tom continued, 'We will need all team members to sign a statement of understanding and waiver. There will be admin to get in place, wills, pensions, updating next-of-kin records, the usual niff naff and trivia, etcetera. I want each Team Leader to be ready for a detailed briefing of their plan by 3rd June. Everyone going on the mission is to have a full medical, tests for Covid-24; we do not want people going down at the last minute. All team members are now on lockdown so no contact with family or friends. We have set aside a training area where we will refine the plans and then refine and refine again. The site will provide all we can in terms of familiarisation training. Any questions?'

Claire asked, 'Sir, those going in if captured, might need to take steps not to be interrogated. Will that be controlled centrally, or will we as operators hold the trigger, so to speak?'

Tom hated these sorts of questions but thought it better if it is raised by an asset going in.

'Claire, we will control that decision centrally, just in case operators are unconscious at the point of capture, but you will always have the choice in your own hands if things go south. Everyone going into mainland China will have a transponder with a suicide toxin, so we can monitor progress remotely, minimising communications. The idea is that unless there are concerns, radio silence will be maintained. Only permitted and agreed codewords are to be passed.'

Claire knew the answer had no happy ending but appreciated Tom's candour.

Yorkie kept his own counsel. He had loads of questions, but these would come out in the detailed planning.

'Team leaders, I want a brief on detailed plans on the 3rd June, but any significant issues are to be dealt with as you find them. Section Chief Rankin is your first port of call. Let's get to it, and thank you,' said Tom.

The meeting was brought to a close, and the Special Weapons Team went for afternoon tea in the canteen.

Yorkie said, 'I am knackered.'

Claire smiled and said, 'So are you going to tell Philip Wong that you've stitched him up good and proper? When you tell him that he's on your team, he'll shit himself. I bet he looks for a transfer to the DVLA in Swansea.'

They both laughed.

Chapter 23

Primed for Action

30th May 2024

A group of key political and military men came together to discuss Operation Fulcrum Storm and its future actions. All arrived surreptitiously through a rear access to Number Ten Downing Street to meet with the PM, Allan Knowles. The time was 20:00 hours.

'Gentlemen, thank you for coming. We have a real situation on our hands, and ordinarily, we would seek to have a full meeting of the Joint Intelligence Committee, but before doing so, I feel that we must have this off-the-record meeting first.'

The Prime Minister continued, 'I need your unequivocal agreement you will not, under any circumstances, now or at any time in the future make reference to this meeting in any form, be it written, verbal or otherwise. The nature of the topic to be discussed and the course of action that may be required are of such magnitude I fear we cannot allow it to be brought into the public domain unless there is absolutely no alternative. The consequences of what is to be discussed could, I feel, bring the whole world to the brink of World War III.'

Allan Knowles looked over the assembled men and said,

'I know you think I am liable to exaggerate and thus am overstating the case. However, I have been receiving behind-closed-door briefings from Sir George, who has been troubled by this matter. Before I go on, do I have your assurances, gentlemen?'

They all answered, 'Yes, Prime Minister.'

Sir George Main, the Chief of Secret Intelligence Service, knew they would agree. No one would walk away from a starting speech like that.

The Prime Minister continued.

'This matter has several technical and scientific aspects which I do not profess to understand fully, but, put simply, we have uncovered absolute evidence that the Chinese, or more precisely a rogue element within the Chinese intelligence hierarchy, has been behind the Covid-24 outbreak. This character also, in all probability, unleashed Covid-19, masking it as a pure accident through the transmission of a source in Wuhan.'

The men in the room looked astounded that they had not heard even a rumour of this.

The Prime Minister continued, 'Additionally, gentlemen, we have clear and unequivocal evidence that there is another strain of the virus about to be set upon us, possibly within months, that will make Covid-24 look like the common cold. The last piece of the puzzle is that the Chinese have a vaccine for Covid-24, with tests for a vaccine for this latest virus, called "Yellow Petal", already underway.

'I will share with you how we have come to these findings, and then we need to discuss our options, and damn quickly, to prepare our best course of action. As you know, Professor King made that bloody awful TV appearance on the 24th May, sending us all into a frightful spin. Well, what you may not know is that a team within the SIS asked Professor King to work with them, and he agreed. Within a few days, they were convinced the Professor's science was solid, and worthy of special attention. A group of dedicated officials within the Special Weapons Section, with the invaluable assistance of GCHQ who played a huge part in this, were able to access all the records and data about this matter. I can also tell you with the strictest sensitivity that we had a man on the ground in Wuhan who facilitated this access. We were able to download their entire database and files. It is this that gives us one hundred percent absolute certainty of the matter I have briefly outlined. I have a full dossier of the intelligence work, original copies and transcripts of the Chinese documents, data, in short, the whole shebang.

'The volume of information is so huge that I have set up a team of leading scientists in the field of microbiology in Vauxhall under George's watchful eye to double-check our findings on the scientific front. Of this, there is no doubt: there is someone, a Major General Lei Wei, who is hell bent on destroying our way of life and perhaps achieving world domination.'

The Prime Minister knew the last statement did not go down well, but all things being equal, that's how it appeared.

Director Special Forces Major General Paul Burns said,

'Bugger me, Prime Minister, this is a hell of a thing to take in with one breath. Do you mean all that bollocks we were getting about this being a naturally-occurring virus is codswallop? Do our friends across the pond know we have this information and come to these improbable conclusions?'

Sir Steven Alexander, the Chair of the Joint Intelligence Committee, then spoke.

'Prime Minister, you surely cannot keep this from our allies or the people. If it becomes general knowledge that we sat on this information, you, we, and our way of life will be turned upside down. At the very least, convene a meeting of the JIC and be seen to follow the correct democratic conventions.'

People around the table muttered in agreement, and then George Main made a brash and controversial statement, as Heads of the Intelligence Services were not permitted to be political in any context.

'I am afraid, gentlemen, this supersedes politics, your individual careers and political party interests. I appreciate the Conservative Party is unpopular just now, but that is not a reason for inaction. If we release any of this information, no matter how it is spun, there will be more questions than answers we can reasonably provide. Therefore, you, sir,' looking directly at the Prime Minister, 'will be portrayed as a fool, and I suspect, that there is a real danger of us all, and I mean the UK, being constrained in taking the right action. If this matter were to be in the public domain, we will be condemned for our inaction in retrospect, and history will mock us for eternity. However, I say again our personal reputations are not the substantive issue at this juncture. What is of pre-eminent importance is our willingness and capacity to do the right thing. We must act and act now.'

The Prime Minister dropped his head with his trademark flop of ginger hair obliterating his face. George Main thought, 'I hope I have not placed too greater burden on his inexperienced shoulders.'

As the Chief of the SIS, he often felt the strain of such responsibility and knew how tempting it was to take the coward's way out and surrender to one's fears. He reflected on his career with some small amount of pride. When hard decisions were required, he would be happy to be judged.

Allan Knowles lifted his head slowly, pushed his hands through his dishevelled mop of hair and said, 'Yes, yes, George, you are right, and my thoughts are in concert with yours.'

He looked to Sir Steven Alexander who had been suggesting some political manoeuvring, saying,

'Steven, this is how I see it. We can take action ourselves, take the credit and at least be judged as men of commitment and courage, or we can take the standard political route and be looked upon as some political weak-willed characters. Opening up this can of worms would lead to God-knows-what. How it would work out, no one can predict. Would you trust the US intelligence agencies to act rationally over something like this? If they were to take precipitative action, do you think they would return the courtesy of telling us? Not a fucking chance. We cannot – and I will not – allow them or anyone else to lead us directly or indirectly into a world war. Esther, I have not heard you say anything as yet. Do you have a view?'

Esther Williams, the First Secretary of State and Secretary, cautiously spoke.

'Well, Prime Minister, this is all a bit of a shock, and to be frank the enormity of what you have said has rocked me. However, I do agree that to release this information on the world and our general public at this time would be catastrophic. Such a step would restrict our options going forward, and, I hate to say it, from a political perspective, the hoops to jump through to take action would be devastating. Disclosure would let the world see our intentions, essentially constraining what we could do. I concur with your thoughts on the Americans. You know my most private feelings about the US President, he would do what is good for the US and the rest of the free world would have to fend for ourselves. He is not a man we can trust. If, as you say, the intelligence on this matter is bomb-proof, then we have no other recourse but to take action. I am not a military person, and therefore in terms of appropriate action in the circumstances, I would defer to others and their greater experience in the practical application of force. However, what I would say, if we are to presume that President Xi Jinping is not complicit in this matter, that may give us some political leverage and options to avoid an all-out conflict situation.'

'Good, Esther, that's what I was thinking,' Allan Knowles said, then paused. 'Indeed, that is what has been proposed by the SIS team. What I would like to do is present you with our two pathways for dealing with this matter. The first, if successful, will enable us to bring this whole Covid crisis to an end or certainly prevent it from deteriorating further. Success will also result in destroying the virus development capacity in China and possibly having the virus and vaccine in our hands. At worse, we would put back China's capacity to develop a biological warfare weapon by years. For this initial option to work, our second course of action would need to bring President Xi Jinping on board with our plans. That will not be a simple sell. I see him as a ruthless man but one who will play a straight game where he perceives benefit for himself and his country. The real and critical downside is China may distinguish our actions as an act of war, and we will still have a conflict to fight. It may only lead to a possible major skirmish, but of course, that would be less than an optimum outcome.

'We are agreed then to keep the Americans out for the time-being?'

The Prime Minister saw everyone nodding in agreement.

'To our plan then, George, you take the lead on this.'

Chief of the SIS went through his proposal. He had already decided to get as much in place as possible: his teams were nominated, and he required support from the SAS which was given without the details being discussed.

George said to Major General Paul Burns,

'Your Major Tim Churchill will contact you tomorrow with a bogus training requirement for five of your best. Staff Sergeant Charlton, who is on secondment, will make number six of the killing element.'

Major General Paul Burns said, 'How is Yorkie getting on in your hallowed halls?'

'He is a shark out of water but a capable and intelligent man. He has settled in nicely and been invaluable in this current situation. I don't think you will see him at Hereford in a military capacity again, to be frank,' said George.

The plan unfolded. RN elements needed to be put in place, and RAF

Strike Aircraft were needed in case "Plan A" went tits-up. It all seemed feasible to the Prime Minister, in terms of the infiltration of China, the securing of assets and the destruction of bio-weapons facilities. However, it all was a catastrophic risk.

George Main then handed the Prime Minister a document which was called "Operation Reel In".

'Sir, this is the detail of what we require from you on the 23rd June. Your role in this is critical. You and I will need to repeatedly rehearse this stage of the plan. We must get President Xi Jinping on his own and elicit the right response from him quickly. You have him at Chequers for lunch and discussions on the 23rd. We have a plan to get him on his own for ten minutes, enabling you to give an elevator pitch. After that, we need him available without his entourage for about an hour. There is no doubt this second phase presents risks also.'

They all knew when risk is compounded by another risk, it increases the chances of cataclysmic failure.

The Prime Minister stated, 'OK, that sounds like a plan and should be achievable with a degree of good fortune. I think you all will agree.'

With an obvious heavy heart, the PM asked the question,

'What if we fail, and the whole thing unravels before our very eyes?'

George calmly responded.

'Sir, we have a whole range of options which are detailed in this document.'

He presented a folder encasing a small three-page document, again annotated 'TOP SECRET'.

'This document highlights our outline options, taking matters from one extreme to the other. Some will be non-starters, but we have left everything on the table. Obviously, some decisions may be taken out of our hands due to the actions of the Chinese. Prime Minister, may I respectfully suggest that you fake a bout of illness and confine yourself to Number Ten, spending the next few days reviewing everything that we have produced in detail? I can give you the support of a learned microbiologist who can explain the technical details. Likewise, my man who has pulled much of this together, Deputy Director Operations Tom MacDonald, would be pleased to offer his wisdom. He is the best of what we are.'

Paul Burns laughed and said, 'Tom MacDonald, the best of what you are?' He paused. 'He is the best of all of us! I know Tom well. He and I were on operations together in Northern Ireland and during the Falklands in Argentina.'

The Prime Minister loved hearing stories of derring-do and suggested that the three of them go through Operation Fulcrum Storm together.

'That would be most agreeable,' said Major General Burns.

After two hours of intense discussion, the Prime Minister felt drained of energy and offered the assembled men a glass of port. It was a working meeting after all. They had been supplied with copious amounts of coffee and nibbles, but the port was unanimously welcome.

The Prime Minister proposed a toast, 'Gentlemen, The King.'

They all stood up and responded, 'The King.'

'I offer a quote if you please; "To courage, which is grace under pressure"; to Courage.'

The Prime Minister held his glass high for the second time. All returned the toast.

'Thank you everyone,' said the Prime Minister talking from the heart, 'I know that there are those who see me as a buffoon, much in the same vein as my predecessor. I can live with that. What I cannot countenance is the thought that some would see me as a coward, looking only at my own interests. In our endeavours during this crisis, we all have to be secure in the knowledge that what we do is for the good of all humanity. We do not do this for ourselves but for all people. Some of our brave boys and girls may die so that many can live in peace without the fear of a lingering death. We must go forward with brave and honest hearts. Do you good men have anything to add?'

George had spoken often throughout the night and had put his ideas and thoughts on the table. It was the time for others to speak. He made the conscious decision to say nothing more.

Sir Steven Alexander asked, 'Prime Minister, are we not being a bit presumptuous in making such a monumental decision on the back of one meeting?'

The PM responded firmly, 'Steven, this is the eighth meeting I have had on this subject matter. This meeting tonight is to authorise our intelligence agencies to put in place those assets and resources that they may need to carry out this operation. As George has said, I do need to review everything, including my role which will be pivotal in achieving the optimum outcome. The Executive Order to proceed has not yet been given, but if and when it is, I want our people to be in the best position to get the job done. We will meet again to discuss the plan and refine the options. What I do not want is any talk of this with anyone outside this room. We will have to think about informing the opposition, but my timing will be based upon the success of SIS ground force and my meeting with President Xi Jinping.'

Looking around the room, Allan stood up and leant over the large mahogany table, and said,

'Gentlemen, are we agreed on the proposed course of action and determined to meet again in, say, four days when we can receive updates on progress and detailed planning outcomes?'

Everyone said, 'Yes, Prime Minister.'

'Gentlemen, any other questions?' was his final call.

Major General Paul Burns made an interjection, saying, 'Prime Minister, you are aware that our armed forces are at their weakest since before Alfred the Great took on the Vikings. We talk of our technological advances, but in truth, our numbers of troops with which to fight a war are pitiful. If we are brought into a war with China, which has millions of soldiers while we only have around 150,000 men and women in all aspects of our defence forces, we will not win; we cannot fight this war alone. How such a war would develop would be beyond our current planning contingencies, and you will need to give this matter some thought.'

'Paul, thank you for that. I know this potential war with China as a standalone nation was never seen as a real threat. Sadly, we will have to trust that in the final analysis, our friends and allies will come to our aid, for without the support of NATO we will be sunk. I know that is a sobering thought, but we have excellent people who we trust can get us through this without resorting to total warfare. If not, this is where hotheads in the US Intelligence Services may play into our hands.'

He looked at each person gathered around the table and said, 'Good night.'

Chapter 24

The Gathering

3rd June 2024

The day before full training was due to start, the SAS boys arrived to have a thorough briefing with Major Tim Churchill. Yorkie was on hand, initially meeting the new arrivals at the training facility which was a disused airfield in Wiltshire. Tim was to follow along shortly with the SIS brigade. Yorkie was known to his companions-in-arms from Hereford. The traditional greeting of soldiers who respect each other is a rigorous handshake and the occasional hug followed by a barrage of banter and abuse. Since the pandemic, the handshaking and occasional hug had morphed into an elbow bump done from as far away as possible. The barrage of banter, however, remained as lively as ever.

'Fuck me, Yorkie,' said Sergeant Steven Lang, known as 'Cockney', 'you have landed on your "plates of meat" here. You are a lucky old sod.'

Yorkie said, 'You'd better park that Cockney rhyming shite here, mate. They all speak the King's English, God bless him. They even eat with both a knife and a fork.'

'Well, I never. Could you "Adam and Eve it",' was the flippant response.

Yorkie and Cockney were peas in a pod. They had served together for years, and it was Yorkie who asked for his old mate to be on this mission. They had fought in Iraq, taking on the Taliban, not single-handed, but listening to Steve, you might think it.

The others came in, greeting each other like long-lost pals. Yorkie knew he had a really good set of lads to choose from. He had been on operations with Sergeant Bill Martin and Sergeant Tony Lane. They were cool and steady under fire and as professional as they come. Both would make solid seconds in command if things went the way of the dodo.

Both Sergeant Geordie Walker and Corporal Terry Williams were

197

known to Yorkie, mainly by reputation. Yorkie had seen them both on training programs back at Sterling Lines in Hereford and was impressed with their attitudes and skills. Although they were not close pals like the rest, he knew they were pretty balanced operators. Geordie was a bit of a clown but as hard as nails. Most importantly, he looked after his people as if they were his family. Yorkie reflected that Geordie's personality was like his dad's: lots of tough love, but there was love if you could get through the thick skin. Counting himself, that made six professional soldiers who had combat experience. The SAS team all had advanced explosive training and experience in fighting in built-up areas, specialists in close-quarters battle, which is what they would be doing if they were uncovered during their mission. Every one of them had an annotation on their file indicating they were Close Protection (CP) qualified; that would be handy as one of their key roles would be babysitting the SIS, or so they thought.

As was standard with many special forces, these men had advanced medical skills. The assembled team members were dressed in green coveralls, looking like a group of motor vehicle apprentices. Each had effective technical communications experience and a raft of individual skills. Steven Lang was a fluent Arabic speaker.

'That'll be about as much use as an ashtray on a motorbike for this Operation,' Yorkie observed wryly.

They had all done advanced Conduct after Capture Training, formerly known as Resistance to Interrogation Training. No one had any experience in handling deadly viruses which was discussed generally.

Yorkie put their minds at ease about this, saying,

'We have a great instructor, but if you get it wrong, you are dead within two days anyway, so the Boss wouldn't be in a position to kick your arse.'

Bill Martin mused, 'Every cloud has a silver lining, eh?'

The group turned to the job at hand. These men had been told nothing because even their commanders were in the dark. All they knew was this one was off the books, a Black Operation. Therefore, the best available team needed to be put forward.

'Yorkie, what's the "Bobby Moore" here? What's going on?' asked Cockney.

'For the score, my old mucker, you will have to wait for Major Tim. What I can say without any doubt, this one is not for the faint-hearted. If you have a good reason to avoid being in harm's way with a real risk of a dead-end, then pull out. You are all experienced guys, and I would be happy to go into battle with any of you, but this is, in practice, the most dangerous babysitting job we will have ever done. That said, it is a job that will blow your minds in terms of what we will be doing. The implications of a successful outcome will be beyond your wildest thoughts,' Yorkie paused, 'except for you, Geordie. God knows where you go off to in that head of yours at times.'

They all laughed heartily, and Geordie punched Terry Williams on the arm and said,

'Fuck you, Yorkie,' while grinning broadly.

Major Tim Churchill swaggered into the room with a roll of maps under his arm and a huge briefing folder. He knew the team to varying degrees. They exchanged a few pleasantries but none of the aggressive banter that was reserved for battle-hardened comrades. They got down to what was required of them as Tim did the briefing. It was unusual to have such a group of people stay quiet after an introduction to a briefing.

After the realisation of the enormity of their task, Sergeant Bill Martin said,

'That's us all going to be pregnant at the end of this, well and truly.'

Tim said, 'We all now know the magnitude of what is asked for here, and any man can withdraw without penalty. This is one of those jobs that is genuinely above and beyond the call of duty,' he added.

'You're "having a bath", Boss,' Steven Lang said. 'Who'd want to miss this one?'

Tim raised an eyebrow, looking first at Sergeant Lang, then at Yorkie.

Yorkie translated, 'Having a bath means to laugh, sir. I have already told him about that Cockney rhyming slang, Boss. He's just a poor, stupid East-end boy, thick as mince.'

Everyone knew Steven Lang was right, none of them would want to miss this gig. The mix of fear, excitement and a bit more fear was what they thrived on. Both the Major and Yorkie instinctively knew no one would withdraw. These men would rather die than look like cowards or exhibit weakness in front of their colleagues. If they withdrew, they would never be able to show their faces in Hereford again and would be ashamed to wear the winged dagger cap badge of the SAS. The mention of expunged IDs and the lethal substance in the tracker raised eyebrows, but it was just part of the deal. Killing yourself as a soldier was always at the back of your mind; no one wanted to endure brutal torture. Death was no stranger to these men. They had all seen it first-hand, and not one amongst them was a virgin when it came to killing the enemy.

Tim finished with, 'Look, guys, the training ahead of you is about a few different things. The key point is to get to know your new teammates. Develop that trust and understanding we just expect of each other. Secondly, this is a different type of job and is critically sensitive. Though some of the skills and training will be "old hat" to many of you, you must take it seriously. I want you to show your professional respect to these SIS people. Every one of them has great qualities, and they all bring something unique to the party. Finally, you will learn new skills, especially surrounding the handling of deadly viruses. I know you will take that seriously. Any questions?'

Given Tim's last words were to take this seriously, they knew banter at this time would be not a good idea. They understood any questions were better put to Yorkie who would give straight answers; the type combat soldiers liked, and nothing would be fudged over. They were all desperate to ask about the suicide toxin.

The team milled around, seeking information about the operation and who these geeks were from MI6. They drank copious amounts of crap coffee. It was the stuff provided in an urn, cheap and nasty with a slightly metallic taste. The rest of the team from London had just pulled up. The SAS and SIS teams were equally nervous about meeting one another. The large minibus and a three-tonne lorry had just pulled up outside, making one hell of a racket on the gravel parking surfaces. Trying to be cool, the SAS boys nonchalantly half-perched on the boxes and tables inside what was to be known as Hangar One. This was the briefing and lecture hangar and where tea and coffee breaks occurred. Another two hangars close by were being fitted out as well, but the men had no idea with what. They could hear loud banging and the sound of industrial tools being used. The final area of interest was the range building, with a classroom and access to the two hundred and fifty-metre range. The accommodation was in the old Officers' Mess where training and support admin staff were housed also. Breakfast and dinner were to be taken in the Mess; lunch was at the training area in Hangar One.

Within minutes, Yorkie and Tim were introducing the SAS team to the MI6 staff, and then Claire took the lead in presenting her people.

Immediately making the point by action that she was the senior rank, she said,

'We are three teams here with two reserve SAS. We will not appoint any reserves at this stage, just in case we have injuries or admin problems, or people are sacked.'

Claire wanted people to know that their places were not a given. Everyone had to earn the right to be on this historic mission. The combat elite were a bit perturbed at the thought that they would be the ones being dumped.

Yorkie shouted out, 'Philip, Bill, Terry over here.' He handed out red bibs with the number two on the front.

'We are Team Two, call sign Romeo Two. I am one. Philip, you are two, Bill, three and, Terry, you guessed it, four.'

Claire who had Scott standing next to her called over to Tony and Geordie, 'We are Team Three, call sign Tango Three.'

She handed out sky-blue bibs and numbered her team.

Peter Goulding from the Consulate in Shanghai walked over to Steven and passed him a vest and said,

'We are for now Team One, call sign Mike One. I am one, you are two, and we will have time to get to know our remaining team members when we are in-country.'

It was time to work. All the SIS and SAS team members were present barring the two SIS in-theatre assets who worked out of the consulate in Shanghai.

Though everyone knew the broad plan ahead of them, Claire covered it again in brief.

'We will be training, and it will be fucking hard. We can only proceed with the mission if we are one hundred percent confident we can pull it off. Anyone, for any reason, who is out of their depth in any way can pull out. Whether it's a problem with skills, attitude, commitment or a personal issue, you can walk away at any time. We have absolutely no room for passengers.'

By now they all understood what was at stake and were silent when she spoke. It was obvious their new boss was a strong and capable leader.

She pressed on, 'We will refer to each other by call sign only in all live target training just to learn good practices. All non-operational personnel will be referred to as Staff. We have a small team of specialist trainers from the MI6 training establishment. I can assure you, gentlemen,' referring to the SAS contingent, 'they are as good, if not better at their craft than anyone else in the world. Listen to what they say, and make sure you do as instructed. If you have any reason to question their techniques, practices or procedures, keep your mouth shut until after the training unless it's a real safety issue. This is not a democracy. Knuckle down and get on with the training. We are not short on time because we are all experienced operators, and much of what we are doing is not new. Any questions thus far?'

No one spoke. Her briefing style was clear and direct. Yorkie had also informally told the boys that the real boss was a woman, and they were to be respectful.

He had said, 'No stupid sexist jokes, but treat her like one of the boys. She is harder than you, Bill, and has a brain the size of a very large planet.'

The lads could see that Yorkie held this woman in high esteem, and that was as good as any reference.

Claire then went on to mention all lectures and briefings would be covered in Hangar One, pointing to the current location.

'All that banging next door is a mock-up of the three target buildings we are attacking. Due to restrictions of time and space, the building work will not cover the whole floor of each target but will be detailed enough for us to practice entry routes one and two, plus putting all charges in place and recovering viruses. The rooms are to emulate the targets. They are not facsimiles, but we have excellent intel which will give you an unequivocal representation of each area.'

She quickly mentioned the range, messing arrangements and accommodation. All communications with the outside world would be cut until after the operation. Mobiles had already been confiscated, and no laptops or iPads were allowed. Tim would relay any messages from Hereford and Vauxhall should anyone need to be contacted. Most on the team were unmarried or separated, and for other family members, it was just a case of thinking they were on a long training exercise in the wilds of Canada with no cell reception.

Tim stepped forward with the training plan.

'Looks like we're back to school,' Bill Martin said to Yorkie.

Today was an orientation day with each team leader going over the plan with their team. Teams Two and Three covered the infiltration into China together up to the point where they separated. They then broke off into their respective teams to chat through the rest of the mission. Team One finished the familiarisation of the plan in one hour. Teams Two and Three were still hard at it two hours later. They all agreed that the plans were thorough and seemed fairly straightforward. Another brew-stop and the infiltrators were introduced to their instructors who were a motley crew: some ex-forces, some ex-field agents and a couple of eggheads. The latter group was the technical team, all of whom were shit-hot at all things wiggly amps and things that went bang in the night. The Chief Instructor was a huge man, and he would be taking training on weapons, explosives and self-defence. Philip Wong would provide some cultural knowledge of Chinese and teach a few words, especially about viruses and place names. The CI and a former SAS soldier would conduct the training in the mock target buildings, and each team would take turns acting as the guard force and intruders. Emulating the guard force would help teams develop a different perspective.

Communications and surveillance equipment training would be pretty straightforward but critically important. The virus handling aspects would be conducted by Claire, and the escape and evasion discussion would be led by Tim with Team Two and Three separately. Team One would do their own thing and probably in-theatre. They would get some physical training, but people would be responsible for their own fitness. The first day would be going through the full equipment list for the operation, both personal and team resources. Every item was to be checked and understood. They would practice using everything until it felt like it was part of their body. Adjustments and readjustments would be made so things fitted neatly which was of paramount importance, especially for weapons holsters, knife positioning and communications equipment. Tomorrow afternoon, they would have a full medical and inoculations.

After a fairly full day, the teams were dismissed to complete an administrative pack. Wills were important, and nearly everyone had made one. Phil Wong, being the youngest and least experienced, asked Yorkie for advice on filling out the form. The waivers, granting the UK Government freedom from civil legal action, were a laugh but completed and signed. Everyone had a non-disclosure statement to sign with the obvious consequence of a breach leading to prosecution under the Official Secrets Act 1989. This was no different than day-to-day work for these people. Next-of-kin notifications would be made through parent units and organisations, if necessary, but new forms were completed for expediency. In the pack-up was a list of items to be handed over for retention by the staff until the operation was completed including all jewellery, watches, wallets, pictures, phones, iPads, personal clothing and actually anything they had brought with them. Dog tags were to be removed, and the SAS boys felt naked without them.

'They would take our tattoos if they could,' said Tony Lane.

'Not yours, mate, only the ones with the correct spelling,' countered Yorkie.

Each person was given a cover story dossier in case they were captured alive and available to question. The stories were flimsy, to say the least and contained an invented new persona. Every detail of the new character had to be learnt by heart. However, at the back of their minds they knew that if they were caught, it would be curtains for them as some muppet in London would pop the toxic substance in their trackers. The cover stories were a comfort blanket, nothing more. That evening they would joke about their new fictitious lives.

Geordie said to Bill, 'I can't believe it, mate. They've given you a grown-up personality transplant. You might even be able to score in the Eagle pub now.'

In the morning, they would each be given a passport in their new name, along with some letters and papers. They would each have a driving license and other new personal items, with nothing of UK origin. Critically, each person would carry an exfiltration plan showing a false route of escape with details of made-up safe houses and codewords for access. The idea was not to fool the Chinese permanently but just bamboozle them for about twenty-four hours. Every person realised the Chinese would, in all probability, be taking this information from their cold dead bodies.

In the words of Major Tim, 'The captured person would be fucked, but the deception might give the rest of the team a chance to get out. Equally importantly, the attention of the Chinese would be drawn either to the south in the case of Team Two or north in the case of Team Three, thus improving the chances of the uncompromised team of get out. If the whole country were put on alert, any movement would be sticky, regardless.'

That evening, dinner in the Mess was pretty rubbish, but they all got down to eating the stodge provided. There was no booze, and most were non-smokers. Only Steven Lang and Tony Lane went out for an "oily rag".

Yorkie whispered under his breath, 'That Cockney twat just can't help himself.'

It was early to bed, but few got off to sleep quickly. Some were excited, others nervous and a few just rehearsing everything they had been told. This was pure unadulterated intelligence work, and they all loved the idea of being part of the mission. They felt fear also, but these guys generally ate fear for breakfast.

Chapter 25

All the Gear

4th June 2024

Most of the assembled teams were up at six a.m. and out for an early morning jog. Claire had arranged to go running with Yorkie, and Yorkie had mentioned it to Geordie, who told everyone else. The gentle run was to loosen up the body, but as usual, the boys started taking the piss early and became competitive. They stayed together as a group, and Philip Wong was elated to be running in such esteemed company. After forty-five minutes, they were back, having covered about seven miles. They showered, put on clean overalls and went through for breakfast.

The staff came in and ate at a table removed from the trainees. This was pretty standard protocol. The trainers did not need to know the details of the mission; they just had to provide the instruction as briefed. The more astute of the trainers would, by the end of the next two weeks, have a broad understanding as to what was going on but would just move on to the next operational training task. In the world of the SIS, nearly everything that was a direct operational training assignment was secret, and one job just blended into another. The faces changed, but the requirements were generally standard. Now and then, they would see familiar faces, but during training, they exhibited no overt friendliness. They simply had a military and intelligence function to perform.

The Chief Instructor, or CI as he was known, had told his team of instructors the previous day, 'Keep the training dispassionate and your distance from the operatives. They are not your friends. They are tools to get a job done, and your sole task is to prepare them for that job. We serve them best by instructing them in a way that they will remember their training. Being a trainer is not about being popular. It is not about us. It is all about the message, the things they need to learn and retain.'

Now in Hangar One, the CI stood tall in front of the three teams. Looking around with the trainees wearing green boiler suits and brightly-coloured bibs, he thought it looked like a kindergarten day out. Such courses always did, but he knew this one was different. He did not introduce himself because he did not want to know their names and didn't care to share his own.

'Right, people, listen in and gather round,' he said.

He gave them a minute to get settled.

'In the next couple of hours or so, I will show you what equipment you will be wearing and using on your holidays. I have a packing list here so that you do not exceed your weight limit. A copy of the list is on your table over there along with generic items that do not need fitting. The items that do require a modicum of tailoring are in the containers behind you. Go and get your size when instructed, try it on and whatever number is annotated on your list, get that number and place the items on your table.'

He was sharp and focused.

'This will be done by coffee break this morning, so we can get on with more interesting things. Copy?'

'Yes, Staff,' everyone replied.

They all knew the drill. It was time to knuckle down, concentrate and get the task done as instructed.

The CI continued, 'On your list are two numbers. The black one indicates the total number of the item you need to take from stores; the red number is what you need to put in the box under your table. The items left on your table will be working and training kit for retention in this establishment for the foreseeable future. You will note you have duplicates of clothing, so you can stop your smelly bodies from becoming too over-powering for my sensitive nose. The staff in the Mess will wash your clothes and have them back to you by six a.m. if you get them to them in a laundry bag by seven p.m. Please remember to put your team number on the bag, no names.

'Back to more operational issues. Once you are happy with a full set of equipment for your fly-away box, and it has been buddy-checked, it will be packed into one of these three crates.' He pointed to the crates the size of a small car.

'Each team has its own crate, and we will get it sent out to your initial Rally Point, wherever the fuck that is. When trying clothing on, do

207

it quickly. I know you SAS boys are all fashion critics but move with a purpose. Those items of operation equipment that need to be adjusted, do it now; make sure you are happy because when you're sunning yourselves on some far-off beach, it will be too late to ask mummy to get you another one. OK so far?'

They responded, 'Yes, sir' or simply, 'Staff.'

He added, 'Take your time to make sure the items are right for you. Any issues are to be raised promptly.'

The CI looked down at his list and said, 'I will now go through your equipment as laid out on the table, and I want you to check you have everything as I call it out. Let me know if something is missing, or if you cannot find it. Do not put weapons or technical kit written in GREEN in the fly-away box until this afternoon. We will undertake a functional check and then pack them. Everything else, put straight in the box. Go stand behind your table, facing me.'

Each table was labelled with the call sign and a number one to four. As the last person reached the table, he called out, 'Glock 19 with holster, silencer and torch attachment.'

Everyone took the automatic pistol from the holster popped out the empty magazine, pulled the working parts back, checked it was safe and made sure it did not have a round in the chamber. They released the working parts, put the magazine back in and re-holstered the weapon, most within a few seconds. Philip Wong was about ten seconds behind everyone else.

'We will test-fire your weapon on the range this afternoon. Moving on, people, a cleaning kit and spare parts for your handgun. We will also check and use these later.'

After calling out each item on the list, he paused momentarily, glancing around at each table.

'Four empty magazines plus two hundred rounds of 9mm ammunition.'

Some people opened the boxes to make sure they had what was on the label.

'Put the magazines and rounds in your box.'

He checked everyone did as instructed.

'You will see two Ari B'Lilah blades with sheaths. Place one of each in the box and leave the others on the table.'

The knife before them was a true weapon of war and was the preferred blade of the Yamam Israeli Counter-Terrorism Unit. It looked intimidating and in good hands was lethal. The boys from Hereford knew any knife would do in a fight. The experienced combat fighters were feeling the weight and balance of the weapon.

'You will have plenty of time to acquaint yourselves over the next few weeks,' the CI said and paused.

'Next, we have two sets of monocular Night Vision Goggles, a head-band attachment and a carrying case with spare batteries. We will test these out this afternoon at which point, you guessed it, one will stay with us, and the other is to be packed.'

The single lens goggle was lightweight and compact, ideal for this mission. The version they had been allocated had digital controls and a built-in infrared illuminator. They were supplied to elite forces around the globe. These particular ones were purchased, should anyone check, on behalf of the Israeli Defence Forces by an independent arms dealer from Tel Aviv.

Pretty soon all the items on the table were listed off, the same drill being repeated over and over again. There were no shortages or questions which was just how the CI liked it.

He called the team over to his central table with several items of clothing plus a few extras.

'I will tell you what we have here, and after a brief description, you will go to the indicated locker behind me and collect the item in your size and preferred colour. Quoting Mr Ford, "You can have any colour you want, so long as it is black".

'What we have here is a one-piece suit covering you from your calves to your neck and halfway down your forearm. This is an ultra-rugged and highly-abrasion-resistant material and is designed to be worn under other clothing. It has reinforced knees, elbows, buttocks and shoulders. This particular design has loops for an adjustable belt,' here he held up the belt, 'which is compatible with your Glock 19 holster and has loops to hang your NVGs and other kit from it. It can also take the knife sheath if you wish. The suit has loops around the thigh plus knife pouches in both legs if you prefer. The outfit also comes with a hood full-face covering.'

Geordie nudged Bill and said, 'That full-face cover would come in handy for you with your new personality when you are on the pull.'

Both men sniggered but stopped immediately when the CI glared at them.

The Chief Instructor, not one for being delayed, carried on,

'The suit has accompanying zip-up boots that require no inner soles or socks. The rugged rubberised bottoms are non-slip, and perfect for climbing. Now go and get yourselves fitted out into one full set of the described items and keep them on. Then get four spare sets of each and put two sets in your fly-away box.'

Bill then nudged Geordie and whispered, 'Look zips on your boots. That's handy for you 'cos your mum won't be around to do up your laces.'

It took about fifteen minutes for everyone to be content with what they had.

When trying on the one-piece outfit, Yorkie asked, 'Does my arse look big in this?'

A muted call came from behind a screen and answered, 'Your arse looks big in everything. You're getting old, you fat fucker.'

The room had a moment of uncontrolled laughter which let off a bit of steam. Even the CI laughed.

Claire saw the CI smile and said to Philip, 'See, he is sort-of human after all.'

Rubberised gloves were next on the list, followed by an outer lightweight stab-proof vest offering additional storage for personal first aid kits, spare batteries, rations, survival aides and four magazine pouches. Within fifteen minutes, the teams were ready for the next surprise.

It was a respirator – M-15 A1T M-15 S80 – of the type and standard used by the Israeli Defence Forces. It was lightweight and would cause minimal interference with performance during tactical movement, employment of weapons or effective communication. This was not a bit of equipment most had seen before, but it was not dissimilar to the types of respirators they had used. Essentially, they all worked the same.

The pile of kit kept getting bigger.

The urns of tea and coffee came in along with a tray of rather boring biscuits.

The CI noticed and said, 'Right, people, that is your lot. If you have any equipment malfunctions during training, let me or your immediate member of staff know. We will now stop for thirty minutes, so grab some liquids, stretch your legs and take a piss. At ten thirty a.m. exactly, the comms lecturer will be in to get your personal comms set up. That will include team equipment and on-task surveillance equipment. Lunch will be at twelve-thirty p.m. in here, and after lunch, we will check your personal weapons out. Clear?'

'Yes, Staff.'

He paused, 'If you are unfamiliar with the Glock 19, I will go through it with you on an individual basis.'

Philip Wong sidled up to Yorkie and said that he had only used the Glock 7 and 9 in training.

'What's the difference?'

Yorkie strode over to the CI whom he knew from a previous life.

Yorkie went back to Philip, and said, 'Grab a brew and come with me.'

They went over to Yorkie's table and went through the weapon.

'Check it like thus. Insert the magazine until it clicks this way. Cock it like this and kill the bastard in front of you. Change the magazine like this and keep firing until all the baddies are dead. Apply safety here. Unload like this,' he ejected the magazine, cocked the weapon and put it down.

A call from the coffee table, 'Watch it, Yorkie, you might shoot yourself in the foot again.'

Philip looked at his impromptu weapons instructor.

Yorkie said, 'Don't listen to those gits. I've only done it twice.'

Philip said, 'Have you really?'

Yorkie punched him on the shoulder, saying, 'Don't be a fucking dimwit. Now you try it. With a magazine of no rounds, load.'

Philip picked up the weapon and checked it was safe, then he put the magazine into the gun.

'Ready and engage,' called Yorkie.

The young man cocked the weapon and killed the imaginary assailants in his front.

'Cease fire, safety on and unload,' were the next commands.

They went through the procedure a half dozen times. Yorkie could tell Philip was capable and confident but was feeling intimidated by the company he was in. Everyone else seemed to be taking things in their stride.

'Philip, you will be fine, just make sure when you need to pull the trigger, you are ready. Just remember when the enemy is in range so are you. I suspect we are going to get plenty of practice.'

Yorkie strode over for another watery coffee.

A short, bespectacled communications member of the staff could be seen at the far end of the hangar putting items on the well-spaced chairs. He was humming away to himself. The contrast in styles between the CI and this weak civilian could not be greater.

The CI called, 'Two minutes, people,' and pointed to the chairs which were formed in front of a large overhead projector and a vast white screen.

Everyone headed down to the area indicated. Individuals were allocated specific seats within their teams.

'The whole set-up here seems so choreographed, much slicker than the training at Hereford,' said Terry Williams to Claire. He was obviously impressed.

The CI introduced Colin in his usual direct style.

'He is a whizz-kid on this technical shit. Do not doubt that what he teaches you will be as valuable as your Glock 19 or any other single bit of instruction you receive. Good communications will save your lives on task. Listen intently, or you will sense my size twelve boot up your arse. Again, no pissing about. Any questions, Colin will clarify as you go along. Colin is not a mean-hearted miserable shit like me, but I will be at the back watching you just in case you decide to be any less than one hundred percent focussed.'

The CI gave a false smile and walked off. However, he was actually smiling inside. He loved play-acting the hard man.

Colin had a nervous disposition, but as he got immersed into the subject matter he knew so well, it was clear that he was in his element.

'Let's start with the easy stuff,' he said in a most uninspiring tone.

He began by explaining the personal comms for each team member, the settings and key points. He told them GCHQ would be listening during the operation and all comms would be transferred to London via a secure link. They would have a comms check every ten minutes by the way of a confidence bleep back at base. Colin instructed the teams to select a training frequency and practice using the handset. The frequency for each team had been set on the handset and numbered according to the team number: T1 for Team One, T2 for Two and T3 for Team Three. They had a second training handset with training frequencies. Each group went off into the corner to put their sets on their newly-acquired belts and talked to each other practising their new call signs. About ten minutes later, GCHQ came online using the call sign, 'Mother Bird.' Each team leader confirmed all communications were good, and that ended the session. The kit was simple but effective.

Claire asked Colin, 'That's all well and good with us standing here, but it's a bit of a false dawn, is it not? When we are in China, will we get the same reception?'

Colin explained, 'These communications are secure but had world-wide coverage because the signal is not a raw radio signal but a digitised one, which, in fact, goes all the way out to space and back again. As a result, the proximity of the sending source is geographically irrelevant to the receiver. If you are masked by terrain or in a built-up area behind really thick walls or a metal box, the signal might not get through. I don't know where exactly it is that you are going, but the boys at GCHQ do, and they are confident there will be minimum interference. They will ensure the correct comms satellites are above you at all times.'

He paused, 'As long as you have them switched on, and you press the right button, they will work.'

The pre-set discreet frequencies made the set soldier-proof which essentially meant it was robust and easy to operate, even for Army grunts, and Colin knew these were no ordinary soldiers.

Colin explained their secondary system.

'This walkie-talkie is for in-theatre use only, still digital and secure but with limited range. Your tertiary comms are the mobile phones. They have been set up so you can only call five numbers: each of the other teams and MI6 headquarters or, if you really get stuck, phone a friend.'

The last comment was a joke, but the response was a bit flat.

Colin thought, 'I must work on my delivery.'

The would-be comedian quickly turned to the notepad device on his table, saying,

'Under your chair is a digital notebook. Please take it out and turn it on.'

He waited for the shuffling of chairs to die down.

'On this system, you will have all your routes to and from the target destinations, basically, a Google Maps type of application. The map can be enlarged or reduced showing individual buildings. The plan of your target will also feature, showing the layout.'

Using the large screen and talking slowly through the functions, he showed them how to find it.

'On this feature, it will overlay your position, that of your team members and anyone else who is in the vicinity, at all times. Active team members will feature as a blue dot, other bodies will feature as a red spot; where we can read their IR footprint. You can add people in as friendlies to avoid a blue-on-blue confrontation.'

Colin went through some of the controls and unique features of the application. He then took out two small cameras and explained how they could be discreetly located and would feed directly into the target plan on their notebooks. When activated, the first camera produced a small image in the bottom left-hand corner. The second camera displayed in the top left-hand corner but always resizing the map on the screen. Placing a camera on the table facing Team Two, Yorkie and his boys all saw themselves on the huge white screen.

Yorkie loudly said, 'Bugger me, my arse does look big in this!'

After the laughter died down, the teams went off and played with their new toy.

Tony Lane said to his team through his radio,

'Bloody hell, we never get kit like this back at Hereford.'

Claire said matter-of-factly, 'How often have you saved the world, Tango 3-3? Also, use the correct RT from here on in.'

'Tango 3-3, copy that,' came the immediate reply.

Scott MacGregor, who was Tango 3-2, was very impressed with his team leader. She was sharp and direct but calm.

Scott boasted a significant resumé of field operations in difficult situations and was already feeling comfortable about the people around him. The feeling was mutual across all three teams. The Directing Staff could sense they had an exceptional special operations force forming before their eyes. The communications lecture and tests were over, and Colin managed a few laughs, but he wasn't going on the comedy circuit anytime soon. He was an impressive man in his own way, and everyone warmed to him and his clumsy humour. The audience was happy to have such good communications facilities, but familiarity and further confidence would develop during training whist carrying out mock attacks. Experienced operators knew the Training Staff would throw in a few curve balls just to see how the players reacted.

What the teams did not know was that all the communications equipment had been purchased through an Israeli cover company. The off-the-shelf burner phones were registered in Israel too. The objective here was if the team or their equipment fell into the hands of the Chinese State Security, their first attempts to ID their captives would lead to Israel. Any in-depth research into where the team's resources came from would also point to the Israeli Defence Forces. The cover stories had subtle elements indicating the saboteurs were from the Holy Land: a few Stars of David, the odd note in Hebrew and a used chocolate wrapper from a Tel Aviv manufacturer added to the misdirection. It had been Yorkie who suggested Israel as the patsy for the operation. He told Uncle Tom, 'those Israeli Special Forces have the nerve to attack any threat and are some of the best in the world.'

That afternoon, it was off to the range, and the cheery CI was front-and-centre again. He did the usual safety brief about keeping their weapons pointing down the range at all times, telling them to follow his instructions to the letter. He then went through a basic refresher of the features of the Glock 19.

'This gun is a good little workhorse for close-in stuff but shit if you have to shoot your way out against overwhelming odds. It's great for close-quarter covert encounters. The silencer is super but makes it a bit unwieldy. On the plus side, unless improperly attached, it offers less muzzle rise, less sound and less concussive effect, all helping accuracy which I am guessing for you might save your bacon.'

The operatives went on the range in team sequence, first firing two magazines of fifteen rounds and then a further two magazines with the silencer fitted. They fired at a target twenty-five metres away and walked to ten metres.

'Don't worry, people, we are going to keep honing your sloppy skills and pathetic reaction times with this little beauty,' the CI added.

After the range came weapons' cleaning and checking the contents of the spares box. The Glocks were put in the fly-away box. The mission communications were also packed; there was a second, slightly different communications pack-up configured for training, set on each desk.

They spent the rest of the afternoon waiting to see the medical team for a full-naked inspection including blood tests, heart rate, and blood pressure; twelve injections for who-knew-what; and dental, sight and hearing checks.

The teams also spent time with a couple of psychologists to assess the mental functionality of each person and to uncover any peculiar or dangerous behavioural traits that might hinder the individual's capability of performing the mission successfully and making rational judgements. When looking at a group of people who are being trained to kill without mercy, it's difficult to spot the normal person. Once the testing was concluded, the only people needing a lie down were the psychologists. All team members were declared fit for duty.

After the evaluations, Yorkie said, 'We will see how people respond to pressure and react under fire in the Target Training Facility.'

Yorkie didn't realise every time he made comments like that, Philip Wong would wrestle with his personal doubts and demons. Claire could sense this in Philip, as she was similar in character but hid it better. As a woman in a male-dominated world, she knew all too well it did not pay to show weakness.

The medical examiners reported superficially everyone appeared fit and well. Any anomalies in blood work would be reported in a few days. They would check for drug abuse and signs of alcoholism, amongst other things. Before coming on-site everyone, including trainers, was required to have Covid-24 tests and thereafter, went into isolation.

Geordie Walker looked like he might be developing an abscess on a tooth, but that was easily remedied the next day.

'The sound of a Geordie with a numbed mouth was like listening to humpback whales going at it,' noted Scott MacGregor.

Claire said to Yorkie in the quiet, 'He's coming out of his box some. That's good to see.'

Yorkie added, 'Everyone is now finding their default personality settings.'

Claire replied, 'It's only young Philip Wong who seems out of sorts, but this is a completely new experience for him.'

Yorkie said with confidence, 'In time he will settle down and fit in better, I am sure. This is a great adventure for the lad.'

Chapter 26

Home on the Range

5th June 2024

It was day two of training proper, six a.m. The operatives were given military sports kit, looking like raw recruits, and everyone was up and went for a morning run. After showering and putting on their new tight-fitting black operational suits plus bibs, the physically and mentally alert troops then went for another unmemorable breakfast. Once they were all in Hangar One, the CI came in, tall, rigid and with a face that read something terrible was about to happen. He smiled at the thought that they looked like sticks of liquorice.

'Right, people, in your chairs to the front. Get a move on, this is not a Women's Institute social club outing.'

They all moved with purpose and took their positions waiting for the next instalment of bullying or, what the Army called training.

'I am pleased to inform you that you have me all fucking day,' started the CI. 'We are going to do a basic course on Chinese small arms and pop off a few hundred rounds per weapon on the range.'

He asked the usual question of who had handled the various weapons, and a few knew most, while a couple more had experience in one or two pieces.

The CI seemed indifferent to the answers and continued,

'In the afternoon, we will hone your unarmed combat skills, and if you are still able to stand after that, we will do a walk-through to familiarise you with Hangars Two and Three. Just to round off the day's entertainment, this evening we have a couple of clowns from the Conduct After Capture Team coming in to test you on your backstories. Teams One and Two, you will be up first. Team Three, you will have that pleasure tomorrow night. Remember, there is no Geneva Convention here, and you will not be treated as soldiers but as the bloody spies or terrorists you are.'

The last statement was said with true passion. Turning as if he had just put in an order for a latté, the CI took a blanket off the table to reveal several small arms.

'I know that your job, sorry, holiday, involves a get-in, get-out-without-incident scenario. However, we are here to give you the best chance of coming home, should you make a complete arse of things. Before you are six small arms in common use by the People's Republic of China's Armed Forces and their State Security Forces. We will have some instructional training followed by some hands-on dry-training, and then we'll go to the range. When at the range, can I ask you to at least try and hit the targets today,' he said mockingly.

The CI reached down without looking and selected the first weapon.

'This is the QBZ-95, automatic rifle brought into service in 1995 and widely used throughout China's armed forces. Over three million have been produced, so you might likely come across one if you encounter non-friendly forces. There are about six variants, but all are pretty similar. You don't need to retain any of the technical specifications.'

He then detailed the weapon's characteristics: overall length, barrel length, weight empty and with a full magazine of thirty rounds, muzzle velocity, and rate of fire. His knowledge was encyclopaedic, and a few of the audience thought he had to be making it up. The CI used no notes and kept giving fact after fact. He went through the actions of loading and unloading showing the setting for safety and firing positions. He explained the rudimentary facts of how the weapon's working parts operated with its short-stroke piston, and rotating bolt. He pointed to the hooded post front-sight and aperture rear-sight. The lecturer demonstrated great dexterity in the handling of the weapon.

'For those inky swots who want to read more on each weapon here, there is an information sheet.'

The CI lifted a piece of paper in the air and causally wafted it about.

He then went through the QBZ-03 assault rifle and Type 81 automatic rifle. The latter was based on the Kalashnikov design with which all present were familiar. After the rifles, they moved to a selection of pistols which were given the same treatment. His knowledge was all-encompassing, and his handling of each weapon was confident and assured.

Team members were given a rifle and a pistol to handle and to get to grips with how they worked. Everyone held the weapon in a firing position, located the safety, and depressed the various buttons to see the empty magazines pop out. The sound of cocking weapons was ever-present.

The CI walked around making derogatory comments,

'Don't hold that weapon like that. It's not your dick, and the way you handle that, the safest place is directly in front of you.'

After ten to fifteen minutes, they swapped weapons and went through the motions again, and then once more. Coffee came, and everyone hastily had a brew and went back to the Chinese small arms. The constant clicking and cocking with the odd clank of a magazine on the floor sounded like an old grandfather clock. Everyone gingerly took the leaflets on each of the weapons and hid them in their suits. They were all too embarrassed to look like 'inky swots' in front of the CI.

At ten-thirty a.m., the CI brought in three more of every weapon type and went through the firing drill for each, whilst the teams replicated his movements. He then called out commands, and the students obeyed. Being familiar with weapons of many different types, most found this to be pretty basic training and easy to grasp. They were attentive because they all appreciated when their own weapons ran out of rounds, the next best source of firepower is the gun of the guy you have just killed. No one was going to resupply them in central China. The teams would be out on a limb and on their own. Most individuals, by now, had realised if they needed to shoot their way out, they were pretty much done for. The SAS boys thought, 'If this happens, I will take as many with me as possible.' This was their training and mentality, regardless that the Chinese were not actually their enemy. Their logic was simply that of any soldier; there were no personal grudges against the Chinese. Winning was all that counted but coming second with a good score counted for something too; especially, if it saved the lives of your colleagues.

They then went to the range and spent the rest of the morning shooting the shit out of Figure 11 targets. These were life-size figures of some hard-faced Nazi bastard in a running pose coming towards you. It was only a paper picture covering over plywood backboards. The handguns were fired first at targets fifteen metres away. The rifles were shot at varying distances up to two hundred and fifty yards and encompassing various shooting positions. They had no major issues, other than a couple of stoppages which were rectified without the need for the CI's bullish intervention. Everyone was safe and competent, and out of the thousands of rounds fired, they hit the targets every time, well almost. Given that each engagement of the handguns required a double tap, two shots, the target would be dead or bleeding out badly. If the person on the ground still posed a threat, another headshot would finish the job. The high-velocity rifles would normally be a showstopper for any target not wearing body-armour. Close-in engagements were always head shots; farther-away engagements required aiming for the centre of the body or whatever was exposed. Counting rounds was important with your own weapon, but if you picked up someone else's, you wouldn't know how many rounds were left in the magazine, and so, time permitting, it was worth checking. It helped if you could pilfer a full spare magazine or two from a bloody target on the floor.

Lunch came and went, and Hangar One had a new padded flooring area. The blue square was obviously a training mat for unarmed combat. Just the sight of it raised adrenaline levels.

Each of the participants in the operation had been through various lessons on the subject of hand-to-hand combat. Some had put their training to effective but brutal use in the real world of espionage and combat. For those few who had held a man and either broke his neck with a distinct cracking sound or watched the breath leave him as they turned a blade, it left mental scars.

The idea of having to take on these trained killers in hand-to-hand combat was intimidating for young Philip Wong. He looked across at Squadron Leader Claire Walters who was the only person he guessed was lighter than he was, and she seemed totally relaxed. She either had balls of steel, metaphorically speaking, or was a tough lady. Unbeknownst to him, she was a very skilled combat fighter. Her early days of learning Judo and Karate helped her understand the principles of unarmed combat training. Since then, she took every opportunity to practice close-in combat, often coming away with cracked ribs, a chipped tooth, various black eyes and fat lips. She thought every injury was another lesson learnt and had no fear of pain from such fighting.

The CI came in wearing his gym kit and trainers. The assembled crowd were in their operational outfits with their combat knives only. Everyone had taken a light lunch because of the concerns of being winded and puking it all up again.

The suits they wore were good for combat, padded in the elbows, knees and backside but light-weight and stretchy. This reduced the restrictions that came with wearing a standard combat kit.

The CI stood on the mat at one end of the blue square, and the team walked across to form a semi-circle around him.

'This afternoon will begin with some warm-up exercises. Then we will go through, in slow-time, hand-to-hand combat manoeuvres. We will not be going in at full force in this training session. I will be gentle with you, as we do not want any unnecessary injuries, and I am afraid I might break some of you. The aim this afternoon is to get your muscle memory working and to hone a few techniques.'

He indicated for the assembled class to move back into an area offering a decent space to move. After the group had spread out sufficiently, the CI put them through a range of mild stretching exercises, starting at the head and neck and working down through the torso to the limbs. A bit of running on the spot got the blood flowing. A few floor exercises put some strain on the muscles. After a few minutes of cooldown, the CI gave his 'get your mindset right' speech.

'When employing hand-to-hand combat, you need to get down and dirty with the enemy immediately. The first few moments of contact in hand-to-hand combat make the world of difference in the outcome. Your aim when engaging in one-on-one combat is to kill the target quickly, whatever it takes. You don't get points for style or coming second. There is no surrender. Either kill or be killed. Your body is a weapon, and you can use any part of it to incapacitate or kill your adversary. The two key qualities that you need to survive are attitude and force. If you apply those attributes to your skills, it increases your chances of survival immeasurably.'

The CI picked up the dummy behind him, and Geordie quipped,

'Look! He's brought his girlfriend along.'

Bill said, 'She might not be a good looker, Geordie, but I bet she has a better IQ than you.'

The CI made fixed eye contact with Geordie who nearly pissed himself. Saying nothing to the childish remarks, the CI went through the vital and vulnerable points on the body, indicating where each was on the dummy.

He said, 'My personal favourite is eye gouging. Two fingers are great, but one will do.'

Vigorously demonstrating, he thrust his fingers into the eye sockets of the dummy. A few of the class felt some empathy for the dummy and were a bit taken aback by the ferociousness of its attacker.

He added, 'There is a technical way to do it, but in moments of desperation, just crush the eyes or pull them out. If you have a sharp object to hand, all the better.'

He worked down the body of the dummy, and at each point he demonstrated the best way to disable or despatch the enemy: elbow strikes to the back of the neck, fist-punch to the front, thumbs to pressure points, disabling open-hand strikes, attacks to vital organs, stomps and kicks to the groin or knees and calves, leverage on limbs to dislocate or break. As a presentation, it was a most brutal but timely reminder. He put the dummy down and asked everyone to pair off. He then demonstrated exercises in the various defensive modes, disarming someone with a knife, and putting an enemy down who is holding a rifle. He demonstrated a hip throw and follow-up killer moves. He went through defensive moves in case the adversary was getting the upper hand and the countermeasures to someone holding you from behind in a headlock. The presentation went on for two hours, and by the end, everyone had gone through the motions of being the attacker and defender.

Nodding at the poor dummy on the floor, Yorkie whispered to Phil,

'There is no way he's getting his leg over tonight, not the way he's treating her.'

Large pads were introduced so individuals could practice punches and strikes to the body without inflicting any lasting injuries. A few mistimed engagements left a couple of minor bruises, but it was all taken in good humour. When the afternoon tea break was called, most people were pleased for the reprieve from being thrown around and throwing plus absorbing punches and kicks. Everyone had spent time on their backs, but no downtime was permitted. The physical demands were exacting.

Scott said to Claire, 'So much for being gentle. I'm knackered and ache all over.'

She smiled; she loved feeling this tired. It meant she had done something challenging. She then said,

'This was gentle. No one is bleeding too badly.'

Before they left the mats, the CI made a few key points.

'Remember: you have trained today against friends, and your instinct is to hold back. This can be a learnt reflex, and you must always follow through in the real situation with force and intent. I will leave the mats and pads set up and the dummy here, suspended, so you can practice your attack posture.'

He pointed to the ceiling where a chain was hanging down.

He continued, 'We will have two more formal sessions of hand-to-hand combat to develop your muscle memory and killing demeanour. Take your break, and your next training session commences at 1530 hours outside Hangar Two in your teams, dressed just as you are.'

The CI about-turned and strode off towards the hangar entrance.

The sun was shining, and it was a pleasant day. Inside the hangars, it was cool and a bit musty-smelling. The CI appeared from Hangar Two and ordered the teams to follow him. The workmen building the apparatus had long gone, and the place was tidy. The Type E Lamella hangars were huge: three hundred feet long, a span of one hundred and sixty-seven feet, a height of thirty-five feet and a clear door opening of forty feet. These hangars were a holdover of the post-Second World War era and built of twelve-inch-thick reinforced prefabricated concrete arches with turf covering and a curved profile; designed not to cast a distinctive shadow. The admiring onlookers were not too sure what they were actually looking at from this dimly-lit angle but saw that tremendous effort had been spent putting it together.

The CI stated, 'We are going to walk around your individual target. There's no point looking at the other teams' targets. Targets One and Three are in here, and Target Two is in Hangar Three, just around the corner.

'You will, of course, get the opportunity to see all the training facsimiles when you are acting as guards or supervising the infiltration training.

'The reserves will be shown all targets and will practice each scenario. This means that you two,' he pointed to Terry Williams and Geordie Walker, 'will be working harder than anyone else with the distinct chance of not going on the operation. Life can be a bitch.'

He glared at Geordie for the earlier girlfriend joke.

Team One was the first to enter their target replica. They meandered around opening doors that led back out to the hangar, and then into the science laboratory which was fitted out just as you would expect a laboratory to be.

'This is a pretty near perfect facsimile of the facilities at your target. Wander around and get to know it,' reinforced the CI.

He did the same with Team Three and then took Team Two to Hangar Three to go through the same process. Team Two had the more complex entry in terms of the area to cover to get to the target laboratory.

The CI then took everyone to the central Attack Simulation Control Room where fixed cameras would watch every movement of friendly and enemy forces in each of the facilities. The role of the supervising team was to make constructive comments on the actions of the attacking force and would be made up of four people, one each from the non-training teams plus the CI and a former SAS operative now working with the SIS.

'The models have their limitations,' the CI stated, 'but it's a great opportunity to practice almost every step of your work. I understand that time is critical in your mission, so tomorrow morning you will be given an opportunity to get your communications up and running. Colin will be on hand to assist. After that, you can organise a walk-through without some miserable shit looking over your shoulder. After lunch, we will then take each team, one at a time, through their missions. The first mission will be a walk-through, with commentary from the Team Leader and each member as they take an action. It will be slow, but that way everyone knows what the others are doing and thinking. We will keep doing this until it's faultless and at the pace required, and then possibly some more repetitions thereafter. You will need to be in a full operational kit. Blank rounds will be issued, and practice knives carried. We don't want you rufty-tufty types getting carried away with yourselves. Any questions?'

'Staff, any chance that we could have a walk-through this evening?' pleaded Claire, anxious to get moving.

'The hangars will be locked and guarded at 1900 hours. If you wish to view the platforms, be my guest, but you will have to be out by that time. We will be in this facility for a good number of sessions, so don't worry, you will all be up to speed.

'That's it for today. Teams One and Two, you will be questioned by the Conduct after Capture Team this evening. You best get your homework done, kiddies. They will be here at about 1900 hours and will call you from your dormitory as required. Just so you know, it will be aggressive questioning, but nothing else, well maybe a bit of banging around,' he walked away chuckling to himself.

'Who the fuck was he calling rufty-tufty? I'll have you know I could rip a tissue or crush a grape,' said Bill Martin quoting comedians of old.

Geordie Walker responded, 'When you're finally thrown out of the Regiment, you can get a job as a bouncer at a children's day-care centre.'

Claire turned to Yorkie and asked, 'Is this what it's like all day with you boys?'

He shrugged.

That evening Teams One and Two were questioned regarding their cover stories. The questioners really went to town without physically assaulting anyone. They threw a few bins, and banged tables, and the air was blue with copious amounts of vulgar language. The interrogators found minor weaknesses in the cover stories which was the objective and gave everyone the time to rethink a few points. The Conduct After Capture Team was generally impressed and thought that a re-visit for these two teams would not be needed.

'Just tell them that we're coming back. That'll do the trick,' one of them said.

It was the same outcome the following night with Team Three.

All the teams went for a walk around the newly constructed targets.

'I can't believe it. Team One only has a small area to cover. It'll only take them ten minutes,' said Philip.

Yorkie said, 'Don't focus on what they've got to do. Get your mind around your job.'

Yorkie knew he would get plenty of opportunity to watch each target being infiltrated as a supervisor in the Attack Simulation Control Room.

The truth was each target had its own little problems. Target One was in a modern building on the sixth floor with one entrance in and out which would be guarded. It would take some gymnastics to get in, get the job done and get out undiscovered. Each participant could now see their own tasks and problems; it was becoming real. Thinking back to the maps they had researched and with the target clearly in their minds, they were becoming utterly aware of how isolated they would be.

Chapter 27

A Few Days Training

6th - 10th June 2024

During the first few days of training, it was self-evident that the group of ten were highly compatible professionals, albeit their characters were disparate. Apart from Yorkie telling his former colleagues to tone down their aggressive banter, things were progressing well. Though the military boys had a slightly different culture from the civilian agents, they were clever enough to know when to be on their best behaviour. Claire liked what she thought of as 'the wayward boys' and chuckled at their juvenile behaviour.

Today was their third day together, and they would now see how the practical tactical elements would come together. It was a bit like dancing: you had to be in step with the rest of your team. Each team member had to know what the moves were and, if someone or something interrupted the choreography, anticipate what to do to get back to the performance and in step with the team. Other people just could not find the rhythm. They lacked the dexterity to become good dancers, and it was the same with tactical movement. It was as much about coping with pressure and mental agility as the physical prowess of the participants. Having one set of skills without the other leads to failure. Failure in training is painful, but it builds experience and knowledge. Training aimed to build many skills qualities and attributes but most importantly trust. Failure in battle was often fatal.

The teams walked into Hangar One in full battle order. As a prelude, they had again been out for the seven-mile run around the airfield. During the run, the three Chinese speakers were teaching their teams some phrases which might be useful during the operation.

Yorkie jokingly said, 'All you need to know is "don't shoot" and "I surrender".'

Geordie, possibly not joking, added, 'All I want to know is how to say "where is the nearest pub?"'

After more light banter, the teams were taught a few Mandarin insulting phrases which might intimidate anyone captive and during tactical questioning, as it was euphemistically referred to. The old sweats like Yorkie and some of his SAS mates called it for what it was: torture. The most unpleasant and distasteful aspect of warfare but a necessary evil.

Back in the hangars, as they manoeuvred, the attachments on their equipment belt and in their pouches meant they were slightly restricted compared to the previous days. By the time they had gone through the next week or so of training, the equipment would be at one with them in every respect. Fidgeting was commonplace. People were adjusting their Glock holsters and making sure the reach was comfortable and that they could present the weapon quickly. At one point it looked like a scene from a wild west movie with cowboys practising being quick on the draw. They could slip their knives into a few alternative pockets or compartments. Each operator had a personal preference. Fighting, like most sports, had to feel natural in movement, instinctive and not laboured. The first reaction had to be the right one. Their profession sometimes did not offer a second chance!

Bill Martin had stolen another identical blade and said, 'If stealth was the aim, I would rather have two options of being able to get a knife quickly in a tussle to silence my prey. Remember: over-confidence kills.'

Often in a knife fight, an adversary would focus on and dislodge the blade in your hand and might think he has the advantage. This is often without realising that a second weapon could be pulled out to lethal effect within seconds. Everyone saw the logic and thought, for the extra weight, the benefit would be worth it. Keeping your options open was always the right decision. Major Tim was tasked to ensure extra knives would be available at their form-up points on the RN vessels. Team One would sort themselves out, as they would be taking a diplomatic pouch with them on their flight.

The communications fitted neatly and were discrete. They carried out tests professionally and succinctly. Colin reminded the troop that transmissions outside hangars Two and Three were open to intercept, and even though the systems were secure, it was best to keep checks to a minimum. Just the pulses of energy might make some foreign eavesdropping agency aware of activity which may instigate a curious look. The facilities within both target hangars had signal suppression systems throughout, incorporating a combination of installed physical and electronic countermeasures. The forty-foot doors to Hangar One were closed, and, apart from emergency lighting, all other lights were extinguished to simulate a night-time approach. They had enough residual light to make out shapes, just as they would at the targets from streetlights and the like. They put on the NVGs, and lo and behold, everyone looked like Martians, all green and glowing. It was still easy to discern who was who.

'Yorkie, even in this light, you are still one ugly son of a bitch,' said Bill Martin.

Chuckles were heard over the RT.

Claire's commanding voice landed in everyone's earpiece.

'Right, people, get your fucking game faces on, keep it focussed until the break, then rip the shit into each other. Understood?'

About half the team confirmed, saying, 'Copy,' while others said, 'Ma'am,' or 'Got it.'

Claire was pleased with the response. 'Equipment check by call sign, Team One, number off.'

Peter Goulding started, 'Mike 1-1; comms good, vision good.'

Next, Sergeant Steven Lang spoke, 'Mike 1-2, all good.'

Then Yorkie Charlton said, 'Romeo 2-1, check.'

Each person reported in, and a few minutes later, all were up and running. The odd-looking bunch were instructed to take out their digital notebooks and switch them on. A few guys struggled to press the "ON/OFF" button with gloves on; it was these minor changes in sensory ability that training ironed out. Going through a few settings, Colin was happy his students knew enough to commence training. As each team went through their attacks, he would watch and provide advice, if needed. Recounting the training protocols, the CI was happy teams were ready to start serious training. He had a handheld radio, and the doors opened to Hangar One. The teams lifted their goggles to get used to natural light. They were pleased with their toys thus far.

Walking to their respective target facsimiles, teams were allowed a thirty-minute familiarisation walk around. It would take time to become accustomed to the new facilities but this was a good start. Tea break was called, and they went back to Hangar One. From here on in, all combat kit was to be left at the target areas unless advised otherwise. The camp was secure with civilian guards dressed as MoD Police at static points and conducting patrols, but there was no point in drawing attention to the area by wearing unusual equipment. The inner training area was on a remote part of the airfield and had a mobile electronic intruder detection system surrounding it. At night, mobile patrols would cease, and static guards with NVGs moved into the training areas. Unbeknown to the ground force, friendly satellites above were quietly watching the training area for unusual activity. Security was tight, and the stakes were extraordinarily high.

All the Team Leaders already had clear thoughts as to how they would approach their targets. Yorkie had been instrumental in advising Peter Goulding and Claire during their desk-top exercise back in London. Uncle Tom also had some minor input but was greatly impressed with Yorkie's clarity of thought on how to deal with issues. That no-nonsense approach and attention to the smallest detail were critical. After the break, teams were expected to walk through the entry plan, review internal transit routes to the target area, and mimic their actions regarding laying explosives and extracting the viruses. Key to their planning was the setting of electronic wireless cameras with movement sensors as remote sentries and the positioning of the third man whose principal job was making sure the team had no surprises from unexpected guests. The Team Leaders selected an order of movement with the central person using the digital notebook to guide the path and give instructions. The front person, the point, was to ensure no nasty revelations were in their path of approach. The last man was to ensure that nothing came unexpectedly from behind. One person was to attend the chamber where the viruses were handled to get samples. Another person's role was setting time-delayed charges. Each function had a designated time limit to get their job completed safely. The longer the teams stayed on site, the greater the chance of detection. Being discovered would compromise their mission and possibly the other two teams' outcomes as well.

Discovery during the task within each target would be a real game changer, and no one wanted to be the prat who let the whole operation falter or even fail. The pressure on team members, even in training, was intense.

Within the training platform, the actual target facilities were replicated in detail so teams could gain familiarity with their tasks as close to being real as possible. Hastily made signs in Chinese were erected, so during training they could learn the specific symbols and their meanings. This level of detail allowed individuals to understand what distracted them and park that thought for the future. If you saw a symbol and wondered what it was, at that particular moment your situational awareness was diminished slightly, causing a reduced reaction time to another event that could be critical. A few seconds' delay here and there would add up, resulting in a slower speed to complete a task which again could be crucial. Small margins made a big difference.

Many of the operatives had not previously seen this level of preparation before a mission. Often agents and soldiers had a few days to get their shit together, and then they were on their way. A quick in-theatre brief and that was you off to the target. Operators might have plans, maps and a smattering of intelligence, but on occasion it was flaky. These operations often demanded the troops undertaking them to make it up as they went along, using their skills and experience to determine the right way forward. It was for this reason that so many operations went wrong or failed to achieve the successes being demanded.

Equipment, even on special forces operations, had limitations. People generally were imperfect too. Combine these two factors into a hostile situation, where an enemy will not do or be in the numbers expect, it can all go to bollocks quite quickly. For Operation Fulcrum Storm, the participants were generally astounded at the time, effort and money being thrown at this mission. The equipment was excellent, the level of tech support was brilliant, and the specialist training input was unheard of. The real winner was the level of intelligence. They even knew the guard rotas and patrol patterns; Yorkie even joked that they knew the names of their wives and tennis partners.

During breaks between run-throughs and debriefs, everyone had a constant thought that was impressed upon them by Major Tim.

"In World War II, the UK lost nearly half a million people. Covid-19 and 24 are expected to kill up to ten million people if a new vaccine is not found. These estimates were not trusted by anybody if Covid-24 continued to be an untreatable virus. The death toll would be greater than any of us can contemplate. If this virus is replaced by a more deadly version, the death toll could be unimaginable. This outbreak would be similar to the Black Death, killing off half of the population of those countries infected. It would put our nation's population back to where it was one hundred and fifty years ago".

The teams needed no greater motivation and accepted that if they had to give up their lives for the greater good, so be it. This was always easy to say in the comfort of home.

Yorkie told his SAS pals that Major Tim had asked to be on the mission, but Uncle Tom had vetoed his participation. Often it was seen by Non-Commissioned Officers that their bosses would rather stay behind and control from arms-length out of harm's way, but that was not true in this case. This increased Tim's credibility in the eyes of the soldiers he was sending into danger.

In training, teams were asked to justify certain actions, most were accepted and even applauded, a few brought criticism, but each person took any comment in good faith. Everyone hated being pulled up, but a mature response led to a better job and increased the chances of success. No one was trying to prove they were better than their colleagues. As a group, they only wanted to be the best they could. The benefit of each team observing everyone else's ingress and egress on the target meant they could pick up on the training points raised and adapt their own plans accordingly. Day one was fairly straightforward: no buggeration factors were inflicted upon the teams by the demon CI.

Finishing the target training at 1500 hours, Claire took the teams through a theoretical lesson on the viruses. She kept the training to the basics, but the demand for knowledge was insatiable. She had already grasped that, despite appearances and inappropriate language, everyone before her was extremely intelligent with strong, inquisitive minds. It would be a stupid individual who would underestimate them. The players in this act grasped the enormity of the danger of handling such lethal viruses. The practical training would be covered over the next two days, as each day would be rehearsing and adding to what they had done thus far. Practice explosives and simulated virus receptacles of the same size as those already on the way to embarkations points would be on-site in the morning to aid and improve training. Both the actual explosives and virus-carrying equipment had to be made or procured especially, and this was where the delay occurred in getting hold of them. Their origins were obscured by a convoluted supply process which, if checked, would lead to somewhere other than the UK. In the case of the plastic explosives, the source would appear to be Eastern Europe, and the flasks Germany – just a bit more deception.

For each person, much of the day was spent sitting on their arses and waiting for their turn to take part in active training. Wearing combat gear with full respirators on and working in near-darkness made everyone hot and sweaty. Because of the restricted areas within their targets, there was little by way of movement once inside. Being quiet and staying still when not doing a specific task was a survival skill in itself. There were few interventions in the early training runs, and, consequently, the lack of exercise was almost as crippling as too much. That evening they all agreed to undertake a spot of unarmed combat training, and the CI was happy to come along and supervise. He was still the same miserable git as he was during the daytime.

Peter Goulding commented, 'That guy is a machine. He must have had his personality removed at a young age.'

Yorkie added, 'He only has three settings: eat, kill and sleep.'

From behind him, Yorkie heard, 'Staff Sergeant, if you are talking shit, you are not focussed on the enemy in front of you. Get a grip.'

Yorkie shouted back, 'Staff,' sounding as if he had just been told off by a Headmaster.

The routine was set for day four of training: run with piss-taking, followed by breakfast. They attended their target maps and were pleased to see that the mock explosives were here at last. The viral canisters were also to hand.

Claire had mentioned that virus snap-freezing was the technique used to rapidly maintain the virus in suspended animation. It reduces the level of water present in the sample and therefore ice crystals, maintaining the integrity of the virus. The freezing element was liquid nitrogen but supplies of this had not arrived as planned. All operatives needed to have practice of handling this substance as "pulling a trigger without fingers could be problematical". She hoped it would arrive tomorrow.

The explosives were presented in a range of shapes and sizes; each one had its own unique instruction and function regarding where to locate it on the designated target. The detonators were integral to the plastic explosive which appeared to be a C4-type compound; a plastic explosive. An aerial wire ran around the explosive ordnance and was hidden by the design. Some were shaped like box-files with Chinese writing on them, some were bits of equipment and others were just slabs.

The first two morning run-throughs were straightforward. Having the replica explosives and virus containers made it feel more realistic. After morning coffee, Team Two was up. Their entry went as expected. They placed the sleeping sentries to cover the two routes into the target area. The systems were working well. They got to the laboratory area, and all comms went down. Yorkie quickly reassigned Sergeant Bill Martin (Romeo 2-3) to guard approach 1, and he would cover route 2.

He instructed Philip, 'Romeo 2-2, you do the virus handling, then relieve me, and I will then do explosive positioning.'

No guards were expected. Target time was eleven-thirty p.m., and the guards were not due until midnight. The team was out without incident with one minute to spare. The debrief was tough.

The CI laid into Yorkie.

'You should have accepted the risk that one route might be open, and the team would have been out with fifteen minutes to spare. Had there been any delay whatsoever in getting the primary tasks done, the whole operation would be compromised.'

He ended, shouting, 'Mission failure. You're all dead. Do it again.'

Yorkie accepted his mistake of being too focused on the protection and not completing the task. As they walked back to set-up point Alpha, he was heard saying under his breath, 'Fuck, fuck, fuck.'

He turned to his team, and said, 'Guys, that was my poor decision-making there. You did really well.'

The control came back, 'Stop talking like you are on some fucking Boy Scout outing. Get ready. You go in 5, 4, 3, 2, 1! Go-go-go!'

The next time round, the Directing Staff introduced a dropped empty glass container which needed cleaning up as part of leaving no trace of their presence. It went well, and the comms worked.

The CI providing modest praise said, 'You did OK that time.'

Team Three had an earlier-than-expected guard patrol, but Tango 3-3 (Sergeant Tony Lane) monitored the situation and stayed cool, telling everyone to take cover. The guard passed without incident, and the task was completed. It took longer than expected to finalise, but the integrity of the operation was intact. Tony was applauded for his sound decision-making. Had he taken the step of eliminating the guard, the alarm would have been raised within a couple of hours, and the whole job would have become more challenging.

Team One knocked over a shelf of glass receptacles whilst climbing down from a ventilation duct. This was not a Staff-induced occurrence but a genuine blunder. Peter Goulding (Mike 1-1) had to kill the guards when they came to investigate. Both guards were dispatched silently using knives.

The CI, in his gentle and caring way, said, 'That was a monumental fuck-up. Do you two know what you are doing here? Piss off, and let's do it again after lunch, but get it fucking right next time. If you don't, you might as well find another career.'

They did it all again and again. Soon, no matter what was thrown at the teams, their actions and decision-making were spot-on. Now and then, teams were put in a no-win situation: comms down, guards early and ready. On one occasion, Philip was told not to hesitate to kill, and he ultimately took his man down.

Yorkie was quick to point out, 'The next time the target might be sharper and have the upper hand. Small margins,' he reminded him.

The team had another gym session on the mats: a tag wrestling match to let off some steam. The outcome of the wrestling was much debated, with no team accepting defeat. In the first round, Geordie underestimated Claire and ended up flat on his back within seconds in a headlock. He stood up slightly embarrassed but hugely impressed with his opponent.

The other SAS boys were desperate to get the taunts in saying,

'Wait until the boys back at the Regiment hear of this!'

Geordie replied with humour, 'I let her win. Normally I have to pay for treatment like this at Mrs Wiggins's house of bondage and pleasure.'

He looked over to Squadron Leader Claire Walters and gave her an acknowledging nod of the head in respect of her well-executed victory.

Day five of training was the same start; run, piss-taking and crappy breakfast.

Scott MacGregor said, 'This reminds me of that movie, "Ground Hog Day".'

It was back to the target simulators, and with only minor issues being raised, all went well as the morning disappeared. The afternoon was back to the range for Glock 19 pistol and QBZ-95 automatic rifle firing. The quality of marksmanship was impressive. Philip was now in his element. He was a good shot and had taken his instruction fully on board. His reaction times at snap-shooting were sharp and accurate.

Then they received some good news of sorts: the liquid nitrogen arrived. An impromptu lesson was put together in target one. The demonstration to show just how dangerous this stuff was involved putting a dandelion into a small amount of liquid nitrogen. Claire then gave it to Philip with the instruction, 'Crush it.'

'If you get this stuff on your hands,' Claire said, 'Geordie, it will be the end of your piano playing days.'

She went on to explain it was important that the job of inserting the virus files into the flask be done quickly and smoothly. The size of their vacuum flasks with the amount of liquid nitrogen meant the temperature would be held constant for four days only.

'If the liquid nitrogen evaporates due to delays, or it is spilt, that time would reduce, making the whole thing more unstable quicker, possibly leading to death. Just another cheery thought for you to ponder,' Claire said jokingly. No one laughed.

The training was over, and everyone still had their fingers.

Training Day Six: Ground Hog Day.

'Same shit, different day,' said Terry Williams.

However, today was different. Tom MacDonald was paying a visit, accompanied by Major General Paul Burns. When the teams heard this, they felt a sense of trepidation. Both intelligence supremos arrived just in time for morning break. Tom MacDonald brought in a massive box of assorted doughnuts and Starbucks quality coffee in vacuum flasks.

His comment on meeting the CI was, 'Apologies, Chief, but I am not drinking that shit anymore. I am too old to put up with horrible watery instant coffee and crappy stale old biscuits.'

The CI smiled and said, 'You're the boss. You do what you want, sir. I'll have the pink-frosted doughnut with the sprinkles.'

Tom smiled. He and the CI went back decades, working together and having each other's backs. Claire Walters introduced Tom to the assembled team, and he, in turn, introduced Director Special Forces. Tom gave a short speech about the great work they were doing, and both supremos wanted to be assured the teams had everything they needed. Major Tim Churchill stood behind his director, hoping none of the SAS boys would come out with anything inappropriate. He was in luck for just now.

When the directors mingled with the assembled crowd, they were impressed with the intensity and specific detail of the training. Team Three were tasked with putting on a show in their target training area.

After twelve minutes' preparation time, the CI called to Tom MacDonald,

'Sir, we are ready to go. Follow me, please.'

Tom stuffed the remnants of a vanilla and raspberry doughnut into his mouth and followed his past comrade to Hangar Two.

'Very impressive,' he said taking in the training environment as he wandered through, whilst munching on the last bit of his pastry.

Before the team got on with their mock mission, both Tom MacDonald and Paul Burns walked around the target area. Both made noises sounding like a mix of pride, envy and, lastly, regret that in their day they did not have such facilities. They took up position in the control centre watching the array of screens in front of them. The CI talked them through what was available to the teams and how they observed such, adding that Colin, who was in the back of the room, could throw in a few communication curve-balls.

'That sounds great fun,' said Paul Burns.

'Ready Team Three,' said the control room.

'Tango 3-1, ready,' was the reply.

'Exercise 5, 4, 3, 2, 1. Go-go-go.'

The clocks were reset 23:15 hours local time in Zhengzhou, China. The team made a swift and silent forced entry, tactically moving to position Alpha.

'Camera 1 set.'

Sergeant Tony Lane looked at his monitor, and an image appeared.

'Tango 3-3, check.'

They moved on Position Bravo.

'Camera 2 set.'

Sergeant Tony Lane looked again at his monitor, seeing another image.

'Tango 3-3, check.'

Tango 3-1 said, 'Tango 3-1 and Tango 3-2 moving to target.'

Two voices said, 'Copy Tango 3-2,' and 'Copy Tango 3-3.'

They stealthily moved to a door and used key-picks to subtly force entry. This is a basic skill that all MI6 field agents know, but the speed of access was striking. Tango 3-3 stayed in his position guarding the door whilst monitoring the remote sentry cameras. After a brief chat in the control room between Tom and Colin, there was a call from the target simulator.

'Tango 3-3, camera 1 down, moving to position Alpha.'

'Tango 3-1, copied.'

It was now exercise 23:37 hours local time in Zhengzhou.

'Tango 3-2, packages positioned.'

'Tango 3-1, copied, babies almost in bed. Two Mikes, repeat Two Mikes to exfil.'

'Copy, Tango 3-2, exfil in Mikes Two.'

'Copy, Tango 3-3, exfil in Mikes Two.'

Tango 3-2 had moved to position Bravo awaiting the order to 'Exfil, Exfil.' The order came, and the team tactically withdrew making sure everything was as it should be. Tango 3-2 and Tango 3-3 lifted the cameras as they left and were outside by 23:43 hours. The whole operation took just fewer than thirty minutes.

Tom could feel himself welling up with pride. This was a perfectly-executed job. He could not fault any action of what he had seen.

Tom quietly prayed to himself, 'Please, God, let it go this well in China.'

After a period of questioning, he congratulated the team and took Claire to one side.

'I am afraid I have some bad news for you.'

She looked shocked momentarily but then realised anything serious would not be mentioned until after the operation. He continued,

'I am afraid that you have been discharged from the RAF.'

'Oh,' she said, understanding that this moment was on the horizon and due to happen.

Tom went on, 'The bad news is you will remain on the Royal Air Force books for two years regardless of what happens, and you have just been promoted to Wing Commander with immediate pensions rights at that rank. Congratulations.'

She smiled knowing that Uncle Tom had pulled strings. This meant if something went wrong in China, her mum, who was her only beneficiary, would be set for life in terms of income.

'Thank you, sir,' she said with true feelings.

Tom smiled. He appreciated how much this would mean to her; it was well-deserved.

'I only wish I was going with you to China. I hate sending people out on operations and staying behind. It plays havoc with my sleep and heart rate.'

Claire said, 'Ah, so you have one, sir, a heart, that is?'

'Careful, Wing Commander, what has been done can be undone. I think you have spent too much time with these SAS types,' he said, grinning, showing his human side.

'Just as a favour for my great generosity,' Tom added, 'would you tell Staff Sergeant Charlton that his discharge from the Army came through also? On similar terms to yours, but he has been given a Commission in the Special Air Service Regiment in the rank of Major, which he will hold for the next two years. You are both on my books now, and when you get back, we will have plenty of work for you.'

'Thank you, sir. It will be my pleasure,' Claire said and about-turned, walking straight over to Yorkie. She was buzzing with excitement and slightly lost for words.

The other three SIS staff were given similar recognition. They were delighted, and Peter Goulding was to tell his operatives back in China similar news. Major General Paul Burns had taken his men to one side. He gave a rousing speech and expressed his gratitude for their endeavours. He then told each man separately they were to be promoted with immediate effect and their new rank and wages were being back-dated two years. For these men it meant a great deal in terms of an immediate small cash benefit in their bank accounts, but their pensions were much better for their families, just in case.

It was agreed training would be suspended for a day. The tenth of June was supposed to be a day of rest, but the teams would do their usual morning run and after breakfast would go into the target areas. Meeting up for coffee at ten thirty a.m., the Chinese speakers agreed to provide a degree of light language training. Also, Teams Two and Three went through an element of escape and evasion planning and covered the landing routes. Peter Goulding chatted through the local area information around Shanghai which was his turf. He also explained key points about how the culture and infrastructure in China differed.

He stated, 'Once on the ground in China, you will need to think about how you will get around. China is vast, and getting out on foot will take ages and, in all probability, would be a non-starter from your target locations. You will need transport. You'll have limited access to the internet as the Chinese government has a firewall that blocks much of it. If there continues to support from GCHQ, that would be a bonus, so keeping hold of your especially-calibrated notebooks would be ideal. Because of your appearance, you won't be travelling through hubs of the population to access train stations, etcetera. Signage in China is limited and seldom in English. For example, even main bus and train stations have virtually no English signs.'

Scott added, 'Travelling by car is not for the faint of heart. Road signs are in Chinese. Also, the culture of driving will be unfamiliar as the Chinese have inconsiderate traffic behaviours. The heavy congestion of before the Covid-19 crisis is starting to build again. The road conditions off the main highways are terrible in places. If you have an accident, apart from the obvious compromise, the police are keen to attend as they exact stiff penalties or bribes or both. Travelling on expressways is precarious due to constant toll points with security guards, greatly increasing your chances of being caught. Travelling off the main highways is also hazardous. Classified as village roads, many are paved, but some marked on maps are gravel, improved earth standards, or merely earthen tracks. These latter roads during inclement weather are sometimes impassable. Poor weather and poor-quality roads will screw with your travel time estimates. Also, the local Police in villages undertake stop-and-search of non-local vehicles to elicit fines and bribes. The good news is that they don't always call in the stops and undertake them in secluded areas so they can pocket the cash. If needs must, you can always eliminate the police and get as far away as possible.'

He moved on to the infiltration of mainland China.

'The entry point for Teams Two and Three is a pebbled beach about eight kilometres north of Chuanlong Harbour. This area is part of the Yellow Sea which is in the East China Sea. Because of the proximity to Japan and South Korea, military patrols historically were more active than in some other parts of the country. However, because of the Covid-19 and 24 crises, the frequency of patrols has reduced markedly, with military personnel acting more and more in support of aid to China's civil community. The jaunt from the RN Frigate to the submarine East of Japan will be fairly straightforward. The submarine will come inside Chinese national waters to about eight kilometres off the coast. There a fishing boat will pick teams up, and it will be a very quick transition by necessity. I understand we hope to have friendly eyes and ears airborne to support the switch from the submarine to the fishing boat and during the landing phase.'

He never said anything further on the who, why and where. Those listening accepted that if it were important, Peter would have mentioned it.

He continued, 'Using a series of local roads, you will get to the highways, secluded in the rear of two trucks. The lorries will be transporting fish, so don't be too surprised if you find the stink rather uncomfortable. The local agents, whom I know personally, are solid characters. They will make their way to a safe house north of Najing. This property is isolated and set within a produce farm. A short stop-over will see the two teams moving off mid-morning to take up lay-up positions near their target areas. Your transport vehicles are moving fresh vegetables to the market in both the cities you are heading for. The markets are open at midnight, so it will not be unusual for such modes of transport to be on the road. You will essentially be hiding in plain sight. Teams will look to arrive in your target cities by nine p.m. and will have a takeaway for dinner, which is pretty common for such drivers in China. You will undertake a drive-by recce of your targets and familiarise yourself with the rendezvous points. The infiltration teams will be dropped off, as per the individual plans, with vehicles waiting close by, ready to make a quick getaway. Infiltrators will transit from the vehicles to the entry points of their targets using the cover outlined in the intelligence reports. Both teams will take no more than fifteen seconds to get to their entry points, both of which are obliterated from general view. Just check via your notebooks there is no one in those areas before leaving your vehicles.'

The rest they knew.

Later that morning, a few of the SAS boys and Philip asked if they could practice on the firing range with the Chinese weapons. The CI was happy to oblige but was still the same grumpy git as always. After the three p.m. tea break, most people found a quiet corner and wrote a few letters to be sent in the case of their own fatality. In the evening, they all went on the assault course set to the rear of the hangars, just for a bit of fun. They did the cargo net climb a few times, just to get used to it, as the jump from the RN frigate to the submarine would be by this method. After dinner, they enjoyed a few bottles of wine, courtesy of Uncle Tom. They had a glass or two, and sat around the large dining table listening to the soldiers telling war stories and funny yarns about one another. The SIS personnel were just as experienced in operations, having worked in equally dangerous covert situations, but their mindset was different. The MI6 spies just sat there smiling and tight-lipped.

Chapter 28

A Man Becoming a Leader

11th June 2024

The past week had been a great strain on the Prime Minister. The leader of the opposition had been calling yet again for his resignation due to the poor handling of the Covid-24 situation, primarily because of the lack of significant Government backing for the poor and less fortunate in society. The treatment of working families in big cities was claimed to be the root cause of the riots but throughout history, the poorest are generally hardest hit by any deprivation. What labour leaders realised, but would not admit, was that the Government was running a near subsistence economy, the cash was almost gone and borrowing was no longer an option; confidence in the world financial markets was near non-existent. The Government coffers were dwindling at a great rate, but Allan Knowles hoped that the end was in sight. He knew however, he was limited to what he could report. Everything his Party did was too-little-too-late. If he instigated greater policing of the lockdown, the left and liberal-leaning parties would cry that the Tories were infringing citizens' human rights. On the other hand, if they relaxed the measures in place, then they were acting for big business and not the average person on the street. This was a no-win situation for the Prime Minister. The resurgence of Covid-24 brought with it new challenges; PPE always had been and continued to be a problem. Whole industries had moved onto a war footing to provide PPE, but the Covid-24 outbreak saw all workforces, including emergency services, decimated by illness and fear throughout the country and world. The number of people in hospitals across the UK was at an all-time high with over seventy thousand in intensive care. Predictions indicated of those in hospital, around twenty-five thousand would die within a week. These numbers were making the Prime Minister ill and having the same impact on the whole country.

It was with this devastating backdrop that the Prime Minister invited

Chief of Secret Intelligence Service George Main, Chair of the Joint Intelligence Committee Sir Steven Alexander, Director Special Forces Major General Paul Burns, and First Secretary of State and Secretary Esther Rennie – whom he thought of as the "Gang of Four" — back to discuss progress on the China situation and Operation Fulcrum Storm. In addition, the Prime Minister had expressly requested that Deputy Director Operations Tom MacDonald join them.

Allan Knowles greeted these influential people and bade them to sit. Coffee was on the table, as was a modest selection of buffet items. The PM had not taken lunch or dinner and was famished but struggled to eat due to a loss of appetite. Having lost two stones over the past three months, Allan Knowles was weak from his previous Covid illnesses, which he tried to disguise without success. His clothes were baggy and his face reflected the overbearing stress.

In his mind, he knew he had to lead the nation forward but it was arduous. Rather than reaching for some sustenance, he started, mustering all his strength and energy.

'Thank you for coming to meet with me again. I feel that given my latest updates on Covid deaths and infections plus the predictions being made, we must consider ourselves in a state of war. The matters we discussed previously have remained constant, the evidence regarding the SIS findings on this matter are irrefutable and, as such, we need to agree on our nation's course of action. We have no room for dithering, indecision or frailty of heart. I will provide an Executive Order within the next few days to take action, but we must search our consciences to ensure we are doing the right thing for the good of the UK and humanity as a whole. I must say, however, I have wrestled with this problem long and hard, reading every document twice and tussled with each fact on numerous occasions. With great trepidation, I can only reach one conclusion and therefore, must provide leadership in authorising one course of action.

'I know you believe me not to be a details man, but I have no choice here. In my consternation, I have had to become enveloped in the weeds of this dilemma and, even surprising myself, to a level I thought I was incapable. I have read the science, and Professor Janet Williams was an absolute gem in guiding me through every detail to ensure I understood it sufficiently. Tom, you kindly took four hours to walk me through the intelligence from Covid-19 to the present day, keeping it simple enough for me to understand. The evidence presented was compelling.'

'Not at all, Prime Minister. You do yourself an injustice. Your grasp of the details was perceptive,' replied Tom with all sincerity.

'You're too kind,' the PM said generously. 'At this point, I see no option other than to give Operation Fulcrum Storm the go-ahead and do my part on Operation Reel In. I wholeheartedly wish we had another less taxing way forward, but I cannot trust President Xi to do the right thing without there being a pressure point to force his hand. Tom, may I thank you again and Mary Westwood for her very comprehensive analysis of President Xi.'

Tom nodded but stayed silent.

'Before we go down that route, Prime Minister, have you given any thought to bringing in the Leader of the Opposition to discuss matters and to gain his support?' asked Sir Steven Alexander.

'As you would expect, I have given this matter serious and near-constant consideration, but I do not feel it strengthens our position one iota, either from an operational perspective or political one. I think that he is an inherently weak man and is too keen on power. As such, I feel if he were brought into the fold, he would be inclined to talk to his inner cabinet, who, in turn, would blab to some of their communist pals, and the whole thing could be scuppered. The matter of involving our allies, especially the USA, has weighed heavily on me also. Again, our tactical advantage of being a small country with an elite compact force has tremendous merit. Secrecy is everything, and, as Tom has told me, most countries are using their intelligence systems and organisations to deal with grievous internal matters, much as we are undertaking with MI5 and GCHQ. If we involve the US President, the element of surprise would be lost, and it would sink any chances of a peaceful outcome. The decision rests with me. I alone will take full responsibility for these operations. Should they prove to be a political disaster, it will be my career ruined and my credibility devastated throughout history. I need your final thoughts on the efficacy of what we are doing. If anyone here tonight feels this is entirely the wrong judgement, I am happy for you to express an opinion.'

The room was quiet. The Prime Minister could sense an underlying tension but attributed it to the gravity of the matter at hand, more than the failing resolve of his colleagues. There was a palpable tension in the room.

The Prime Minister, turning to Major General Paul Burns, said,

'Thank you for your support. Before we go into the other matters, Paul, I understand that you were present at the training centre yesterday. How did you find things?'

Major General Burns calmly said, 'Prime Minister, we have a group of people of the finest calibre. They are supremely well-trained and motivated. The trainers and operators have applied themselves diligently to the task of this enterprise and understand their place in history. Both Tom and I were there yesterday, and I am proud to say that both aspects of this operation, the SAS and SIS, make me proud to command such sterling people who are the best of this generation. They have everything they require to make this mission a success and that includes the moral fortitude to do whatever is needed.'

The Prime Minister commented, 'Paul, it is so heartening to hear such eloquent praise of our men and women.'

General Burns added, 'They are all prepared and willing to make the supreme sacrifice, Prime Minister, should they be required to do so.'

The PM reflected openly, 'Such people are the ones making history, and it will be their endeavours which require recognition. We here are putting nothing more than our reputations on the line. Those brave souls are putting everything they have at our disposal. They are inspiring.'

Allan Knowles, looking moved, pulled himself together and continued.

'The aim of the next debate will be the consequences of our actions should the Chinese government wish to treat them as an act of war. The dossier that George left with me essentially pointed to two scenarios with which we could potentially be presented. George, would you like to cover these off?'

'Surely, Prime Minister,' George replied. 'If we sense that the Chinese government will not accept our terms under Operation Reel In, we will find ourselves in all probability either needing to call on our NATO allies, who may not wish to be drawn into a conflict at this time, or seeking solace from our American friends. In the latter case, it is impossible to know which way the US President might jump, but his abject disdain for the Chinese increases the chances he would be pleased to stand by the UK. If so, it might lead to a political stand-off. However, he is highly unpredictable. Potentially, the ace up our sleeve is that we could be holding the only source of the vaccine in the world for Covid-24 and "Yellow Petal". The US President sees himself as an astute negotiator so he will no doubt want a quid pro quo for helping us, and that might be a fifty percent share of all benefits from the vaccine production and sale. Because of the state of affairs in Europe and North America, there is a chance they might just cut us adrift. Standing against the Chinese might seem a monumental task, but, given the geography and distances they would have to cover to attack us, it would make it almost an impossibility. It is my assessment they would more likely attack us in a similar way we attacked them, to save face in the eyes of the world.'

George continued, 'We have modelled possible media reactions to the outcome of the operations, and one such negative response could be that the UK destroyed the vaccines in China to get a monopoly on the vaccine market. The Chinese will no doubt deny all our evidence as propaganda and claim we are thieves. It would be a fair certainty they will demand the return of all the vaccine samples. We suggest the correct political and humanitarian way to avoid being ostracised by the international community is to share the vaccine with our friends and allies and possibly even some countries we might not wish to see flourish.

'However, we must understand the risk that the Chinese might not seek to make a proportionate response and could resort to tactical nuclear weapons. This would leave us in a genuine quandary: would we respond and therefore risk escalation? We assess the likelihood of such a response as less than one percent, but this option would be on the table for them. It is worth pointing out here that our figures indicate that a nuclear war will kill fewer people than "Yellow Petal", if it ever were to be released on the world.'

'Prime Minister,' said Esther Williams, 'if we get to the point that the Chinese have declared war on the United Kingdom, we will have no option other than to appraise the NATO partners of our actions and the reasons for going it alone. Without equivocation, we would need to make samples of the vaccine available. We could not be seen to be doing this for political or economic advantage. Any sign of ambiguity on our part would have severe repercussions. For our Party to come out of this untarnished, we would need to publish all, or at least much, of the intelligence to prove our righteous actions. Our system of politics is that the opposition will make some outlandish claims, and we must be prepared for that. If there has been any point since the Second World War that we need strong unwavering leadership, now is the time. Prime Minister, I have every faith in your ability to lead us through this crisis.'

'Here, here,' said the assembled intelligence men, but without great gusto, apart from Tom MacDonald and Paul Burns.

The PM responded, 'Thank you all for your generous words and support. I will give the go-ahead for the operation to proceed. It will be with a heavy heart, but I feel entirely justified. In the next few days, George, I want to go through the meeting we are orchestrating with President Xi Jinping. It would be remiss of me not to say my role in this matter is causing me some trepidation and sleepless nights.'

Tom MacDonald turned to him, and said, 'Prime Minister, I have only been in your company four times now, and each time you have grown in stature. You are a man of many great qualities, and, I believe, if you can muster the faith and courage in your own abilities, you have every prospect of succeeding.'

The meeting went on with other words of encouragement for the PM. It was agreed that they would rehearse Operation Reel In as many times as it took to make it flawless. The Prime Minister knew every wordplay of the plan, but he could take this no less seriously than those brave people he was putting into a hostile environment in China.

When the five visitors left together via a back door, George Main, Sir Steven Alexander and Esther Williams had a short discussion as they contemplated throwing the PM on the fire, discrediting him and taking a more conciliatory path. Both Tom MacDonald and Paul Burns highlighted the risk of such a plan if anything were to be leaked.

Tom MacDonald asked, 'Who of you would stand in his place at this time?'

They muttered, but no one took a step forward. Uncle Tom's retort rocked them.

In their car on the way back to Vauxhall, Tom said to his friend Paul, 'Political cowards, the fucking lot.'

He was furious. He was not one to be disloyal to his boss, but he had just seen him being entirely two-faced. In Tom's mind, he was not worthy of his position. They were at war and needed war-time style leaders, not PC bureaucratic mandarins. He continued his rant, and his friend listened and agreed.

Quietly inside Number Ten, Allan Knowles had sensed a slight distancing from a few of the men present. It was unnerving to him that the three senior advisors had been unusually quiet and restrained. Esther Williams's comments sounded genuine, but she was ambitious with the ability to deceive. Equally, he had detected Tom MacDonald's and Paul Burns' resolve.

'These two are men of true steel whom one can trust,' Allan said later to his wife.

Chapter 29

Downwards Stretch

11th – 15th Jun 2024

Claires teams were all set, and the repetition of training had been comforting. At this juncture, the focus was on language training and preparation for dealing with 'what ifs', such as what if the night vision goggles failed, or what happens if one person loses comms with the rest of the team. They practised first aid, knowing that a life-threatening injury would probably result in death for the casualty. If there was an engagement of any type, no first aid would be administered until the engagement was won and over. They agreed they would not surrender and, if needed, would call in the suicide capsule activation. They all contemplated ending their own lives if things looked hopeless. They talked about the possibility of having to take the lives of the Chinese soldiers with whom they were not at war and agreed to minimise conflict away from the target areas. However, if they had to eliminate a potentially compromising person, they would. Their lives and, more importantly, the mission took precedence. Talking about all the scenarios was as important as the training itself. It led to an understanding of thought processes and provided a level of moral justification that underpinned trust. The whole group was in concert with each other and supported every course of action but judgement would still be needed. The unknown was the greatest threat.

At this point, exercising regularly helped to keep their minds fresh and active plus it honed their physical prowess. To improve their reflexes, they went for runs throwing tennis and rugby balls back and forth. They worked on upper-body strength and teamwork on the assault course. Moving over high obstacles gave them confidence and enabled them to deal with issues of height exposure. They put the unarmed combat mats, pads and the dummy, whom they agreed to name Uncle

Tom, to good use. Their reaction times on the mat were sharper, their interventions were more powerful and the accuracy of their punches and kicks improved. The intensity in all aspects of the training was starting to peak. Philip got a black eye wrestling Geordie, but it was entirely unintentional. Tony Lane dislocated his finger through a mistimed punch during an extreme session on the pads; he sorted himself out, immediately getting back to the training despite being told by Claire to take a rest.

'There is no rest in battle, ma'am,' he said.

The next day his finger was swollen like a balloon, but Tony did not slow down; he just kept pushing through the pain. They expended tens of thousands of rounds on the weapons range. Someone put pictures of various personalities on the targets which generated a negative comment from the CI. The SAS boys also set up a killing house like the one back in Hereford but of slightly smaller proportions. It was a disused married quarter on the south side of the airfield. They used the Glocks with blank rounds to refine the techniques of moving around buildings and engaging targets at short range. Claire and Philip found Yorkie's and Steven Lang's experience and training to be of great benefit. They improved their posture and balance when moving from room to room whilst being ready to engage but, equally importantly, knowing when not to shoot. They had become so close to each other in terms of the cross-training that it would be difficult to know who the professional soldiers were and who the MI6 'pen-pushing pussies' were, as Geordie referred to his new colleagues.

For the routine entry into the targets, the record time to undertake tasks with no problems and exit was nineteen minutes. The worst timing was thirty-five minutes. The kit they carried and the suits they wore felt normal now. Reaching for their combat knives was second-nature. The Glocks in their hands felt as natural as a steering wheel.

The reserves constantly watched each training platform and at no notice were pulled in to replace each participant. Leaders swapped teams just for a change so that they could see team members operating and possibly pick up something useful to use themselves. They even switched targets as a whole team. The competitive nature of participants drove them to do a great job, but the principal learning point was familiarity did take minutes off the time on target. This cross-training made for real respect amongst the whole group. The Directing Staff had become admirers of the force they were training, and they kept on notching up standards and pressure to keep them on their toes.

By the 13th June, the teams were feeling impatient. The routine of constant training was becoming a stale habit. Over-familiarity generated a lack of concentration. They did ambush drills to mix it up and to provide insight into a different aspect of what they might encounter. The CI took them back to basics. They went over methods to facilitate escape if they were caught or hunted. They reviewed ways to take the inexperience of Chinese troops and use it to their advantage.

On the 14th June, Claire managed to obtain a few movies on DVD. Star Wars was democratically voted the first choice. They used the CI's big training screen and his rather expensive high-definition projector. Claire had purloined popcorn, and the Field Catering Unit on-site made hot dogs in proper soft white finger buns with darkened fried onions and provided the usual ketchup, mustard and mayonnaise. It was culinary heaven and a real spirit-lifter.

Late that afternoon a team of two arrived out of the blue from SIS Headquarters. They had a couple of small suitcases and not a smile between them. Colin spoke quietly with one of the chaps whom he knew from GCHQ. Claire recognised the other as the medical technician from SIS Headquarters. They asked each team member to step forward one at a time. Peter from Team One went first. They took a finger prick of blood and tested it against a small hand-held device. After a few bleeps and squeaks, the details of the man with a picture came up.

The med tech said, 'Roll down your top to your waist.'

After a moment, he said, 'Turn sideways.'

The sullen med tech reached into the briefcase and took out the largest hypodermic instrument any of them had ever seen. A capsule was lifted, and the details were checked against the electronic identification device. Once happy with the verification of the ID, the capsule was loaded in the hypodermic gun. Using his forefinger and thumb, the medic grabbed a chunky bit of flesh just above Peter's buttocks, pressed the gun against the fold and pulled the trigger.

Peter Goulding let out an almighty yell.

'Bloody hell, could you not find a more painful place to put that?'

The medic retorted, 'Don't be a pussy.'

He wiped the area with an alcohol solution which also burnt, slapped on a plaster and shouted for the next person.

'Mr Lang, you are next,' was the matter-of-fact call.

Steven got to his feet and said, 'If that twat calls me a pussy, I'll deck him and arrange a visit to the hospital for him.'

He said it just loud enough so the medical technician heard him and stopped being quite so brash with his comments. All the remaining team went up, and each was injected with a tracker and suicide capsule. The second visitor called over each of the newly-injected subjects and checked to make sure the bio-readings coming up on the screen of his computer were the correct ones. There were no glitches.

Squadron Leader Walters was the only member called by her rank and name. The injection proceeded without a murmur or smart-arse comment from her.

She thanked the medic who smiled back.

'Just one question,' she said. 'How robust are these capsules?'

The medic said quite seriously, 'Ma'am, you can hit them with a small hammer, and they won't break. They can only be activated by a coded signal. They cannot be triggered by accident.'

The next day was a run-through of each target operation in front of Deputy Director MacDonald and Director Jacobs from GCHQ. After that was completed, they had the full briefing, the last time that they would be all together until after the job was completed. Tom once again went over the mission and the secondary missions for each of the teams. He discussed the explosive charge that would be in each of the virus containers, instructing personnel to self-destruct the flasks if they thought they might get back under Chinese control. A forced entry into the flasks would ignite the explosive, and if the flasks were not in friendly hands by 24th June 2024, they would self-ignite. He discussed with the teams the importance of not letting the Chinese know of their presence, and they talked through one more time what they should do if the mission for any reason had to be aborted.

David Jones of the Far East Desk said,

'The overarching command and control of this operation rests with the Deputy Director Operations SIS. He has appointed me and Section Chief Rankin as his co-second in commands and Watch Officers for this Operation. In the Operations Room, we will be supported by Lee Ford, our GCHQ Liaison Officer, and Major Tim Churchill, 22 SAS liaison Officer. The only other staff allowed in the operations room during the live operation will be Mrs Joyce Young of the China Desk, who is a language specialist, and Peter Tomkins of the Specialist Weapons Section. Only these Officers will hold the authority to initiate the Abort Order from Headquarters SIS. Team Leaders on the ground may order the Abort Order or their deputies in the case of a fatality or incapacitation of a team leader. Finally, the Naval commanders at Sea can abort at their own discretion.'

David provided an up-to-date intelligence brief that included current photographs from aerial satellite reconnaissance, guard positions on the sites, the number of guards, their weapons and their training. He then went over the Operational Security (OPSEC) measures for a final time. Coordination of communications was essential to the success of the mission. Local communications with in-theatre agents would be by handheld encrypted radios. The comms with headquarters were to be controlled via GCHQ. Derek Jacobs would maintain a visual watch on ground forces by satellite, obviously subject to weather and cloud cover, but they would know where people were even if the visual spectrum was taken out of the equation. During the hours of darkness, a contact could be maintained, and even when they were in a building, they should be able to pick up infra-red images. The transponders would give a signal within two feet of their location. Likewise, any untagged bodies would be identified as hostile. Images would be passed to SIS Operations. All three teams knew all this, but again, it was comforting to know people were watching their backs, albeit from over five-thousand miles away.

Codewords and call signs for the operation had been learnt by heart. The key code words were:

Abort mission - Abraham

At target and initiating ingress - Abel

Mission complete - Cain

Mission compromised - Judas

Samples retrieved - Jerusalem

Teams secured - Joshua

Call Signs were allocated as:

Team One - Mike 1

Team Two - Romeo 2

Team Three - Tango 3

Controlling Director – Condor 1

Ops Watch Officer 1 (Bill Rankin) – Condor Ops 1

Ops Support 1 (Peter Tomkins) – Condor Support 1

Ops watch Officer 2 (David Jones) – Condor Ops 2

Ops Support 2 (Tim Churchill) – Condor Support 2

Director Jacobs said GCHQ would stage mock minor police incidents in each of the target areas on the night of the operation to divert local Chinese police units away from target areas. The deception techniques employed the week before the attack on the buildings included minor comms failures and false alarms being set off which would make the guards less likely to take an alarm seriously. More importantly, the alarms would be neutralised, and they would provide false images on the cameras so when the teams received the signal to enter the buildings, they could do so knowing that the guards would not see them. For the last time, they went over the ways the teams would be inserted into the country and would travel in-country to their targets.

Yorkie spoke up, directing his question to Tom.

'Sir, this young lad working in Wuhan that's on the team so to speak. If he is compromised, I take it he has not been prepared to take his own life should he be captured?'

'That's correct, Yorkie. I will leave this matter to your discretion. I am sure you understand what's at play here.'

'Right, sir, leave it to me,' Yorkie acknowledged.

Tom added, 'But, Yorkie, bring him back here if you can. He's a good lad.'

Yorkie nodded, accepting this clear direction.

The room quieted as Tom gave his final words before their departure.

'All of you, I want you to know that I sincerely wish I was going out there with you. I fully appreciate the dangers you face and the courage needed to undertake such a mission. When I say this, I truly mean it,' and here he paused, his voice cracking with emotion.

'Both that old fool at the back of the room there,' Tom pointed to Derek Jacobs, who grinned at him, 'and I have undertaken a great many covert operations, and we both agree that in all our time a better group of people has never been put together for any mission than this one. You have trained hard and are the best of what we can offer in the way of the defence of the UK. Please come back home safely and make us all proud of your tremendous achievement.'

From table two a Yorkshireman said,

'Oh, stop it, you'll make us all weep.'

A more feminine voice retorted in gruff tones emulating Winston Churchill,

'We shall defend our island, we shall fight on the beaches, we shall fight on the landing grounds.'

'Fuck you lot,' Tom retorted, laughing.

'Finally,' Tom said with grave sincerity, 'one piece of wisdom from an old operative with many missions under his belt. As you will be in confined spaces for days, make sure you do not each too much crap. There's nothing worse than being stuck next to a "farter" for hours on end. Remember smells can compromise the team.'

The room erupted in laughter. After everyone calmed down, Tom asked,

'Any last questions?'

As he expected, no one spoke. He approached each table and shook the hands of all present. He hugged both Yorkie and Claire.

Chapter 30

Go Position

15th – 16th June 2024

After the briefing, Team One said hasty goodbyes and wished everyone good luck. They had their bags set to the rear of the briefing room, and a security Landover would take them to the MI6 car waiting at the airfield's main guardhouse to transport the duo to Heathrow. They arrived at the airport in good time as the roads were still quiet, and Heathrow was essentially a ghost town. Of the thirty flights due to leave, most were only twenty-five percent full. Their diplomatic cover allowed them to be rushed through customs and security. Their diplomatic bags were not checked and were put straight onto the aircraft hold. Taking off from Terminal Five, it was now 1335 hours local on the 15th June, and the aircraft taxied on time. It forged its way down the runway and lifted into a clear blue sky with infrequent fluffy white clouds. This was it: the two men were on their way to Shanghai Pudong International Airport.

After an uneventful flight, they landed at Terminal 2 in Shanghai on the 16th June 2024, at just after 0755 hours local time. They were streamed quickly through a special customs desk and cleared with no fuss, minimum paperwork and a cursory check of passports. They were heading into Shanghai City centre in a Consulate car by 0835 hours local time.

Teams Two and Three mingled with the briefing team and their senior bosses, but they were keen to get on their way. Today was a rest and relax afternoon for them with no training. The truth was no one could unwind; they were all on edge and ready to go. The countdown had begun.

M Day Minus 5

The next day after a run and breakfast, the UK teams began to get their kit together, waiting impatiently for their departure times. They wandered around the practice target areas one last time, chatting with the training staff who were packing up the site and thanking the behind-the-scenes support staff. It was strange to see the practice mats being put on the back of a three-tonne lorry. They had spent hours on them being bounced around and dropping faux enemies with a well-timed throw, kick or punch.

Each person on Teams Two and Three arrived at Heathrow separately. Some used genuine taxis, and others were MI6 vehicles. The passengers went through the whole process of checking in and going through security without any contact whatsoever with their colleagues. They all had papers from Japanese immigration to authorise their journey. The travel restrictions were strict for non-diplomatic passengers. Once in Japan, other than transport from the airport to their hotel and their meeting venues, they could not move around freely. Even these restricted travel permissions came with the absolute requirement to wear full-face masks when outside their hotels once in the country. In truth, the Japanese Home Office knew that they were participants in the UK military training exercise being conducted in the waters East of Japan, but neither nation wanted attention being drawn to the multinational, if smaller than intended, exercise.

Like Team One, they would leave Heathrow Airport, London from Terminal Five. As business class passengers, they went to the British Airways lounge, slowly arriving one by one. Boarding was at 1500 hours, and take-off occurred on time at 1530 hours local on the 16th June. They arrived at Tokyo International Airport, commonly known as Haneda Airport, some eleven hours and thirty-five minutes later, just a slightly longer flight time than Team One had to Shanghai.

The non-stop flights in business class minimised the impact of fatigue. They would benefit from being able to sleep on the aircraft, as their seats converted into a six-foot fully flat bed. They had the capacity for two 32kg checked bags, plus carry-on hand luggage, but they were nowhere near this limit. They had all brought reading materials and the odd puzzle book. The seating arrangements on the aircraft were such that, unless you were travelling with a family member, each person would have a space on either side of them for Covid safety.

Due to being in Business Class, check-ins were less rushed, but the wearing of face masks and gloves was a bit of an inconvenience. Passengers had their temperatures taken and provided with a three-page document to fill in regarding health and previous travel history. The gloves would come off once on board the aircraft, but masks had to be kept on unless passengers were eating or drinking. Hands were sanitised every time anything new was introduced to the passenger. The British Airways flight was on the Airbus A380, a double-deck, wide-body, four-engine jet that was the world's largest commercial passenger aircraft. It was also one of the greenest aircraft in service. Most people were now more interested in day-to-day living and not so much the planet. It was one of the societal changes brought on by the prolonged and deadly pandemic.

Back in Shanghai, Team One's car was followed to the Consulate and seen entering the vehicle compound which had ten-foot-high security mesh fencing and armed Royal Marine guards. Consulate cameras watched the car enter what was classified as UK National soil, but they also recorded the Chinese State Security tail they had picked up. This was the game of cat and mouse that embassies around the world played. The more the Consulate made this look like it was just a routine replacement of a member of staff, the better. They leaked the details of the new arrival early so the Chinese could run their checks in plenty of time and put their minds at rest. The replacement man was a low-ranking Marine who was new to the country but was due to stay on a two-and-a-half-year tour of duty. He was told to make a few blunders with paperwork coming through the Customs desks just to look like a newbie. He called everyone sir, and when the Chinese customs official asked him the reason for being in the country, he looked perplexed and, sounding unsure, replied, 'To work at the Consulate, sir.' The art of not drawing attention is to be a grey man: not clever, not threatening, no personality and presence – be someone others would not remember.

Once inside the consulate, Sergeant Steven Lang was introduced to a few key personnel. First, he met the MI6 Head of Operations, who went under the guise of Head of Trade Mission, and then two individuals who would be taking part in the operation in a few days. They were not introduced by name, just their call signs Mike 1-3 and Mike 1-4. After the operation, these men were staying behind unless expelled by the

Chinese, being declared persona non grata. The truth is that the Chinese had a bad habit of aggressively interrogating Embassy and Consulate staff if they thought they were spying. The capturing State Security would take their time to check the diplomatic credentials of the suspect spy to give them a going over, and in more than one case, Embassy staff had broken under questioning.

Both Peter Goulding and Steven Lang went to the Consulate's basement and checked out their equipment. They tried on everything, undertook functional checks and then left all the paraphernalia on two tables. The area was secured for now.

M Day Minus 4

The next day, as part of a standard reconnaissance and orientation, Mike 1-3 took the new boy on a jaunt around the city of Shanghai. They were out for three hours in the Consulate car. Mike 1-3 was driving and providing a running commentary. At one point they passed the target and then took the direct route back to the consulate.

There was a KFC just around the corner from the Institute of Microbiology & Immunology, and that evening, Peter (Mike 1-1) and Steven (Mike 1-2) went for a walk, stopping at the fast-food outlet. They were out for about five hours but did not notice any tails from the Chinese Secret Police. Two other groups of pedestrians had left the Consulate just fifteen or so minutes before them to act as a decoy. With black hoodies, jeans and white trainers plus full-face masks, which was the local fashion of choice, they were inconspicuous. Neither man was exceptionally tall, and both were well-built but not enough to look out of place. They carried nothing except their wallets and IDs. Arriving at the Institute of Microbiology & Immunology, Shanghai Normal University, in Xuhui District, they found it to be surprisingly busy. A few students were milling around, keeping the prescribed distance of two metres, and all wore face masks. Some had the full-face sealed masks that were required by law in Japan. These were like low-grade military respirators with inter-changeable filters. The boys decided they too would wear these the next time they went out as they gave better coverage of facial features for being disguised and probably better protection. They also agreed that these lightweight masks could be used in place of the military respirators they had been issued which were more cumbersome, but they would check this out with Operation Headquarters back in London. The other good news was there were a few white European faces mingling around. This put Steven somewhat at ease. They walked in the front entrance of the Institute and up to the sixth floor where the military facility was located. They could see from the external corridor that the atmosphere was different on this level with keep-out signs. Through a glazed door, they could see everyone was in overalls and the armed guards, in disruptive pattern material uniforms, stood out from all around them. It was just as Steven had seen from the photos. They did not press their luck by hanging around too long or going into the Secure Area. They walked to the Seventh Floor and found Room 712 which was directly above the laboratory. This was where they would be accessing their target in a few nights' time. They observed the air-conditioning duct they would use to lower themselves down to one of the offices of the main laboratory, thereafter, gaining access to all they needed. Room 712 was an empty study area, but as a precaution, they surreptitiously placed a small camera which they could view to ensure that on the day of the assault were not walking into a dead-end.

Though in practice the College was busy, most students did their lectures online. The Chinese were undertaking their secret vaccine development by hiding in plain sight, only the guards gave the game away. Mike 1-3 and Mike 1-4 had already reconnoitred the target a few times and had put a small mobile camera down the ducting which was how they knew its exact size and which allowed for the copy to be built back in the UK for training purposes. After their quick look around, Steve was told to navigate back to the consulate on foot without using a map, remembering the waypoints that Peter had alerted him to on their outward journey. This was just in case something went wrong on the night, and the Team had to disperse without transport. He made it home without a problem.

In addition, Peter pointed out a safe house.

'If needed, go in there and lie low. This will be our Emergency Rendezvous.'

Peter had not shown his colleague this previously in the UK because he did not want to risk compromising it should one of the Teams operating in-country be taken alive, however unlikely that situation was

262

to occur.

Peter Goulding said, 'If we are separated, make no further communications contacts, as the Chinese may have access to our systems, and do not go back to the Consulate. The Chinese will be on alert, and as part of standard protocol, their counter-surveillance teams will be fully active and have it covered. They can put thousands of bodies on the ground within a couple of hours: police, military and civilian-clothed State Security Agents. Any incident of significance will make them likely to stop anyone on foot and bundle them into a van. No questions and these people will not be seen for at least a couple of days, some perhaps never again.

'We will both head for the safe house, and you should check to make sure you are not being followed. Mike 1-3 and 1-4 will go to other locations which will form part of any alibi they have. We have our own cover stories which, if needed, will be sufficient until the diplomatic immunity kicks in.'

One of the important tasks, if compromised, was to dead-letterbox the flask with the vaccine. Throughout their route, there were several stashes they could use. If the Consulate was being aggressively watched, the team could drop the package in one of these locations and have another team retrieve it. If they were found with anything on them indicating they were spying, they would be tortured within an inch of their lives, diplomatic immunity or not. This was a deadly high-stakes game and the losers would pay a hefty price.

It was the middle of the afternoon in Tokyo, and it was a glorious sunny day. About an hour into the flight, the team had been given Covid-24 test kits which were analysed on the aircraft to see if they had the virus. The results were not surprising: all were clear. They filled in the now onerous immigration paperwork which indicated where they would be staying and what they would be doing. There was a list of regulations, each of which required a signature. Fines for non-compliance were the equivalent of thousands of pounds. Just before coming into the approach, air stewards came around with a small BA-branded medical bag. They said it was complimentary, but the cost of airfares was now more than triple what they used to be, so that was debatable.

The bag contained a full-face mask which was to be worn before leaving the aircraft. Also, there was a one-piece suit of lightweight plastic material which was to be worn over the passenger's clothes. The instructions suggested that all unnecessary clothing which could be removed should be placed in the blue resealable plastic bag and washed immediately upon landing. The white coverall was supplemented with blue latex gloves and shoe covers, to be worn on exiting the aeroplane. Other items included hand sanitiser, anti-bacterial wipes and a thermometer plus a testing kit for self-checking every six hours. Once the aircraft landed, passengers rushed to put on their new hazmat-style suits. They could only change out of these once at their destinations, where again the suits and all items of clothing should be washed in the anti-bacterial wash solution in the freebie bag. This product could be used as a body wash also. It was this compulsive and strict enforcement of behaviour that kept Japan's death rate down to one of the lowest in the world.

Upon leaving the aircraft, all passengers were processed through a carwash-type contraption in which anti-bacterial spray was misted all over them, and a team of cleaners in full hazmat suits brushed gently with sponges on sticks.

'This is a surreal experience,' thought Yorkie. It reminded him of his training at The Defence Chemical, Biological, Radiological and Nuclear Centre at Winterbourne Gunner in Wiltshire, many, many years ago.

After the shower, came an area of warm air blowers which, mixed with the ambient warm temperature and the stifling suits, made beads of sweat trickle-down Yorkie's back and into the crack of his backside.

Muttering, 'Great, just bloody great,' he had not slept much on the aircraft, watching some old movies to help pass the time and munching over-cooked food in between them to get him through the flight. Yorkie was now a little tired and could do without this carry-on but forced himself to focus.

They were processed through customs with all officials wearing full PPE within plastic booths. The passengers collected their luggage which was also in plastic bags with just passenger names in black marker pen on the side to differentiate them. It made finding luggage harder, but the low number of passengers minimised the hassle. Walking out to the arrivals area, which was almost deserted, the team members were collected in several vehicles and taken to their hotel. They would stay there until 0700 hours the next morning, never leaving their rooms and having no contact with each other. Dinner was pre-ordered and delivered to rooms, as was breakfast. That afternoon and night, each team member slept as much as they could but it was good to have a long shower and feel clean. Everyone played the next few days in their heads over and over again. Philip Wong, after being surrounded by teammates for the past two weeks, felt a wave of insecurity and solitude. He worried about oversleeping. His inexperienced brain kept replaying things that could go wrong on the mission, over and over again. Eventually returning to the to the same conclusion, 'We know what we are doing, and Yorkie will keep me straight.'

As part of the ongoing deception, Sergeant Steven Lane completed the standard induction paperwork to be registered as having all the correct credentials for someone of his station and function with the staff of the Consulate. His false details were entered into the HR computer which, it was believed, the Chinese had compromised, but that was a small matter. The Consulate was obligated to pass much of the information over to the Chinese authorities anyway. Steven went through the standard induction process and was introduced to his team and his new boss. As part of familiarisation, he was shown the perimeter of the Consulate. All in-house security measures, gates, and cameras were pointed out as well as the exits and entries. This was all being carried out under the watchful eyes of Chinese State Security. The Chinese Counter Intelligence agents observing matters thought it all looked pretty normal and only worthy of a few benign comments in the counter-surveillance team's daily log. A selection of photos was taken by the Chinese observers and electronically passed back to their Headquarters, but no one was interested in a lowly guard. They had done the standard checks, and no flags were raised.

On another warm Tokyo morning, Teams Two and Three received their early morning calls at six a.m. as arranged. Breakfast arrived trayed and covered with cling film. It was a mix of cold meats, a warm boiled egg, cereals and milk. The makings for coffee and tea were already in the room and in plentiful supply. Despite the heavy use from the previous day, they still had sufficient beverages left for breakfast. The meal was spartan but good. Another shower got everyone alert and ready to move; this would be their last quality shower for a few days. They would wait for the concierge to call, letting them know their transport had arrived. Mingling in the foyer was not permitted. The team members were wearing jeans and hoodies plus the PPE required by Japanese law. At 0700 hours, the cars came, and one by one the team was driven to the harbour and deposited in the coastguard lounge. There they were offered more coffee, and waited quietly, saying nothing and taking no interest in their surroundings. At 0930 hours, a Naval Lieutenant Commander came in and asked Task Force 21 personnel to follow him; this was the team's designation for this aspect of their journey. They picked up their bags without uttering a word and followed him to the seaward side of the building. A walkway led onto an old Japanese Coast Guard patrol vessel named Nagura with the numbers in large print on its side reading, 'PL28.' Within ten minutes of the team being secreted below decks, the ship was readied, cast off and proceeded out of Tokyo harbour at a very leisurely pace.

This was the first time the teams could chat. The topics were mundane: the food on the aircraft, the movies they had watched. They had a sense of increasing purpose now that they were on their way. When they cleared the harbour and were beyond the Chiba peninsula, the sea state became slightly rougher and uncomfortable. Staying below decks for a few hours until the boat was clear of land, the teams then decided to take in the sea air. After about ten hours, they were arriving within view of Hachijō-jima, a small volcanic Japanese island in the Philippine Sea, about two hundred and ninety kilometres from Tokyo. The exercise area was some two hours further southeast. The coastguard crew offered some light snacks which were gratefully devoured. The chat was lighted-hearted. At about seven in the evening, the Japanese Coast Guard vessel started up its helicopter. The seas were light, and there was little wind.

Without any ceremony, the teams and their escort transferred to the HMS Richmond, a Type 23 frigate of the Royal Navy. Once again, the visitors were put below decks, offered refreshments and shown to the ready room where they would be re-associated with their equipment. They took no time to toss away their civilian bags, get their fighting kit out and undertake functional checks. Everything was as it should be. They were due to meet the RN submarine in about seven hours so they agreed to six hours of sleep and then get ready to move. Tensions were rising, and heart rates increased ever so slightly, but they were all in control and eager to get to the next stage. Waiting was the hardest part of any job.

Yorkie told Philip, 'It's not like in the movies, you know. Most of our lives in the Special Forces is training and waiting. The work itself is intense, but as a proportion of our lives, it doesn't take up a huge amount of time. Waiting and keeping yourself one hundred percent ready for action is the hardest part of it all. That's where the dedication comes in.'

Philip smiled nervously.

'I know,' he said, and thought, 'I am learning.'

Sergeant Tony Lane looked around, wide awake.

'Can someone go and tell the captain of this tub to turn the engines off and stop this infernal rocking? It's playing havoc with my beauty sleep. If I don't get any, I'll end up looking like Yorkie.'

Everyone burst out laughing apart from Scott MacGregor who appeared to be asleep.

Bill Martin suggested, 'Let's draw a Chinese moustache on his face, just to help with camouflage.'

They had not realised that Scott had been awake and heard the laughing. Everyone laughed even harder when he surprised Bill by saying with complete sincerity,

'You fucking do, and I'll shoot you myself, drop you into the sea and feed you to the bloody sharks.'

He closed his eyes again and feigned sleep. Everyone grinned, and the tension lifted somewhat.

Back in London, the Operations Room was cleared of non-essential personnel. The Fulcrum Storm Operations Team had assembled and run through comms checks with GCHQ, establishing all satellite links on the main screens. The centre screen was for Team One, and the blue dots marked all four call signs. The left screen was dedicated to Team Two, and the target area was shown, but the blue blobs of Team Two and Three were still shown in the middle of the East China Sea in international waters. The right-hand screen was for Team Three's target area. The Captain of HMS Richmond sent a signal asking for a fuel top-up at map reference Foxtrot Sierra 6. This was code that he had the six operators on the vessel and was heading for intercept with the submarine. There was to be one comms check en route to targets by Teams Two and Three at 1200 hours local; Team One would contact SIS HQ at 1800 hours local. This would confirm links, and then they would go to radio silence unless there was an operational imperative. It appeared the technical aspects were working as planned. Director Jacobs confirmed no unusual comms traffic by the Chinese, plus work patterns at each site remained unchanged and predictable. He reported that superficial access to the systems at the target sights confirmed computers, and therefore security systems, were still controllable from his location in Cheltenham.

It was two a.m. and Teams Two and Three were dressed and ready to move. Having been given bright orange life-preservers and a harness, each had a rope to carry to the side of the ship. Netting had been put over the port side of the vessel, and they were required to climb down with a naval hand securing and guiding their rope, belaying them until they were inside the hatch of the submarine. At that point, they would take off their life vests and harness, which would be hauled back onboard the frigate. They went over the side two at a time, and once the first ones were on the deck of the smaller boat, the second pair would start their descent. Moving swiftly, and with the uneven pitching of the two vessels, Philip lost his footing and almost fell but managed to hold on. The rest of his climb down was more cautious but, he gratefully noted, uneventful. The last two unclipped their life jackets which were hauled up and the submarine hatch was sealed. Diving straightaway, the sub tilted to the right, turning towards the West and China. The new transport was cramped and smelly; it stank like a mix of an old house that had not been lived in for years and a decrepit workshop. The diesel craft was a great resource to get you where you needed to be, but provided a very basic home for the crew. The sailors on the vessel looked at the six passengers with wonder and awe. It was evident these were incredibly fit and capable guests. The ratings looked over their non-standard kit and guessed they were SAS.

Claire, passing the Captain, said, 'Thank you for the ride, and I hope that someday you and your boys will come to know what a great part in history you have played.'

'You are welcome, ma'am,' he said.

The Captain had no idea what rank this lady was, so he played it safe.

The teams were taken to the Officers' and Senior Rates' Mess where they had more coffee and another wait.

'Fuck me,' said Bill Martin, 'Now I wish we had parachuted in. My arse is numb with all this bloody sitting around.'

'Stop your moaning, Billy boy. Cheer up. You could be dead in the next few days,' said Yorkie.

Bill looked across and grinned, 'Not fucking likely with you covering my back, me old mate.'

Claire looked at the team and demanded, 'Anyone wanting to get off just say so. Torpedo tube four has been kept clear for such an eventuality.'

'That's not fair, ma'am,' said Sergeant Tony Lane. 'You know Yorkie and his fat arse won't fit in there.'

Yorkie muttered an obscenity in response, and everyone chuckled.

Philip picked up a pack of cards on the side and said,

'Pontoon, anyone?'

Before anyone could blink, all were taking part and for small stakes: toothpicks. After a couple of hours, they put the cards away and took cat naps. They were all rested and well-fed. Apart from a few visitors who said little, it was a dull journey.

The participants in Operation Fulcrum Force going in-country were now approximately one hour from the RV coordinates. They were to meet an indigenous fishing vessel. A Japanese early warning aircraft was on station and reported the all-clear code word. The crew of the aircraft didn't know what was going on but knew they had to report any other surface vessels in the vicinity. The submarine Commander came down and told the team that they would be surfacing within the next thirty minutes and that things might get a bit bumpy due to a small sea swell.

Everything required by the team members was attached to their bodies. They had all been given a black survival suit to keep the wind chill and water out and would sustain them if they fell into the cool waters. With lightweight life preservers too, their movement was restricted somewhat. These floatation devices would accompany them to the shore. Once on dry land, the dry-suits and lifejackets would be cached with other items near the beach landing point.

The sub was pitching and rolling far worse than when they got on. They waited for the "GO" signal, and Yorkie felt distinctly queasy.

'Confirmed contact signal,' came a call from the coning tower, 'five minutes to off-load.'

A machine gun was set to cover the fishing boat in case anything was amiss. The Japanese E767 AWACs gave a confirmatory all-clear as the frighteningly small fishing vessel approached bouncing on the waves.

'This looks like jolly fun,' Bill said in a piss-take posh accent, watching the even smaller vessel bob about like a piece of driftwood.

The team was now on the deck of the submarine and attached to a lanyard by a carabiner, clipped to the life preservers. If they slipped overboard, they would be soon pulled back to safety. They would be wet, cold and miserable but safe.

Yorkie looked at their next ride and thought, 'Bloody hell, we are all going to die. If this thing makes it safely to shore, I am going to mass when we get back.'

Claire turned to Yorkie and sensed from his facial expression he was having some rueful thoughts. She offered a bit of comfort, saying,

'It does look like a shipping disaster in the making, but that engine sounds brand new.'

Team members nodded in agreement. Getting on board required effort, and when within the confines of their new water-borne taxi, they were instructed by their new Captain to take specific positions.

Scott laughed saying, 'The Skipper said if we move around too much, the boat will capsize and sink.'

The uncomfortable journey to shore took about seventy minutes, and the ride was wet and chilly. The time passed slowly and the passengers felt vulnerable. A pungent smell of fish did not help Yorkies slight nausea. The boat suddenly landed on the shore with a jolt and a loud crashing sound. The pebbles raking against the sturdy wooden frame sounded like they were doing serious damage, but the Captain was unconcerned.

Scott said, shouting above the waves and wind,

'Over the side and get to shore.'

When off and with everyone safe, they helped unload the cargo of freshly-caught fish. Once landed, everyone helped push the boat back into the water, taking advantage of the incoming swell. The small vessel would head back to the harbour with a disappointing catch, but the Captain had made a year's wage in one night. Smuggling was a fairly mainstream occupation in these parts, and no one gave a crap about what the cargo was as long as the money was good.

The team moved quickly off the beach to the awaiting vehicles. Everything was being done in the moonlight to avoid drawing attention. They squirrelled away all their surplus kit in the vehicles. The expensive items of kit had a residual value to the drivers and could be hidden more effectively and safely at the lay-up point. Just like the boat, the lorries looked like they were on their last legs, but the engines sounded solid. The guests were offered an array of baggy Chinese clothes to wear over their own outfits. The clothes were worn and torn with spatters of mud, but they did not smell recently used. If the vehicle had to stop, and people got out, they would be less conspicuous. The traditional Chinese conical farmers' hats and facemasks would help cover their European features. The teams were separated and put into lorries. The vehicles had a false back wall which would hide the passengers from a superficial search. The fish crates were placed on the floor between the partition and the rear door. The smell, exacerbated by the lack of circulating air, physically assaulted the field agents' senses.

Claire joked, 'This has to be the worst Uber I've ever taken.'

A hatch opened to the front, and Scott asked the driver to leave it ajar for now to let in some fresh air.

The driver and passenger spoke in Chinese and laughed. Then Scott laughed.

'Come on, what was it?' asked Claire.

'These fellows here said they preferred the usual smell of fish to the peculiar catch they have landed tonight,' he answered.

They all laughed quietly.

Scott had taken time to speak with the two men driving them away and was assured everything was going as per the plan. Both lorries would take different backroad routes so as not to draw attention. The journey on the rough roads made for a restless but uneventful ride. The safe house was ready, and, once there, the teams would be fed and rested. In the other vehicle, poor old Philip had been sick, the fumes and smell of fish on the back of the motion sickness from the boat having caught up with him. Yorkie told him to splash water on his face and take on some liquids. No one was taking the piss today, but there would be time later. Yorkie was simply relieved it was not him being ill.

The two lorries arrived within minutes of each other at a darkened rural location. The vans opened, and the clayish smell of the ground was most welcome. The fishing catches were removed from the vans and put in the ice room; the team of visitors helped with this task. After being shown into the farmhouse, they were left with tea and a meal of rice and vegetables. The men outside were talking as if angry, but Scott explained they were just having a regular chat about what to take to market. The courtyard now had four lorries and eight locals. The amount of movement and noise was alarming.

Yorkie said in a whispered annoyed voice,

'What fucking happened to stealth and silence?'

Scott leant over and reassured him in a quiet tone,

'This is a standard day for these boys. The nearest house is about one click away. They would hear this racket most mornings. Most of the peasants in this area work for our guys. There is nothing to worry about.'

Yorkie gave him a hesitant thumbs up by way of thanks for the explanation.

After a period of banging and clattering, Mr Wang came in and introduced himself in not perfect but understandable English. Wang was one of the most popular names in China and meant King. Both Philip and Scott guessed this was not his real name, given the livery on the sides of the vehicles had a different designation. It was still dark, so Mr Wang wanted to show both teams how they would be concealed in the lorries and joked it would be less smelly than the fish vans. He laughed loudly. The fruit and vegetable vans had a false floor allowing the human cargo to lie down but get out quickly without having to climb over the produce.

Four vans, as usual, would set off to the markets, two each to Wuhan and Zhengzhou. The lead van would attend the market, drop off its produce and then meet at the RV which had been designated in both locations. The second vehicles were to assist in case of any technical issues with the primary vehicles. The drivers would take their regular route along the highways, paying the usual tolls and possibly bribes. Once in the target areas, the drivers would go for a takeaway meal at their normal food-stops. At the allotted time, the van with the passengers would go to the target area, undertaking a reconnaissance. The other would deliver the goods to the market. Mr Wang invited them not to worry, as this was a fairly routine matter for them. Outwardly, nothing would change or appear different. They had done these routes hundreds of times. They even knew several toll booth managers by name and many more by sight.

After the job, once both lorries were at the RV, they would drive back in convoy. They would split the remaining produce between the vans before setting off, as it was a usual practice not to sell all your goods at the market. Leaving at midday from the farm, the teams would arrive in their target cities at around nine p.m. A bit of dinner and a recce of the target area would bring them close to the time to get in position and ready.

'For now, just relax and eat what you need,' he said and showed them to the very basic bathroom facilities, a hole in the ground in an outside shed.

'If you go out, keep covered up,' said Claire.

Mr Wang's wife had made chicken and rice soup which looked unappealing but tasted fabulous. They had plenty of bottled water and Chinese protein bars for the journey. The time slowly wound by, and every noise put the SAS boys on alert. It was now daylight and the Chinese speakers were relaxed, their drivers laughing and joking. This was a big payday for them if all went well. If it went badly, their lives were on the line and their families would die too. For these peasants, the risks were worth the rewards.

In Vauxhall, the duty operations team noted that Teams Two and Three had landed safely and as planned, were now at the safe house North of Nanjing. The communications sets were also working as they sent a confidence signal every ten minutes which resulted in a pulse generating a bleeping sound of three pips. The bleep was a nano-second signal sent on a frequency hopping mode to avoid direction-finding equipment. All the satellites were in position with redundancy, if required. The in-house MI6 teams changed over at six a.m. local and every twelve hours thereafter. Section Chief Rankin – call sign Condor Ops 1 – was the senior man on shift just now. His number two was Lee Ford – call sign Condor Support 1. Peter Tomkins was in situ as general support for the two men, covering desks for short periods of absence and food. Claire would love the idea that Peter was the tea boy. As it was, all three men were just watching stationary assets at this time and monitoring voice communications in case a ground situation developed. Nothing was heard or happened. The tension made the tedium feel painful.

Everything was in place. The lack of incidents or activity was making Bill Rankin nervous, but he realised in these cases no news was always good news. Everyone was jittery but ready for the next phase of action.

Chapter 31

Let the Condor Fly

21 June 2024

It was a sunny day in Shanghai with partial clouds and a projected high temperature of 24° C. Rain was predicted for later in the day, continuing into the evening. June was the wettest month of the year in this part of the world. In the countryside around Nanjing, the rain had just started, and the temperatures might even reach 28 °C.

Steven Lang said light-heartedly, 'Being restricted in a tight compartment of a lorry for up to eight hours was no fun.'

He certainly got the best deal in terms of infiltration. Both he and Peter would meet up at midday and go through the operation one last time. In the afternoon, they would travel the route to their dinner venue for the evening and then onward to the target area for parking. Nothing was being left to chance. Peter had even arranged to pick up some dry-cleaning close to the target parking area so the drive past might appear normal and not look like he was checking out the route for some clandestine reason.

To the North near Nanjing, Teams Two and Three were wishing each other good luck inside the farmhouse as they were due to depart to their target locations in fifteen minutes. Yorkie had given Claire a good old hug, and she responded with a peck on the cheek which elicited a childish response from the other SAS lads.

The boys too got a hug, but Yorkie said, 'Anyone else tries to kiss me, they die now, mission or no mission.'

Claire took Philip to one side and said, 'You are making history. Your family and Britain will be proud of you. I have no doubt you will do a great job. All the best, and when we get back, we'll order a massive celebration dinner.'

She winked at him and hugged him as well.

'Thanks, Claire. I hope it all goes well.'

She said reassuringly, 'Of course it will. Remember your training. Things will be fine. Look after Yorkie for me.'

The teams had stowed their equipment and were wearing their peasant clothes on top of their operations attire. Their hats were too bulky to place in the hidden compartment and so were left covering a bumper crop of green apples. They each had ferreted away plenty of water and snack bars next to their crawl-in spaces and were as ready as they could be. A drizzle was falling. It was hot, but the rain made it bearable and freshened the air.

Bill Martin joked, 'I am going to smell like a wet dog with these clothes for the next few hours.'

Philip retorted, 'You have always reeked like a wet dog, from day one.'

Everyone laughed at the young man's humour.

The floor of the lorries had been padded with rough and well-worn quilted blankets. The journey would be uncomfortable but bearable. The Chinese speaker in each team would ride in the support vehicle, upfront with the drivers, and had been told the game plan for the day. It was a simple and eminently plausible story; they were off to market. They had the required papers to travel and plenty of yen to bribe the guards if stopped. Both Philip and Scott would provide a commentary on the local short-range, secure walkie-talkies, so there would be no surprises for those hiding in the rear of the vehicle. Just in case of a tactical surprise, their in-theatre hosts had provided a couple of Type 81 automatic rifles which were similar to the AK-47. Each weapon had two magazines of thirty rounds. The team members checked the weapons for safety. The magazines were loaded, weapons cocked and safety catches applied. The cocking of a weapon might give them away and would slow down reaction times in the rush to action, if required. The rifles were stowed in the secret compartments alongside the intrepid operators.

'That would even things up in a fire-fight,' Yorkie said, hoping against having to engage in one.

The two bodies secreted themselves into their cosy space and prayed they didn't need the call of nature any time soon or were liable to get cramp. Stops had been planned to stretch legs and have a toilet break, but each time they pulled over presented another possibility of discovery. This wasn't training now. This was for real, and if they got it wrong or were just unlucky, someone might die.

The vehicles were about to set off and then came a call at midday local time.

'Condor One to all call signs. Let the condor fly. I repeat, let the condor fly.'

'Romeo-2 copy,' and, 'Tango-3 copy,' responded Yorkie and Claire. On the local frequency, Claire asked her team to confirm the order. Everyone responded, and Yorkie did the same with his people.

Within minutes they were on their way. Claire could see on her digital notebook where they were and the progress of the other Team. Looking at it every twenty or thirty minutes helped to negate the feeling of isolation. Also, she found Sergeant Tony Lane to be a very bright companion, and he discussed a couple of operations he had been on. It was generally taboo to do this, but he thought, 'Here I am with a cool chick who makes Lara Croft look like Mary Poppins on sedatives.' Claire found his stories funny but unexpectedly eloquent. She told him about what she had done thus far in life, and he seemed genuinely impressed. Claire found herself liking this man. Tony kept on talking and entertaining her. She listened intently, laughing at his punchlines from time to time.

Scott, at the front of the support vehicle which was ahead of theirs, would give brief reports on distances and points of interest. They were coming up to the first toll which was an automatic system. The driver pulled out a card, and the barrier lifted, letting them through uninhibited. Two minutes later they were away from prying cameras, of which there were many, and Scott gave a quick resume of progress.

They could hear the Chinese chit-chat going on at the front, but they spoke so fast, a non-native Chinese speaker would struggle to understand.

Scott reported, 'The first few tolls are like that last one. When we change roads and are a bit further from the big cities, we have a greater chance of being stopped for security checks but mainly for the police to elicit bribes. Apparently, it's a good run if they don't get scammed.'

Team Two was having the same general experience. It was now three p.m. in China and very warm. The rain was coming down harder, a constant tinny drumming noise that, every now and then, built to a crescendo. This coupled with the sound of the road, only inches away from the hidden soldiers, meant that talking in the confined space was no easy feat. As promised, the vehicles did look like shit, with a few holes in the substructure caused by rust. Unfortunately, these gaps allowed spray from the wheels to periodically find its way into the hidden compartment. Parts of the floor covering were damp and added to an irritating lack of comfort. Yorkie was hoping that it didn't look like he'd pissed himself.

In London, the time was 0800 hours local. Tom MacDonald walked into the MI6 Operations Room and got an update from Bill Rankin, who reported,

'Progress is as expected and planned. No traumas. The vital signs of all team members are good. The communications are all live, and we have eyes on the vehicles.'

Tom said, 'I am staying on-site until the operation is over, and everyone is back in safe hands. Should anything of significance happen, let me know soonest. Text me, and I will come down immediately, ring if it is mega-urgent.'

He went back to his office and turned his sofa into a comfy sleeping space. He knew he would not have a deep sleep, but then he also understood that neither would the operatives on the mission in China. It was going to be a long couple of days for everyone involved. This was not the first time he had stayed for days on end at the office which always drove his wife crazy with worry. She was used to his irregular working patterns but did not like them.

The Teams pulled over, hundreds of kilometres apart, but within minutes of each other for a comfort break. Their legs were stiff, despite the regular but limited exercises they did to maintain circulation whilst lying down. Taking in the fresh air, they each did what was required, had a very brief face-to-face chat, and scurried back into their hidey-holes once more. After a couple more hours most of the hidden passengers had managed a cat nap. The noise of the rain and roads was hypnotic. The side roads joining the highways were more akin to off-road driving. Even the highways now and then would provide a huge bump because of potholes.

Yorkie said to Philip, after a rather aggressive thud in the road,

'You are supposed to tell passengers when we hit turbulence, twat.'

Philips's response was, 'Fasten your seat belts, and trays in the upright position and stay seated!'

About ten minutes later, the Team Two vehicle, in which Yorkie and Bill were hiding, swerved and then pulled over off the main road onto the not-so-hard shoulder composed of compact loose earth. Dust was now coming in where the rain spray had previously entered, and the two men coughed. They heard excited garbled Chinese voices.

'You have a flat,' Philip said over the RT. 'The lead vehicle will be back around in three minutes. Stay put for now. Do not move.'

Both men in the hidey-hole were cursing their luck. The fine dust was getting in their eyes and throats. As it settled, Yorkie took a swig of water and passed it to Bill. The van had stopped on the verge of the highway. Traffic was light but still passing at a fair lick. The second van arrived with a scraping of tires and more dust. Both men shook their heads but kept quiet. They heard anxious voices and a clunking sound outside.

Philip said over the RT, 'You are going to have to get out. You're lying on the spare and the vehicle jack. Don't worry. My vehicle will block your movement from cars on our side of the highway. Once out, hide behind the bushes to your left until the job is done. It should take ten minutes. I suggest we use this as our official stop.'

Both men moved quickly into the cover afforded by the foliage. In turns, they took a leak. Instinctively, they kept a watch on the terrain around them but without drawing weapons. The wheel was almost done when a local police car came to the rear of the second vehicle. A quick burst of the siren and flashing lights increased tension all around. The stress levels of all the operations staff went through the ceiling. As it approached, the vehicle made a crunching sound on the gravel, throwing copious amounts of dust in the air. Two rather officious but young policemen got out of their car with hands resting on their side-arms.

Philip whispered to his team leader, 'Let us deal with this.'

Instinctively both Yorkie and his colleague unclipped their Glocks ready for action. Yorkie attached the silencer. Bill felt down to where his combat knife was nestling; he lifted it out and slid it back in for reassurance. They heard raised and excited Chinese voices. It took a further ten minutes to explain to the police what had happened, where they were going and what they were doing. There was a cursory check of the vehicles, with more shouting by the Chinese officials. The police issued fines for stopping on a highway and being overloaded; the last fine was a total fabrication. No receipts were given for the payments, and the police went off after confiscating a handful of fruit and vegetables. Using this as their last stop before hitting Wuhan, they were now twenty-five minutes behind schedule, but could make that up. Yorkie did not call in the stop or the police intervention to Headquarters. For him, it was a non-event, as both he and Bill had kept well out of sight down an embankment. It was now 1800 hours local and about two and a half hours to the centre of the town. Traffic was becoming even lighter. Team Three were just pootling along, stopping as agreed and experiencing no ordeals other than aches and pains in the backside.

In London, the Operations Room had eyes on Team Two's vehicle pulling off the road. This was an unexpected stop. They saw the second Team Two lorry pull up behind, and a few moments later call signs Romeo 2-1 and Romeo 2-3 take off into hiding while Romeo 2-2 stayed with the vehicles. When the police turned up, they put a call to GCHQ,

'Can you intercept the transmissions of the vehicle behind Team Two's convoy?'

GCHQ control came back and said, 'We have the frequency of the police radio, but nothing has been called in yet.'

That was a good sign. The police were doing a routine stop. They watched the bodies move around the lorries and could make out waving arms. No weapons were seemingly drawn. They observed the pass-off of what they assumed was cash, and the police car left the scene. A note was made of the incident but Bill decided it was not of enough consequence to disturb Tom.

In Shanghai, Team One members were dressed in loose-fitting casual Western civilian outfits and wore the single-use paper masks that were used by many in China. It was just after 1800 hours, and they jumped into the work's car and headed out for a spot of dinner at one of Peter Goulding's favourite haunts. They served Western-style dishes which would suit Sergeant Steven Lang's tastes. They ordered a fairly light meal and observed their Chinese intelligence tail from the Consulate in the car park.

'Nothing unusual there,' Peter told his colleague.

At the restaurant, the black car with two men in it knew they were in for a wait, so they chatted away and took their meals themselves. The two UK operatives intentionally sat just out of the gaze of the Chinese counter-surveillance team. After about an hour and fifteen minutes, two men got into the Consulate car and set off back home. These characters were dressed just as the two operatives were with the same baseball caps and masks. They drove back to the Consulate. The two imposters were careful not to drive too fast as they could not risk being pulled over. The tail followed behind at a discreet distance, monitoring the activity of the Consulate car but in all honesty, not really taking too much notice of events. This was a routine occurrence they had been through many times, and it was barely worthy of note. They had nothing to report as they saw the black vehicle pull into the security gates of the Consulate compound.

Back at the restaurant, Peter and Steven both went to the washrooms and changed into more typical Chinese attire which had been stashed there earlier. In their new garb, they walked to a replacement car parked at the rear of the diner. This was a standard-looking local car, a bit battered and not particularly clean. The door was open, and keys were behind the sun visor. Their tools for the night were in the rear under a dirty old blanket. Driving off at a leisurely speed, they made their way to a construction site which they knew was not occupied. Checking the surrounding area using the night-vision goggles and digital notepads, it was all deserted as expected. They got dressed for the evening's activities and put back on the Chinese clothing over the top. They checked their equipment to ensure everything was working. Another slightly dishevelled car pulled up. It was call signs Mike 1-3 and Mike 1-4. They spoke in English, saying they had just passed the target area, but apart from some small social gatherings, the Institute of Microbiology & Immunology was as it should be. It was now 2200 hours local, and Mike 1-3 and Mike 1-4 would go back to the target. Mike 1-3 was working as a janitor, and tonight he was looking after Floor Seven. He had started a course at the University and asked if any jobs were going. He needed to supplement his income. Cleaning was the only option which he took reluctantly as the pay was poor. He was on shift tonight from eleven p.m. until three a.m. tomorrow. The second car would be parked across from the entrance to the University with Mike 1-4 acting as eyes and ears on the outside. He would also be the get-away driver picking up the infiltration team and whisking them away from the target area, all being well.

The two other operatives would affect an entry to the target via the front door which would be open, as usual. Once inside they would make their way to Study Room 712 and prepare for the agreed start time 2315 hours local. Before Pete and Steven set off, they checked their comms. They reviewed the camera they had concealed in the Study Room. All was quiet. They had confirmation from Mike 1-3 that there was no one home which was the code the Seventh Floor was clear. The infiltration team drove their car to a public parking garage about a one-minute walk from target. At 2250 hours local, they were in Study Room 712 with the cover off the ventilation shaft and standing by. The remote cameras had been placed in the corridor showing access routes to their location. Cleverly, Mike 1-3 had put a camera just outside the doors leading to Level Six showing the two guards sitting down beside the secure laboratory access. They were chatting and laughing, both holding magazines. If they continued to talk, their noise would assist in masking the team's movement one floor above them. All being well, Mike 1-3 would pick up the camera on his way out before setting off home at 0300 hours tomorrow.

In Wuhan and Zhengzhou, the convoys of fruit and vegetable lorries arrived within the required time-frame. The SIS agents switched vans with one of the local boys, and the decoy vehicles proceeded to their respective markets to offload the produce. The target-bound vehicles, as planned, went to a takeaway restaurant commonly used by lorry drivers.

There they picked up an assortment of takeaway food and drove to a pre-designated secluded spot. After reconnoitring the area, the teams took the opportunity to take a leak, grab a bite to eat and shake down their equipment. They were stiff but otherwise fine. It was now 2130 hours and had no abort calls.

'That's good,' said Yorkie. 'No abort call indicates everything is OK.'

The older agent had long forgotten about his raised heart rate when the police vehicle turned up. The option to despatch the Chinese police officers to the next life had gone through his mind, but the outcome achieved was far preferable. Philip and the local boys handled themselves really well, given the pressure.

As Yorkie was deep in thought, the local Chinese driver was applying new livery to the front and side of the vehicle. He changed the number plates plus made a few minor adjustments to the van's appearance. It was a black van which was most common in China. The make and model were also highly popular. Should the van be observed at the scene, it would at least point the authorities to a fruit and veg dealer in the south of the country.

Yorkie looked over his team. Philip looked on edge, but that was to be expected. Bill Martin seemed like he was having a day by the sea with his family. That was his stock in trade; cool and thoughtful. The driver was also looking a bit anxious. Yorkie pulled the team in; it was now 2205 hours.

'This should be a fairly straightforward in-and-out job. As rehearsed, Philip, you get the viruses, I will set the charges, and, Bill, you cover our arses. Our Chinese friend here will keep a watch outside. All OK?'

Everyone nodded. The driver spoke English, but it was a bit stilted so Philip repeated everything, and the Chinese man smiled and bowed towards the Team Leader.

Yorkie reciprocated and continued, 'Now remember; we may be picking up a new contact, call sign 'Baby Bird'. He should be at the target as we arrive or close by. The passwords have been told to everyone, so let's not get jumpy and kill any friendlies.'

Philip said, 'The driver told me we are about twenty minutes from the target and suggested that we undertake a drive-by as planned.'

'Perfect,' Yorkie replied. 'I will sit in the front with you, Philip, and the driver. Bill, let's get you in the back of the van for this last push. Masks and hats on. You will be able to see the locality for orientation purposes.'

Everyone looked happy and focused. They got set and concluded their drive-by recce. The streets were empty, and from the notebook, they could see no red spots depicting anything other than the expected guards at the target area. The rain persisted, but it was only a light shower.

Yorkie said, 'Watch for leaving footprints when we enter. We do not want to leave a tell-tale sign that they have had visitors.'

Philip thought, 'This was not raised in the training as all the target areas were inside and undercover. This is where Yorkie's experience counts. Small margins.'

In Zhengzhou, the story was similar but no pick-up of a friendly. The drill had been discussed many times, and nothing they had done was out of the ordinary. The recce went well. It was pissing down in Zhengzhou which added to the cover. Fewer people were out and about. Guards tended to be less diligent in their duties during such inclement weather, and less likely to want to go for an external wander. Guards all over the world missed the odd patrol but annotated the log as if it had been undertaken. The lorry parked in a lay-by close to the target, awaiting the signal to get the job done. It was dark and the only hazy illumination was from streetlights and external building security lights. The shadows would also help with their cover during the movement to the target entry point. All three teams were in the holding positions.

Tensions were rising back in London also. The MI6 clocks showed the time as London 1558 hours local and Beijing 2258 hours local.

Tom MacDonald demanded, 'Confirm lights out with GCHQ.'

Thirty seconds later he heard, 'Confirmed, lights out and no one home.'

'Condor 1, Condor 1, lights out and no one home,' said Tom MacDonald into the radio.

A few seconds later, 'Mike 1, copy.'

'Romeo 2, copy.'

'Tango 3, copy.'

All teams knew it was a go for the operation. No turning back now! GCHQ had taken control of the alarm systems and disabled the cameras watching the three laboratories and surrounding areas. The images of the infiltration routes were set to pre-recorded imagery taken ten minutes previously, running on a loop. This would bamboozle the guards into thinking all was clear.

'It's just a case of in and out,' Tom reminded himself over and over.

Just after 2300 hours, the Operations Room saw a small figure approaching the lorry of Team Two.

Tom MacDonald said, 'Do not call it in. It could be 'Baby Bird'.'

Back in Wuhan, a man was walking in the shadows and moving quite slowly and deliberately. The movement was not natural and was spotted by the Chinese driver. Philip had picked him up on the notebook imagery as a red dot approaching somewhat erratically. Philip alerted Yorkie.

Yorkie said, 'If he stops, it might be 'Baby Bird', and that's fine. If it is not him, just get rid of him and quickly.'

Yorkie pulled his hat down as if he were having a nap to hide his Western features. The young man knocked on the passenger window which Yorkie opened slowly, tilting his head away.

Looking terrified, the young Chinese man said in a strongly accented voice,

'You don't get many condors here, do you?'

Philip answered in Mandarin, 'Only in the summer.'

Everyone relaxed, it was 'Baby Bird'. Philip climbed past Yorkie and out of the van. The two men had a brief discussion in Mandarin, bowing to one another. Then they walked towards the target, disappearing behind some signage. The lorry cautiously pulled over to the other side of the road, reaching the designated delivery area and parking. The rear of the van opened, and Bill jumped out. Both he and Yorkie made their way to join the two younger men at the rear of the building which was secluded from general view. They were now all positioned at the fire escape door which had a corridor leading to the research institute.

Yorkie made the call.

'Romeo 2, Romeo 2. We are Abel. Repeat we are Abel.'

'Condor 1, copy,' said Tom MacDonald.

Yorkie could see that the building was heavily alarmed and presumed cameras covered all aspects of the structure. He trusted GCHQ to do their bit, and in reality, they had cock-all option just now. The door was breached using a small drill and a wire pull to activate the handle on the other side of the fire door. With a loud creak, the door opened just enough for the team to slip in and rest on the other side. It was pulled closed behind them.

'Thank fuck,' they all thought, 'no alarms.'

Yorkie had his Glock drawn, as did Bill. Philip was number two of three surrounded by trained killers and Chen Lau, their new team member, call sign 'Baby Bird'. Looking at the tablet, Philip observed only the three blue dots of the team on the map plus one red spot next to him. As he expanded the map on the screen, he saw four extra red dots about two hundred yards away. They seemed static for now, and they had not moved from when he checked upon arriving at the Wuhan Institute.

Yorkie transmitted, 'Romeo 2. We have 'Baby Bird' in hand. Repeat 'Baby Bird' in hand.'

'Condor 1, copy,' came the reply.

Yorkie turned to his three companions and said,

'Let's get the job done quietly and as we practised.'

About five hundred and twenty kilometres to the North in Zhengzhou, Team Three had pulled into their target area, and Scott MacGregor had noticed a small red marker indicating a life form by their entry point. This set his pulse racing, and back in London they could tell from the biometrics on his tracker, he was stressed.

He pointed this out to Claire and Tony saying, 'This could be a guard or a member of the public or just a large dog.'

The latter was unlikely because there were few strays in China.

After a brief discussion, Claire directed Scott to approach the area in Chinese dress and assess the situation. Condor 1 back in London had also noticed the unexpected heat spot and called it in, just in case the team had missed it. Team 3 acknowledged. As Tango 3-2 moved cautiously down the alley to the entry point of the target, he heard a rustling sound ahead. He took out his knife, for now keeping it concealed from view. As he approached the entrance steps that led down to a covered doorway, he noticed a vagrant, smelling of rice wine and urine, had located himself there for a few hours of sleep. As Scott took a further step forward, the startled drunk leapt to his feet in fear. The frightened small man believed he was being mugged and quickly brandished a small farmer's knife with a wooden handle and short steel blade. In panic, the peasant started to raise his voice but was quietened by a swift and powerful thrust to the throat. The insertion of a hard blade into the man's neck caused him to gurgle on his own blood, and his eyes were wide open, showing great fear and shock. Scott had hold of the man's arm with the knife in hand. The man's eyes closed as he exhaled his last gasp, and a smell of stale wine and bad breath wafted in the air. Within seconds, the vagrant went limp, slumping to the ground in a pool of blood. It was silent again. Back in the van, no one had been aware of the killing that had just taken place.

'Tango 3-1 and 3-3, proceed to my position,' said Scott dispassionately.

Within seconds, both Claire and Tony were by his side and realised what had happened.

Tony said, 'You get in that door. I will put our friend here in the wagon.'

Blood was still oozing from the dead man as Tony pulled him to the lorry, and, with the help of the driver, put the lightweight man in the hidden compartment. The rain was heavy and would help erase the signs of the dead man's presence in time. The blood would wash away quickly and, with luck, before the guards noticed anything. As Tony arrived back at the infiltration point, the door was open, with Claire and Scott waiting inside.

'Boss,' said Tony, 'let's get our driver to drop the body off at our lay-up point and meet us back here in thirty minutes.'

Scott said, 'No. I suggest we get the second vehicle to come here, and our man can dispose of the body after meeting us at the RV.'

'Good idea, Scott,' said Claire nodding.

A quick call on the secure local walkie-talkie got everything in motion. The only problem was that they'd have no external cover, but would have to risk it.

'Tango 3. Tango 3,' she voiced into her comms with London. 'We are Abel. Repeat, we are Abel.'

'Condor 1, copy.'

She recognised Tom MacDonald's voice and found it comforting.

They proceeded further into the building. Cameras were set as per the training. Though the fatality had not changed the plan, it made it more complicated. With Tony securing the laboratories' approaches and monitoring the position of the guards, the other two were at work doing their magic, Claire with the viruses and Scott with the explosives. Scott almost repeated a training accident by nearly knocking a glass jar to the floor, but his lightning reflexes saved the moment. Claire noticed inscriptions on some vials which didn't match up with her notes of what should be in there. She asked Tango 3-2 for assistance. The labels read IV34HS, which was an unknown element, so she took it anyway. All the other target samples were located and put in the vacuum flasks. What she did not consciously realise was she had the "Yellow Petal" vaccine, which had been labelled incorrectly.

Back in Shanghai, Peter Goulding said, 'Mike 1. Mike 1. We are Abel. Repeat, we are Abel.'

'Condor 1. Copy,' Tom MacDonald said for the third time.

Mike 1-1 was now in the ventilator shaft crawling along the ducting and making sure he only placed his weight on the joints and fixed points. They knew from training the conduit would only take one man's weight at a time, and that was only with careful negotiating. The flimsy panelling would easily dent and possibly come away under the full pressure of a man's body mass. It was slow progress, but there was no point rushing. They had all the time they needed because at their location no guards were patrolling. The Chinese guards just sat outside the laboratory door reading magazines and talking nonsense, the way most bored guards do. The only way they would know something was up would be if they repeated the accident which occurred in training, when a careless foot knocked a shelf full of glass to the floor. Both men knew this and had learnt to pace their movements. Just like crawling through undergrowth stealthily, you looked at every placement of your hands, elbows, knees and feet, whilst keeping your head down. To rush would court disaster. Time was on their side.

Once Peter arrived at the ducting that bent downwards to the Sixth Floor, he set in place a brace on which he could lower himself six feet on a short rope using a descender. His movements remained deliberate and under control. Upon arriving at the bottom of the duct, he could see the lab through the grating he would need to remove.

He called back to Sergeant Steven Lang in a whisper, 'Mike 1-1 in position Bravo.'

'Copy,' was the whispered reply.

Mike 1-2 followed Peter's steps into the ventilation shaft, taking care to replicate the steady and purposeful movement of his colleague. He was aware that the noise being generated by the movement reverberated more than in the training set-up. He could only think it was due to the echo effect of the longer pipework. Steven slowed his pace, taking a few seconds between movements so any sound generated would not be compounded with the sound of the next movement.

A few minutes later, the janitor on their level was quietly going about his cleaning tasks when a young man and young woman, obviously intent on some form of sexual encounter, came into his corridor. The trendy-looking young man was surprised to see the lowly cleaner and took his hand off the breast of his younger-looking companion.

The janitor looked up and turned off his mechanical polisher and said in Mandarin,

'You cannot be here. The place is being cleaned.'

The man laughed at him, demanding, 'Shut up, or you will be sacked. My father is a senior party member and knows the Principal.'

Completely ignoring the pleas of the janitor, the adolescent tried Room 712s door, but it was locked, and the blinds were closed. He staggered five paces and found Room 709 open. Both the young people were intoxicated. The aggressive youngster proceeded into the open classroom and unceremoniously dragged his companion in behind him. Room 709s door was slammed closed and locked from the inside. The janitor heard a scraping sound of tables and chairs and a great deal of laughing from inside.

After a few moments, Mike 1-3 called in the development to his fellow saboteurs but said he had eyes on the situation, and there was no immediate threat. Mike 1-3 started his polisher once more, the noise being a useful cover for both his colleagues and unintentionally, the love birds. The guard's downstairs had not stirred from their relaxed seated positions. Mike 1-1 looked at his notebook and saw two red hot spots across from their entry room and the two guards about fifteen metres away from him who had not moved position all night. Peter acknowledged the call and proceeded to remove the plate covering the extraction unit access panel. One of the small screws dropped to the floor. The noise was almost inaudible, but he knew it was that sort of clumsiness which might be a showstopper. Removing the remaining screws without incident, he rested the square of aluminium inside the ventilation system with the remaining screws set into a piece of putty. The putty was an idea developed in training as the screws were always rolling away, generating more movement and noise: a simple solution to a vexing problem. Next, he lowered down the empty viral flasks on a lanyard onto the table immediately beneath him. Mike 1-2 was now directly above him. The whispered instruction was to lower away, and the explosives were manoeuvred down in three distinct transactions. As each was received, they were, in turn, lowered to the table in the office beneath Peter.

Training had taught both them and their supervisors that by the time Mike 1-2 had gotten into position to lower himself into the laboratory, Mike 1-1 had completed his tasks with the viruses. Therefore, Mike 1-2 was to lower down to Position Bravo and await to receive the flasks with the vaccine. His other job was to keep eye on the guards and warn of any movement. Just as Mike 1-2 was about to put out his head through the hatch, Peter was back with the vaccines.

Semi-startled, Steven commented softly, 'That was fucking quick.'

Peter replied with a whisper and a confident smile, 'I told you the training would pay off.'

Two canisters with a foam outer covering and a stainless-steel top and bottom painted matte black were handed over. Steven secured both canisters into the pouches on his belt and double-checked the fasteners were tight. Preparing to set off back the way he came, he reached on to his belt and took out two mechanical ascenders. Attaching these to the 9 mm rope hanging in front of him, he started to climb up. Back up to the level, as he shimmied along to the first opening, he could hear Peter climbing into the ventilator. The noise echoed in the chamber, they both halted and hoped the guards did not hear it.

Steven commented, after checking his monitor and seeing the camera shot of the guards still sitting and talking,

'Keep going. They did not hear or are too lazy to react.'

A few moments later Mike 1-2 was lowering himself back onto the table in Room 712. He looked around. Nothing had changed, and confirmed he was at the starting point. Mike 1-3 also confirmed all was quiet apart from the love birds in the opposite room. Back on the Study Room floor, he put on his indigenous outer clothes and placed the canisters into a small rucksack and waited. After five minutes, Peter's head filled the opening in the ventilation shaft, and one minute later, he was on the floor. Steven stood on the table and reaffixed the ventilation shaft cover whilst his comrade put on his native civilian clothes to cover their working attire. The baggy outfits allowed access to the weapons if needed. Four minutes later they were ready to extract themselves from the target.

In Wuhan, the team was almost finished when Bill Martin called,
'Guards on the move.'

They were not expected to undertake a patrol until midnight. It was only 2325 hours.

'What's their twenty?' asked Yorkie.

'It looks like they are going for an external sweep of the building; a perimeter check,' replied Bill.

Yorkie said, 'Keep doing your jobs, but, Philip, quickly let the driver know he might be getting a visit.'

Alert, Philip notified the driver of the situation who hastily turned off and hid his walkie-talkie. He then picked up a box of food plus chop sticks and started casually eating some noodles in his cab. The food was cold by now, but no one could tell. As the operatives inside kept working, the driver outside had his dinner rudely interrupted. His lorry door was yanked open, and he was aggressively pulled out of his van. Dropping his noodles on the floor, the driver cried out in pain.

The guards kicked him repeatedly, yelling, 'What are you doing here? What is your name? Why have you parked here?'

The driver struggled to get the words out as repeated kicks winded him and replied, as in shock,

'I am only eating my dinner, sir. I apologise. I don't know the area well and thought this just looked a good place to have my meal. The parking bay was empty and off the road.'

Then one of the guards said, 'He has a knife.'

The other guard clumsily pulled his weapon to his shoulder and pulled back the cocking mechanism.

He then ordered, 'Do not move, or I will shoot. Keep your hands where we can see them.'

The driver acted even more scared now and said,

'It's a fruit knife. I sell fruit and vegetables. I am on my way to the market not far from here, the open-air market over the bridge. Let me show you.'

The man feigned terror, and the guards were taken in that this man was a peasant who knew how to grovel.

Whilst being held by the scruff of his neck and being slightly choked, he sidled around his vehicle and opened the back door to show them the fruits and vegetables. The guard not pointing his rifle struck the man around the head and called him a peasant pig, throwing him to the ground once more.

Laughing, a final kick to the ribs came with a warning,

'If you are not gone from here in five minutes, we will shoot you.'

Desperately trying to catch his breath and not having to fake tears, the man promised,

'I will go. I will leave now. Sorry, sir. I am leaving now.'

The guard said with a hateful chuckle, 'Pick up that mess before you go,' pointing at the noodles strewn across the floor.

'Yes, sir, yes, sir,' came the panicked response.

One guard gave him a final kick in the side. The driver restrained himself from drawing his knife. He would have dearly loved to kill these young bastards who respected nothing. They reflected everything that he hated about his country. He was incensed but realised that doing nothing was the right thing. If he appeared weak, they would walk away.

Team Two had finished their tasks and were waiting to leave the building.

Philip saw on the notebook that the guards were heading back to their original positions and would not pass their exit point. The guards were now wet from the rain and had dealt with a situation which would look good in their logbooks. They probably thought it was time for tea.

The driver scrambled to his knees and turned on his walkie-talkie. He also started picking up the noodles to waste some time. He wiped the blood from his face.

Philip radioed the driver asking, 'Is the coast clear?'

The driver confirmed in a calm but cracked voice,

'All clear.'

The team returned to the vehicle swiftly and silently, running in a crouched position. Yorkie and Bill were quickly in their hidey-holes with the vacuum flasks and all the spare kit. Philip and Chen Lau were in the lorry cab with the driver. Within a few seconds, the team was extricating themselves from the target area. The intervention by the guards had almost cost them the mission, and their pulses were racing again.

Yorkie said to Bill off-mike, 'That's two fucking close run-ins today. We have been lucky.'

Bill responded sarcastically, 'Since when have you believed in luck? You always said, "Those that train hard and plan well, putting every endeavour into something, make their own luck".'

Yorkie glibly said, 'You're right. I will shut the hell up.'

Yorkie put in the call saying, 'Romeo 2. Romeo 2. We are Cain and Jerusalem. We are Cain and Jerusalem.'

Uncle Tom's voice had a definite jubilant note when he replied,

'Condor 1, copy that, Romeo 2.'

Team Three's secondary van pulled up just in the nick of time. They had taken a few moments longer to clear all the blood from the floor in the hallway and laboratory using water only. The paper waste was being carried off-site, as were the two canisters full of viruses. Everything else was as it should be. The van pulled up, and Claire and Tony jumped in the back, hiding behind some empty crates which offered little cover. Scott was riding shotgun again. As the lorry pulled away and conscious there was a long drive back, Claire transmitted,

'Tango 3. Tango 3. Cain and Jerusalem. Repeat Cain and Jerusalem.'

That familiar voice replied, 'Condor 1. Copy, Tango 3.'

Within the SIS London Headquarters, there was a quiet celebration. So far, the operation was going well. The Operations Team noted there had been an incident upon their arrival but did not seek clarification of it because they were helpless to act. They saw Tango 3-2 engage the target and observed Tango 3-3 move the lifeless body to the vehicle. Listening to the RT calls, Condor 1 was content the right decisions were arrived at, and the team was acting in a calm and collected way. Keeping your eyes on the prize was always important, and Claire put the mission first.

The boys in Shanghai were now ready to leave their target. The janitor went into Room 712 and explained that the couple were still in Room 709.

Peter said, 'Let's just move. They could be there for hours, and if they are pissed, what would they say if they saw us?'

Both he and Steven Lang walked down the corridor as if just finishing a lecture. They proceeded down the stairs, not passing a soul, out the front and into the car. A few people were milling around, but it was too easy. They drove directly back to the Consulate keeping their heads down. A call was put to security guards at the gate who knew something was on-going but had no idea what. The car slowed as it reached the gate and was admitted without impediment. It went through the first gate and then the inner gate to turn around, without seemingly stopping, to come straight back out. On the way out, the driver stopped for a matter of seconds, went to the boot and took out some food cartons, got paid, and he was on his way within a few minutes. The Chinese State Security were caught on the hop, and a counter-surveillance car followed the delivery vehicle as it left the Consulate. It was pulled over a few hundred yards down the road. After a few aggressive questions with badges and guns being shown, the actions of the driver and the food order seemed genuine. Mike 1-4 was sent on his way without further questioning. What the Chinese Counter-surveillance Team had not noted was as the car was turning slowly two bodies slumped out and rolled to the side of the road under some bushes and lay there unmoving. The two agents were safe, but the driver still had to convince those outside the gate there was nothing suspicious going on, which he did. Once the counter-surveillance car moved away, the two men quietly walked around the back of the consulate and entered a trades entrance which had been left open.

Gaining access to the safety of the Consulate, Peter put the call in, saying,

'Mike 1. Mike 1. Jerusalem and Joshua. Repeat Jerusalem and Joshua.'

This was the key target with the vaccine secured.

Uncle Tom said, 'Copy that,' and let out a yell in celebration to the Operations Room. He shook the hands of all those present, and he could feel himself welling up with both pride and relief. The operation had gone supremely well thus far. He felt exonerated for being a hermit over the past month or so, planning this whole escapade. His heart was racing, and his head was pounding, but he was enjoying the relief of the moment.

He knew two teams were still on the ground, and plenty could still go wrong, but the main prize was theirs. It was now twenty-eight minutes past midnight in China and 1728 hours local in London. Tom knew the etiquette was for the Chief of the SIS to let the Prime Minister know the outcomes, so he went to see his boss George Main and gave him the good news. George offered hearty congratulations, and Tom could sense he still had doubts about the next phase involving the PM.

Chapter 32

Home to Roost

22nd Jun 2024

It was now the early hours of the morning in central China. Four vehicles, two full of agents, were heading either south or east towards Shanghai. The natural urge was to drive quickly away from the target sites and put time and distance between those areas and the attack force. The sensible action was to keep within the speed limits and act as if it was just another day at work. This was not a time to allow their bodies and minds to switch off. The operatives still needed to be prepared to react to any unforeseen situation. This remained vitally important.

The roads in China in the early hours of the morning were very quiet. The teams were tired, having not slept properly for days on end. Covert travelling, even with friendly forces, seldom allowed operatives to rest properly, and it was taking its toll. The group had mixed feelings of jubilation and trepidation. They knew the technically challenging part of the operation was complete, but that would count for nothing if they did not get back home with the viruses and, more importantly, the vaccines. Teams Two and Three maintained radio silence but were desperate to know if Team One had secured the first prize. The best clue that everyone had completed their tasks was the lack of a call to suggest a change of plan.

Scott MacGregor sat in the front of the lorry watching landmarks come and go. He considered what happened leading up to him killing that poor peasant. Replaying the scenario over and over in his mind, he could see no alternative, and he needed to believe that deep down inside. The consequence of not taking swift and decisive action might have been devastating for the mission and his newly-acquired friends. Scott had killed before but regretted it with all his heart. This was a sad aspect of his work, and he had to reconcile his thoughts that this man gave his life, if unwittingly, to prevent the deaths of millions of others. The saving grace of this man's demise was that it was quick, and the man felt no real pain, just momentary panic and then nothing. However, experiencing the smell of the peasant farmer and sensing his last breath made it all more real. Killing from range using a rifle, or even a handgun, was very different from feeling a man's life-force departing his body whilst you held him. The body was dumped in a layby some miles out of the city. With no ID and possibly no criminal record, his murder would never be solved. The authorities would see the victim as someone who was an undesirable and therefore would put no effort into solving the crime; possibly not even recording it.

In the solitude, what was occupying Tony's mind was his pent-up fear of being captured. This was not a subject that he spoke about to anyone. It was the terror and great burden he carried around with him. Nothing that war makes you do compares to the ordeal of being tortured by a remorseless enemy. Having been caught by the Taliban in Afghanistan and tortured for days on end, he never wanted to go through that again. His nightmares came back from time to time. That feeling of being completely helpless and the fear building every time a new person walked into the cell was incomprehensible to anyone who had not experienced it. Tony knew fear and felt less than whole because of it. His liberation came at a cost to his comrades, but they had destroyed the Taliban stronghold. On his return, Tony had lost both his wife and his child, having taken months to attempt to readjust to family life. It was too late for his wife of eight years who had borne the stresses of being an SAS soldier's wife for too long. Now, he had to stay calm and deal with his anxiety.

The rain kept on coming, and the only difference between the drive to the targets as opposed to away from them was that it was completely dark. The traffic was very light, and therefore noise levels were not so irritating. The tolls were easily negotiated as they were not so congested. Their vehicle paid one minor bribe, sought by a young police officer looking to supplement his wages. The drivers' fatigue only served to increase their desire to get home, increasing their willingness to cough up the small amounts of cash being extorted.

The roads felt even rougher than the morning's journey. One saving grace was the temperature was cooler at a respectable 15° C, so it was less stifling for those concealed away. The vehicle occupants were encouraged to eat to keep their strength up and take on plenty of liquids. Keeping hydrated maintained alertness. The extraction should be uncomplicated if all the players were as up to their game as the current crop.

'Condor 1. Condor 1. To all call signs, Starlight in position. Repeat, Starlight in position.'

London was passing the codeword to indicate that an RAF Aircraft was on the runway at Shanghai Hongqiao International Airport. The aircrews were expecting a special cargo of PPE which had been agreed as part of the deal to hold a state visit for the Chinese leader. In addition, there was a late addition to the manifest as one of the Consular staff from Shanghai had been taken severely ill with what seemed like Covid-24. The Chinese medical authorities had seen the casualty and confirmed the medical findings. Now in what appeared to be an induced coma and, on a ventilator, he was being flown out with a medical team from the Royal Navy forces exercising in the Sea of Japan to assist with the recovery of the patient back to the UK. They were to arrive at Shanghai Hongqiao International Airport by helicopter by 0900 hours local.

The operations teams were making good progress, and it was evident that no alarms had been raised at the target sites. Had there been any alerts, GCHQ would have notified Condor 1, who in turn would have alerted the teams. If the presence of the teams was detected, the explosives would be detonated prematurely. Just now, the mission was still covert which was making the whole extraction possible without the need to take up the range of contingency plans that had been drafted. If anything had gone wrong, in all likelihood, no one would be going home. However, plenty of time still remained for things to go sour, and that is why it was important to stay alert and responsive.

It was 0855 hours local, and Team Two's vehicles were first to arrive at the rally point with the PPE carriers. They pulled in cautiously at a truck stop north of Shanghai in the town of Danyang, where hundreds of lorries were waiting to go either to the port or the airport. The whole place was bustling with people. The smaller lorries pulled up and parked in an area away from the bulk of the other larger lorries and people waiting. After a quick discussion, one of the drivers went for a wander. They were at the RV in good time, if a little early. Forty minutes later, Team Three entered the truck-stop and pulled alongside. Both teams were where they should be. The smaller produce vehicles attracted no great attention, but it was still thought best to keep the European contingent interred as long as possible. Just ten minutes later, three large articulated lorries pulled up next to the diminutive grocery vehicles.

The sound of airbrakes assaulted the eardrums of those in hiding, as the articulated vehicles stopped right by them, and they were at a level adjacent to the engaged brakes. The smell of burning oil was almost overpowering as the brakes were applied. The commotion that followed was a typical greeting from friends. After a further ten-minute wait which seemed to last forever, the RT came alive.

Scott said over the walkie talkie, 'Two of the lorries have the PPE with concealed spaces for the teams. The drivers suggested that one team gets on board the first vehicle followed by the other on to the second lorry. Team Two, you are the first to climb into the rear of the first PPE lorry.'

Yorkie and his team moved quickly and were covered from view by other vehicles and people milling around. Once they were inside, the rear doors were closed with a squeak of metal on metal. The rear storage areas had dim internal lights, just enough to see once the players' eyes had adjusted. Within each lorry were three pallets of PPE, and each pallet had a storage area for one person.

Yorkie said, 'Now that Chen Lau is on the team, two people will need to be in one space. It will be tight but OK; it won't be for long.'

Yorkie told Philip to convey the instructions to the new recruit.

'You and 'Baby Bird' go into unit one, as you are the smallest. Also, you can explain to him in Chinese any instructions that might follow. That would be easier. Agreed?'

It was agreed. The first pallet was approached by the vehicle's driver who moved one of the boxes at the bottom and took it out of the pile. This small entrance was just about enough of a gap for Yorkie's huge frame to access the vacant space inside the construction of PPE boxes. The internal void benefitted from all-round cover. The idea was that a person could slide in on their backs, sitting up in the space. There was room for a crouched standing position. The stress on the legs would be too much over a long period but would be good for a while to stretch. With little room to move, their real issue was muscle cramps, especially if they had to exert themselves at no notice.

Yorkie went first to look in and came back out stating, 'Perfect,' in a confident tone.

'Right, Philip, you and 'Baby Bird' in this one,' he pointed and continued.

At that point, it was evident they had a problem. Philip and the new arrival were whispering back and forth in anxious tones in Mandarin.

Taking Yorkie and Bill to one side, Philip explained,

'Chen Lau suffers from claustrophobia and cannot, will not go inside the boxes. He said he is already feeling sick, just at the thought. He will not go.'

'What?' said Bill feeling the strain of an unexpected problem, 'You are having a bloody laugh here. We haven't got all fucking day.'

Yorkie put up his hand and said, 'We have three choices. He goes in under his own steam. We put him out with morphine and hope for the best. Lastly, we kill him. I do not think putting him back to Wuhan or just letting him go here is a sensible option. It could expose everything. I have authority to take him out if he looks like he will compromise the mission. I do not want to do that, but that is an option.'

Yorkie paused, 'Philip, speak to him again and impress upon him that we can give him a sedative, but if it looks like he is going to give us away at any time, we will kill him. Can you do that? Also suggest to him we could leave him behind, and we could ask the lorry drivers to return him to Wuhan.'

In Yorkie's mind that last option would not happen. If 'Baby Bird' wanted to stay, he would require Bill to kill the boy. Despite Yorkie's admiration for what Philip had achieved, he suspected the young agent would not be able to kill in cold blood. Philip went off and calmed Chen Lau down. He spoke with him explaining their predicament, that something had to be agreed and now.

In the meantime, Romeo 2-1 spoke with Condor 1 and was ordered to take whatever action he thought was best for the completion of the mission.

'That's no fucking help,' Yorkie said to Bill, feeling the pressure of his predicament.

'Yorkie, if you need me to sort it, you know I will, but let's see if the boy will settle down. We have twenty minutes before we leave,' replied Bill trying to take the pressure off his pal.

Team Three was now installed in their PPE cocoons without any issues. The enclosed rear of the lorries was stiflingly hot and uncomfortable. It was a two-and-a-half-hour drive to the airport, and once on a sealed and airborne aircraft, they would be let out. In total they had about three to four hours to endure this particular ordeal. They all had plenty of water and snacks, and if they needed a piss, the instruction was to do it in the bottle. It was small inconvenience to endure for home and freedom and, of course, success.

Philip returned to Yorkie saying, 'He said he will try but would like some sedatives.'

Bill extracted his first aid kit and immediately produced three ampoules of morphine.

'This will do the trick,' he said to Philip. 'Give him one, and if he needs it, give him another. Any more just now might kill him.'

They agreed. 'Baby Bird' apologised and took the morphine and injected it into the fleshy part of the thigh. He quickly started to go limp, and they manhandled him into position.

Just before the cover box was put back in place, Bill took hold of Philips shoulder,

'If he is going to compromise us, kill him. Do you understand, mate, if it's him or the mission, he dies! Get that clear in your mind now. Do you understand?'

Philip nodded his agreement and understanding. Now concealed in amongst the PPE, Philip looked at the boy opposite using the torch on his handgun. He sat facing this fellow he hardly knew, realising the enormity of what he might have to do. Chen Lau was asleep, and Philip knew he would need to make sure he stayed that way until they were on the aircraft and safe. They had considered Chen Lau could stay out of the hiding place until the vehicles arrived close to the Airport, but the risk of having to deal with a distraught person with guards close-by was far too dangerous.

At 1035 hours local time, the convoy of three lorries left for the airport. The relief for those hiding in the rear units was profound.

Looking at her watch, Claire thought, 'We should be at the airport by 1300 hours, with take-off at 1400 hours. That's not too much of an ordeal.'

Everyone had their digital notebooks out which gave a bit of light, and they could monitor progress.

They all quietly thought, 'All being well, we will be safe by mid-afternoon.'

In terms of comfort, the journey was worse than the fruit and vegetable lorries. It was hotter with hardly any air movement. It was dark and the floors were hard. The consignment pallets had cling film wrapped around them for rigidity which only made matters worse. It was like sitting in a plastic bag. The only positive was that, when the vehicles braked, the boxes shifted which brought in a waft of fresh air.

Being physically and mentally strong, the teams would not find this an issue. However, for 'Baby Bird', Yorkie had his concerns.

Yorkie's voice sounded in Philip's ear, 'How's the boy doing, Phil?'

Philip put on his torch, 'He is still out like a light.'

'That's great. We have been on the road for an hour, so in thirty minutes give him another morphine just to be sure he remains that way.'

'Copied,' responded Philip.

Thirty minutes later, Philip reported, 'Morphine given.'

Yorkie acknowledged the message. Almost everyone inside the boxes was feeling travel sick which was exacerbated by the extreme heat and lack of fresh air flow. The constant jostling wasn't helping either. The sitting posture was almost as bad as a stress position prisoners endure during torture. The pain being felt was a real struggle.

'The boxes are good sound insulation,' Yorkie said encouragingly over the RT, 'and unless someone knew you were here, there would be no indications giving you away.'

He wanted to reassure his team and let them know he was still there and thinking about them.

Tony Lane was struggling being on his own too but knew he would get over it. He had found Claire's presence on the outward stretch of the journey a great comfort. Now alone, he was wrestling with his own demons once more. Not the physical pressures but the mental challenges and it took all his efforts not to break radio silence.

The lorries arrived at the airport and got straight through the outer security cordon. The inner security, giving access to the taxiway, was a bit stickier. The cargo was expected, but it was a few hours late. The lead driver apologised humbly and said one vehicle had a minor technical issue, and he lifted up a dirty old hose waving it around as proof. After some aggressive words from the on-duty guard, things settled down. As this consignment was classified as a priority cargo, the vehicles were reluctantly given the OK to proceed. An airfield escort vehicle was sent to guide the three lorries to the waiting military aircraft off in the distance. Parked away from the passenger terminals, the lorries took ten more minutes to navigate their way to the huge transport aircraft waiting. As they pulled up behind the C-17 Globemaster III aircraft, the rear ramp was down and ready to receive the goods. Royal Air Force personnel were waiting patiently and were accompanied by airport logistics personnel and an officious customs man with his two security guards, both of whom were armed.

A forklift was on-site ready to off-load the pallets from the lorries to the aircraft ramp. After checking the delivery paperwork and cross-checking export documents, the customs officer, after a period of posturing, gave the order to off-load. The concealed teams had sensed they were at the airport due to the sounds around them and the intermittent driving. When the rear of the lorries opened the rush of fresh air revived them but set their hearts racing. The noise levels outside were excessively loud with the aircraft idling engines and the sound of motors running plus shouting voices. Small streams of light pierced the eyes of the hidden. The assault on the senses set everyone on edge.

The first pallet to be taken was that of Team Three's lorry; each unit took about seven minutes to be placed on the tailgate lift, dropped to ground floor level, picked up by the large forklift and positioned on the rollers on the aircraft. The next pallet on the lorry was moved by manual trolley to the edge of the door and on to the tailgate, being dropped to the ground level ready for the large fork-lift to carry it away. The Chinese customs official with his armed guards were presently checking over each load of goods, just to see that it was what the paperwork said it was.

The squat official unceremoniously kicked the boxes to see that they felt like masks and gowns. On one pallet he opened a rectangle box with a blade to confirm what was inside and found no surprises. The bespectacled official seemed generally content. Pallet number three had a major wobble, and Claire who was hidden inside almost felt herself gasp as she thought the whole lot was going over. After twenty-three minutes the first lorry was empty, closed up and moved to one side of the tarmac taxiway.

The next lorry reversed a small amount into position. The hissing sound and stilted motion of the air-brake system kicking in rocked and alerted everyone inside their refuges. It was their turn to move. The rear door opened, and the gust of fresh air hit everyone cowering inside like cold water to the face. Philip Wong's unit was first to be lifted by the large forklift. Small shards of light penetrated just enough to see that Chen Lau had his eyes open. Philip turned on his torch to assess the state of his new friend. Chen looked as if he were sick, and his eyes were those of a madman. As the pallet was being jostled on the forklift, 'Baby Bird' was clutching and pushing at the sides of the boxes and making a murmuring sound.

Philip said in Chinese, 'Quiet, friend. We are almost home.'

His audience wasn't hearing him. The young man suffering from claustrophobia and general disorientation was also having an out-of-body sensation. He didn't know where he was or who was this man in front of him. The light being shone in his face was adding to the confusion and increasing the boy's panic. Chen's noise level increased. Philip was alarmed that this man would alert the guards to their presence. He learned over and put his hand over Chen's mouth, but the Chinese lad was strong and wrestled him off. The boxes were shifting somewhat and murmurings became louder. Outside the customs official thought he had heard something above background noise of the aircraft and vehicles, but shrugged when he didn't hear it again.

The pallet was unceremoniously dropped on the aircraft's tailgate, and after a walk-around a few seconds later, the customs agent waved on the loading. The second and third pallets were loaded without incident. The teams were on board the aircraft. The last lorry was unloaded, and as planned, the second to last pallet lost a few boxes falling to the ground.

The loose items were picked up and stowed. The last pallet was now on. The Loadmaster and his team quickly got everything lashed down securely. The patient from the Consulate was already loaded and secured at the front of the aircraft and was being monitored by a team of uniformed medical staff. The paperwork was signed off by the UK contingent and all seemed in order. The customs official was happy, and the Chinese team started walking off the ramp. Looking down, the last guard saw something that looked like blood on the aircraft's ramp. Just as he was about to investigate, the ramp started moving upwards. The guard jumped off and looked back. The Loadmaster was waving goodbye with a John Wayne type of salute and a cheeky grin. The guard turned and walked away at a pace to catch up with his colleagues. The Loadmaster had seen the blood and hoped the Chinese staff would not notice it. When the ramp was fully up and secured with the lights indicating full closure, he breathed a sigh of relief. There was no need to inform the Captain of this minor issue, well not just yet.

On the internal RT, the Loadmaster told his Captain,

'We are ready to roll, boss, the sooner the better I would suggest.'

Ten minutes later, the aircraft was taxiing into position on the runway. The aircraft Captain called,

'Tower, this is United Kingdom military aircraft November Echo Two Six requesting take off from Runway Eighteen Lima.'

There was a long pause.

'Tower to UK military flight November Echo Two Six. You are requested to hold in your current position.'

There was no obvious reason to hold the aircraft. No planes were in the circuit, and no ground movements were observed.

The Captain said over the intercom, 'Everything OK in the back with the cargo?'

The Loadmaster was about to explain that there was a blood leaking from one of the pallets, but the air traffic controllers came back on.

'Tower to UK military flight November Echo Two Six, you are cleared for take-off Runway Eighteen Lima.'

The Co-pilot answered, 'Roger,' and before he even finished the word, the Captain was applying eighty percent power, then the brakes came off with a jolt, and the aircraft started lumbering down the runway.

Within minutes, wheels were up, and the aircraft was climbing and turning to the east under one hundred percent power. It would only be a matter of minutes before they were in international airspace.

Six minutes into the flight as they were still climbing, two Chinese fighters came alongside. The Chengdu J-20, known as Mighty Dragon, flew side by side with the Royal Air Force transport aircraft for about one minute.

The co-pilot said, 'Captain, we have an escort.'

'That's brilliant,' said the sarcastic Captain. 'Give the bastards a smile and a wave. That's why the tossers kept us on the ground.'

The flight deck crew all waved with big cheesy grins. The Chinese fighter pilots returned the salute and, putting their fifth-generation stealth aircraft into after-burner and a ferocious climb, disappeared into the clouds.

'Fucking show-offs,' said the Captain. 'They wanted us to see that they are almost as technologically advanced as we are.'

The Co-pilot said, 'That's true. We have six dozen F35B lightning IIs which are better aircraft, but these people have hundreds of their J-20s.'

The Captain came back smugly, 'But ours are better quality.'

The cocky Co-pilot not wanting to be outdone added,

'Remember what Nikita Khrushchev of the Russian Army said, "Quantity has a quality all its own".'

The Captain responded, mockingly offended, 'Shut the fuck up and concentrate on doing your crocheting or something. On second thoughts, go and make yourself useful. Put the coffee on.'

The flight deck laughed. The senior pilot winked at his younger Co-pilot.

Down at the back of the aircraft, the Loadmaster got the call from the flight deck,

'Let the chicks out. We are over international waters.'

The flight crew pulled away the plastic covering over the boxes and shouted,

'You can come out. We are in international airspace and heading for home.'

Firstly, Yorkie appeared, muttering under his breath. Then Bill.

After that Claire, Tony and Scott.

'Where is Philip?' asked Claire, gathering her thoughts and posture.

A box was kicked from the side of a pallet, and Philip's head popped out.

'Here he is,' said Yorkie with gusto, but they all soon realised he was covered in blood; lots of blood.

Yorkie grabbed him and helped him to his feet, guessing what happened.

'How is Chen?' asked the big man.

'Dead.'

Yorkie took Phil by the shoulders and forcibly walked him a few steps down the aircraft, away from the crowd.

He turned and gestured to Bill and mouthed, 'Get him out,' pointing to the blood-spattered entrance in the pallet.

Bill went straight in and pulled the boy out unceremoniously. The medical team on the aircraft came rushing and attended the young Chinese man. The dark stain of blood totally consuming the young man. Everyone held their breath.

After a few seconds, the medical staff shouted,

'He's got a pulse. He's alive, barely, but he's still with us.'

Suddenly, four medics surrounded him, setting up drips and bandaging the wounds. Bill told them about the morphine and why it was administered. Two of the medical team gave him a look of disgust at his reasoning. Sergeant Steven Lang from the Consulate was up and about, greeting his colleagues. The medics put the real patient in the ventilator and gave him oxygen. 'Baby Bird' was stabilising but remained in a serious situation. They had the bleeding under control, and his vital signs were OK, if weak. The decision was made not to jeopardise the mission for a medical emergency.

Steven Lang jokingly protested, 'Shit, that was supposed to be my bed for the way home.'

No one laughed, especially the two RAF nurses who looked scornfully at him.

Claire staggered down the aircraft and told Yorkie and Philip,

'Baby Bird' might still make it. The medics say you missed anything serious, but he'll need some blood and soon.'

Yorkie said supportively, 'There you go, mate. Pop along and give a few pints. That will make amends, Phil. Do it now.'

The young man's spirits visibly lifted, but he still looked terrible. Stabbing a man just to quiet him down was not something he had ever really contemplated, but Yorkie's hard-hitting 'welcome to the real world' speech had made him realise his actions had potentially saved everyone. Phil left, walking uneasy with the pitching of the aircraft, towards the nurses.

Claire suggested, 'Let's get some coffee and decent food inside us, but first, let's call it in.'

Without comment from Yorkie, she pressed her mike,

'Condor Control. Condor Control. This is Tango 3-1. Do you copy?'

She expected and received an immediate response.

'Tango 3-1, this is Condor 1. We copy loud and clear. Send your message.'

'We are Jerusalem and Joshua. Repeat. We are Jerusalem and Joshua. That's Tango 3 and Romeo 2. Confirm.'

'Copy that, Romeo 2 and Tango 3, Jerusalem and Joshua. Any mishaps? Condor 1 over.' Asked the controller, who knew all their call-signs were on the aircraft and exactly where the aircraft was.

'Condor 1. No, all birds are alive and well. Tango 3 out.'

That wasn't quite true, but all the team members were sound. The whole Fulcrum Storm Operations team met at the front of the cargo bay, hugged and congratulated each other. They were too knackered to sound overly jubilant. They were still mindful of security and had to be careful as to what they could discuss openly. Two of the medical team were the newly-promoted Staff Sergeant Geordie Walker and Sergeant Terry Williams, who were passing round excellent hot coffees and lunch boxes with sandwiches, cake and chocolate bars. The sugar rush was excellent.

The proper medical team of two RAF nurses and the RAF aircrew looked upon this motley group with disbelief. However, they knew they had just done something remarkable that would never hit the news and of which they could never discuss. The team stank and were armed to the teeth, walking around with their Glocks and knives and Chinese assault rifles. After about ninety minutes, Yorkie pulled the team in and disarmed everyone, and all non-essential kit was stowed away in a locked box. The flasks had already been retrieved and stored within a restrained container which provided extra insulation for the duration of the flight. It would take about eighteen hours to get back to the UK with one stop at Dubai Airport to re-fuel, get some fresh rations and then be off again. No one would leave the aircraft, not even the patient regardless of how he was getting on.

Claire strongly suggested that everyone get some rest as best they could. The debrief would be challenging and immediately undertaken once they were back at base. The teams found the best place to sleep during their flight was on top of the pallets of PPE. The boxes were more giving than the seats on the aircraft and they could stretch out. Exhaustion had set in, and after mugs of coffee and a mix of sweets and cakes, many just wanted to flop.

Yorkie was snoring, as usual, having decided to sleep inside the hidey-hole. The insulation of the boxes drowned out the incessant rumble of the aircraft's engines and Geordie's constant chatter. He kicked the boxes so he could fully extend his full frame.

Scott was soon sound asleep as if he had no cares whatsoever in the world. Philip quietly cried himself to sleep, still coming to terms with his first field venture. Claire knew he would either come out of this a stronger man, or it would break him in a subtle but profound way. Steven Lang, Tony Lane and Bill Martin were comparing notes and still taking the piss out of each other. Geordie and Terry Williams were just taking it all in, laughing at the tops of their voices and swearing as if it were a badge of honour.

Claire thought, 'This is going to be one long flight,' and sought solace in her own hidey-hole of PPE using some blankets she purloined from the Loadmaster to make her space as comfortable as possible in the circumstances.

Touch down at Brize Norton occurred at one a.m. local time. An ambulance took Chen straight to a hospital in London, and a minibus took the real medical staff away. Uncle Tom met the returning operatives as they staggered off the aircraft. He thought they all looked terrible but shook everyone's hands. He went and thanked the aircrew for their services and said that there was a case of Champagne Bollinger special cuvée brut for them and the medical team, courtesy of His Majesty's

Government and Secret Intelligence Service.

His joy and satisfaction were obvious to them all.

'You lot, I am afraid will need to go back to the training base, get cleaned up and be ready for debriefing. We will start at midday tomorrow. Take all your personal equipment and weapons but leave the flasks, and I will see you tomorrow afternoon. Just a very big thank you. You have done a bloody marvellous job and made it look easy. We know it was not.'

Tom took Claire and Yorkie to one side, saying, 'I will need to see you both in London at eight a.m. Do you feel up to it?'

'Yes, sir,' was the reply, they had both slept well within the confines of their cargo.

'That's great. I will take you back with me to Vauxhall. There is some late-night supper on if you need it, and you can get some sleep.'

Before they left, Professor Johnathon King and Professor Janet Williams arrived to meet the teams and collect the virus flasks. They had a three-vehicle armed convoy to escort them and the precious cargo back to Porton Down. Johnathon was especially pleased to see Claire and Yorkie with whom he had a strong bond. He had not slept well since he knew they had left the UK and his relief was there for all to see.

A bus collected the operations team plus all their equipment, minus Yorkie and Claire, and they slid off into the darkness yet again. Yorkie had told his muckers that he would be with them at some point tomorrow, probably late afternoon. An MI6 luxury minibus pulled up, and Uncle Tom and his two dishevelled passengers climbed on board. Within minutes of pulling out, they had large brandies in hand as they toasted the success of the mission.

'Now Wing Commander,' said Deputy Director Operations returning to his formal self, 'tell me about the whole thing from getting on that fishing vessel to being pulled from your concealed space on the aircraft.'

Claire hardly stopped talking for the whole hour and thirty minutes of the journey. Yorkie chimed in once in a while when she sought a point of clarification, but every detail was recounted and, not surprisingly, recorded. The typed report was presented to Tom MacDonald by seven thirty a.m. on the 23rd June 2024.

Once back in a laboratory environment, the viruses and vaccines would be separated into three lots and dispersed, just in case of reprisal from the Chinese. Unknown to the operations team, a whole new set of protocols was in place for what was going to happen next, and the key was the quick testing of the vaccine and its mass production. Already suitable facilities had been clandestinely prepared to start making the vaccine. It would take many weeks to produce enough for the UK, but plans had been drafted to draw in other major and international manufacturers depending on the outcome of the meeting with the Chinese President. They still had massive hurdles to overcome.

Chapter 33

A Different Battle - Part 1

23rd Jun 2024

It was eight a.m. local time at the SIS Headquarters in London where a full staff was working. The Chief was in his office, and the Operations Room had been re-set to monitor an elaborate surveillance network at Chequers, the country house of the Prime Minister. This afternoon at midday, the President of China, Xi Jinping, was planning to lunch with Allan Knowles at this sixteenth-century manor house located in rural Buckinghamshire.

The luncheon was categorised as an informal event and would give both men the chance to speak privately. It was an opportunity to detail any final points regarding their more formal discussions held earlier during the State Visit. The truth was that such Heads of State visits were well-choreographed, and each side ordinarily knew what they would get out of it long before the visitors landed on UK soil. Mounting pressures on both leaders meant they required a win-win result, as each had their own but very different growing domestic issues. By its very nature, such lunches were never deemed to be the key part of the political dance of statesmanship but rather window dressing. After lunch, both men would ordinarily shake hands and thank each other for the benefits of the visit, wishing great prosperity on each other. That was the normal state of affairs, but today was going to be different; very different.

Allan Knowles had been working on something much more convoluted than a flaccid farewell. Indeed, the outcome could be life-changing for both men, their countries and, possibly, the world. This was to be the greatest or worst day of their lives, depending on the perspective taken by each leader. As yet, the Prime Minister did not know which one it would be. Much of what would transpire was now out of his hands, and for this non-practising Christian, who was quoted as saying "his faith comes and goes", he was searching for a sign, any sign, that he was doing the right thing. President Xi Jinping was due to arrive by helicopter at midday, but before then the Prime Minister was expecting a few other callers.

Back at the SIS Headquarters, George Main, Chief of the Secret Intelligence Service and Sir Steven Alexander, Chair of the Joint Intelligence Committee, were looking at the summary report of Operation Fulcrum Storm. It was impressive to the point of being almost unbelievable. They were both shocked and pleased in equal measure it had all worked out so well. They had thought the mission highly unlikely to succeed and had prepared statements denouncing the Prime Minister's actions in undertaking it against their better judgement. Tom MacDonald had been asked to support his superior in this stance but refused outright. He had complete faith in the judgements made and the team whom he had selected, along with others, to carry out the tasks. He was sworn to secrecy on his honour which he now regretted agreeing to.

Standing before his boss and the Chair of the JIC, Tom MacDonald reported.

'Sir, we achieved every single objective we hoped to do. Thus far, we had only one casualty which was a Chinese national. Regrettable as that loss is, it will never be seen as part of our mission. We also have one of our friendlies in hospital with a stab wound, but he should recover in due course. Of key importance is that the viruses and vaccines are now under our control. As per the Operation Plan, these have now been dispersed as a precautionary action, in case of reprisals. The boffins at Porton are already making positive noises about the haul, and we hope to hear good news within twenty-four hours. There is little more the field operation could have hoped to achieve. Our people did a sterling job, and in time, we will look to make the appropriate awards. For now, sir, I would recommend that we focus on the next actions.'

George Main, for all his ambition, was happy to distance himself from Allan Knowles, and he had made his position fairly widely known, not always the wisest action. He saw no need to risk being ruined by a temporary leader of the country. Consequently, he had instructed Tom MacDonald to stand beside the Prime Minister today at Chequers, his stated logic being that Tom was immersed in the operation at a level of detail he would struggle to grasp in such a restricted period of time. Sir Steven Alexander, too, was a canny slimy political type and, as such, wanted to be on the periphery in case crumbs of credit were to be had but just far enough removed that if the Prime Minister failed and fell, he would not be dragged down as well. One does not get to lofty heights in politics by being outwardly brave and committed. Esther Williams had also managed to step sideways at this eleventh hour. She saw herself as the next Leader of the Conservative Party, especially when the Prime Minister made what she was sure would be an inevitable fatal error, propelling his political career in a downward trajectory. She wanted to be wearing the Conservative Party crown when the country was coming out of the Covid crisis, but not just yet.

George Main conceded, 'Tom, you have everything in place. We could have not been more thorough in the planning of this matter, and I leave it to you to guide the Prime Minister at Chequers. Will you be taking Squadron Leader Claire Walters with you?'

'That's right, sir. Wing Commander Walters will accompany me,' he corrected his principal.

'Great. You had better get going. It just needs you, and everything else is in place, I trust?' George Main, who hated being corrected, replied cuttingly.

'It is, sir, and I will report back as soon as the right moment presents itself,' said Tom in a way that was unusually vague for him. He was normally so precise. George Main had purposely had no input into Operation Reel In, apart from handing the dossier to the PM. It was evident he did not want his fingerprints on the evidence, should there be any formal inquest or enquiry.

Claire was in her Number One ceremonial uniform with medals. The newest addition was the unexpected Conspicuous Gallantry Cross (CGC) with which both she and Yorkie had been informally presented the night before. The formal award would be made by the King in due course, but Uncle Tom thought it would be a nice addition to her other two general service medals. He had also gone to the trouble to have her uniform tailored with her new rank braid and as a special treat, formally recognised her freefall parachute training with the parachute wings insignia of the SAS. The latter was more about appearances than substance, but she loved the idea of being seen as a warrior alongside such an elite force.

The Director Special Forces gave his permission for these to be worn, but said,

'We will, in due time, have to get Claire on a proper SAS-accredited jump course. She can meet up with some of her new chums from Hereford.'

Yorkie had a whole new uniform waiting for him also, as he was now a Major in the Special Air Service Regiment. He had an array of medals including the Military Cross and Military Medal, plus mentions in despatches oakleaves on his general service medals for Afghanistan and Iraq.

Yorkie said, 'All I need is the VC, and I'll have a full set.'

Claire responded, 'Any stupid jokes today, and you could be getting it posthumously!'

Tom MacDonald looked at his two protégés and remarked on how smart they both looked. If they were his children, he could not be prouder.

'Major, with all those medals you look like a blooming Christmas tree,' he said in hearty spirits.

They both looked exceptionally presented and professional, as they were to be paraded at Chequers to the Prime Minister. Both had full ceremonial swords, gloves and accoutrements. Major General Paul Burns congratulated the two returnees on their awards and a job well-done. He was especially proud of Yorkie, one of his own, who had led one of the teams.

Paul Burns said to Claire and Yorkie, 'It is often the case that great deeds are done by ordinary people with great ambition. For people of our ilk, we must content ourselves that the actions we take, and the outcomes we produce are gratitude enough for much of what we do is lost to the greater world within our lifetime.'

Tom said, 'I could not have put it better myself.'

Paul laughed, 'But you did, Tom, back in 1989 after our trip to East Germany. These were your words to our team when we were back in RAF Gutersloh. Do you remember? You are losing the plot, you doddery old bugger.'

Everyone laughed. Tom was a tad embarrassed but thought it funny too.

The helicopter, an AgustaWestland AW159 Wildcat, was waiting to take Tom, Claire, Yorkie and Paul Burns to meet the Prime Minister at Chequers. It took off at 0925 hours and landed in the grounds of Chequers some twenty minutes later. The team disembarked, and the helicopter, which took off straightaway, repositioned itself at RAF Halton, three miles away. The team from London was escorted in, ready to meet with the Prime Minister. Already present were Mrs Joyce Young of the China Desk, SIS, plus another interpreter from the Home Office. Bill Rankin was also waiting and greeted both Yorkie and Claire, offering somewhat stilted congratulations. It was ten a.m. when the Prime Minister sauntered in. Without focusing on anything else, he walked through the itinerary and proceedings for the lunchtime visit. Nervous as hell, the PM took enormous pride in meeting the two warriors back from China.

'I do not have enough time to thank you properly just now, but I will take the time to meet the whole crew that supported your mission in the next few days. I promise.'

The team of Intelligence Specialists were to be on hand to support the Prime Minister and only become involved if summoned to do so.

Tom explicitly told Yorkie, 'Say nothing, Major, but look like you mean business.'

It was now 1100 hours in the UK and 1800 hours locally in China. At midday UK local time, the explosive devices in the three target areas would be ignited by remote signal. Just before ignition, the fire alarms would go off in an attempt to clear the buildings and minimise the loss of civilian and military lives. It would be seven p.m. local at each target site. The SIS had eyes on the ground at each location plus satellites to monitor the extent of the damage. The devices used were designed to generate maximum heat with a devastating charge that would restrict, to some extent, collateral impacts. Everyone was constantly looking at their timepieces.

The team was offered coffee, but they only asked for water. They all felt the weight of the moment at hand.

'Sir, what are the chances of us getting a result here?' Claire asked

Tom during a quiet moment.

'Truthfully, Claire, I would give it a fifty percent chance of success, but I am hopeful we can pull it off. I have seen how hard the PM has been working on his delivery, and our boys on the China desk have been trying to aid him with the nuances of Chinese culture. We have a good profile on President Xi Jinping. He has a known aggressive streak; he is supremely smart and a survivor. It is that latter trait that we will be looking to stimulate and nurture.'

He paused wondering if there was any benefit, continuing,

'From our detailed analysis of him, the greatest thing we have to do is allow him to maintain face.'

Yorkie covertly listening, interjected, 'Pardon, sir. Face?'

Claire said with a degree of exasperation, 'Yorkie, you were not listening to those cultural briefings we were given, were you?'

Tom MacDonald smiled and continued, 'The Chinese have many idiosyncrasies of culture and the concept of face is perhaps one of the most difficult for Westerners to understand. This notion refers to a cultural understanding of respect, honour and social standing. Actions or words that are disrespectful may cause somebody to lose face, whilst respectful actions may save face. In all we do today, we cannot take away from the President his pride, dignity or prestige. Saving face is a prime motivating force in Chinese politics and losing it will undermine him and turn him against anything we offer. That is regardless of whether or not it is smart to do so. However, he must see this, not as him personally maintaining face, but rather as the whole of China. In this matter, he and China are one, and that is where the challenge lay.'

Claire stated quite abruptly, 'In our politics, our leaders are quite often embarrassed by various disclosures but seldom feel the need to resign. They just bluff it out and hope the country forgets. In China, their culture would not allow this to happen.'

Whilst they waited in silence, Tom had another quick mental run-through the proceedings. The sound of a helicopter was heard in the background. Yorkie looked at his recently acquired Omega watch, another present from Tom, and saw it was 1159 hours.

He said, 'I would think that's our guest, sir.'

No one replied. It was accepted it could only be President Xi Jinping and his entourage. Then a second helicopter was heard. The first had landed, and Chinese special agents got out and formed a perimeter of guards. The second helicopter landed and out came the President of China and his lovely wife, Peng Liyuan, who was referred to as the Chinese First Lady by her country's media. The intelligence team could see the Prime Minister and his wife walk out to meet their guests. The initial contact was undertaken with great warmness. Mrs Knowles was pregnant with her second child. It was early on as yet, but she was visibly showing. One Chinese cameraman and two British pressmen were present, so the whole event was unencumbered with too many prying eyes. The President's staff included his Secretary of State, a PR guru and an interpreter. They went into an anteroom and sat for pictures, and then all the photographers were dismissed to allow some unrecorded and relaxed moments.

It was now 1210 hours local. Deputy Director MacDonald received a call on his secure mobile.

'Sir, lunch is now served.'

'Copy. Lunch is served.'

This was code to indicate that all three sites in China had been obliterated. No further details were required just for now, but a full post-attack assessment would be carried out in due course.

Major General Paul Burns heard some movement and said,

'That will be the group going into lunch. We might as well get a coffee and relax for a while.'

He knew all too well that no one was going to relax one iota.

Chapter 34

A Different Battle – Part 2

23rd Jun 2024

The Prime Minister was careful to show great respect to President Xi Jinping and his charming wife, Peng Liyuan. Each principal had an interpreter, and the wives had a dedicated interpreter too. The President could speak English and, though he was educated at a university that taught subjects in English, it was believed he never attended such lectures. President Xi felt more at ease expressing his great intelligence in Mandarin Chinese, letting his capable staff translate his thoughts. From relative humble beginnings, the President had shown true qualities to rise to his position of near absolute power, and for those who closely watched China's growth and development, it was evident, he was a shrewd individual. Not known as an extrovert, Xi possessed a well-adapted sense of humour plus a character and personality possessing both great warmth and remarkable strength. He was a feared adversary and a great advocate for modernising China. His ambition was to see China grow and become a great nation on the world's stage with increasing prosperity and cultural freedoms for his people. In this latter context, he had to move cautiously.

His wife, China's first lady, Peng Liyuan, possessed elegance and grace all of her own. She also had a good level of fluency in English and was comfortable in any company. Her speech was slow and graceful but distinctive. With her presence and stunning beauty, she held her audience captivated. As a former performer, Peng gained popularity as a soprano singer with regular appearances on China TV. Peng displayed the character and charm her husband kept hidden. It was clear to see why the President admired her so.

In preparation for today's important work, it was necessary to bring the Prime Minister's wife in on the proceedings. She had received copious amounts of guidance on how to conduct herself and the ingratiating things to say. The food was perfect, and the meal was gratefully appreciated. Throughout the meal, Allan Knowles knew he was in the presence of a great man. Not a stupid man himself, the Prime Minister appreciated his life had been littered with immature actions and a series of quite inexplicable cock-ups. To emulate the man in front of him, and those other great characters of history, he would have to raise his game even further. He owned the capability and desire to do this, and not for himself. For the first time, he felt the pride and duty to serve his country, even if it ended up being to his personal detriment. The magnitude of the situation and the realisation of his part to be played reminded him of his classical education and the sacrifice that great heroes made in those early times. He was also moved by the feats of this generation's heroes who were in his outer lounge, looking to him for leadership. The Prime Minister did not wish to be found wanting in these circumstances. He had not realised, but his wife who adored him had seen him blossom in recent weeks and was now gazing upon him with admiration. Katie Knowles had observed him growing in maturity, determination and stature. The childish game of politics had given way to a greater understanding of what his legacy could be, if only he showed the authentic courage required in these situations.

The President's personal bodyguard was no more than two metres away, and for the plan to work, Allan needed President Xi Jinping on his own. The Prime Minister knew the President's penchant for art and history, and after lunch, he suggested they progress to the drawing room so that he could show him some of the house's ancient Chinese pieces. Allan won the moment by suggesting that they were priceless both in value and historical culture. Simultaneously, Mrs Knowles suggested that Peng join her in the family wing where she would like her views on the new baby's room. These displays of personal openness warmed the President and his wife; both agreed to the suggested informal tours. The close-protection guard was sent to accompany the ladies. As the Prime Minister pointed out, 'We can see your men on the lawn to the front out the window.'

He added, 'Anyway, my chaps have the place surrounded. Trust me. No one is getting in here without our men seeing them coming.'

The President smiled and nodded in acquiescence but spoke into his collar in Mandarin. From the corner of his eye, the Prime Minister noticed two of the Chinese secret service agents turn to face the mansion. Unperturbed by this, Allan sauntered into the main lounge and in a relaxed manner explained a range of Chinese artefacts to his guest. The President's interpreter gave a running commentary. They were some of the rarest pieces he had seen outside China, encouraging a natural flow of conversation. As planned, the Prime Minister praised the Chinese culture and craftmanship which was not hard to feign as he genuinely believed in the words he was expressing.

As the leaders ambled around in deep conversation, they reached the far end of the room where a small double oak door was open. The Prime Minister walked in quite nonchalantly, and President Xi followed instinctively. He was now in the spider's web. It was just a case of holding him here until the spider convinced the fly of his good intentions. Once inside the room, the doors quickly but quietly closed behind them.

The gentle click of the door closing and the presence of others in the room made the President change from a relaxed guest to a trapped animal. Xi was faced with four military-type people and an interpreter. His instincts were kicking in.

'Do I need to summon help?' he thought.

Before the President spoke or gestured, the MI6 interpreter stepped forward and bowed.

'Honourable President, we humbly apologise for this intrusion, but a matter of great importance will be brought to your attention by Prime Minister Knowles. We obligingly seek your agreement to have five minutes of your time without interruption. I will translate for the Prime Minister and your interpreter can advise if my words are falsely given.'

She bowed again and took three steps back. The Prime Minister took half a pace forward and asked the President to sit. Xi sat cautiously tilting his head in curiosity, and then the remaining players in the room sat in their allotted chairs.

The Prime Minister wasted no time in outlining the unscrupulous actions of Major General Lei Wei and the activities going on in China in secret. He exonerated the President by highlighting he knew Xi was oblivious to the situation. The Prime Minister stated that given the UK's extensive knowledge in this matter, he was almost one hundred percent sure no one else in the higher echelons of the government of The People's Republic of China was implicated. Putting all the cards on the table, he summarised how they were alerted to what was going on. Then in a totally unprecedented ploy, he explained in detail to the President how they could prove their findings beyond any doubt. He disclosed GCHQ's ability to tap into the computer systems at Wuhan and other places. He passed over documents that surely could have only been produced by the President's staff. President Xi found himself feeling as if he were being humiliated and the structures of his country being ridiculed. He could sense anger rising inside him, experiencing disgraced that these Westerners could so easily break his nation's codes and bare all their secrets. The Prime Minister detected the man was under great pressure and could see the anxiety present on the formally smiling face.

Allan Knowles went on to explain, 'My friend and fellow leader, for the sake of world peace, I unilaterally ordered the destruction of the facilities and the annihilation of the viruses within your country.'

The President looked outwardly shocked, leaning forward as if to stand.

Raising a non-aggressive hand, the Prime Minister said,

'Sir, Mr President, please hear me out. I am being completely honourable and respectful both to you as a man of courage and vision and to your great nation. Your security people cannot hear you just now, but you are not under any threat. I give you my word of honour on this. The actions I ordered were undertaken, not as an act of war, but of friendship and peace, for your country and greater humanity. This is not an act of hostility but one to prevent aggression and foster stability in your country and around the world. Our operation was designed so that no one would be killed during our mission, and we have done everything possible to ensure lives would not be needlessly taken. The explosions which you will undoubtedly hear about will only damage the viruses and the buildings in which they were being developed. These people behind me were the ones who planned and executed the elimination of these viruses. It was not an attack on your country but a strike against a threat to both your leadership and world peace. If you can see our actions in that way, Mr President, we have a solution which will give both our countries a way to make amends and save face.'

'What I tell you today, on my honour, and I offer you my life should I ever break this pledge, will not be shared with anyone but you and the people here today. We do this in good faith because we both know if this information were to be leaked, there would be condemnation and calls for retribution. The details of what I have explained would ruin your country and many countries around the world. The response to what I have told, if published, may lead to other nations demanding a war footing against China, and many hundreds of millions of people may die needlessly. The outcome would be the near destruction of many societies as we know them. You understand that the UK has a strong bond with the USA, but this matter will never be disclosed to the Americans. Again, you have my solemn promise on that.'

The Prime Minister took a deep breath and continued with sincerity in his voice.

'My pledge to you, Mr President, is that these people here will give their lives to the preservation of this information; they are people of courage and honour. What I am going to propose is that the UK will develop the vaccine for Covid-24, and we will, in a joint endeavour with your country, provide the cure to the world. You will maintain the honour of your country, and together, in equal partnership, we will eradicate this pandemic. This I know is important to you, and together we will succeed. My proposal, to come to this glorious victory for China and the UK, is fairly detailed and will need your further consideration.'

He wanted to keep talking, but he was told to keep it relatively short. Stay on message and not try to win the argument but let the President see the path for himself.

The Prime Minister stood.

'Sir, I have taken too much of your time, and your men will be anxious. Can I respectfully suggest that we adjourn just now, and I will leave you to consider what I have said? I reiterate we will be the only ones who know how we came by the vaccine, and your position will never be threatened or impugned on this matter.'

The interpreter finished three seconds later.

The Chinese leader spoke in stilted English, 'Prime Minister, this is a great burden you have placed on me, and I have to give the matter some considerable thought. I will take my leave, and I will let you know my thoughts within a few hours.'

The Prime Minister replied off script, 'Mr President, I am grateful for your forbearance on this, but I hope you can believe that the way in which we have raised this difficult subject is out of genuine friendship and respect. We have been open with you and shown our hand in matters which leave us exposed to some extent. We intend no deceit or dishonour. As an act of good faith, I will offer my resignation as the leader of this great nation, if you require me to step down to allow both countries to move forward in peace. All I ask in return is that you take action to remove Major General Lei Wei from his post to curtail his naked ambition.'

The President stood up and bowed to Allan Knowles who returned the bow. As the President looked around the room, those present came to attention in unison. President Xi bowed slightly in respect, for he knew that the men and woman before him had defeated his country in the matter at hand. These were extraordinary characters, true warriors of the nature he read about in the history of his beloved country. The President was not storming out and was taking his time to think.

He turned to the Prime Minister.

'I may decide to delay my departure tomorrow. Maybe we could meet again to discuss a pathway to peace, possibly here where no one can hear what is being discussed.'

President Xi smiled in his usual enigmatic way.

The Prime Minister said, 'Mr President, I am wholly at your disposal.'

Both men left the room and walked to the front of the lounge where the President announced it was time to leave. His wife was smiling as they entered the majestic hallway, having had a most pleasant time. The President was shown to his waiting helicopter, and bade the Prime Minister farewell.

Re-entering the house, Allan Knowles went directly into the dining room and sat down on the seventeenth century dining chair. He loosened his tie, his default gesture when he was stressed.

His wife came in and asked, 'How did it go, darling?'

'I don't bloody know. That man has a poker face from hell, but I sensed he understood my sincerity. From here, what happens is entirely in his hands.'

Katie simply said, 'If the ball is in his court, all we can do is wait to see if we get it hit back to us. You now need to muster your energy and thoughts. Go and speak to your people out there.'

He looked up and staggered to a stand. The past few days had drained him mentally.

'Allan, tuck your shirt in, do your tie up and flatten your hair. Shoulders back and walk like a statesman. You are a great leader; show the world you are one.'

Mrs Knowles walked in to the family's private areas. Allan went in the other direction. Upon arriving in the anteroom, he was greeted with silence. All eyes were on the Prime Minister.

'Right, Tom, you have a reputation for giving it straight. How did I do?' he asked, looking directly at the Deputy Director Operations.

Tom MacDonald smiled and said, 'Bloody marvellously, Prime Minister, absolutely spot on. If President Xi does not respond favourably, this will not be a consequence of your performance today. You can rest assured, sir, you played your part well. Bloody well-done, sir.'

The rest of those assembled nodded in agreement and offered comforting smiles. They had all been worried about this part of the plan, but the PM had played his role perfectly.

The Prime Minister said, 'Bugger me, I was a bit worried I had not come across as genuine, but I meant every word of it, every word, you know.'

The group relaxed, and though the Prime Minister did the lion's share of the talking, everyone made positive and supportive overtures. Lunch arrived for the guests, and they all sat down and ate in the presence of the PM; it was a surreal moment.

'The President said he would contact you in a few hours, so not too long to wait,' concluded Tom MacDonald.

Tom then, in his typical, non-conformist way, asked if the Prime Minister would be happy to present some medals this afternoon in an informal setting without the trappings of publicity. It was suggested that it would help the time pass less stressfully. The AgustaWestland AW159 Wildcat from RAF Halton was en route plus a Special Forces Chinook was in-bound. The Prime Minister agreed to Tom's request. A small entourage was put together, and the necessary security agencies were informed. The Chinook landed. Tom, the Director Special Forces and the Prime Minister clambered aboard, and as it took off, the small Wildcat landed and then was away with the three other intelligence staffs.

Yorkie was sitting in the rotary aircraft blushing, and said,

'What the hell are those boys going to say, seeing me like this and in the company of the Director Special Forces and the PM?'

For Claire, this was one of the proudest days of her life, and she was barely getting to grips with what had happened over the past month or so. As the AgustaWestland AW159 came into the approach, the Chinook was on the ground, and the Prime Minister plus his support staff were being blown about. The PM's ginger hair was misbehaving badly. Three minutes later, the second group was on the ground heading for Hangar One.

The Operation Fulcrum Storm Team had been given just thirty minutes' notice of their pending visitors' arrival, but no names were given over the RT. They were showered and dressed in their training outfits; the same kit used on the operation. They had their weapons attached plus all the operational equipment. They had no idea what or who was in store for them.

The whole Team lined up in their operational groupings. Peter Goulding, who had flown back on a civilian aircraft, was asked to step forward, and the Prime Minister presented him with a medal: Conspicuous Gallantry Cross. Peter thanked the Prime Minister and stood back in line. Peter was taken aback by the award and nodded to his Deputy Director, who winked a smiling response. The Prime Minister then made a joke about Claire and Yorkie being too impatient to receive theirs, as they already had them, but he made a point of congratulating them and patting them on their shoulders. The men of the SAS thought that was it, only the big cheeses and officers get the medals. Then Staff Sergeant Steven Lang was ordered to step forward. It was strange to be called Staff Sergeant as he was only newly-promoted, but he did so in true military style, coming rigidly to attention and calling out, 'Sir.' He was the pleased and proud recipient of the Military Cross. Then followed Philip Wong and Staff Sergeant Bill Martin from Team Two and Scott

MacGregor and Staff Sergeant Tony Lane, all now decorated with the Military Cross. The reserves, Staff Sergeant Geordie Walker and Sergeant Terry Williams had to be content with their advancement in rank and a mention in despatches and the award of a silver oak leaf. These two characters were part of the medical team from the UK task force in the Sea of Japan, or so the Chinese were led to believe.

Deputy Director Tom MacDonald read out the abridged citations for each recipient of the awards. He did not make Claire or Yorkie go through this ordeal. After the brief formalities, Major General Paul Burns and the Prime Minister heartily congratulated each man and impressed upon them the significance of their actions.

Allan Knowles told the assembled team, 'We are not out of the woods just yet, but we are hopeful that, thanks to the efforts of Operation Fulcrum Storm, our lives can resume some sort of normality in the not-too-distant future.'

Paul Burns said, 'Gentlemen, when you have finished patting yourself on the back, you will need to get down to the serious matter of debriefing. Mr Rankin and Mr David Jones, who will be over tomorrow, will need your best endeavours, but for now, here are a few bottles of Champagne and a couple of slabs of beer to celebrate your successes and awards.'

The PM and his entourage promptly withdrew to Chequers, taking Bill Rankin and Paul Burns with him. The Wildcat took the SIS intelligence officers back to Vauxhall, but they hung around for a small glass of bubbly. Both Yorkie and Claire might still be needed, and Tom MacDonald wanted them close to hand. Their stock as professional operators had increased markedly in his eyes and that of the Prime Minister.

On the flight back to Chequers, the Foreign Secretary contacted the PM.

'I know this will sound strange, Prime Minister, but President Xi has asked if he could extend his stay one day and meet you at Chequers tomorrow morning.'

'That is perfectly fine,' the PM replied casually. 'Let my secretary know. All appointments for tomorrow are cancelled. We'll reschedule the meeting with the select Committee on the Coronavirus for next week.

Matters of State take precedence over over-sight committees.'

On landing at Chequers, the PM went in and saw his wife, imparting what could only be seen as good news. He then asked to be put in touch on a secure line with Deputy Director MacDonald, immediately after he was back in London. It was only fifteen minutes later that the two men were deep in conversation yet again.

'Prime Minister, may I respectfully suggest that you should be speaking with George Main before you determine how you want to press on,' said Tom MacDonald.

'Look here, Tom, I know your boss put you front and centre today because he needed to have a plausible excuse if it all went belly-up. If he did not have the faith in me or our plan, he should have the balls to say so and not leave you and me holding the baby. I like the cut of your gib, and I can recognise that you and those two operatives of yours, the Wing Commander and Major, have a bond. The Head of Section fella, Rankin, he's a nice bloke but lacks the leadership or drive to see this through. We need to have a winning team on the pitch tomorrow, and I think I have just outlined it. Now tell me what else we need to do to prepare for tomorrow.'

They spoke for about an hour. The next phase was prepared, but Tom was not looking forward to seeing George in the morning. Men of Bill's age and experience still respected their superiors and the sway they held over all beneath them.

Chapter 35

Co-operation and Peace

24th Jun 2024

The team from SIS Headquarters was called to the Chief's office overlooking the Thames. Looking furious with his Deputy Director, he sought a 'fucking explanation' why this next phase did not involve him and who authorised his team to go to Chequers this morning. Tom explained the events of yesterday and the directions he had been given by the Prime Minister, purposely leaving out the slur that Allan Knowles had made regarding George Main and his loyalties. The Chief believed Tom had manipulated his position to curry favour for the betterment of his career.

Tom's response was, 'Sir, with respect, you know that is absolute bollocks.'

The discussion continued with both men knowing that regardless of what was said here and now, the Prime Minister held all the cards and called the shots. So off Tom and his two junior agents went to Chequers to support the PM.

The helicopter took off from SIS Headquarters and flew directly to Chequers. The arrivals were in their best uniforms and regalia for the second day running. They were escorted to the lounge by one of the house staff who asked, 'Coffee, ladies and gentlemen?'

Tom answered for the group saying, 'That would be most welcome. Thank you kindly.'

A short while later, a black saloon car was seen progressing down the long drive to the main house, having already passed through one set of security checks. It stopped at a second security point with armed policeman and was allowed to proceed. A host of specialist fire-arms officers were on the premises and had the car in their sights, tracking its progress. Such intense security was pretty standard for a State Visit. The sound of the car swinging round in front of the main house was dramatic. Five minutes later, Professors Johnathon King and Janet Williams entered the lounge. When they saw familiar faces, they relaxed. Coffee was served all round amid an air of excitement. It was nearly nine thirty a.m., and the Prime Minister was due at any moment.

All yesterday evening, the intelligence staff had discussed the game plan for today. It was a detailed set of actions with well-considered consequences. Whilst the Operation Fulcrum Storm Operations Team were training and focussing on the covert mission to China, Johnathon and Janet had been tasked with reviewing all the intelligence from Shanghai, specifically in terms of the research on the vaccines and their ability to replicate them. Their objective was to determine confidence levels in the Chinese scientific outcomes. This was very much an academic exercise, and the findings were highly promising. After much deliberation, they were eighty percent confident, give or take five percent, that without a live virus they could replicate the science undertaken by the microbiologists in China and produce a workable vaccine. They had already started this process, and progress was being made to develop the vaccines. A full study over the past thirty hours of the live vaccine purloined from the Chinese meant they were now almost one hundred percent confident they had a viable vaccine. The important realisation was that it presented an authentic opportunity to develop a mass-produced cure for Covid-24 and "Yellow Petal", should the latter surface, in one vaccine. The two scientists, plus others at Porton Down, were going to offer the Prime Minister a quick win but one which could blow up in his face. The balance of argument was if the Chinese trials had gone as they were reported, they were on to a winner. If, on the other hand, they had been fudged, this would be a false summit, and the implications would lead to political ruin for the PM. That in turn, would generate social disharmony on a level not yet seen in the UK. Their recommendation was to start using the vaccine as soon as possible without further trials, taking the risk and getting it out there. The worst-case scenario would be some people who contracted Covid-24 would die that otherwise might have survived.

Claire stated what most were thinking, 'Desperate times require desperate measures. We have never in modern history been in a more

330

desperate situation than we are now.'

The Prime Minister came in holding a union jack mug of tea and wearing tartan slippers. The assembled crowd stood, and he waved them down saying,

'Relax. Please sit.'

Tom MacDonald said to the Prime Minister, 'Sir, if I could be so bold as to kick things off, it might save a bit of time. I know we are on a tight schedule.'

'Carry on, Tom. We are on the clock here, and the President will be with us at eleven a.m. sharp. Crack on.'

The PM sounded relaxed and looked less tense than the previous day.

Tom summarised the science and confirmed that in all probability the live vaccine in hand would work. He highlighted the small risk involved but stressed the rewards were immeasurable and worth the endeavour. Tom then asked Professor Janet Williams to provide an assessment of her work on the production of the vaccine.

'Prime Minister,' Janet started, 'it is my belief that we could commence production of the vaccine immediately. As you know, it takes time to build stocks, but I would assess we could start rolling out treatment samples within two weeks. If we split the acquired samples into four or five separate containers and distribute these to our allies and the Chinese, we could generate about six million vaccine treatments in one month. After that, production would increase exponentially, with a target date of September 2024 for all high-risk patients being treated and thereafter, starting an immunisation programme worldwide. The reality is that death rates should start falling rapidly within three months and thereafter, there should be a huge reduction. A target timescale for the worldwide eradication of these viruses is two years, and that is a cautious, not optimistic, prediction. Our experience in producing the first Covid vaccine has given us the capacity to act quickly.'

The Prime Minister was as excited as a teenage boy but kept his dignity intact. He beamed.

'Janet, that all sounds absolutely fabulous, fantastic, bloody marvellous. I trust the vaccine provided to our allies will be under licence, and we will see some income to our exchequer?' asked the Prime

Minister.

Tom said with an unequivocal tone, 'You are completely right, Prime Minister. We have a back story as to the development of the vaccine which was done in tandem with Chinese scientists. The research we have pilfered from Shanghai has been translated into English, so that it purports the UK has done the work but obviously in secret. The Chinese will have their test results given back, so they can justify their findings which by no coincidence will substantiate ours. The return of the data will obviously be part of any deal with President Xi. We must hope the Chinese come on board with our demands.'

Janet then added, 'The team at Porton Down is ready at your instruction, Prime Minister, to open up the research to a few selected universities around the UK. This would be in conjunction with the commencement of vaccine production. Our new production facilities are in Oxford, Bristol, Cardiff, Liverpool and Inverness, and all are ready to roll. If we can use military couriers, work could commence in two days.'

Tom said, 'We would need to beef up security at each site, but we have plans in place, Prime Minister, and for an operation of this magnitude, we would not risk any possible compromise.'

The Prime Minister said, 'Don't delay getting this stuff on the street as quickly as we are able. I do not want to hear of any hold-ups because of funding issues or logistical problems. The production of these vaccines is a national priority, Chinese participation or not. I would like a press release prepared for this afternoon, nothing fancy. We just need to let the population know that there is light at the end of the tunnel and we are highly confident of our research. Janet, would you be so kind as to assist my press secretary in stitching something together, and would you please be present at the press conference? I may ask you to say a few words. As you know, the science is a bit beyond me and had it not been for your help previously, it would still be mumbo jumbo.'

The Prime Minister paused, 'We would, of course, need to be able to include President Xi, should he come on board as expected.'

He looked around at the assembled group, his eyes resting on Johnathon King. Tom took this moment to make an observation.

'Prime Minister, as you have been briefed, you are in the presence of a dead man,' said Tom MacDonald, pointing over to Johnathon King.

'Ha! Yes,' said Allan, 'like Lazarus of Bethany, we need to bring him back from the dead. Do we just say his death was falsified to protect him whilst he was undertaking this sterling work with Janet and the team at Porton Down?'

'We have cobbled a press release together along those lines, and Janet can discuss this with your PR people,' said Tom.

'Grand stuff,' the PM responded.

'With your permission, sir, I would ask that both Professor King and Professor Williams go ahead and meet with the Press Secretary to get this moving forward,' Tom suggested.

The Prime Minister got to his feet and escorted the scientists to his in-house offices, where the Press Secretary was slouched reading a newspaper. He made the introductions and left them to their task.

The coffee was replenished, and the Prime Minister returned, having put on shoes and combed his hair, leaving him looking a bit more professional. The next hurdle to overcome was the possible demands and positioning of the Chinese President. They had worked on this previously, and the key issues were no reprisals and the removal of Major General Lei Wei. If the Chinese were content with that, in exchange for the UK's silence, it would have to suffice. However, the astute person that Xi was, he would not leave matters there. He would want something in return, an ace up the sleeve which might be needed in the future to justify a passive response to an attack on China. They were prepared for a negative and aggressive response but were hoping for a conciliatory approach.

'This is a matter for China to cogitate. We cannot be too prescriptive, or Xi will just up sticks and leave,' the Prime Minister observed.

One other matter was still in the process of investigation; the identity of the General's accomplices. Major General Lei Wei was a clever and devious man, but they suspected someone else was standing beside him or leading the process. It appeared that cash had been brought in from outside the Chinese government. Funding schemes had been set up through secret bank accounts, but the incoming cash had been well-laundered through criminal Chinese gangs and externally to China. GCHQ had tried to break through into Lei Wei's personal and work computers and the systems he had at home and in the office, but the firewalls were complex. They would get through eventually, unless it was too late, and the Chinese State Security already had his hardware. On the matter of the firewall, Tom remembered what he was told by Derek Jacobs, who had said, 'This is not the usual code that the Chinese use. It looks almost Western but has been manipulated to look like authentic Chinese. There could be a double-bluff going on here, but I doubt it.'

The question was, if it wasn't just the Chinese, then who else was involved?

It was 1045 hours, and the Prime Minister excused himself. The team moved to the anteroom. This room had been rigged with a number of features that interrupted signals in and out.

The sound of the first helicopter and then a second one could be heard in the distance. This was President Xi Jinping and his wife, Peng Liyuan. The press had speculated about the extended stay of the President, and they were scrambling for a motive. One speculation was a pending trade deal which was not so wide of the mark.

At 1110 hours, President Xi Jinping walked into the anteroom with his interpreter. Mrs Joyce Young of the China Desk, SIS, was there to support the Prime Minister. Everyone came to attention, and with a smile on his face, President Xi bowed. The Prime Minister and assembled team bowed in return. The President took the same seat as before and begged everyone to be at ease. It was a distinct change in stance from the previous day which seemed to bode well. The Prime Minister also was upbeat and thanked the President for gracing them with his presence.

Xi lifted his hands and said speaking in English, 'I would like to start today. My intelligence teams in China have told me that there were explosions at three academic sites yesterday. Each target, it was reported, was related to biological research that had no military value. All were destroyed by a simultaneous explosion. Their assessment is that it was from the growing disaffection within our country for animal testing. The explosion caused no fatalities although four security guards were injured, one seriously and the rest minor. They have also indicated the damage to the testing facilities did not encroach on to other buildings nearby. Hearing these reports, I can only assume that certain aspects of commentary yesterday were honest and honourable. I am heartened the terrorists who conducted these crimes left no trace of their presence. My senior intelligence staff are at a loss regarding the perpetrators of this act. Even those people who speculate about potential sources of the attack do not suggest UK or Western involvement. I congratulate you.'

He paused, getting the next batch of phrases together in his head.

'I therefore commend your military ability and thank you for being precise so that casualties were minimised. For these reasons, I am prepared to listen to your proposal. I apologise, but from here on my assistant will translate. My English is insufficient to understand the complexities of what you will be saying.'

He broke off into Mandarin, and his words were translated.

'I now respectfully call upon you to detail your proposal. You will understand nothing of this meeting can ever be recorded or repeated outside this room, except those matters we agree to use to cement our friendship and develop trade, if that is our chosen path.'

'President Xi Jinping, what I would like to do is approach matters logically. I think as a starting point, we can put the unfortunate attacks on these laboratories behind us. It would serve neither of our countries to discuss these matters further. Do you agree?'

Xi said, 'Yes, I agree,' in English.

The Prime Minister continued.

'Thank you, sir. What I would wish to cover first is a token of our openness and willingness to build a unique relationship between our two great nations. In this matter, we would coordinate our scientific work in relation to the production of the vaccine to eradicate all forms of Covid from the planet, once and for all time.'

He continued and recounted the briefing he had earlier in the morning. Claire was asked to fill in a few gaps, and it was clear President Xi was pleased with what he had heard.

Tea was summoned and delivered, allowing a short but relaxing interlude, during which the Prime Minister spoke off the cuff.

'I believe this meeting today will have meteoric consequences for our two nations, and humankind generally, for decades. It will elevate both our countries beyond their current standing in the world.'

President Xi Jinping smiled and gave a gentle nod, waiting to hear what was coming next.

The Prime Minister got back on script.

'President Xi, the first matter on which we request reassurance is that Major General Lei Wei be removed from his current position and not allowed to operate in any capacity with your armed forces or political echelons.'

Xi responded in Mandarin, 'Be assured Major General Lei Wei has been arrested, and all his staffs down to the rank of major have been detained or are being hunted. We will deal with this matter firmly and decisively. Our intention is to find out who was responsible and complicit within his organisation. These people will be executed without trial.'

As difficult as execution without trial sounded to Western ears, no one batted an eye. The devastation wrought by Lei Wei and the enormity of his crime warranted the summary execution.

The Prime Minister nodded, happy with that response, and added, 'Sir, we are also aware that funds were being passed to Lei Wei, and we suspect but have no irrefutable evidence, they came from outside China. We have indications that the office computer used by this man and his home system had security settings which were far in advance of most Chinese systems. We would, in cooperation with your people, like to see if we can identify the sources of these funds and other parties who were in league with the Major General.'

It took a few minutes for the full extent of this question to sink in.

'Tell me, Allan, what do you need me to do in this respect? If I hand over what you want, can you assure me that all information recovered will be shared and China as a nation will be allowed to take whatever steps we deem necessary on the basis of such information?'

This whole last statement was in English.

'This we can agree,' said Allan without any hesitation, and he asked Deputy Director MacDonald to interject.

'Mr President, if we can get access to the hardware and any information on disks, pens, memory-cards, or remote hard drives that this criminal used, we will report fully to you on this matter as the Prime Minister said. I can contact you or one of your trusted staff to arrange to pick-up these computers and items in Beijing. We will provide all intelligence from these systems to your people.'

The President smiled, 'I am sure you have the means to be very resourceful, Uncle Tom. You and your qualities are known to my people, and we will arrange something before we depart today.'

'Thank you, sir,' said Tom, thinking, 'You have done your homework. You sly old dog.'

Claire felt a smile sneak on to her face, and she saw a similar grin on the face of the Chinese leader. This wasn't an ambush by the UK side, more a crossing of intellectual swords. Xi was very well-briefed and was capable of holding mountains of information in his head, and in a foreign language too. It was very impressive.

The Prime Minister continued, 'Sir, as sign of good faith on your part, we ask that your government sign the Convention on the Prohibition of the Development, Production and Stockpiling of Bacteriological (Biological) and Toxin Weapons. This would enable you to undertake an audit of your Armed Forces to ensure that a repeat of the behaviour of the Major General would be entirely unlikely in the future. For our part and in consideration of your agreement on this matter, we will agree to destroy all the samples of viruses taken from your research facilities. As you know, sir, such matters require a leap of faith.'

Again, the President nodded and then spoke in Mandarin,

'We will make this one of our joint announcements today, Prime Minister, if all else proceeds within the same spirit.'

The PM was on a roll.

'The only remaining matter of importance is the production and distribution of the vaccine. My team has suggested China could be responsible for the production and selling of the vaccine to the continent of Asia with its population of about four and a half billion people. We, the UK, will be responsible for the production of the vaccine to the rest of the world, giving us a target audience of around three point four billion people. Our teams here in the UK will welcome a delegation from your country, as soon as they can be mustered, who can help increase the volume of vaccine production to a critical level. In that time, you can prepare your nation to develop the facilities to mass produce the vaccine and, say, in one month's time, your scientists can return with sufficient vaccine to undertake a massive reproduction programme within China. The details can be worked out later, but if we have broad agreement and work in good faith, we can draw up a simple agreement to ratify matters.

Obviously, we will have vaccine stocks fairly imminently, and should you require an immediate supply for key personnel, we would be happy to oblige.'

President Xi said, 'I think your proposal is fair and just. I suspect, had you been less honourable, you could have easily just manufactured these vaccines for your own benefit. It would have been a simple matter to deny any involvement in the attacks.'

The Prime Minister smiled his acceptance of the President's praise.

'President Xi, I also will ask you to consider two other points which are not related to the situation before us today, but in all conscience, I feel it my duty to raise. Firstly, I would ask that you restrain any future military build-up in the Pacific Ocean. We and our staffs have corresponded on this many times, so I will say no more except that Western governments are being pressured to spend more on arms. As you know, this is the time for rebuilding, not an arms race. Your nation is militarily strong and is under no threat from anyone.'

'Finally, I know you are a man of vision, and therefore I ask you to review your country's attitude to human rights. We do not wish to inflict our culture on your country, but building a fairer society makes the country stronger not weaker. We are aware there are many factions within China who would relish the chance to start a counter-revolution. This would serve no one's interests at this time. Strong leadership in bringing your people into the world's fold of free countries will make you the greatest of all China's leaders. These matters are for you to consider in due course.'

'Is there anything you would like to add, Mr President?'

Xi smiled and said, 'No, thank you, Prime Minister, but I would like my Press Advisor to speak with your Press Secretary to pen a joint news release.'

'Of course. Perhaps this could be done whilst we enjoy some lunch.'

'That would be most welcome. Prime Minister, I would also be happy for your team here to join us, if that is permissible.'

The Prime Minister bumbled a bit at this unexpected inclusion, saying,

'Um, yes, that should be fine. I am sure the team would be honoured, Mr President.'

At 1230 hours, the Prime Minister took President Xi through to a private lounge where he could converse with his staff privately and give instructions. At 1300 hours, luncheon was served, and the three intelligence officers were completely flabbergasted and honoured to be sharing a light lunch of cold meats, Scottish salmon, salad and a range of rice dishes with the Chinese President and the Prime Minister.

Claire thought, 'This is so unreal. How can I ever explain this?'

Then she realised that, of course, she never would because of the Official Secrets Act.

Chapter 36

A Pressing Conference

24th Jun 2024

After the luncheon, Tom MacDonald contacted SIS Headquarters and had his call put through to the Chief who was still in his office. George Main took a formal and slightly aloof tone. He was obviously still furious with his Deputy Director Operations. Maintaining his own professionalism, Tom explained the events of the morning, omitting mention of having had lunch with the PM and the President of China and their wives. The conversation was stilted and awkward, with George Main ordering his subordinate to come straight back to Vauxhall to provide a full written brief and to bring the recordings of the meeting. Tom apologised to his superior and reported that the Prime Minister, who was conducting a press conference at four p.m. at Chequers in conjunction with President Xi Jinping, had asked for his team to remain behind until its conclusion.

'What?' said the Chief of the SIS. 'Has he cleared his statement with the Cabinet? Has he consulted the Chair of the Joint Intelligence Committee? Of course not. He is a fucking loose cannon and will screw up the whole operation if he is not careful.'

Tom's instinctive reaction was to tell his boss he was talking bollocks, but restraining himself, he said,

'Sir, the Prime Minister and President Xi have reached an accord, and everything that we hoped has been achieved. This is a great coup for the UK and the role the SIS had played within it. I will pass on your sentiments to the Prime Minister, but for the avoidance of confusion, sir, can you tell exactly what you would like me to say?'

Before slamming down his phone in total rage, the Chief yelled,

'Do not, I repeat, do not convey any part of this conversation to the Prime Minister. That is a direct order, Deputy Director. Do you understand?'

The tone when he said 'Deputy Director' was derisory, making the point that his subordinate was an underling, and he was going to redress this lack of loyalty. Tom had seen people like this all his life, having no respect for them.

To the empty room, Tom said, 'Fuck you.'

It was a low moment at a time when they all should be exceptionally proud and euphoric about their achievements. Instead, he was feeling ashamed about his boss's tantrum and lack of honour.

Tom reflected and was mortified by George Main's behaviour, 'This unscrupulous man may not leave it there and will seek some form of retribution against me. Or worse still, the Fulcrum Storm Team. I can't allow such a travesty of justice.'

A few seconds later, Claire walked in and seeing Uncle Tom obviously deflated and looking all his sixty-plus years, asked,

'Are you all right, sir? Do you need anything?'

Tom's red face displayed an anger she had not seen before. He was sitting slumped on the Chesterfield sofa, and said,

'Sit down, Claire. I just need to let off steam for a while.'

The Wing Commander asked again, 'Are you alright, sir? What is it?'

He looked at her and changed his mind about unburdening himself, trying instead to reassure his young protégé.

'Nothing more than petty internal politics. What can I do for you, Claire?'

She reached over and handed the Deputy Director Operations a printed script saying,

'This is the proposed press release which will be given at four p.m. this afternoon. The BBC and China's National TV are on their way. The Press Officer is setting up a briefing area in the main hallway. He has everything he needs, but the PM insisted you read through this draft.'

Tom refocussed and glanced down at the notes and started to read,

'Whose are these comments in manuscript?' he quizzed.

'The comments in green are the PM's and the ones in red are mine,' she replied self-consciously. 'I hope you don't think I was being too presumptuous in putting my thoughts down, sir?'

He continued reading and then said, 'Not at all, Claire. I concur with all you have amended and with the Prime Minister's comments too.'

He took out his pen and made a few minor changes. He looked up at her and said, 'Let's not paint ourselves into a corner with absolutes. If we say we are ninety-five percent confident of success, it leaves a bit of wriggle room, just in case we have unforeseen setbacks.'

It was a small but important point.

'That is a great piece of work. I must thank Johnathon and Janet for their input. How are they both?' he enquired.

'Well, between you and me, sir, I think we have a budding romance there. I caught them holding hands, and they quickly pulled apart and blushed,' Claire replied.

'Now that's good news. It's nice to see people in love,' said Tom.

It was now three thirty p.m., and Tom was gagging for a cup of tea. Just then, as if by magic, a house servant came in and said tea was being served in the main lounge. The whole team gathered, and Tom made his feelings known about everyone's sterling work. The Chinese Press Officer was introduced to Tom. Passing over the changes to the Prime Minister's Press Officer, Tom pointed out his small change and explained his rationale. The moment of truth was looming, and tension was building again. It had been a day of constant pressure and stress. Could both men pull off this great deception and coup? Tom was almost certain it was a foregone conclusion but was crossing his fingers just in case.

The Prime Minister and President left the room at 1545 hours. The press vehicles had turned up twenty minutes prior. The media crews were small and basic; one questioner plus a cameraman. Long gone were the days of a soundman and producer plus hangers-on. The chairs in the hallway had been placed to reflect the social distancing requirements. Lecterns with plastic screens were set to the front but were more for show and solidarity than real protection from the virus. All personnel in Chequers were screened for the virus on a bi-daily basis, so the house was as clear of Covid as could reasonably be assured.

At three fifty p.m. local time, BBC correspondent began recording, stating to the camera,

'The BBC has an exclusive live broadcast from Chequers with the

Prime Minister and President Xi Jinping of China. We have not been pre-briefed on the subject matter but... ' and she went off at a tangent speculating what might be announced.

A few minutes later, both leaders stepped forward into the press conference, walked in front of the lecterns and shook hands for photos, a dramatic gesture as it was in direct contradiction to the normal Covid-24 protocols. Both men looking supremely relaxed.

The BBC correspondent tried for a quick question.

The Prime Minister put her down sharply, saying,

'Lorna, you are here to witness and report, not make the news. Let's stick with the usual convention of letting us make a statement, shall we?'

The two men took their positions behind the Perspex screens. The Prime Minister led off with a statement. The usual platitudes came first with details of how well the visit had gone. He praised his honoured guest for his wisdom and intellect.

'Nothing much to report on here,' thought the correspondent who was still smarting from her very public and personal rebuke.

The Prime Minister then said they had a number of joint announcements with agreements on trade coming first.

'Pretty standard bullshit,' thought Lorna still disgruntled.

Then came the revelation that shocked the nation. Lorna's notes went like this,

Developing a vaccine in secret with Chinese partners since March 2024.

Proven to work well – ninety five percent confident of success.

Plans to mass produce in UK and China.

First vaccines will be on the streets in weeks.

Within six months the whole of the UK and China would be vaccinated.

In two years, the pandemic would be potentially eradicated.

Will offer vaccine under license to other nations.

China would service Asia.

UK would support the rest of the world with its allies and friends.

The Prime Minister said, 'This is a momentous occasion which has been only possible to achieve through the co-operation of our two great nations. We have been working tirelessly within our countries to find a vaccine. We needed to maintain full secrecy on the research because previously there had been too many false dawns and dashed hopes. Testing has proved positive, and we are now ready for the last battle with this pandemic. The final victory is still many months off, but to quote a great man, "This is the beginning of the end".'

The Prime Minister passed over to his new friend who repeated much the same in Chinese with nuanced differences. Then the Chinese President added an additional comment. After discussion with the Prime Minister, it was agreed his country would sign the Convention on Biological Weapons and would be vociferous in meeting its obligations. The President then went on to say, not having forewarned the Prime Minister,

'As part of the new world in which we all must now live, the Chinese Government will halt any further expansion and modernisation of its armed forces to place greater emphasis on the social and cultural development of our great nation. We must beseech the peoples of the world to reflect on the cultural differences in our nations and learn to see the dissimilarities as opportunities and not challenges or threats. I sincerely hope that other world leaders will see this as part of a new rationale of thinking which would focus on trade, the betterment of mankind and sustenance of the planet.'

Lorna sat with her jaw hanging limp.

Questions followed from both the Chinese and UK press, and every answer was fully and eloquently delivered. This was truly breaking news and offered hope to the beleaguered world.

Professor Janet Williams, the Leading Scientific Advisor on the vaccine, explained that the Chinese scientists would be arriving in the UK to help set up and develop the production facilities, and she recounted the next few steps and processes to get the vaccine out to those that needed it most.

The BBC correspondent then asked the question in millions of people's minds across the world who were watching this newsfeed.

'How is it the UK and China are working in tandem on this project?'

Janet turned and introduced Professor King.

Jon said, 'I discovered the building blocks of the virus and incorrectly assumed the virus was manufactured. My science was picked up by an eminent team in China, and it was agreed, in conjunction with both governments, that we would coordinate our research in secret for the betterment of humankind.'

To the person on the street, the assertions made by Professor King sounded plausible and commendable. However, some in the scientific academic community would not grasp the connection but would struggle to contest the findings. The now completed and detailed work would be open for the world to review and benefit from it.

'This is not a UK or Chinese success but a triumph all peoples can revel and share in,' Professor King concluded.

The press conference ended abruptly with many questions hanging. Both men were pleased with their outcomes, and the swift decision-making ability of President Xi was the key factor in many of the results achieved. It seemed that everyone would win. The UK news outlets copied the BBC News story, and it was re-transmitted worldwide. People on social media were going berserk with joy over the claims. Within minutes, UK Government officials were being asked for comment, and they were all dumbfounded, apart from Esther Williams, who was trying to put herself forward as one of those in the know.

The Government issued a strong message to stop people from thinking the protective measures in place could now be lifted. They could not, but some people just couldn't help themselves, and deaths increased over the next few weeks as sections of the population prematurely partied and celebrated.

It was five p.m. in Chequers and midday in Washington D.C. The significance of the British reports had landed almost instantaneously on the desk of US President. He had a number of reports before him. However, the news that the Chinese and British had collaborated on a vaccination project, and no one had told him about it was, in his estimation, criminal.

He asked, 'How could it be that the British could develop a vaccine, yet we are nowhere near having a workable solution? Surely, we would be aware if either of these countries was making a breakthrough. Aren't the British our friends? They talk of our special relationship but then do this behind our backs!'

He continued to rant, and all his immediate team looked flabbergasted. This genuinely had come out of the blue. They quickly checked and saw that no communique had been issued from the Washington British Embassy, and when they spoke to the Ambassador, he could offer no explanation or further details. It was the same with the US Embassy in London; they knew nothing. There was a media and intelligence blackout as far as the Americans were aware.

'Get Allan on the phone. He's my friend, and he'll tell me what is going on. This can't be right,' said the President.

The CIA was looking at this announcement by the British and simultaneously holding in the other hand the reports of explosions in three separate bio-weapons locations in China. The facility at Wuhan was constantly on their radar, especially since Trump wanted proof that the Chinese were behind the initial Covid outbreaks. However, CIA staff were unable to find any correlation between the pandemic and the People's Republic of China. Then another report came in announcing Major General Lie Wei had been arrested along with some two hundred of his staff. All were being held and questioned, so sources leaked, in connection with the terrorist attacks on the three microbiological centres. Were all these incidents related? No one had any clear idea.

This had set a number of people within The George Bush Center for Intelligence, located in Langley in Fairfax County, Virginia, rushing around trying to get answers. The Director of the CIA, Bill Whittaker, called in his senior staff.

'I want to know what the heck is going on here, people,' he demanded. 'We have been caught napping. John, do you have anything on any of this?' he asked his Head of China.

'Nothing, sir, we have no indications of any covert activity nor have there been any leaks regarding the work the British have supposedly done with the Chinese.'

Sounding more annoyed, the Director of the CIA shouted,

'Get our people on the ground to find out what the hell is going on and who is running this fucking show. Doug, you get on to our cousins in MI6 and see if they can tell us anything. Also, see if our liaison team in GCHQ is aware of any British Ops in China. Don't we have some troops embedded in their Special Forces in England? Find out if they know anything. Rattle some cages and see if we have anything at all that will throw some light on this mess. I want this on my desk in four hours.'

The atmosphere at the CIA headquarters had changed in the space of ten minutes. They were looking like the poor relation, and only God knew how their political masters would dress this up.

Back in the UK, people experienced an instant rising sense of optimism. Every mainstream news channel was having newsflashes, showing the joint press conference from Chequers. Questions were aplenty, and detailed answers were in short supply.

The President of China was already at RAF Brize Norton ready to depart. Due to the changed plans, there was little pomp and ceremony. Allan had insisted on flying with President Xi during the short helicopter flight to see him off. Both men had much to do to cement their positions and to keep the momentum going. They agreed to speak in a few days' time to ensure dialogue continued, and the promised actions were dutifully completed. A final photoshoot took place on the steps of the aircraft from the few UK newspapers who were astute enough to pre-position cameramen. These would be the front-page images in tomorrow's press.

The Prime Minister returned to Chequers at six thirty p.m., drained but elated. He walked in from the lawn where the helicopter had landed. Yorkie saw him walking under the rotor blades of the Merlin helicopter, his hair flying, his jacket over his arm and his shirt tails hanging out.

'He looks like a bag of shit, tied in the middle,' he said speaking softly to Claire.

'That may be the case, but today he has averted war and set the UK on the path, with China, as being the saviours of the human race from Covid. I think we can cut him a bit of slack,' Claire suggested.

Tom MacDonald was also looking less alert than usual, slumped in a chair with another coffee in his hand. The past few days had taken their toll on this spy puppet master.

'You are so right, Claire, we owe this man much, but remember that our actions and those of many support staff got us here. No one ever does it on their own, but we always praise the man at the top. It's the way of things.'

The Prime Minister disappeared into the private quarters, keeping the intelligence staff waiting. Tom had decided he was going to forewarn the Prime Minister of those who were considering overthrowing him. It was the least he deserved.

At 1900 hours, the PM came through looking refreshed. He had a clean shirt on and different trousers. He was relaxed, carrying two bottles of champagne and glasses. He cracked open the bottles and toasted the King and then the assembled crowd plus all those who had worked so valiantly for today's successes.

Only twenty minutes later, Johnathon and Janet were ready to leave for Porton Down.

Tom took both scientists to one side and thanked them for the hundredth time.

'You have both been superstars, and I will recommend to the PM that you two receive the accolades you both so richly deserve but more on that after I have spoken with him. Johnathon, I must tell you now you are resurrected, Jackie, your next-door neighbour, was assaulted during a Chinese investigation and break-in at your house.'

Johnathon looked shocked and was expecting the worst news.

Tom continued, 'She is fine and fully recovered. She thinks it was a burglary gone wrong. Please don't dissuade her from her belief. Sadly, your dog was killed during the same attack. We tried to save her, but she died of internal bleeding. We all know how much you loved your Willow, and we are very sorry for that loss.'

Johnathon's eyes welled up. He loved his dog more than anything. Janet squeezed his hand, and he tried to regain control of his emotions.

'Thank you, Tom, for letting me know. I suppose there are casualties in every conflict. I take it, now I have been brought back from the dead, I am free to live my life again and go back to my house?'

Tom said, 'Yes, and you had better ring your father and sister, but please remember security. Also, you need to be mindful that you will, yet again, be in high demand from the media outlets. You are now, with Janet, scientific pop stars.'

'I will remember the security requirements. I was told you would have my balls if I slipped up on that front.'

Tom laughed and bid them both goodbye, watching them leave

hand-in-hand.

The wildcat helicopter was in-bound to pick up the three intelligence officers. The rest of the PM's support staff had left the gathering. Claire took Yorkie outside to admire the rolling countryside of the Chilterns, knowing the Deputy Director would appreciate some alone time with the Prime Minister.

Tom took the opportunity to tell the PM of his misgivings of those around him and that they were ready to put him to the sword.

The PM thanked Tom for his honesty and courage in telling him this, saying,

'I am not greatly surprised, Tom. I had grave doubts myself. I wondered if I had what it took to get this job done. Also, politics does not generally attract the most honest souls. Some are genuinely motivated to start with, but in politics, if you are not political you are cut adrift. Politicians crave power and influence with often dubious motives.'

The PM smiled, 'I know, I was one of those people, but now I see that without honesty and integrity, we are all just shuffling seats around aimlessly. I like to think I have not done a bad job overall compared to my peers in Parliament, but on balance I think we do a pretty poor job. China is undoubtedly going to reform, and so must we. We can talk more on this later, but for now, go home and rest. We all need to recoup and rally for the next battle. I will be in touch, my good friend.'

Just as the helicopter was lifting off to go back to London, the Private Secretary rang through and said,

'The President of the United States for you, Prime Minister.'

'Put him through.'

"Hey Allan, how ya doing? I saw your press conference with President Xi. It seems like you worked him over a good bit. Tell me, buddy, what was it you have on him to get him to the table like that?'

The President was trying to ingratiate himself, but the PM was having none of it.

'The truth is, Mr President, Xi basically came here to sort out some minor trade tiffs, and of course, we had been working together on the vaccine which miraculously came to fruition late yesterday. It was all luck. Pure luck, I tell you.'

'Come on, Allan, don't kid a kidder. There has to be more to it than that. What about that stuff on not expanding his military, the bio-weapons agreement thing? It looks like he just rolled over for you. I am not buying it. Spill the beans,' said the US President.

A few seconds passed, and the President was thinking, 'Here it comes,'

'Mr President, you will hear from my Foreign Office in the next few days regarding the vaccine we have produced. Because our countries have a special relationship, we will do you a good deal. For now, I need to brief my senior team, so if you want to chat over the next day or so, give me a call back.'

Allan Knowles put the phone down on the President of the United States of America, and it felt good to have the upper hand for once.

Within forty minutes the US President tweeted, 'Just spoke to Allan Knowles. Good man. The US will secure get a great deal on the vaccine.'

When the PM saw the tweet, he thought, 'You are going to help pay for the rebuilding of my country, you arrogant son of a bitch.'

Chapter 37

Drawing to a Close

25th June 2024

Tom MacDonald reported at eight a.m. to see his boss, the Chief of the SIS. Both men had mental scars from their previous conversations, and George Main realised he had better mend the bridges or at least appear to be reconciliatory. In his heart and mind, he would never accept the actions of his subordinate as being anything other than an attempt to undermine his position.

He greeted Tom saying, 'Tom, do come in and sit down. I must apologise for my short-tempered outbursts over the past few days. We have all been under a great strain. However, I must commend you and your team for pulling this off. It was a triumph of great proportions, and you should be rightly pleased with yourself. The credit will fall to you and your people of course.'

Tom said, 'Not to us, sir, but the country and the Prime Minister.'

The Chief said, 'Well, well, we will see.'

Tom sat down, reflecting on the preceding days and wondered what game his cunning boss was up to. He knew the measure of the man before him, whom he had never really trusted. Throughout his career, he observed Alan Main worm his way to a superior position, not through honest endeavour, but by being the right person in the right place saying the right things that his audience wanted to hear. He was a true political animal, and, like most animals, he embraced survival of the fittest, expecting to encounter casualties along the way. Tom saw himself as a survivor but not in the same callous way. He preferred to take the pack with him, rather than throwing them to the wolves once their usefulness had been depleted. As such, Tom did his upmost to keep away from the Chief. He knew a greater response was needed.

'Sir, we can be justifiably pleased with ourselves, but the job is not quite completed yet. We need to finish the debriefing of the operational teams which should be done by tomorrow. It will be important to distance these people from the timing of the operation, just in case anyone decides to look into a possible correlation with the recent détente between ourselves and the Chinese and the explosions in China.'

It was evident the Chief had not considered this matter.

'Do you believe there is a real danger of someone snooping around?' he asked.

Tom said bluntly, 'Yes, I do, sir. Already a Green Beret of the US Special Forces on secondment to 22 SAS has been asking if any of our boys were involved with the China attack. We have noted calls to our China Desk from our CIA counterparts asking for updates on our operation in China. Therefore, sir, we need to step cautiously. We must keep our involvement away from public and hostile intelligence service gaze. In this respect, I also mean the CIA.'

The Chief answered, 'I was not aware of these interventions. Of course, I totally agree. We need to brief all our staff involved in Operation Fulcrum Storm to be watchful for such tricks.'

'I have already briefed Wing Commander Walters to speak to all involved. Also, Derek Jacobs at GCHQ will tidy up his end,' Tom said with assurance.

He noticed that the Chief was wrestling with his temper, once again feeling undermined by his junior.

'I never really got on with Derek Jacobs,' he said. 'He is just too much of a by-the-seat-of-his-pants type of operator. Too cavalier for me. Not someone for modern senior intelligence roles.'

Tom remained silent before broaching the matter about accessing Major General Lei Wei's computers and software. It was clear the promise made by President Xi was genuine but getting hold of the valuable equipment might be tricky and politically difficult for him to justify. Xi's own people would surely want to keep their hands on it.

'Sir, I will put in place a localised operation through the Beijing Embassy to affect collection of the IT materials used by Lei Wei, and once back in the UK, I will task Derek Jacobs to wring it out for as much information as possible.'

He was pleased he could make a positive comment about his friend and wondered if the Chief knew they were long-standing buddies.

George nodded his approval and smiled in a forced way. Tom had spent many years around people who were trying to keep the truth from him, and his superior was playing that game with him right now.

'Tom, I got your written report which was scant on detail, and there were no recordings with it. Surely, we have recordings?' asked the Chief.

'Actually, sir, the Prime Minister ordered me to suspend recording as he had given his word to President Xi that no such records would exist. It's in my report, sir. Paragraph three, I believe.'

Tom watched his boss's face turn purple.

'He did fucking what? Did you advise him against this action? What possessed his tiny fucking little mind?'

'Actually, sir, I think that he was trying to be honourable, to do the right thing for the right reasons. The Prime Minister said our written accounts would be the only record of the meeting. I complied with his instructions.'

The Chief was fuming again. He could hardly believe his ears. This was not how a Secret Intelligence Service was operated. A brief and rather tense discussion unfolded about closing down the operation and cleaning all IT systems and the storage of files off the server.

Still annoyed and doing nothing to hide the fact, he said,

'That should take a few weeks for you and your team to complete, Tom. After that, you and your Special Weapons Sections take a few weeks' break. You all deserve it. Also, I wonder if you have thought about taking early retirement, given your recent exertions,' said the Chief.

'Actually, sir, I am considering staying on. Regarding leave, there is not much point taking it as we can't travel anywhere just now. I will mention it to the team though and thank you. Maybe once the pandemic is sorted, I might throw the towel in. That should be a couple of years yet.'

Tom left his boss's office again, once more feeling vexed at the way things went. He was worried that this personal spat between the Chief and himself could impact his operational personnel. He called in Far East Section Chief David Jones and Special Weapons Section Chief Bill Rankin for a post-operation run down. He instructed David to put together a plan for the pick-up of the computers from the Chinese; he passed over a contact provided by President Xi's personal assistant.

Bill Rankin was asked to supervise the completion of debriefing and resettling the troops back to their units and desks. He reminded him that the SAS boys had background stories to justify their absences, but it would be worth speaking to Tim Churchill, SAS Liaison, to give them a few days' break. The SIS personnel were to be offered two weeks' leave, should they want it. Philip Wong should see Mary Westwood from the Behavioural Sciences Team, as should Scott MacGregor; they were both involved in killings or near-killings.

Tom mentioned to David to watch his back, as he believed the Chief was looking to discredit some aspect of the operation. David was a loyal and honourable operator.

Tom said, 'Protect your people, Dave.'

'Will do, boss,' he replied.

Tom MacDonald did not have the same conversation with Bill Rankin, as he guessed he was made of the same stuff as the Chief and would seek to benefit from reporting the discussion to his ultimate superior in the hopes of having his loyalty rewarded. Tom was not being disloyal to his boss but simply looking after the future of the SIS.

Wednesday 26th June 2024

Both Claire and Yorkie were wrapping up at the training site. All operational equipment and weapons were handed over and packed and paperwork destroyed. The SAS team was given written course reports for the Advance Free Fall Course they were on as well as past course notes and other materials. They were once more told this was an illegal operation, and as such, the Government would deny all knowledge of it, and should anyone ever mention it, the consequences would be swift and permanent. Everyone knew the score, but these things had to be said. Each person was given two weeks' leave, not to be taken from their annual entitlement and advised not to go back to Hereford. They were given dispensation to travel anywhere in the UK and do whatever they fancied. There was talk about a trip to the Highlands of Scotland, renting a self-catering unit and undertaking some walking and climbing. Most were up for it. A few had families to get back to. They were reminded not to make mention of the awards or promotions until they were made official. The gongs they received would never be made public knowledge, or at least the citations would not.

They had their trackers and toxin capsules removed. It was more painful than the initial injection, causing more than a few coarse words to be spoken. The medic they had dubbed 'Grumpy One' seemed to take pleasure in their pain. Colin the comms geek collected all the capsules. He boxed up all the comms plus digital notebooks, offered his farewells and went back to GCHQ. Director Derek Jacobs came down to pick him up, wanting to congratulate the team as a whole one last time. The CI recovered all his training aids. Once everything was gone, the wooden structures in Hangars Two and Three were demolished and burnt. The training area looked pretty spartan at the point the military transport and MI6 wheels came to take the teams back to units or for their onward adventures. Everyone felt sad to be breaking up the team, but a fair chance existed that they could get back together in some form or other in the not-too-distant future. Yorkie was dreading going back to a desk.

At Downing Street, the Prime Minister was receiving visitations all day from Heads of Governments and signing agreements for the production of the vaccine, under license, in foreign countries. The income from these deals would be lucrative and would go some way to offset the huge debts the country had taken on to minimise the effects of Covid. The report from Porton Down indicated production was going well, and some localised tests were being carried out on family members with Covid-24. Everyone was confident of a positive outcome, but prayers were said all the same.

The Prime Minister went to see the King in Windsor Castle to update the Monarch. King Charles was alert and appreciated the greatness of what had been achieved. Allan Knowles told him everything, leaving out no detail. His Majesty thanked him for the actions of his teams.

With genuine tears of joy, the King said, 'These young people remind me of the character and bravery that so many showed in the second war. Most importantly, they have restored some of the respect to the United Kingdom in the eyes of the international community.'

In truth, the King had felt a deepening sorrow for the way the country was going previously and was much relieved that for many the end was in sight. He had lost family during Covid, and it would not be long before the country could be rebuilt.

The Prime Minister said, 'Sir, I do think you should make a statement to your subjects to ask them to hold off on rejoicing too early and to get behind the country's endeavours to rebuild a better and fairer society. I solemnly pledge I will work tirelessly for that whilst keeping our institutions intact.'

The King agreed, and the PM said he would send over some thoughts on the matter for him to consider. He bowed with ultimate respect.

Back in Downing Street that very evening, the Prime Minister had an audience with Sir Steven Alexander, Chair of the Joint Intelligence Committee. Also present were the Head of the Civil Service and National Security Adviser. The Prime Minister called in Sir Steven and explained the reason for the meeting and the need to have a witness present. It had come to his attention that Sir Steven was engaging in sexual relations with a woman out of wedlock. This of itself was not an issue, but this woman was a known Soviet agent. It was not a fleeting relationship but one which involved 'many dalliances,' as the PM put it. As a consequence, Sir Steven was asked to tender his resignation, using whatever pretext he wished. Sir Steven was told if any other further extra-marital liaisons were brought to the PM's attention, he would not be bound to stay silent on this current matter.

The Prime Minister added, 'We will of course wish to have our chaps at MI5 debrief you on this affiliation, and I will do my best to protect you.'

The last statement was said tongue in cheek.

The Prime Minister then took this opportunity to really stick the knife in.

'Also, I am wholly aware that you were the key voice in considering tossing me and my career under a bus during a recent meeting. If I hear you speak in any derogatory way about me, my family or my governance, it will be you looking to avoid the bus by way of the aforementioned scandal. I believe other affairs are known as well. When I receive your resignation tomorrow, I will, of course, thank you for your invaluable service, but I do not want to see you in public service anymore.'

Sir Steven Alexander said, 'Prime Minister, I must protest. I was present at such discussions, but it was George Main who was looking to have you removed. He has long considered your presence in Number Ten was undermining the UK's stance within the international community.'

The Prime Minister nodded, thanked him and pointed to the door. A figure came from behind a slightly open door to the rear of the room. The Prime Minister smiled at Tom MacDonald.

Tom said, 'That went well, sir.'

'Now,' said Allan, 'what about that sleaze-ball of a boss of yours? I am happy to sack him for not being front and centre when his country and I needed him. But there is the thorny issue of a replacement. I was thinking maybe five years at the helm for you, Tom.'

Tom was flattered but declined. He knew there were better and more appropriate individuals who would have a greater impact on the SIS. MI6 needed someone at the helm who could work hard for its people and make the right judgements for the country. He had a list of names in his pocket, all who would make good bosses. The list did not feature his own name, but his pal, Derek Jacobs, was at the top. He was also thinking that Lee Ford, the SIS - GCHQ Signals Intelligence Liaison officer, could fill Derek's shoes in Cheltenham, and that would be his recommendation.

At the next Cabinet reshuffle, Esther Williams was gone, and the Prime Minister decided he wanted only intelligent and honourable people around him, resulting in a few other notable casualties. His recent successes meant he dared to take hard decisions. He proposed a reshuffle of the House of Commons, reducing the number of MPs. Too many fat cats took the cream but added nothing to the mix. The House of Lords was also going to be changed, meaning a reduced number of Peers sucking money out of the country. People needed to see that those who represented them did so out of duty, not purely for financial gain. He would freeze pay for any politician who had income from other sources over a set limit. His wife agreed. The King also wholeheartedly agreed such reforms were long overdue, and the Royals should also be duly reformed.

'It is a new world. Let's make it a better one, Allan,' were Charles' words.

27th June 2024

A meeting was held in Beijing at Ritan Park (South Gate) between a member of the United Kingdom Embassy Trade Mission and a member of the State Security of the People's Republic of China. They discussed the weather in Mandarin and talked about the fruit of a recent harvest being very good. The Chinese secret agent suggested that maybe a delivery would be acceptable given the new friendship between the two countries. It was agreed that later that afternoon a delivery would be made to the Embassy four hundred yards and a short walk away.

The computers belonging to Major General Lei Wei were delivered with some fresh fruit and vegetables. The latter were gratefully received into the kitchen. The former was moved by military transport aircraft flying back to the UK with a further consignment of PPE, an additional gift from the People's Republic of China.

28th June 2024

Once at RAF Brize Norton, Derek Jacobs collected the computer items and took them personally to the National Cyber Security Centre (NCSC) in London. He popped in to see Tom MacDonald to let him know of developments thus far.

Derek said, 'With fingers crossed, we will be able to extract something useful in the next few days. It is the Cyber Centre's one and only priority, and its best people are on it. Philip Wong and a Mandarin Linguist from GCHQ have been sent over to assist with language issues and, where possible, restrict the intelligence the Cyber Team comes into contact with.'

Derek mentioned he was hearing rumours the Chief was resigning because of family issues. He also said that he had been called to the Prime Minister's Office on Thursday for a meeting regarding the operation. Tom lied and said he knew nothing.

Claire entered the office, saying, 'I'm sorry, sir, I didn't realise you had company. Your secretary said to just go straight in.'

He welcomed her and motioned for her to sit down, but she remained standing.

'I am here to report that Operation Fulcrum Storm is complete. All files have been lodged in the Top-Secret Depository, Wire Room Two is scrubbed and all SIS systems have had files removed and deleted. All SIS personnel are back at their desks, except for Mr Rankin who took the two weeks' leave offered.' Claire had a sparkle in her eye and ended with,

'Just give me and my boys a call if the world needs saving again, sir.'

She came to attention, about-turned, and walked out.

Both men laughed in admiration.

Chapter 38

New Dimensions

It had been over a week since Major General Lei Wei's computers had been at the NCSC. Daily progress reports were provided, but the security systems on the computer were some of the most up-to-date firewalls seen. The complex hacking had taken longer than anticipated. However, once behind the intricate layers of code, they found a treasure chest of information. Director Jacobs got the jackpot call late on during the evening of the 6th July and wasted no time in calling an emergency meeting. It was sensible to hold it in the Deputy Director Operations Conference Room as most people were already working in London.

Attending were:

Tom MacDonald, Deputy Director Operations, SIS

Derek Jacobs, Director GCHQ

David Jones, Section Chief, Far East Desk

Claire Walters, A/Head, Special Weapons Section

Yorkie Charlton, Special Weapons Section

Philip Wong, Operation Desk (China)

Lee Ford, GCHQ Signal's Intelligence Liaison

Everyone arrived promptly for the briefing at 0900 hours. Derek Jacobs summoned this group because they were the ones in the know. Unfortunately, the dramatic turn of events had only scratched the surface for now. The Cyber Security Team working on this project had managed to get into the hard drive of Major General Lie Wei's work and home computers. The information was so sensitive he had all the systems brought back to the SIS Headquarters and lodged in Wire Room One. The truth was the actions of this man were the tip of the iceberg. Even now, they had not been able to fully uncover the extent of outside influences. Also, the plot had an intricate twist.

'To cut a long story short,' started Derek, 'there are documents, emails and photographs which indicate that the principal contact with Lei Wei was an organisation called 'Blue Planet Reborn'. This is essentially an ecological organisation whose main aim is the restoration of the balance of nature. Quite commendable, one might say. However, members of the hierarchy of this group are fundamentally eco-terrorists who believe they have the moral right to redress the damage people have wrought on planet earth. A superficial review of the group as a whole reveals a considerable collection of eco-misfits with a pretty standard agenda, but even without digging too deeply, the rhetoric becomes much darker and sinister. Their agenda is more extremist. They see the destruction or, at best, the curtailment of humankind as a possible solution to restoring the planet's balance. 'Blue Planet Reborn' is a seemingly small organisation with a few well-placed and wealthy supporters but not so well-funded that they could finance the level of activity we saw in China. Their activities seem to centre around the Far East which logistically makes any action against them challenging. In addition, we struggled to grasp how they could have become involved with someone like Major General Lei Wei.'

Derek paused and gulped water. Surveying the room, he realised he had captivated everyone's attention.

'As you would expect, we followed the money trail back from China to its point of origin. This was a convoluted route. It was laundered dozens of times. However, we have no doubt whatsoever that the source of a chunk of cash was the CIA budget in Langley. We found instructions and undertakings which clearly showed an off-the-books operation. To our eyes, their operation seems to have an aim of at least undermining but possibly overthrowing the Chinese leadership. We can only assume the objective was to replace the existing leadership with Lei Wei who would be more progressive and Western-leaning, at least to start with.'

Yorkie said, 'Just like all those democracies in Central and South America which the US willingly put into positions of power all those years ago. Look how well that turned out for them.'

Derek smiled and continued, 'There are indications in correspondence this operation went up to senior levels in the US government. The President was not named, but there were strong references that he was fully behind this coup.'

The discussion centred around accessing definitive evidence of who was behind the plot and how much they knew in terms of the steps taken to generate a pandemic. It was obvious the only way to verify official US involvement was by accessing the CIA central system and seeing what was on their records. It was agreed that they had hit a near-brick wall about the US involvement until then. It may well be the Americans would have set up a sub-unit working independently of the main organisation as their way of ensuring plausible deniability.

The only other avenue of attack was to see if they could find an unofficial audit trail of contact by CIA personnel with 'Blue Planet Reborn'. To find this connection, action would be required to break into the various email and systems used by the group. Once in, it would be a case of seeing how they received the cash and instructions, following the email trail back to the source. Even if the CIA used aliases, the UK agents had worked with many of the American agents and that might lead to identifying them going forward.

Derek Jacobs said, 'Whatever we do, it will be fraught with danger, but we do have a new ally; China. They have enormous resources and a strong connection with the UK now. Given our target may be in their neighbourhood, they might be happy with a joint task force.'

Tom MacDonald talked about the need to put a compelling case together to take to the Prime Minister.

'If we thought that our security protocols needed to be tight on Operation Fulcrum Storm, this will need to be water-tight if we take it any further. I can assure you if the CIA is involved, and again, we don't know if it is a renegade element, they will have counter-surveillance conventions in place at every level of their participation. Their eyes and ears, plus electronic tabs, will be watching every aspect of their laundering transaction. It would not surprise me if they had an agency presence within the 'Blue Planet Reborn' organisation. I would like to have a thorough look at those documents and do more research into these eco-warriors. We will want to brief the Prime Minister before doing anything against an ally, but I think it is sensible to consider an off-site unit made up of joint agency personnel with the single aim of determining a course of action. Thoughts, please.'

Everyone wanted to speak but was mindful of etiquette. It seemed pretty obvious that the two senior men at the meeting had already discussed this but were looking for ideas or even ratification this was the way to go. Claire Walters looked to David Jones as if to say you have seniority, but he offered her an open hand, signalling she should proceed. Yorkie noticed the gesture and knew what was about to happen.

The only female at the table spoke up.

'Sir, if you are intimating security at this Headquarters is not as it should be, or we have such a familiarity with our cousins across the pond that would make it more difficult to investigate them from London, you are right. We need to be elsewhere. However, to move would be extortionate in terms of cost, and the footprint or waves caused might be difficult to disguise. A team of such people would have to be so secret that even our own people would be oblivious to the new formation, otherwise, it would be a pointless exercise.'

'You are right, Claire, and as such, we'll have challenges and complex issues to overcome. The nature of this beast would be such that the only people outside the Team itself to know about it would be the Prime Minister, the Chief, Deputy Director Operations SIS and Director Operations GCHQ. These individuals would be the only ones who would have oversight and provide resources and funding,' said Tom MacDonald.

'The team would need stand-alone comms specialists, language assets, weapons support and the bank balance of a small country,' Claire added with some humour.

Yorkie spoke up.

'You would need a team of operators, should affirmative action be required, access to transport and a whole raft of in-theatre support facilities, just as we had for the last mission. That would make the formation not so small.'

'Again, you are both right, but the threat from the current situation is not yet assessed. If we are going after the Americans on their soil, we need to distance the operation far from the UK establishment, indeed so far that its base will appear to be on the moon,' Derek Jacobs interjected.

'More bloody suicide missions,' Yorkie said.

'But we love them, don't we?' said Claire jokingly.

'Sir, I hate to be a damp squib on this matter, but will the Chief be happy with this, given his recent, dare I say, tantrum at the loss of face over the Fulcrum Storm outcome?' Claire sheepishly mentioned.

'I think he will be happy, and the new Director Operations GCHQ will be happy too,' Tom said with an element of fun in his voice.

Everyone looked around the table, and all but two people were thinking Director Jacobs was resigning. After another pregnant pause, the curling lips on the faces of the two directors indicated that something underhanded was in train. This was MI6, and often things were not what they appeared.

Yorkie could wait no longer, 'Come on, boss, tell us what's going on here?'

Tom looked at Yorkie and poking fun, said, 'It's your reticence to ask difficult questions that holds you back, you know that, don't you? This is not a matter of public record yet, but it will be very shortly. The current Chief is standing down with immediate effect, and I will be covering his desk for about one month or so.'

They were all expecting him to announce he was the new Chief.

'My appointment as Acting Chief will not be permanent. There is also to be a new Director Operations GCHQ, as Derek here will also be relinquishing that appointment. So, there will be several significant job changes and an element of restructuring to boot.' Tom added, 'Though both jobs have not been formally put to the new incumbents yet, the Prime Minister has signed off on the appointments and will, out of courtesy, be putting them before the Chair of the Joint Intelligence Committee; the Committee will ratify the appointments. So, you will have to wait to find out who these new people are.

'For now, Special Weapons Section, you take the lead on reviewing the data we have on the matter before us and come up with a detailed analysis and options for action,' Tom instructed. 'Philip and Lee Ford will provide support as needed, and if you require any specialist support, go through me and only me at this time.'

David Jones, Section Chief Far East Desk, asked,

'Sir, is there anything you want me to do?'

'Yes,' said Tom. 'I want you to do two things. Firstly, ask our American friends what they were up to in China, you know, blowing up the facilities in Wuhan, etcetera. Sound dumb, they like that. If we ask them the question, it will look like we had no involvement. We will play them at their own game. Next, I want you to see if we have any leads on the ground in Asia regarding 'Blue Planet Reborn'. We know they are sailing around the Pacific and South China Sea, but let's get some tactical intel on them. Let me have a breakdown of the group members, and let's see if they have a formal recruitment process or even an informal one for that matter.'

Tom turned to his friend and said, 'Derek, any chance we can get some Comms intel on these boys and track their every move?'

Director Jacobs nodded and intervened, 'This is the end of Operation Fulcrum Storm and the start of Operation Red Kite. Let's get to it, people. Never a dull day in intelligence.'

As the new Chief-in-waiting, Derek Jacobs had great confidence his first years in charge of MI6 were going to be anything but dull.

Claire left the briefing wondering who would lead the new unit? If she were to lead it, from where would she like to operate? She longed to be closer to the Highlands and her mum. The training areas were vast, there were few people and she knew just the base to use but would need a big budget. Then she wondered how her new team would take to living in Scotland.

Yorkie saw his boss with that glint in her eye and hoped this new unit would come to fruition. He was already assembling the Operations Team in his head. If they were to relocate, his boys loved the Highlands of Scotland, and it would give them the freedom to train and operate without too many watchful eyes.

Tom shouted, 'Wing Commander, Major, in my office now, if you please.'

The last time they were both in the Deputy Director Operations' office was when he informed them they were off to China on a mission. Maybe, just maybe, it could be another mission. Yorkie half-hoped it was not China again, but in reality, he didn't care. Anywhere on operations was better than being stuck in an office.